Dear Reader:

I'm delighted to present to you the first books in the HarperMonogram imprint. This is a new imprint dedicated to publishing quality women's fiction and we believe it has all the makings of a surefire hit. From contemporary fiction to historical tales, to page-turning suspense thrillers, our goal at HarperMonogram is to publish romantic stories that will have you coming back for more.

Each month HarperMonogram will feature some of your favorite bestselling authors and introduce you to the most talented new writers around. We hope you enjoy this Monogram and all the HarperMonograms to come.

We'd love to know what you think. If you have any comments or suggestions please write to me at the address below:

HarperMonogram
10 East 53rd Street
New York, NY 10022

Karen Solem
Editor-in-chief

"HOW CAN WE TALK ABOUT LOVE?"

"We barely know each other. We're pupil and teacher," Jessica protested, refusing to meet Mark's eyes.

"You don't believe that!" He pulled her fiercely against his chest and held her desperately, drowning in the fragrance of her hair, sinking in the soft warmth of her skin. "I may not know much," he admitted, "but I know I love you."

At her sigh, passion tore through him like a roaring, inexorable spring flood, sweeping reason, fear, and caution before it like twigs in the current. He found her lips, and when he felt her response—tentative at first, then strengthening to rival his own—there was nothing in the world except the woman in his arms and the desire that demanded he follow where it led.

———

SEASONS
OF THE HEART

MARILYN CUNNINGHAM

HarperPaperbacks
A Division of HarperCollinsPublishers

This is a work of fiction. The characters, incidents, and dialogues are products of the author's imagination and are not to be construed as real. Any resemblance to actual events or persons, living or dead, is entirely coincidental.

HarperPaperbacks *A Division of* HarperCollins*Publishers*
10 East 53rd Street, New York, N.Y. 10022

Cover photography by Herman Estevez

First printing: November 1992

Printed in the United States of America

HarperPaperbacks, HarperMonogram, and colophon are trademarks of HarperCollins*Publishers*

❖ 10 9 8 7 6 5 4 3 2 1

Prologue

The rough-hewn wooden chair on the veranda of the rambling old ranch house was precisely positioned so that Jessica faced the stark, untamed visage of Packer Mountain as she waited for the sun to dive behind its rock-capped peak.

With half-shut eyes she gazed at the horizon, a stark silhouette of pines and boulders against the soft sky. From years of observing the mountain from this vantage point, she could have closed her eyes completely and still seen its every aspect, from the bleak scowl it wore in winter, when snow clung tenaciously to its ridges, to the smile it wore now, blazing with the gold flame of aspen leaves intermingled with the crisp green of firs.

No, she didn't have to look. She could feel the mountain as the sun disappeared behind it, feel its strength and solidity. The mountain hadn't changed, she thought, moving her gaze from the ridge line and glancing down at her slender hands, white-knuckled from grasping the arms of the chair so tightly.

She made a conscious effort to relax. This wouldn't do; she couldn't afford to be nervous. Not now. Taking a deep breath, she resolutely uncurled each finger until her hands floated on the chair arms as lightly as lilies on a pond.

So many seasons spent at the foot of this mountain, watching the changes, realizing her own life was flowing in a rhythm as timeless as that of the earth around her. April is the cruelest month, they said. Thinking back on a long-ago springtime, she agreed, remembering the sharp wounds, the roller-coaster emotions, the days of ecstasy that had seemed destined to last forever.

Then was this winter? She smiled slightly. Not if winter was deemed a season of death, of endings, of frozen hearts. But if one remembered that under the snow tender shoots of hopes and dreams await the return of the sun . . . then perhaps this was winter.

No, the mountain hadn't changed, but she had. How many years had it been since she first came to this valley? Thirty-five? It didn't seem possible that so much time had elapsed, and then again it seemed she had been here forever. Thirty-five years of love and misery, of hope and desolation. Thirty-five years of fighting.

Well, she still had the strength for one fight more. She pressed her lips firmly together as she listened for the sound of the automobile that would soon be purring up the winding road from the small town of Hope twenty miles away. And as much as she dreaded the coming confrontation, Jessica knew this was one fight she had to win.

She felt the house hulking securely behind her, familiar as an old friend, its rooms quiet now in the gathering twilight. She supposed she should switch on a light, shake off this melancholy mood, but she liked sitting alone in the darkness. For a few more moments, perhaps, she could still hide from the past that was even now speeding over the winding gravel road toward her.

Maureen, her granddaughter, was in her room, probably playing her latest Beatles record. The sound didn't reach this far, Jessica was glad to note. Her ears, attuned to ranch noises, caught an occasional snuffle from the horses in the corral, the shrill cry of a nighthawk, and the faraway yap of a coyote cutting through the stillness. Otherwise the ranch belonged to the encroaching night.

She shifted slightly to look out over the valley floor, wincing as she always did at the line of houses faintly visible in the dimness to the east. In a few years she would be completely surrounded by the ticky-tacky dwellings. Even now she felt as though she were an isolated survivor in an embattled outpost in a struggle whose conclusion was already determined by forces beyond her, or anyone's, control. It was only a matter of time.

She straightened her spine. No one could touch her land, she reminded herself, and it covered a good share of the county.

"I didn't know you were still out here."

Jessica couldn't suppress a start of surprise at the melodious voice. She hadn't been aware of the girl's soft footsteps until Maureen spoke from right behind her.

"You're sure edgy tonight, Lady Jess. What gives?" The girl touched her lightly on the shoulder, then passed in front of her and leaned against the veranda railing, throwing her head back to catch the evening breeze in her long dark hair.

The familiar catch tightened Jessica's throat as she looked at her granddaughter, and a rush of love swept over her. At sixteen Maureen was taller than Jessica, with a slender athletic body that seemed built for the running she loved to do. Her strong, clear profile was outlined against the gathering dusk, and her brown eyes, with their slightly almond shape, were closed as she drank in the night, allowing her thick dark lashes to sweep against her high cheekbones.

Jessica smiled at the girl. She had fallen in love with the screaming, red-faced baby the first time she saw her, and she'd never changed her mind.

"Edgy? I thought I was sitting here quite peacefully."

"Don't try to fool me." Maureen's severe tone was belied by her fond glance. "Who is this man, anyway?"

Jessica tried for a light touch. "Surely you know who he is—perhaps the richest and most powerful man in Idaho. Why shouldn't I be a little nervous?"

Maureen frowned, her eyes still on Jessica's face. "Because it's not like you to be nervous about seeing anyone. Especially a city slicker." The girl moved from the railing and placed a slender hand on Jessica's shoulder; the woman felt the warm pressure through the thin fabric of her shirt. "Do you want me to hang around?"

Jessica raised her hand and placed it over the girl's, giving a warm squeeze. "Not necessary, angel. I'll call if I need you. Why don't you get back upstairs to your homework?"

The girl pursed her lips. "Because school was out a week ago. You *are* uptight." She hesitated as though about to say something else, then shrugged and walked back into the house.

Jessica took a deep breath. The breeze, sharpened with the foreknowledge of winter, cut through her shirt and lifted her hair from her shoulders, blowing it across her cheek. She shivered. Still, she didn't go inside.

Sighing, she ran her fingers lightly over her cheek and along her jaw. Her skin was still in good shape, unlined in spite of years of ranch work, of hours under a hot sun and the assault of winter cold. Her hair, which she was wearing loose tonight, felt heavy on her shoulders, and she reached up to lift it from her neck.

She isolated a strand, twisting it absently in her fingers. Although she couldn't see the color in the darkening night, she knew what it looked like: pale gold, almost white, its lightness effectively hiding any gray that might be lurking there. She had always been proud of her hair; it had changed very little since she was twenty and had first come to this valley. Her waist had thickened a little, her skin was less resilient, and she knew her deep blue eyes had paled, taking on a shrewd, direct expression. But her hair—her hair was the same as it had been more than thirty years ago when she had stood on the schoolhouse steps and watched him walking up the path. . . .

SPRING

1

She brushed her hair back from her face as she watched the last of her eight pupils disappear down the trail that wound between two enormous fir trees before disappearing into a ravine. Shouts and giggles cut into the crisp February air, and like a caged animal suddenly freed, one of the boys leaped over a log that had fallen across the path. No one looked back at the small frame building where she stood motionless in the doorway.

The school day was finally over. She relaxed into an uncharacteristic slump, leaning against the doorjamb that was scarred with the initials of her current students and those who had gone before them, many of whom might not be able to recall that the capital of their state was Boise, but who were, every one of them, adept with a knife.

Keeping the young people corralled in the schoolhouse all day, as required by state law until they successfully completed the eighth grade, was like riding herd on wild mustangs. It was especially hard now that the first glimmering of spring was melting the snow on the south slopes of Packer Mountain and sweeping the ice from the creeks. At seventeen two or three of the boys were already young men, nearly her own age of twenty, and made no secret of their impatience to put folderol like book learning behind them.

Although this was one of those rare Idaho days when it was possible to believe in summer, Jessica shivered slightly. She hadn't expected her first teaching assignment to be like this. When she had attended Teachers' College in Lewiston, she had been full of enthusiasm and energy. She'd had every reason to expect an assignment in a reputable school closer to Boise, where her family lived. Instead she was in this isolated backwoods valley where cattle outnumbered people at least a thousand to one, and where the people were barely out of the hunting-and-gathering stage of human evolution.

She sighed and bit her lip. She had expected a lot of things, but the crash of the stock market over a year and a half ago hadn't been one of them. October 28, 1929. Black Friday. The date was seared into her brain, and the echoes of the crash were still reverberating around her.

The lance of remembered pain came so suddenly that she gasped, clutching the doorjamb to steady her trembling body. Still, she was getting better; sometimes entire days went by when she was able to forget what that crash had done to her future. At other times the memories washed over her in all their ferocious intensity.

Scenes swept through her mind: the dormitory in Lewiston where she had been putting the finishing touches on a term paper; the teacher who had come in, sat beside her, spoke the halting words that had forever changed her life. Her father had hanged himself after learning that his life savings were gone in the debris of the Wall Street debacle. Next went the comfortable home in Boise, sacrificed to creditors. Three months later her mother, evidently unable to face the losses and disgrace, slipped away in her sleep. And Jessica was alone.

In the panic of the ensuing months she knew she was lucky to get any job, even one as lowly as this.

Now she took a deep breath and straightened her shoulders, willing herself to think of something else. Anything else. Absently she raised her arm and lifted her pale hair from her neck, absurdly comforted by its familiar weight. She knew the style was old-fashioned; everyone was wearing short bobs these days. She supposed the flow of shining hair didn't really go with her long-waisted knee-length dress, but she needed at least one thing that was unchanged. When she wore her hair in a loose knot at the back of her head, it didn't really look so out of place.

She was turning to go back inside the schoolhouse when a flash of movement caught her eye. A man had come out of the surrounding forest and was striding up the trail toward her.

She hesitated in the doorway, her start of surprise giving way to curiosity. She thought she knew everyone in the valley, but she didn't remember seeing this man before. He was about six feet tall, she judged, with wide shoulders on a lean, rangy body, and he moved with the unconscious grace of one accustomed to the outdoors.

As he came nearer she could see his features: thick, dark, unbarbered hair tumbled over his high forehead and curled along the back of his neck, where it had evidently been hacked off to clear his denim collar. His eyes, a warm brown under heavy black brows, were alert and observant. She noticed that his cheekbones were high and broad, his nose strong and straight, and she wondered if his craggy features hinted at an Indian heritage someplace along the line.

His manner, though, was quite at odds with his powerful appearance. He approached with a hesitancy, a diffidence, that bespoke the youth beneath the manly exterior.

"Are you Miss Whittaker?" He stopped a few feet away on the dirt path; since she was standing on the schoolhouse porch, her eyes were nearly level with his.

"Yes, I am. Jessica Whittaker." She nearly smiled, but

she kept her voice grave. Who else did he imagine she could be? She had only been teaching here since the term started last fall, but everyone in the valley was aware of her presence. A new schoolteacher was an event. This man would have to be a hermit not to know who she was.

A small smile softened his harsh features. "I'm Mark Hardy. Pleased to meet you."

"Oh!" Her eyes widened in surprise. No wonder she hadn't seen him before. She'd heard a lot about the Hardys. It was common knowledge that they didn't mingle with the other folks of the valley. She'd been told that they lived way back in the woods, coming out only a few times each year to buy flour and sugar. Sometimes one of them showed up at the schoolhouse for a few months, then disappeared back into the wilderness.

Before now she had seen only one of them. A girl, Alice Hardy, was among her current crop of pupils. About four months ago the girl had drifted in, thin and timid. Resisting all efforts at communication, she did her lessons and then vanished each afternoon into the forest that ringed the schoolyard.

The man in front of her—boy, really; he couldn't be much older than she was—was obviously ill at ease. He shifted from one foot to the other and seemed not to know what to do with his hands. But his gaze was unwavering.

"I have an Alice Hardy in school," she said, breaking the short silence. "Is she any relation?"

Another smile crossed his face, erasing the intensity of his expression. "That's my sister."

"Well, uh, she's a good student. Seems to learn quickly." Was that why he was here, to talk about Alice?

He shrugged. "She could be, but she's not too interested. She'll probably learn to read and write, then quit. Anything more isn't worth fighting the old man."

"The old man?" she echoed. She thought she detected a trace of bitterness in his voice.

"My pa. He thinks knowing how to sign your name

should be enough for anyone. He never learned to read and write himself, and he's suspicious of anyone who can. He says it puts ideas into their heads."

She listened carefully to what he was saying, paying as much attention to his manner of speaking as to the actual words. There was something odd about it, something careful and controlled, as though he were speaking a language with which he wasn't totally familiar. The formal cadence to his words was unusual among the more casual speech of the valley inhabitants.

"Did you go to school here?"

He lowered his eyes, a flush of embarrassment showing through his bronzed skin. "Some. Off and on, when I could get away from the old man. When he found out, he made me quit."

He raised his eyes, and she felt the defiance and anger in them almost as a physical jolt. "But he can't tell me what to do anymore. He tried." His mouth stretched in a mirthless grin. "Oh, he sure tried. But he couldn't do it."

Jessica gave an involuntary shudder. She suspected those simple words covered a lot. Her gaze fell to Mark's hands, clenched in fists at his side, and she remembered that she had detected an occasional bruise on Alice's white skin. The "old man's" discipline apparently included violence.

Smiling warmly, she stepped back and motioned him ahead of her into the classroom. "You wanted to talk to me, Mark?"

He didn't answer as his eyes roved over the simple room: the row of windows along one wall, a wood-burning stove in a corner, a floor of wide scuffed planks. A blackboard stood behind Jessica's straight-backed chair, and her desk faced rows of student desks arranged with the smallest at the front, graduating into those of the eighth graders. A small bookcase held the school library.

As though he hadn't heard her question, Mark moved to the bookcase and trailed one hand along the first row, a vague smile on his face.

Jessica moved to stand beside him. "Not too extensive a library, I'm afraid," she said, glancing at the familiar titles. "A set of Shakespeare, a few volumes of Emerson."

"And the Shakespeare set isn't even complete." He grinned, pointing to the top shelf.

She gave him a sharp glance. "I noticed there was a volume missing when I came here. It didn't take you long to see that it's gone."

"That's because I knew it was gone." He stepped back and looked into her face. "I stole it, Miss Whittaker."

"Stole it! But—but why?"

"To read, of course." His voice had an edge to it. "You'll notice an Emerson is missing, too. I probably know both of them by heart."

He walked to a chair and leaned against it, shoving his hands into his jeans pockets. "'Shall I compare thee to a summer's day? Thou art more lovely and more temperate by far—'"

He broke off suddenly and glanced down in confusion, a red flush coloring his skin. "I'm sorry. I didn't mean to be familiar. But with your blue eyes and your hair and the way you move—well, the sonnet just jumped into my head."

She smiled at him and moved behind her desk, trying to ease the embarrassment for both of them. One mystery was solved, at least. His strange, almost archaic way of speaking was based on a thorough, though limited, reading of the classics. But she still didn't know why he was here.

"So have you decided to bring the books back?" she asked lightly, her eyes on his face.

She wasn't prepared for the sudden transformation. His mask of disinterested friendliness dropped, giving way to a look of sheer hunger and desperation.

"No! I came because—because I want you to tutor me, Miss Whittaker."

"Tutor you!" Her first thought was that he was asking the

impossible. He was older than she was; not by any stretch of the imagination could he be considered a student.

The words poured from him as from a pressured dam finally broken. "I want to learn, Miss Whittaker! I *must* learn! Not just reading, writing, and a few sums so they don't cheat me at the general store. There's so much more. Geography, history, literature! And everything that's going on outside this valley!"

"But . . ." she stammered, a vision of what she had heard about the Hardys leaping into her brain, "what good will it do you here in the valley?"

"That's just it!" He struck his open palm with a clenched fist to emphasize the words. "I don't intend to be here in the valley forever."

He began striding about the room like a jungle creature confined to a cramped cage, his energy shrinking it to lilliputian proportions. "There's nothing for me here, nothing at all. The best I can do here is get a job with some cattle rancher, punching cows. People may think that's romantic, but they never spent all day looking at the backside of a cow, then coming in at night so tired they could hardly sleep. It's nearly as bad outside the valley now, with the Depression on, if you don't have an education. There's men standing in breadlines, Miss Whittaker, men watching their families starve. I've got to be better than they are."

The urgency in his voice made her wish she could help, but she didn't see how she could. She knew the bony fingers of the Depression had reached into every crevice of society; after all, she was a living example. Every news broadcast told of unemployment, want, desperation. Judging from their pallor, their listlessness, she suspected many of her own students came to school hungry.

Jessica flinched as Mark again assaulted one hand with the other. "My only chance is to learn something here, then get out. I know it will be hard, but it can't be worse than staying here. Looking at Pa, knowing that in twenty years I'll be the same—"

He broke off and turned dark eyes full of entreaty to her averted face. "I wouldn't take up much of your time," he said softly. "An hour a day . . ."

Something stirred in her heart; he was nearly begging. She knew even then that begging didn't come easily to this proud man. Biting her lip, she looked down at her desk, thoroughly shaken by his raw emotion. She recognized the familiar face of pain when she saw it; pain, anger, and frustration were her own companions as well.

Suddenly she wanted desperately to help him. This was what every teacher hoped to find: a pupil eager to learn, with an intellectual curiosity and fervor that was sadly lacking in her present students. So what if he wasn't formally enrolled? That he was well over the age when everyone else here thought education should be complete? Was she a teacher or wasn't she?

There was something compelling about Mark, something unusual. Although he floundered some in stating his appeal, she sensed in him a deep core of confidence. He was sure of what he wanted, sure of what he could do if he got the chance.

Yet an hour out of her day was not to be taken lightly. She was required to arrive at the schoolhouse early and get the fire going. The school day was painstakingly divided into sessions appropriate to the individual students— she had one in each elementary grade—and then she spent the late afternoon and evening grading papers and preparing lessons for the next day.

In fact the Blalocks would be wondering right now where she was. They kept close track of her; boarding the schoolteacher was a serious responsibility.

Mark seemed to read her hesitation and correctly assessed the reason. "Old Sam Blalock doesn't need to know. You can tell him you're staying late to help Alice. She'll never say different—differently."

Still, she hesitated. Subterfuge wasn't part of her nature. Yet if she helped Mark, it would be necessary. She shrank from what the Blalocks would say if they suspected she was staying after school alone with a man.

Especially this man. She had been here long enough to be aware of the feuds that were rife in the valley, and she had never heard Sam Blalock say a good word about a Hardy.

Mark grinned at her, transforming his face to an expression of boyish mischief. "How did you get stuck with the Blalocks, anyway?"

"How not to?" She shrugged slender shoulders and grinned back. "I have to stay with someone—it's in the contract. And the Blalocks take their position of leading citizens seriously. They donated the land for the school, I understand, and certainly their taxes pay most of my salary."

"Well, you certainly earn it, just by boarding with them," he retorted. His grin faded as his eyes darkened with anger. "Someday old Sam will get his comeuppance. He'll find out that just because he owns the whole valley, that doesn't mean he owns everybody in it!"

There was a hard resolve in his voice, and Jessica felt suddenly afraid for the brash young man and his dreams. As far as she could see, the Blalock cattle ranch looked rock solid. It would take more than a ragged boy in patched jeans and a denim shirt and a chip on his shoulder to bring it down. Even a boy as intelligent and determined as this one.

A boy with no education.

She made up her mind. "I'll do what I can, Mark."

Impulsively he reached for her hands, barely managing to stop just short of touching her. But although he clenched his fists at his sides, his joy was clearly written on his face.

"You can't know what this means to me, Miss Whittaker. You'll never regret it—I promise you!"

She smiled at his exuberance. It remained to be seen whether she would regret this decision. She might regret it very much. But it was a risk she was willing—no, had—to take.

"Can you be here after school tomorrow? As soon as everyone leaves? We should be able to get in an hour before anyone starts missing me seriously."

"I'll be here."

The promise sounded as though it were written in blood. He stood looking at her for a long time, as if memorizing the sight of her. Then he turned abruptly and strode out the door. A few feet away he began whistling "Old Dan Tucker"; she could still hear the tune echoing after he was out of sight in the woods.

She gathered up the papers she would correct that night and went quickly out the door and through the yard. Soon she was on Blalock land. The huge ranch dominated the county; it was bordered on one side by public forest and on the others by a few small farms and homesteads, where most of her students lived.

She had a two-mile walk ahead of her, but she moved slowly now, reluctant to reach her destination. Almost absently she noticed the first signs of spring, as red-winged blackbirds trilled melodiously from a stand of cattails alongside her, and her feet crushed a carpet of buttercups and bluebells. But even though she dragged her feet, the ranch house eventually came into view.

She paused, shrinking back from the imposing structure. Sam Blalock hadn't spared money on the two-story frame building, but it, like its builder, lacked the slightest touch of charm. Stone chimneys rose from a steep roof, narrow windows marched in a military line across the box-like front, and even the veranda failed to soften the building's hard lines.

If she were lucky, she might be able to make it across the yard and into the house without being seen. It would save explanations she wasn't ready to give.

Then she saw the tall, angular form and sighed. No such luck.

"You're late." Carrie Blalock stood on the veranda like an avenging harpy, squinting into the sun, as she watched Jessica across the yard. The woman's dark hair was pulled so tightly into the knot atop her head that her unnaturally tautened brow accentuated her sharp features. Jessica noticed her hands smooth the apron over her plain gray dress. Mrs. Blalock didn't believe in giving in to vanity; it was an affront to the Lord. "We've been waiting supper."

Jessica suppressed an irritated reply. The woman's tone conveyed her disapproval not only of the hour, Jessica suspected, but of Jessica herself. She had a hard time accepting Mrs. Blalock's habit of treating her like an irresponsible child.

"You know Sam likes to eat by five," Mrs. Blalock stated. She seemed to realize a softening smile was called for; it barely creased the stiff surface of her face.

"I'll be right there." Jessica gave her a quick smile as she brushed by and hurried on upstairs to her room. She placed her papers on her desk, then shrugged off her coat, barely glancing at her sparsely furnished room. She had seen the brass bed with the quilted coverlet, the braided rug on the plank floor, the cotton curtains at the one window, too often to need to peruse them now. It couldn't be much past five, but she knew they would all be at the table waiting for her, accusing eyes scanning the door to record her late entrance. Sam Blalock, his upright wife, and Norval.

Well, Norval's eyes wouldn't be accusing. They would be amused, as though he alone knew a rather unpleasant joke. As she did nearly every night, she wished she could have boarded somewhere else. The atmosphere at the Blalocks' was oppressive. Anyplace else, though, was unthinkable. The Blalocks *always* boarded the schoolteacher. Her contract stated that she must board with a family of good character, and no one in the valley would dare challenge the Blalocks' character—or their right to have her. Not with Carrie rounding everyone up for church on Sunday and Sam employing most of the men on his ranch.

She hurried down to take her place at the sturdy table, hoping she wouldn't face too many questions.

"You're late." Sam Blalock looked up from his plate and gave her a long, speculative glance. In spite of her annoyance she nearly smiled at the limited repertoire common to the rancher and his wife.

"I had a few things to take care of before I could leave today," she said, seating herself in her accustomed place across from Norval.

The rancher smiled expansively, and she relaxed. She knew he liked to be sure he was getting value for his money. Sam Blalock was middle-aged, short and stocky, with close-cropped hair and skin toughened by years and weather. While Carrie seemed as dried up and bloodless as a winter branch, Sam had an aura of raw power, of ruthless energy.

"You know, I don't much like you walking all that way home by yourself," he muttered, spearing a steak from the platter Carrie held in front of him. "Norval, here, would be glad to come and walk you home." He gestured at the blond young man who hadn't even glanced up at her arrival. "God knows, he doesn't have anything else to do."

Jessica glanced at Norval, wondering again how a couple like Carrie and Sam could have produced an elegant, sophisticated son like Norval. He lounged gracefully in his chair, his narrow face with its aristocratic features seeming to owe nothing to his parents. He smiled at her now, the slight smile that seemed to find everything faintly amusing, although his pale eyes were cool as usual.

"That's not very subtle, Dad," he said softly. "Are you implying I could do a little more around here?"

His father gave him a distasteful glance. "Around here, anyplace. When I was your age, I'd have jumped at the chance to walk a young woman home. Been waitin' at the door! I swear, I don't know what's wrong with you!"

There was a moment of tense silence. Mrs. Blalock's chest heaved, and she looked down at her plate. The young man picked up his water glass and put it to his lips with exaggerated care, then gave his father a glance of pure malice. "But you think you know what's wrong, don't you, Pop? Just a niggling little suspicion?"

Mrs. Blalock's lips tightened, and she shot a frightened glance at her husband. A bright flash of anger shone through the bronze of the older man's weathered skin, and he half rose from his seat, then sank back down heavily.

Jessica hardly dared breathe. The tension in the room was almost palpable, thick and heavy and poisonous. There had been hints before, innuendos, that something was different about Norval, but she didn't know what it was. She rather liked his sardonic manner, his quick, cutting wit.

Now he idly buttered a biscuit, apparently immune to the charged atmosphere, then lifted his eyes to Jessica. "Let's leave it to the lady in question. Do you want an escort home every night?"

"No! I mean, I'm quite capable—"

"Quite." Norval turned his eyes to his father. "The lady wishes to walk by herself."

Sam Blalock swallowed, struggling for control. Then he slumped back into his chair, capitulating for the moment at least. "Well, there can't be much to hurt her in broad daylight, I guess." He skewered Norval with flinty eyes. "But there's a box supper at the school next Saturday. I want you there, Norval, and I want you to be sure she gets home all right."

Jessica opened her mouth to protest, but before she could speak, Norval grinned and arched a thin eyebrow in her direction.

"Were you planning to go to the supper?"

"Oh yes, of course." It was as much her job to attend certain social functions as it was to teach.

"I'll fix your box." Mrs. Blalock's words came in a rush. "I don't imagine you'll have much time for cookin'."

Again Jessica started to protest, then sighed and reached for a bowl of creamed corn. It would be useless. The box supper was a well-established tradition in the valley. All the women prepared a boxed meal to show off their best cooking. The boxes were auctioned off to the men, who presumably didn't know to whom which box belonged. Whoever had prepared the box became the top bidder's partner for supper. Half the fun was in the stratagems to which the men resorted to discover the anonymous owners.

Jessica's eyes met Norval's, and she saw his slight wink. Mrs. Blalock would make sure Norval knew exactly what Jessica's supper box looked like.

On the other hand, supper with Norval wouldn't be too bad. He was witty in a brittle sort of way, and at least he read a book now and then.

Her attention wandered, and Mark Hardy's image flashed through her mind. She would see him tomorrow. She wondered if anyone had detected the slight flush she felt rise from her throat to color her cheeks as she visualized Mark's wide shoulders and lean body.

Would he come to the box supper?

Immediately she realized how ridiculous the thought was. The Hardys didn't mix with the valley people. And a man who had to steal books would hardly spend what little money he had to bid on a dinner partner.

2

TECHERS GOT A SWEAT ASS! SCRU YOU! JOEY SUCKS …

The words jumped out at her from a welter of similar phrases that covered the blackboard. Jessica sighed and reached for an eraser. She wouldn't mind the scrawled obscenities quite so much if only her pupils could spell. What Joey sucked was completely undecipherable, and she certainly wasn't going to try to figure it out. She had no idea of the meaning of some of the other words, either, and wondered if it was her naïveté or the adventurous spelling.

She shouldn't have forgotten to lock the door last night. The schoolhouse was the only structure in the valley that required a lock, precisely to forestall occurrences such as this. Most of the group hated to write in their exercise books, but she'd already found they had a penchant for anonymous adolescent obscenity. True, she had been exhilarated by her meeting with Mark and concerned about being late at the Blalocks, but that was no excuse for laxity.

She started to wipe away the scrawls, then paused. The

students would be arriving in a few minutes, avid for her reaction. She could picture their quick glances at the board, their sly murmurs, their grinning faces. One or two of them might be the actual culprits, but they would all know about it and wait eagerly to see what she did.

Frowning thoughtfully, she put the eraser down, sat at her desk, and waited for them to come in.

Jeff Deeter was first, which was somewhat unusual in itself. The oldest boy still in school, he had a mop of tousled hair, close-set eyes, and shoulders broad enough to carry logs. At seventeen he was a full-grown man—physically at least, she amended.

He glanced quickly at the board, and surprise widened his eyes. Jessica bet it was because the words were still there. He was followed by Jim Simpson, his buddy, a boy of nearly equal size and sensibility, and Jessica didn't miss the furtive look that passed between them. One by one the others filed in. Last was Alice Hardy, who went quickly to her seat and kept her eyes on her thin white hands crossed in front of her on her desk.

Jessica waited until the silence became uncomfortable. Then she rose from her desk and went to the board. "Who can tell me what's wrong with these words?"

There was not a sound. She swept the assembly with a stern gaze, then picked up her pointer and aimed it at the board.

"Jeff. How do you spell *teacher*?"

Jeff mumbled something, never raising his eyes from his desk. Jim Simpson giggled nervously, and she swung around to him. "Is this word supposed to be *sweet*, Jim? If so, can you tell me what's wrong with the way it's spelled?"

"Uh—s-w-e—"

There was a snicker from the back of the room, and Jessica swung around. "You, Jerry. Come to the board."

No one ever approached the gallows with more reluctance, but eventually Jerry was at the blackboard. Jessica handed him a piece of chalk. "Now, I think you can do better than whoever wrote this. Please correct it. 'Teacher has a sweet—'" She paused. "Perhaps *manner* would be a better choice."

As Jerry began to write she turned again to the squirming students. "I'm ashamed of whoever did this. Misspelling words a second grader would have no trouble with. The first thing we're going to do this morning is have a spelling bee. Starting with *screw.*"

Leslie Bond, a fourteen-year-old girl with long dark braids and sharp, malnourished features, raised her hand. "Miss Whittaker, are you going to tell our folks?"

Jessica pretended to consider. Although the children would undoubtedly be punished at home if their misdeeds at school were reported, she wasn't at all certain the community would approve of the way she had handled things, either.

"No," she said. "If it won't happen again, we can forget about it—and get on with learning to spell."

There was a collective sigh of relief, but Jessica wasn't fooled. She'd have to be sure to lock the door from now on. Still, whatever else they retained from her instruction, she was sure there were a few words they'd never forget how to spell.

The day dragged on, and when the last pupil was finally out the door, Jessica sank into the chair behind her desk. It had been a tiring afternoon, and Jeff Deeter had seemed determined to make amends by hanging around doing all the little chores he could think of. She pulled some papers across the desk and stared at them, but she couldn't concentrate.

"Hi. I hope I'm not late."

At the sound of his deep voice Jessica glanced up from the papers she had been pretending to grade and saw Mark's tall frame outlined in the doorway. She had been waiting for him, her ears straining at every slight noise, but she'd heard nothing. How had he arrived so silently?

She raised her head and gave him a warm smile. He was like a burst of summer sunshine, chasing away her fatigue and replacing it with purposeful energy. "You're not late. Right on time, in fact. The last pupil just left."

"I know. I waited until I saw that everybody was gone." He left the doorway and walked into the room, looking for a moment like a vulnerable, gangling adolescent. "I thought that Deeter kid would never leave!"

Jessica smiled and shook her head. In spite of the way she'd put Jeff on the spot this morning, he still seemed to have a crush on the teacher. This afternoon she'd thought she might have to shovel him out the door to get rid of him.

"It's his age. He thinks it's unmanly not to give the schoolmarm a whirl."

Mark grinned, white teeth flashing against the bronze of his skin. The vulnerable adolescent vanished, and a virile, exciting man took his place. "Can't fault him for that. Most men would feel the same."

His restless energy filled the small room, and Jessica raised a hand to brush her hair back from her suddenly hot cheek. Mark conveyed a feeling of urgency, as though he knew exactly where he was going and was in a desperate hurry to get there.

She straightened in her chair and pointed to a seat opposite her. "Maybe we'd better get started. Should I ask you a few questions and see what you already know so we can tell better where to begin?"

He sat down as though he were on springs, then pulled a sheaf of papers from his pocket. He handed them to her, his expression a combination of bravado and concern, as though he were giving her a gift he was not sure she would appreciate. "I thought maybe you'd take a look at this. I wrote it so you could get an idea of my grammar and spelling and such."

It had to be better than what she'd seen so far today, she thought, straightening out the crumpled sheets. She glanced at the title and quickly perused the first page, frowning slightly. Then, slowly laying the pages on the desk, she raised her eyebrows and shot him a quizzical glance.

"'The Power Structure Behind Economic Policies in the West'? This is almost in the form of a law brief."

He ducked his head and grinned, looking again like a mischievous boy. "Well, I stole a law book, too, by a man called Blackstone, and I've pretty well got it memorized."

"Where did you steal a law book?"

"From old Kincaid, the guy who runs the general store. He used to dabble in law."

She dropped her head into her hands, then raised her eyes and gave him a fierce look. "You've got to stop that! If you stole—and read—a law book, you must know you can go to jail for it!"

"Yeah." He twisted in his seat, trying to look repentant and not in the least succeeding. "But Kincaid won't complain. And I'm going to pay him back—pay them all back—just as soon as I can."

Afraid to ask what else his library consisted of, she returned to the essay, aware of his anxious eyes on her face as she read. His ideas were clearly, almost brilliantly presented, uncompromisingly logical, coherent—and disquieting. Sighing, she put the paper down on her desk and faced him, completely ambivalent about what she had just read.

"I don't know what to say. This is fantastic writing. It's full of strange spellings, of course, and there are some omissions that come from your limited reading. But it's powerful." Her mouth twitched as she held back a grin. "Not so much Blackstone, though, as Thomas Paine."

Thomas Paine at his most revolutionary, she thought. She felt a quick stab of foreboding. Mark was so eager, so optimistic, and so vulnerable—and he was bound for trouble if he stayed in the valley.

He didn't notice her slight hesitation, and a relieved smile spread over his face. "I'd sure appreciate your helping me fill up those holes you mentioned."

She returned his smile, her flash of concern for him giving way to excitement. It was so unexpected to find an intelligence like his in this out-of-the-way place. Or any-place, for that matter. The logic of his arguments, the range of knowledge revealed, was incredible for one of his limited background. Mark was what every true teacher dreamed of: a superior, willing student, hungry for what she had to offer.

Impulsively she reached across to touch his hand, then drew back in confusion. In every sense this was no ordi-nary pupil. This was a vital, virile man, physically com-pelling as well as intellectually exciting, and if she tutored him, she would have to be extraordinarily careful to keep things on a formal basis.

She placed a tablet in front of her and picked up a pen-cil, giving herself time to steady her voice. "The first thing we'll do is set up a study plan. You could use some help with spelling. Your grammar is fine—you probably absorbed it from all those classics you've been reading. And you seem to have picked up a good grasp of history. At least, economic history. I don't know whether I'd be much help in science, but—"

"Economics!" He leaned toward her, his brown eyes blazing. "Everything boils down to economics. The cattle-men have had a death grip on this valley for years, ever since they chased out the Indians. Two big ranches con-trol everything. There has to be a way to shake them loose, give other people a chance."

She put her pencil down on the desk, unable to tear her gaze away from his hypnotic eyes. "I don't think you're talking economics, Mark," she said slowly. "It sounds more like revolution. Some might even call such talk communistic."

"Some? Like Sam Blalock?"

"Well, yes. And he's a powerful man."

For a long moment he held her eyes, then smiled sheepishly. The tension left his body, and he settled back in his chair. "I know—old ideas are hard to change. And a nobody like me isn't going to change them. That's why I want to get out of here. Everyplace can't be as hidebound as this. I want to learn about the world outside—the world you came from."

She smiled in relief. "Well, that's easy enough. Let's start with geography."

She rose and took a fat volume from the bookcase, then pulled her chair around to sit beside him. For over an hour the two heads, blond and dark, bent over the book. Both were so immersed in reading that Jessica only gradually became aware of her shoulder brushing his as she turned the pages of the text. Once she was aware of it, though, the sensation intensified until it filled her entire consciousness.

Abruptly she pulled away. "I had no idea it was so late," she said, knowing her voice sounded too breathless. "I think that's enough for today."

He straightened, too, a rueful smile on his face. "I didn't mean to keep you so long. I've been starving for . . ." His voice trailed off.

His face was only a few inches away, and as Jessica looked at him she became aware of his faint woodsy aroma, a mixture of pine and fresh air and clean, healthy skin. She saw the pulse beat in the hollow of his neck and noticed that his lean jaw had a freshly shaven look. There was even a tiny nick where the razor had slipped.

Simultaneously they stood up, nearly knocking over their chairs, their eyes still locked in passionate awareness. Then slowly, very slowly, she managed to tear her gaze away.

"That's enough for today," she repeated. Was that squeaky little voice her own?

He didn't reply, and she wondered if he had heard. Finally he took a deep breath and slammed the book shut. "Tomorrow?"

"Tomorrow."

He spun around and almost ran out the door. She moved to the threshold and stood watching him until he vanished into the pines.

Then she walked slowly back to her desk and fumbled with the essay while she waited for her pulse to return to normal. What a strange mixture of naïveté and intelligence he was. She wasn't sure just what he was, but he was no ordinary country bumpkin.

The moment of intense awareness that had sizzled between them wasn't ordinary, either. She felt that the essence of his personality had touched her physically, marking her in some indefinable way. True, she had very little experience with men, but instinct told her that her response to Mark had been anything but usual.

If so, it was dangerous. Teachers were required to be as pure as Caesar's wife. The eyes of the community took in her every move, discussed her every act. She could not afford even the appearance of the slightest impropriety. What would the school board think—what would Sam Blalock think—if it became known that she was spending an hour every afternoon alone with a man?

Yet should she let her affinity for Mark deflect her from her duty? How could she, a teacher, turn her back on his desperate desire to learn? With all her other students she felt as though she were trying to stuff information into minds preoccupied with whether it would rain before they got the hay in or whether the first frost would come before the cattle could be brought in from the summer range. Mark Hardy made her remember why she had become a teacher.

And life wouldn't be easy for Mark. Even with all the help she could give him, he might be battering fruitlessly against an impenetrable stone wall.

Suddenly she thrust out her chin in a gesture of defiance no less real because no one was there to see it. She wouldn't be doing anything wrong by tutoring Mark. She had her values; she didn't need the community to keep her on the straight and narrow path of virtue.

The sound of hooves clattering against rock broke through her concentration, and she glanced out the doorway, expecting to see one of her pupils returning. As she recognized the tall, slender man in the courtyard, her eyes widened with surprise and annoyance. He was riding a large buckskin horse, and a small bay, saddled and bridled, trailed behind him. She walked quickly to the door.

"Norval. What are you doing here?"

He pulled slightly on the reins, and the buckskin stopped in front of the steps, dancing impatiently.

He glanced up at the sky, which was clouding over, then back at her. "It looks like it might rain. I thought you might like a ride home, even if you didn't want company on your walk."

There was a faint grin on his face, a sardonic look in his eyes, that told her he had thought no such thing.

She assessed him briefly. He wore the wide-brimmed hat, flannel shirt, jeans, and chaps that were almost the uniform of the county, yet they looked somehow different on him. He had an easy air of elegance about him that seemed out of place in his rustic surroundings.

She returned his grin. "You thought? Or your dad thought?"

"Can't put a thing over on the schoolmarm," he said, swinging from the saddle and joining her on the front porch. "You know the old man has you all picked out as a daughter-in-law."

She didn't answer. Could that be true? Certainly Sam Blalock took every opportunity to throw them together. But surely Sam must see that Norval wasn't at all attracted to her. And although Norval's cynical wit often amused her, for some reason she couldn't define she was uncomfortable around him.

"Well, at least that's up to us, isn't it?" she finally said.

"Don't sell him short," Norval answered, a hint of bitterness in his cultivated voice. "He's used to getting what he wants."

"I don't see why he would want me," she said lightly, hoping to get off the subject.

"Don't you?" He looked at her for a long minute, and she knew he was cataloging her. He spoke almost to himself. "There's that long, pale hair, that translucent skin, a figure that at first glance looks slender but is surprisingly full in the breasts and hips. I can see the attraction."

Even though there was nothing at all suggestive in his appraisal or in his calm, detached assessment, she was acutely nervous, and her cheeks burned. She began an angry retort, but Norval cut her off.

"There's no reason we can't use it to our advantage, though."

"What do you mean?"

His shrewd blue eyes never left her face. "Just think about it. There are times I'd rather be someplace else—places my old man wouldn't like a bit. You must feel the same. A young woman like you can't really be happy with only kids around for company. We could leave the house together, then go our own ways and do whatever we wanted."

She straightened her spine and glared at him. "Forget it, Norval. I don't know what you want to do, but I have nothing to hide. I'm not about to get involved in some charade that—"

"All right, all right!" Laughing, he held up a hand to stop her words. "You'd better ride home with me, though. You're late now, and if you don't want to be cross-examined, you'd best get up on that horse." He looked thoughtfully over her shoulder at the schoolroom. "Why are you so late, anyway?"

She threw him an angry glance, not deigning to reply. He was right, though: it would be much better if she arrived at the Blalock ranch with Norval. It was fortunate that she had worn trousers today. She didn't usually, but there had been a lingering nip of winter in the air this morning.

She locked the door, then grudgingly swung up on the bay and cantered down the trail beside Norval.

He edged his horse a little closer. "You didn't tell me—why *are* you so late?"

Her pulse jumped, and she tried to control the faint flush coloring her cheeks. He wasn't going to let go. Perhaps she could satisfy his curiosity without telling a direct lie.

"I had to stay late to help a pupil."

"Oh? Which one? I'm surprised you get any of those mustangs to come to school, let alone stay late."

"It was—it was Alice Hardy," she floundered.

"Hardy?" He gave her a sharp glance, then frowned. "Better stay away from the Hardys. They're nothing but trouble."

"Trouble? You know them all personally?" She knew there was an edge to her voice.

"It's no secret," Norval said, jerking his horse's reins so viciously that the animal danced backward a couple of steps. "They're all a bunch of backwoods hillbillies. Old man Hardy got here about the same time Pa did, and he holed up in some hollow in the woods and raised a bunch of hungry, snot-nosed brats. Take any one of them to town and put a necktie on him, and he'll stand still all day, thinking he's tied up!"

"I gather the Blalocks aren't too fond of the Hardys," she said slowly.

"And vice versa," Norval snorted. "Old Jeb Hardy knows he's not welcome within a mile of the Blalock ranch. And those ignorant kids—"

"Not everyone's father can afford to send them to college, as yours did," she said sharply.

Norval grinned, apparently pushing the Hardys out of his mind. "I'll just bet Pa wished he hadn't sent me. He thinks it's college that ruined me!"

"Are you ruined, then?"

He lifted an aristocratic brow. "I guess it all depends on your point of view."

She glanced at his face and saw the usual sardonic expression. She decided she didn't want to pursue the subject. She knew there was some problem between Norval and his father. She sensed an unspoken undercurrent of anger every time they were together. But she had no idea of the cause. She returned to the topic of greater interest to her.

"Are you simply repeating what everybody says about the Hardys, or do you actually know them?"

Norval's expression changed from aloof, self-mocking irony to bitterness. "Oh, I know them. The oldest one, Mark, is about my age. We went to school together—when he went, that is. He only came about half the time. He's a brawler, a roughneck. He ought to be in jail."

He raised a hand and absently stroked his jaw. Jessica hid a smile. As plainly as though he had said so, Norval had indicated that he and Mark had fought, and that he hadn't gotten the best of it. The prince of the county and the ragged hillbilly. It must still rankle.

The Blalock ranch house loomed in front of them, effectively stopping the discussion. Jessica slid from the horse and handed the reins to Norval, who tossed them to the ranch hand who walked from the barn to meet them.

"See you at supper," she called over her shoulder, walking quickly toward the house. He nodded briefly and trotted his horse toward the barn.

Carrie Blalock's angular face was visible from a front window before the woman drew back quickly, letting the curtains fall in front of her. Jessica couldn't suppress a smug smile. Her arrival with Norval had been satisfactorily noted.

Pine needles crunched beneath his boots, and the wind nipped around his shoulders and across his back, sliding easily through the thin material of his oft-washed denim shirt, but Mark ignored its chill as he covered the ground in long, loping strides. He shouldn't have waited so long before starting home; it might be dark before he got there, and the forest trails were hard to follow at night.

He stared unseeingly at the trail in front of him, avoiding rocks and holes with a sureness born of familiarity. He wished he had been able to pull himself away from his hiding place behind the school before Norval Blalock had appeared in the schoolyard. The man's arrival left a bad taste in his mouth. He'd had a hard time controlling his anger when he saw Norval riding that buckskin with all the smugness and superiority that old Sam's money could give him.

A faint smile eased the harshness of his set jaw. Norval hadn't looked so smug the time he'd knocked him across the schoolyard. And Norval hadn't called him a mongrel again, either. At least not to his face.

Well, let them smirk and sneer all they wanted. He knew he was better than they were—more determined, more intelligent. When he had made his money, he'd come back—and see what they had to say about Mark Hardy then!

A wave of despair hit him, a force so strong that he stopped and leaned his head against the rough bark of a pine. Who was he kidding? What was the use? What good had it done to knock Norval down? It hadn't gotten him to college. It hadn't gotten him a decent job. It hadn't changed Norval's—or anyone else's—opinion of him. He was a Hardy. A no-good, backwoods hillbilly.

He pulled ten crumpled dollar bills from his pocket and looked at them bleakly. He was twenty-two, and this was all the money he had in the world, money it had taken him years to save. And he had to carry it around with him so the old man couldn't find it.

To Jebediah Hardy, that money would represent danger. The old man was well aware that his eldest son wanted nothing more than to get out of the valley, and he was prepared to do anything in his power to stop him. Mark had heard Jeb's harangue often enough to know his father's feelings on the subject. Kin stuck together. A man's oldest boy didn't desert him.

He clenched his fists and pounded the unyielding bark,

then lowered his head until his brow rested against the tree. The sharp scent of pine assailed him, and he took a deep, resolute breath. He would get away—he would. Away from his home, where his deep hunger for knowledge was looked upon as betrayal. Away from the valley, where he would always be known as one of the no-good Hardys.

The pretty new schoolteacher was the key. He didn't know much about the world beyond Hope Valley except what he had heard in snatches over the radio and read in the occasional newspaper, but he knew enough to realize you needed all the armor and ammunition you could get. If he could make it out, get rich, he would be judged for who he was, not who his family was.

Jessica Whittaker. Her very name sounded cool and elegant, like the freshly ironed scented sheets he had only read about. And she seemed to care. She seemed willing to help him.

A faint uneasiness curled like invasive tendrils of morning glory in the pit of his stomach. There had been moments today when they had looked at each other and he'd had to exercise every bit of willpower he could command to keep from crushing her in his arms. Him! The thought was laughable. Mark Hardy, who still lived with his ma and pa and had ten dollars to his name.

His fingers worked convulsively as a vision of Jessica Whittaker's shining head, bent like a flower over the geography text, swept into his mind. He had hardly been able to keep his mind on the lesson. The lemon scent of her hair floated to his nostrils, and out of the corner of his eye he saw her long, dark lashes sweep her high cheekbones. Her slender shoulder was not quite touching his, but he was so aware of her that he began to sweat.

She was so beautiful.

But she was not for the likes of him. He straightened his shoulders and loped off down the trail at the brisk pace that could cover the miles almost as competently as a lean, hungry wolf.

3

"*Can't be much fun for you,* coming back here at night after you've been here all day." Lydia Adams made an ineffectual effort to control her wild mop of curly red hair, then gave Jessica a sympathetic glance and placed yet another box supper on the already laden desk.

"It really doesn't seem like the same place," Jessica replied, glancing at the gaily decorated boxes stacked on the white linen cloth that covered her scuffed desk. "So much more festive."

She smiled at Lydia. The woman's round cheeks were flushed with activity, and her blue eyes sparkled as she brought order out of chaos. Her cotton dress, which fit a little too snugly in places and which Jessica suspected was made out of flour sacks, was sprigged with delicate embroidered flowers, and she moved quickly on surprisingly tiny feet. Lydia had been the friendliest of all the women in the valley, and Jessica liked her.

"You've done a marvelous job," she said sincerely. The room had been transformed. Nearly every available surface was festooned with red ribbons and white linen. Children's desks were lined against the wall, leaving the middle of the floor free for dancing. Kerosene lamps cast a soft yellow glow over the wide planks, which had been newly waxed and polished. The far corners of the familiar room were cloaked in mysterious darkness, and unrelieved blackness pushed against the row of windows from outside, a blackness that seemed to float in from the forest as though curious about the sudden activity. Jessica glimpsed her reflection in the shiny panes, and it accentuated the feeling that the schoolroom had become an oasis of light in the surrounding dark.

The most obvious difference in the schoolhouse tonight, however, was in its occupants. Some of her pupils were there, but they were outnumbered by adults—adults whose daytime faces were known to her, but who, in their best clothes amid the festive shadows, were suddenly strangers.

She turned back to Lydia with a laugh. "I didn't know so many people could crowd into one room."

"Well, it's the first social affair we've had since you've been here. A new face always brings out a crowd." Lydia leaned close to Jessica, trying to be heard above the plunking sounds of a fiddle being tuned. "Every man in the county is here—and the women sure wouldn't let them come alone." She gave her a quick wink. "I'm certainly going to watch my Jake."

Before Jessica could reply, the old man who had been sitting on a stool by the door readying his fiddle struggled to his feet and launched into the clear and haunting melody of a waltz.

Lydia nudged Jessica. "Ben always starts them out slow. It will take a few more trips outside to nip at the bottle before the guys warm up enough to two-step!"

At a light touch on her arm Jessica turned from Lydia and looked up into Norval's face. He was smiling, as though the two of them shared a private joke.

"Would you like to waltz before I turn you over to the yokels to step on your feet?"

"I didn't know dancing was among your many talents," she said tartly, reacting to Norval's smug, superior tone. She suspected he was right about the dancing ability of the local men, but she found herself wanting to wipe the cynical smile from his handsome face.

"There is no end to the things you don't know about me." He put his arm around her waist and moved her out onto the impromptu dance floor.

They were silent as he guided her around the room in long, smooth strides. She was glad she was able to follow him; she knew they were the focus of every curious eye in the place.

She supposed they looked good together. She had taken care in dressing, and she knew her pale green taffeta dress with the low waistline, accessorized by a long strand of authentic-looking pearls, was more fashionable than anything that had been seen in the valley for years.

She placed a hand on Norval's back, feeling the smooth texture of his white linen shirt, as he bent his blond head above hers. He *was* a good dancer; he moved her in graceful patterns, holding her carefully away from his body in a very correct waltz. They might look like one unit, she thought, but the slight rigidity in Norval's stance reminded her that he had no desire to hold her any closer.

Out of the corner of her eye she saw Cam and Ted Beale move onto the floor, followed immediately by another couple, and she relaxed. At least she and Norval were no longer providing a floor show.

He caught her faint exhalation and grinned. "Got to give the yokels their money's worth."

She stiffened. "If these people are so far beneath you, I'm surprised you're even here."

"No, you're not." He twirled her expertly. "The folks are determined that you and I are going to become an item. And loyal son that I am, I wouldn't want to disillusion them."

"Why not?" She tilted her head back so she could look

into his face. "You're an adult. You're educated. I *know* you have a mind of your own. Surely you can pick your own girl."

An amused look crossed his face. "Or not pick her." He seemed about to say something else, then changed his mind and asked instead, "How are you coming along with your tutoring?"

Her heart skipped a beat. Had there been some innuendo in his words? She and Mark had been meeting daily for the past two weeks, and she had thought their secret was safe. The Blalocks had accepted that she would be an hour later and no longer questioned her so closely. Although Norval always smiled cynically when she mentioned Alice Hardy, she had thought he believed her.

"Everything's fine," she said, turning her head and setting her lips in a firm line. Norval didn't know anything. He was just fishing, and she wouldn't blurt out any damaging admissions.

Not that she was doing anything wrong. Still, it would be hard to convince people of that. Gossiping tongues were often more active when there was little to feed on, and she knew her every move was scrutinized and discussed.

But she and Mark attended strictly to business. They were studying history now, and Jessica was continually amazed at his understanding of the forces that shaped their world. His quick mind was such a delight that she wondered sometimes who was the teacher and who the pupil. He had an unerring grasp of the interrelationships of subjects. She had always seen them as separate: geography, history, economics, literature. For the first time, under Mark's penetrating questions, she began to see all knowledge as interrelated—geography affecting economics, economics affecting history, history demanding literature to mirror the turbulence of social upheaval and change.

Mark's most insistent questions were about the privileged social milieu in which she had lived before her father's death, and she was surprised at his hunger for even the minutiae: the menus at dinner parties, how people dressed, what they talked about. He was almost as eager to shed his backwoods accent as he was to learn about Adam Smith's theory of economics.

Even to herself she could not admit how much she looked forward to those sessions. All afternoon, as she listened to the students' recitations, she felt a rising tide of anticipation. Lightness permeated her. He would soon be here. Her cheeks felt hot, her throat tight, and she couldn't control her frequent glances at the clock.

Then the last pupil was gone. She would sit at her desk, ears alert to catch every sound above the pounding of her heart. Finally she would hear the wooden porch steps creak under his boots, and she would raise her eyes to see his tall frame filling the doorway.

The hour would pass in a kaleidoscope of excitement and confusion. The sight of his muscular forearms mixed with the discussion of the reign of Claudius. The intensity of his eyes vied with the map of England. Her own voice explaining a passage from a textbook sounded as though it belonged to someone else while the sweet smell of his sun-warmed hair enveloped her.

Occasionally their shoulders touched, and they both became rigid, caught as swiftly in the currents that surged between them as though roped by invisible lariats. During those silent moments she became excruciatingly aware of everything: the buzz of flies against the windowpane, the breeze fanning through the open door to cool her hot cheeks, his chest rising and falling with each breath.

At such times her face would flush and her throat constrict. She would clench her hands in her lap, unable to look up from the page, where words swam unintelligibly under her eyes. She was aware of his own struggle as he sat motionless, rigidly controlled.

Norval's voice brought her back to the present. "The music has stopped."

"Oh." Her arms fell, and she backed away in confusion. "I guess I wasn't paying attention."

"Obviously."

"Where are your folks?" She quickly changed the subject. "I thought just about everybody would be here tonight."

"Not them. They don't dance. I'm to uphold the family honor. Buy your box supper and take you home."

Annoyance edged his voice. What was the source of the pressure they were putting on Norval? He was obviously not in the least interested in her.

She tried for a light touch. "How will you know which one is mine?" She had brought the box in herself, smiling at the intricate crosshatch design Carrie Blalock had colored on the lid.

"Now, you know better than that." It was Norval's turn to smile. "Mother didn't go to all that trouble coloring the thing for nothing."

Before she could reply, the musicians burst into a fast rendition of "Golden Slippers." A hand touched her arm, and Jeff Deeter's father bashfully asked her to dance. After that she didn't sit down at all as one man after another claimed a dance. The floor was soon crowded with couples two-stepping and jigging as the surreptitious sips of whiskey and the beat of the music worked their magic.

She looked around as she went from one pair of enthusiastic arms to another, but she wasn't really surprised that she didn't see him. The Hardys didn't attend these social functions, and she hadn't expected Mark. Nevertheless she felt a sense of loss. She was glad when the music stopped and Lydia's husband, Jake Adams, ambled to the front of the room to begin the auction. He picked up a box from among the profusion on the desk.

"Okay, men, this is what we've all been waiting for." He held up a hand, and the buzzing voices quieted, finally falling silent. "What lucky man is going to have supper with the beautiful lady who fixed this box? What am I offered for a chance to sit and talk"—he winked—"or whatever with her?" He held the box aloft, turning it so it could be seen from every side.

"Twenty-five cents."

"Thirty."

Hearing no more bids, Jake handed the box to a rangy man who opened the lid and took out a slip of paper. Apparently it was the wished-for name; he grinned widely as he made his way to the side of the room where the woman waited, a shy, proud smile on her face.

"Now, this one—" Jake stopped in midsentence, his mouth still open with surprise as he stared toward the door.

Alerted by his expression, all eyes followed Jake's gaze to the schoolroom door. There was a collective gasp of surprise. Then all was unnaturally still as the crowd gaped at the tall, broad-shouldered man who stood framed in the doorway. Jessica's heart thudded against her chest, and she put her hand to her throat as she stared, along with everyone else, at Mark Hardy.

The golden light caught the angular planes of his face while the darkness of his shirt and jeans echoed the blackness behind him. He paused, glanced briefly at the crowd, then strode into the room. Here was a Mark Jessica had never seen before—confident, almost arrogant, as he ignored the stares and whispers, clearly returning his neighbors' contempt with interest. As his swift glance located her, then swept on around the assemblage, he seemed to dominate the room.

Jessica heard the murmur of embarrassed greetings as people said hello, then edged slightly away, leaving Mark as solitary as if he had been alone in the woods. Irritation surged through her. Surely Mark had as much right to be here as anyone! Defiantly she raised her chin and gave him a warm smile as his dark eyes returned to her.

Tension drained from his lean body as he returned her

smile and leaned indolently against the wall, his eyes holding hers above the heads of the crowd. For a long moment there was just the two of them, united by an invisible skein as strong as steel.

She felt someone else's eyes on her face and glanced away from Mark, her cheeks flaming. How very obvious she had been. Her gaze met Norval's, and a cold shiver went down her back at his shrewd expression. A half smile on his patrician lips, he arched an inquiring eyebrow. She disregarded his smile. His eyes weren't cool; they were angry, and the set of his shoulders indicated he was anything but pleased by Mark's sudden entrance and her unguarded response. Suddenly she knew that Norval had been suspicious for a long time, and that he had just had his suspicions confirmed.

Jake recovered from his shock. He lifted another box and inquired what he was offered. Talk started again. The bidding was swift, and soon only about six boxes remained on the desk. Of all the men only Norval, his lips now twisted in a cynical grin, and Mark, who still lounged against a far wall, had not bid.

"This is sure a little beauty." Jake lifted a box, and Jessica caught her breath. The intricate cross-hatching was plainly visible, and she knew she was about to acquire a supper partner.

"Let's start the bidding. And don't be bashful, men."

Norval lifted a languid hand. "Fifty cents."

There was a rustle of excitement. Norval was starting the bidding high; fifty cents was the top that had been paid so far. He obviously knew whom he was bidding for.

Jessica glanced at Mark. His eyes searched Norval's face, and then he smiled, a slow, knowing smile. "One dollar."

In absolute silence all eyes turned to Mark, then swung back to Norval. In the uncertain lamplight Jessica thought she saw Norval flinch. His face lost its customary cool expression, and the look he shot Mark contained pure hatred.

"Two," Norval retorted, his features contorting into a sneer as he stared haughtily at Mark. There was no mistaking the challenge, or the dislike, in the look he gave him.

Mark's expression didn't change. He retained his smile, although Jessica saw immediately that it didn't reach his eyes. The two men were like stallions squaring off for a fight, she thought, resentment coloring her face an even deeper red, and it was painfully obvious that she was the prize!

"Three dollars." Mark's voice was cool, and Jessica clenched her hands into fists. She would have bet he didn't even have three dollars, yet here he was, spending a fortune on a box supper!

Uncertainty flickered in Norval's eyes, and he flashed Mark a venomous look. Jessica winced. What was Mark thinking! She remembered Norval's mention of their rivalry as children, and the antipathy was obviously still alive and well. Yet it was insane to challenge Norval on the basis of money. He had the entire Blalock ranch behind him.

"Five dollars."

Perspiration shone on Norval's forehead, and Jessica saw the moisture gleam faintly in the lamplight. Not one voice broke the silence; she could even hear the slight rustle of the breeze under the eaves of the building, and the faint hoot of an owl. Norval's bid was more than a week's wages for many of them, and the crowd was now well aware that something most unusual was happening.

Mark stared back at Norval, his dark eyes unreadable. Then he grinned. "Ten."

The crowd gasped, then relapsed into silence as they waited for Norval's reply. She knew they were confident of the outcome. It was unthinkable that a reigning prince would back down from a backwoods upstart. But he was certainly taking his time in upping the bid. In fact, he seemed to have a hard time raising his gaze from the floor, and his angry flush had faded to a sickly pallor. Seconds ticked by. Then, without a word, he turned abruptly and stalked angrily out of the room and into the night.

It seemed to Jessica that everyone let out a collective sigh. She knew she did, and she clutched the desk behind her for support, her eyes never leaving Mark's face. He gave her a quick smile, then walked to the front of the room, where Jake still held the box with the crosshatch design.

"I guess that's mine." He reached for the box, his voice low and firm.

"Sure is!" Jake handed him the box, then shook his hand. "And you paid a record price. Can't wait to see who the lucky lady is." His quick glance at Jessica told her he certainly had his suspicions.

Mark slowly opened the lid and took out the slip of paper. Then he bowed slightly in Jessica's direction. "I'm honored to have supper with you, Miss Whittaker."

Unable to answer, her heart still hammering in her throat, Jessica could only nod. She took Mark's outstretched hand and, with every eye in the place on her, walked beside him to the far corner of the room, where he pulled two chairs together and motioned her to a seat.

As though to make up for the previous silence, the crowd began to jabber. Disconnected phrases floated to her ears. "Imagine—the nerve!" "Where did a Hardy get ten dollars?" She resolutely ignored it; at least the racket was enough to cover a low-voiced conversation.

"Mark, are you crazy? Why on earth did you do this?"

His confidence ebbed away, and he looked like a little boy being chastised. "I wanted to see you. See you as a person, that is. Not a teacher."

"But here? That dramatic entrance in front of everybody . . . and bidding for me like I was a horse!" Several curious faces turned her way, and she lowered her voice even further. "It's embarrassing."

Concern darkened his expression. "I'd never do anything to embarrass you. I didn't think of it like that at all. I just wanted to have supper with you."

She had to smile at the perplexity in his voice. He was more than ever like a little boy whose big surprise had backfired. Jessica relented. "Anyway, how did you know that particular box was mine?"

"I didn't know—but I figured Norval would. And he wouldn't have bid for any other box."

"Oh, Mark." Impulsively she reached out to touch his arm, then drew back quickly as she realized eyes were scrutinizing her every gesture. "You took a chance. You spent so much money. How did you know you could out-bid Norval?"

"I didn't know that, either." His devilish grin was back in place. "But I figured he wouldn't be carrying much money around with him. No reason to—a few dollars, maybe. And I guess I was right."

"I guess so." That was undoubtedly the reason Norval had stopped bidding: he wasn't carrying cash. She suspected he would have spent every dime he had before he let Mark Hardy beat him at anything.

"I don't like it that you made an enemy because of me, Mark."

His face became very still; only a muscle twitched in his jaw. "I haven't *made* an enemy. I have an enemy. I've had one for a long time. Norval and I have hated each other since we were kids."

A shiver sent cold prickles along her skin. This talk of enemies, of hatred, seemed so out of place here. For the first time she sensed quite viscerally the deep, twisting currents of the old feuds that ran under the facade of cheerful friendliness the people turned toward her.

"Whose side was everyone on tonight?" Absently she took a delicate chicken-salad sandwich from the box.

"They had a devil of a time deciding," Mark said cheerfully. He reached for a sandwich, his hand just happening to touch hers and sending a wave of little shocks along her arm. "They dislike me—think I'm too big for my britches. I've heard more than one say water can't rise above its source. But they don't care much for the Blalocks, either. Sam has ridden roughshod over most of them at one time or another. He didn't get his huge ranch by being kind and reasonable. And since he's almost the only employer around here, he can put wages wherever he wants them."

As the evening wore on she and Mark continued to talk quietly, more or less ignored by the others. When Jessica saw coats being gathered, children wakened, she realized that it would soon be time to go.

Mark realized it, too. He leaned toward her. "May I walk you home?"

She averted her face. She'd had no choice about Mark as a dinner partner; after all, he had bought her box. But agreeing to walk home with him was a bigger step. It would cause more talk. But Norval hadn't returned, and she didn't really want to walk alone at night. Nor would she be expected to.

She broke off the line of thought. That wasn't it at all. She wanted to walk home with Mark, and she was still angry at the treatment he had received. She was a grown woman. She could walk home with whomever she wished.

"All right. Wait outside. I'll get my coat."

Mark grinned happily and walked toward the door, and Jessica went to the line of hooks along one wall and reached for her wrap.

"Are you sure you know what you're doing?"

At the soft whisper Jessica turned to look into Lydia's worried eyes. "What do you mean?"

Lydia gazed at the floor, then back at Jessica. "Leaving here with him. That Mark Hardy, he's different. He shouldn't have come in here like that. It was out of place."

Asperity sharpened Jessica's voice. "Why out of place? Doesn't he have a right to come to a community supper?"

"Well, he never does. I hate talking to you like this, but someone has to. You don't understand—there'll be talk. . . ."

Jessica bit back an angry retort. Lydia meant well; she could see it in the woman's worried eyes. She was a friend—she considered it her duty to warn her.

Jessica spoke softly. "There shouldn't be. After all, he's only walking me home. It's the polite thing to do—the expected thing to do after supper."

Lydia shook her head doggedly. "Not with Mark Hardy. Besides, he never does the expected thing. Please be careful."

Impulsively Jessica reached over and squeezed the woman's shoulder. "Thank you, Lydia. I'll be careful. It's only a walk home." She slipped on her coat, said the necessary good-byes, and walked out into the night, ignoring the eyes that followed her.

Mark was waiting by the door.

Mark strode briskly through the woods, the trail so familiar he didn't even have to think about where he put his feet. There was a most delicious fragrance in the air, a burgeoning of new leaves and sweet grasses, and he drew it in with deep breaths. He hadn't seen Jessica since the box-supper social, and he was in a fever of impatience to be with her again.

It was early afternoon—much too early for his lesson. He would have to hang around in the woods until the last student left. Probably that Deeter kid, if he could judge by the past.

He hoped she wouldn't be angry about what had happened at the social. Perhaps he'd been wrong to surprise her. They hadn't talked much when he walked her home. She'd seemed to be in a thoughtful mood. Maybe even apprehensive.

He had parted with her outside the yard of the Blalocks' ranch house, unable to bring himself to say much to her. Probably he had stepped out of line in going to the supper, walking her home. She was way beyond his reach. She had never agreed to do anything but teach him, and he had uni-laterally tried to change the relationship.

Into what? He didn't know. Any relationship other than teacher-pupil was impossible. He clenched his teeth, swept by the familiar wave of angry frustration. It had been a dumb, impulsive thing to do. He still didn't know how he'd gotten up the nerve to step inside that room and face all those people as if he belonged there; it had taken every ounce of courage he had. And he'd spent every dime he had buying that silly box supper.

A grin spread over his face. It had been worth it, though, if only to see Norval Blalock's expression when he realized he had run out of cash. He hadn't seen that vicious look on Norval's face since he had held him down in the schoolyard and pounded his head in the grass until he yelled uncle. And it was gratifying to see all those people smiling at him when he knew they were really wondering where a mongrel hillbilly like Mark Hardy had gotten all that money.

A quick frown erased the grin. He had been a fool to spend his only ten dollars like that. It meant he would have to postpone leaving the valley that much longer. But to sit beside Jessica Whittaker, to proclaim that he was just as good as anyone there, had been worth it.

He only hoped she would think so. Perhaps he shouldn't have asked to walk her home. Yet from any other supper partner anything else would have been an insult, and seen as such by the group. Still, she had to be so careful about relationships. Her reputation would suffer enough if it became known that she spent every afternoon alone with a man; it would be disastrous if anyone found out *he* was the man.

He watched from his vantage point until the last pupil had left—as he'd suspected, the hulking Deeter kid—then walked slowly toward the school. The door was open to the soft afternoon breeze, and he could see her sitting behind her desk, her slender shoulders bent slightly, her beautiful eyes lowered to a paper in front of her.

He paused and caught his breath, a painful band constricting his heart. The late-afternoon sun filtered through the leaves of the cottonwood tree just outside the window, shining through the panes to dapple her pale gold hair with dancing shadows of dark and light. Her hair was brushed back from her delicate oval face, and in the soft light her skin looked translucent. A faint flush colored her cheeks, and her full lips were parted slightly, giving her a gentle, vulnerable appearance that went straight to his heart. She was incredibly, unbearably beautiful.

Suddenly, as though becoming aware of his presence, she raised her eyes and looked straight into his face. He couldn't look away from their clear blue depths. He was mesmerized, a butterfly on a pin, as the moment stretched on and on. A shaft of fear shot through him at the thought that arrived full blown in his mind. He struggled to push it away, knowing it was hopeless. But as surely as he was standing here, he knew that this was the woman he would love forever.

He tried desperately to crush the knowledge. This was not the time to fall in love. He had to avoid anything that tied him to the valley. Yet he was helpless; all rational thought paled before the sureness of his vision. It was a moment of insight stronger than anything he had ever felt before, a blaze of certainty so blinding that he was unable to move as he stood looking at her. It was powerful. It was riveting. It was terrifying. It was inevitable. Against all reason he was in love with this woman.

She appeared startled, apparently alarmed by the forcefulness of his gaze, and he made a determined effort to shake off the unwelcome vision. He would think about what had just happened later. Now it was time to get on with his lessons.

"You're early, Mark." She flashed him a quick smile, but her voice had a tentative note that told him she was aware that something had just happened between them.

"I didn't want to waste a day like this. It's almost like summer out." He forced a calm tone to his voice as he stepped inside the door and glanced around the room, then out the window, where the cottonwood leaves flickered against a backdrop of pure blue sky.

Suddenly he felt almost claustrophobic. He couldn't stand the confining walls of the schoolhouse a minute longer.

"Why don't we take the books outside today," he said impulsively. "Nothing says you can't learn history with the wind on your face and the leaves rustling in your ears."

She was silent a moment, as though considering the suggestion from every angle. Then she pushed back her chair and clasped a history book under her arm. "That sounds like a perfect idea. I've been hoping for an excuse to get outside."

They walked silently, side by side, along the trail that Mark had traversed a few moments earlier. Occasionally his arm brushed hers, and he drew back, feeling her soft skin burn his hair-roughened arm. His emotions were in complete tumult, the revelation that had come to him a moment ago vying with the need to maintain a calm demeanor of simple friendliness.

"How's this?" He stopped and pointed to a faint path overgrown with bracken and willow that branched off from the main trail, leading to a creek swollen with spring runoff rushing through a draw a few yards away. She nodded, and he took her hand and led her down the bank to the mossy edge of the rivulet.

She glanced around the green enclosure, drinking it in, then took a deep breath and lifted her hair to allow the breeze to fondle her neck. "This place is so beautiful," she said softly. "I feel as though I'm in another world."

He knelt to touch the tender grass along the creek bank, his nostrils catching the moist, sweet smell of moss and early-blooming crocus. "It's pretty wet. . . ."

Quickly he stripped off his flannel shirt and placed it

on the grass in front of a sun-warmed rock. "This should do it. Sit on the shirt and lean back against the rock. Perfectly comfortable. I hope." He raised a dark eyebrow solicitously.

She looked startled, but she sank down on the shirt and leaned back against the rock as he had suggested. The history book remained unopened on her lap. Only then did he consider that she might be uncomfortable with him partially undressed. Damn. Once again in his eagerness to be gallant he might have offended her delicate sensibilities. Would he never get it right?

He stood looking down at her, hoping that the frustration and hunger tearing him apart didn't show in his eyes. He had never known a woman like Jessica, never even suspected one had existed. She brought him visions of worlds he had known only from books. Her slender body, the aristocratic tilt of her head, her eyes full of warmth and intelligence, all combined to beguile his masculine senses and assault what little confidence he had. She was so far beyond him; he could never hope to possess her.

He pushed the unsettling thought away. He could accomplish anything he put his mind to. That's what all this studying was about, wasn't it? Well, he would find the way to make himself worthy of her, he vowed silently. He would enter her world and become a man she would be proud of. It would take time, but he would do it!

Finally she smiled up at him, and his heart churned. "Come on, no playing hooky," she teased lightly, recovered from whatever lapse of composure his impulsiveness had cost her. "Just because we're out in this beautiful weather doesn't mean we can ignore our history lesson. Yesterday we left off with the barbarians storming the gates of Rome—let's take it from there."

He sank down beside her and reached for the book. "I've been wondering about that. Just who were the barbarians?"

"Well, the Celts, the Gauls, the Visigoths—"

"No. I mean, the Romans called them barbarians. But doesn't the bunch that writes the history decide who's a barbarian?"

She smiled. "You do have an interesting way of looking at things. And the Goths might have agreed with you. But"—she hesitated—"are we still talking about Romans?"

He glanced down at his hands and smiled sheepishly. "Probably not. I know I felt like a barbarian Saturday night, storming the walls of the civilized world. An outsider, anyway." The book slipped unnoticed from his hand, and he picked up a pebble and twisted it between his fingers, not noticing when it crumbled to dust.

"Sometimes I think I can't stand another day of it! I've got to get out of here. Leaving Hope Valley is all I've ever dreamed of." His voice was husky with passion. "That, and getting rich and coming back to show them who the barbarian really is!"

Perhaps the intensity in his voice reached something deep inside her. Her blue eyes deepened to midnight and searched his face, and he felt the light touch of her hand on his arm. "You'll make it. I know you will."

Her voice, soft and melodic, flowed through him like warm honey, and suddenly he was trembling. Propelled by a force that rose from somewhere deep within him, he leaned toward her. Hardly breathing, he looked into her wide eyes. He was fascinated by her full lips, soft and slightly parted. He felt her breath warm on his cheek. He hardly knew when he put his arms around her waist and pulled her against his bare chest. As in a dream, he sought her lips, and he felt her slender body straining toward him.

He had no idea how long he was suspended in that moment. But for a heartbeat—or an eternity—there was nothing else in the world, just her soft flesh burning into his, the scent of her hair mingling with the moist fragrance of rushes, her fingers digging into the muscles of his back. His pulse pounded like a hammer in his head, and he felt her heart beating through the thin material of her dress.

Finally he managed to pull away and meet her eyes, recognizing the same fright and consternation he knew must be in his. Her breath was coming in short little gasps, and he saw the pulse pounding in the hollow of her throat. Never had he even imagined such beauty and warmth as hers. It reached out to him, enveloped him like clear water pouring over parched desert sand.

He recognized the calm core of certainty that he had experienced earlier. He loved her. She was his woman.

But how could he take advantage of her like this? She trusted him, or she never would have come to this secluded place. Probably she had never dreamed anything like this could happen. Her sweetness and innocence would preclude even the thought of a passionate embrace.

Yet, on another level of his mind, he knew that what was happening was as inevitable as the rising and setting of the sun. It had been foreordained since the moment he had first seen her in the schoolhouse door, the sun dappling her pale hair. They had gone through a fated passageway, and there was no retreat.

"I guess this changes things," he finally whispered.

He barely heard her words, and he saw her lips tremble. "I guess . . . I guess it does. . . ."

"You know I love you." He whispered the words against her throat, tasting the slight moistness of her skin.

"Oh, Mark . . ." She moved away a little, straightening her blouse, refusing to meet his eyes. "How can we talk about love? We barely know each other. We're pupil and—"

"You don't believe that!" He pulled her fiercely against his chest, holding her so tightly that she gasped for breath. He was drowning in the fragrance of her hair, sinking in the soft warmth of her skin. He held her desperately, as though she might vanish if he relaxed his grip for a moment. "I may not know much," he ground out between gritted teeth, "but I know I love you."

She gave a deep sigh, and a wild elation surged through him. She wasn't pulling away; she must feel something of the same fierce desire that was pulsing through him. He found her lips again, and when he felt her response, tentative at first, then strengthening to rival his own, he was lost. There was nothing in the world except the woman in his arms, and desire that demanded he follow where it led.

Passion tore through him like a roaring spring flood, inexorable, sweeping everything—reason, fear, caution— before it like logs tossed in a wild current. Yet even then he could have stopped if she had pulled away; she could have tamed the frenzy with a word.

But she was as mesmerized as he by what was happening, her mouth as eager for him as he was for her. When he pulled slightly away and ran his hand down her side and along her hip, she gave a long, quavering sigh and raised her eyes to his. They were dark and shadowed, drawing him to the center of the whirlpool. In the back of his mind some remnant of thought whispered of danger, of caution, but he was beyond caring.

Then all thought was gone as he followed the demands of the primeval necessity within him.

4

Gurgling with spring runoff, the stream charged the sandy banks that confined it, swirled around rock outcroppings, leaped over the boulders it had carried miles from the crumbling granite cliffs where they were born. Tiny finches darted like winged golden coins through the thicket of pine and willow that enclosed the clearing, and a gray water ouzel perched on an exposed rock and shook sparkling droplets from its wings. From the meadow near the schoolhouse the melodious cry of a killdeer floated like a ghost on the soft spring air.

Tender spring clover studded with buttercups and woods violets edged the creek, and the fragrance of the flowers mixed with the moist, sweet smell of moss and lichen covering the sun-warmed rocks. The afternoon sun was still high in the azure sky, flooding the secluded clearing with warmth and glinting off the sheen of perspiration on Mark's bare brown shoulders.

The breeze, teasing the tops of the willows, didn't penetrate to the two people stretched out on the warm grass in the shelter of the granite slab rising out of the aromatic earth. Jessica might have been dazzled by the sheer exuberance of nature, but the most dazzling reality of all was the man beside her—the intoxication of his lips, the strength of his arms, the pressure of his thighs burning through her dress as she spun dizzily in a maelstrom of sensation.

For one fleeting instant she might have been able to stop, rescue them both from the torrent sweeping them along. Fear lodged like a rock in her stomach, nearly overwhelming the building desire. She felt his fingers fumbling with the buttons on her blouse, and she shivered as he slipped it off her white shoulders. What were they doing? This was going too far. This was going much too far, and she put her hand against his chest in a feeble effort to hold him away. She was forgetting everything she had been taught, every value she had.

Then all her doubts vanished. The feel of his warm skin under her trembling fingers fed her need to draw him even closer. A sweet, warm languor flowed through her limbs, and her entire body became one seeking, searching mouth.

Oh, she didn't doubt that it was wrong. In the part of her mind that even then stood apart, watching, evaluating, she knew that she should be doing anything in the world but what she was doing now. But her body was in command for once, in the grip of an age-old instinct, surging ahead with blithe disregard for the consequences.

Yet if it had been only the demands of her body, she could have managed to pull away. The constraints of her upbringing were powerful. Nice women didn't feel what she was feeling, or if they did, only the most depraved let it get out of control. She had never questioned that. No, her response was more than the clamoring insistence of her aroused body.

There had been something deeper between her and Mark from the very beginning. With his first tentative smile he had touched her soul. Even his eager intelligence and fierce enthusiasms weren't sufficient explanation for what she had felt from the moment she saw him.

It was recognition. She had looked at him, and some veil had dropped from her eyes. She had seen him in his entirety, and the rhythm of her being had vibrated with his. They had recognized each other. And from that moment of recognition doubtless both of them were helpless to change anything that was to follow.

They fumbled awkwardly at restricting clothes. Mark crushed her lips with his, and she felt his hands on her hips, urging her toward his hard body. Then they were finally together.

She gasped at the sharp lance of pain that ended her maidenhood, and for a split second both were still as the barrier fell. Then, instinctively, she arched her body, meeting Mark's frenzied movements, until at last the unbearable tension burst in a long, quivering spasm.

For endless drugged moments neither moved. Mark lay heavily against her moist body, his chest moving with his ragged breathing, his mouth soft against the hollow of her throat. An incredible feeling of tenderness flooded through her, a tenderness so intense it was almost pain.

Along with the tenderness came a premonition. She pressed even closer to his sheltering form as unshed tears stung her eyes. She had crossed a bridge that had no return. Everything was changed. Forever. Her intuition told her the bond she had forged with Mark was unbreakable, come better . . . or worse.

Mark raised his head and gave her a crooked grin. His eyes held a dazed, incredulous look that made her want to pull his mouth back down to hers. He lifted himself on his elbows, bent to kiss her gently, then moved away. With his absence a breeze chilled Jessica's exposed flesh, and she shivered. And when she gazed at Mark, a second shiver—this time of apprehension—coursed through her body.

With a stifled groan, he dropped his head into his hands. His bright ecstasy of a few moments before had faded to a darker mood, and the change in him alarmed her. There was a dejected set to his shoulders that frightened her, silencing anything she might say.

As though he felt her confusion, he turned to face her, and she saw raw torment in his eyes. Instinctively she reached to touch him, to bring him back to her, her own conflicting emotions momentarily forgotten.

"Mark . . ."

He gave her a slight, bitter smile. "I've done it now, haven't I? Ruined everything. You trusted me, and I acted just like any other valley yokel. Weak. Without honor. But, oh, my precious, I couldn't help it. I really couldn't."

So that was it. He was blaming himself for what had happened. "Mark, don't. I wasn't exactly fighting you off, you know."

The self-reproach in his face made him look so young and vulnerable that she felt years older than he. She probably should feel regret also. And she probably would— later. She struggled to a sitting position, smoothing her skirt down over her knees, trying to understand what she did feel. She knew she should be ashamed, frightened, even angry, but she wasn't. She felt . . . she felt triumphant!

He turned to her and gently stroked the grass from her hair, then pulled her head to his shoulder. "That was the first time for you, wasn't it?"

She caught her breath in astonishment. "Of course!"

He placed his hand under her chin and tilted her face so that his lips could touch hers gently. "Me too," he whispered, his tone an uneasy mixture of shame and pride.

The bashful admission startled her. She took virginity in women for granted, but men were supposed to be knowledgeable, to seize any opportunity for sexual experience. Mark's admission made him even more lovable in her eyes. He trusted her enough to be vulnerable.

She had known, of course, that he was different from the others in his drive for knowledge, his ambition, but now she realized how very unique he was. Her heart stirred with pride, and a calm certainty flooded through her. What she had done was right. She would worry later about the problems that were sure to arise for them.

Suddenly he grasped her shoulders, turning her so that he could look directly into her eyes. Fervor blazed in his eyes, his chin had a firm, stubborn set, and he spoke slowly, deliberately, as though he would imprint the words on her heart forever.

"You know I love you."

"Yes," she whispered. "Yes."

"And I swear to you that you will never be sorry for what happened. I don't have anything to offer you now, but I will, I will! You are my woman, Jessica. Don't ever doubt it. You are mine."

Her skin prickled at the ferocity with which he pronounced the word *mine*. It had a finality that frightened her even as it thrilled her. It was a solemn oath, an irrevocable promise. She knew he did not make promises lightly, and his honor demanded that he keep those he made.

She lifted her head proudly and met his eyes with a steady, direct gaze. "And I love you," she said solemnly.

He crushed her against his chest, holding her so tightly that she could barely breathe, and she felt his desperation, as though he were trying to ward off some unknown calamity that hovered above them.

She patted his shoulder. "Don't worry," she whispered. "Everything will be all right."

"Will it?" His lips tightened. "In the long run, maybe. But what about now? What are we going to do?"

She tried to ignore her sense of foreboding. He was right. Somewhere down the road—and more likely sooner than later—there were going to be choices, demands, problems, that neither she nor Mark was equipped to handle.

But for now there was the present. She spoke briskly, as much to reassure herself as to comfort him. "We don't have to worry about anything right now. I love you, and

I'm happy to be with you. Let's not spoil things by worrying and courting trouble."

In answer he pulled her closer and buried his face in her tousled hair. It had come loose from its pins and fallen over her shoulders. They clung together wordlessly, neither wanting to leave the clearing. Here was love and safety. Outside was the world.

The shrill voice must have been calling for some time, but it penetrated their consciousness only now when they were quiet. Jessica stiffened, straining to hear as faint words reached her ears. Someone was calling Mark's name.

He stiffened and asked uneasily, "What was that?"

"I think someone is calling you."

They stared at each other, recognizing the same question in each other's eyes. Then Mark spoke softly. "It sounds like Alice."

Springing to his feet, he pulled Jessica up beside him, and they hastily adjusted their clothes, brushing away the leaves and grass that clung to them. "Over here," he called in the direction of the ghostlike voice.

A small form materialized a few feet away on the trail, and Jessica recognized Alice Hardy. The girl was probably about twelve, but she looked younger. Striped overalls covered her thin, undernourished body, and her feet were bare. She had about her that same air that Jessica noticed in school: a pervasive timidity, as though the slightest word would send her scurrying away like a frightened rabbit.

Her short straight hair was the whitest Jessica had ever seen, and her pale, translucent skin was probably the result of a poor diet. Her eyes, a startling blue, were now red-rimmed from crying, and her small mouth trembled. She stared wordlessly at Mark.

He bounded toward her and put his hands gently on her shoulders. "What's the matter, Alice?"

"It's Ma! She's—" The words ended in a sob.

Mark's shoulders stiffened, and he sucked in his breath. "What's happened?"

"She's sick. Awful sick. You got to come right away! Oh, where have you been? I've been looking for you for hours!" Sobbing uncontrollably, she grasped Mark around the waist and buried her face in his shirt.

Mark swore softly, as if at some unseen presence, then turned to Jessica, his hand stroking Alice's unruly hair. His face was a mixture of fear and anxiety, along with a strange anger. "I've got to go," he said, biting off the words. "I'll take you back to the schoolhouse."

"No, don't waste time on that. I can get back on my own just fine. Don't worry about me." She forced her voice to steadiness as she bent to pick up the textbook that had fallen from their hands earlier in the afternoon. Then she gave Mark a direct glance and an assured smile. "You go along now."

He stood indecisively, an internal debate raging, conflicting emotions warring in his expression. Then, with a weary sigh, he shrugged his acceptance and started up the trail, one hand on Alice's thin arm.

At the top of the rise he stopped and turned to face her once more. "Remember what I said." For a long moment he held her eyes with his dark, forceful gaze. Then, without another word, he strode away, Alice trotting beside him as she tried to match his pace. Jessica watched until he was out of sight around a bend in the trail.

Even then she watched the spot where he had disappeared, trying desperately to get her emotions under control. It hurt incredibly to see him leave. Too much had happened, and she couldn't assimilate any of it. Their mating had caught them both like an unexpected hurricane, beating down any resistance, leaving her bewildered and shaken.

But it had happened. There was no turning back. She, who had expected to be virginal until her wedding night, had given herself freely and joyfully to an idealistic young man who seemed to mean trouble for everyone who knew him. A firebrand in more ways than one. Where was her shame, her regret?

Strangely enough she didn't feel any. When she remembered how she had melted into Mark's arms, she felt exultant. A wild, singing ecstasy coursed through every sinew of her body. Her mating with Mark was as natural, and as impossible to stop, as the waters of a river flowing to the sea. She took a deep, quivering breath, alive with an incredulous but deeply sincere joy. Mark was her man.

But where was he now? What emergency had taken him away? A glance at the sun brought anxiety flooding back. The Blalocks would be wondering where she was. She had better hurry.

The thought of sharp-nosed Carrie Blalock waiting at the ranch house brought Jessica crashing all the way back to reality. It was well and good to tell herself that Mark was her man, but what people would say if they knew of this afternoon sent waves of fear flowing down her spine. A fallen woman would not be allowed to teach children. If a single suspicion reached the valley, she would be instantly ousted, and she would find it impossible to get a job elsewhere. If there was one question on which the people of Hope Valley were in complete agreement, it was that no woman of uncertain morals would ever teach their children.

She squared her shoulders and pushed back the cloud of despair that threatened to engulf her. Who would ever know?

A twinge of uneasiness followed the thought. Norval was already suspicious. And why had Alice come directly to the school to search for Mark? Of course, Mark must have told his sister that Jessica was tutoring him, in case she had to find him or cover for him to their father. But there had been a sly, almost condemning look on the girl's face when she came around the bend and saw them in the clearing.

Jessica forcibly shrugged the thought away. She would worry about the future when it came.

◦   ◦   ◦

Only someone familiar with the outer circles of Dante's Inferno could have imagined Sunday dinner at the Blalocks, Jessica thought as she patted her hair into place and smoothed her simply cut white blouse and ankle-length black skirt. For Carrie Blalock the Sabbath was not to be profaned by levity or frivolity—by which she meant laughter or light conversation—and one's dress must also fit the austere occasion. The uncompromising attitude made for an interminable afternoon.

Dinner was also a command performance, no excuse whatsoever accepted from either Norval or Jessica. And the food matched the mood perfectly, Jessica thought as she approached the living room, comparing memories of her mother's lavish Sunday dinners with Carrie's plain fare. At least the Blalocks often had guests in on Sunday, which somewhat alleviated the dreary atmosphere.

She paused in the doorway. Although the day was bright, heavy drapes over the pair of wide windows evinced an air of gloom. The furnishings—a long sofa, side chairs, and end tables—were in the Victorian style, managing in their ornate stuffiness to make the fairly spacious room appear small and stifling. A dark Oriental rug covered the polished floor, muffling sound and reminding people to keep their voices at a decorous level. The only concessions to the twentieth century were the radio console in one corner and the gramophone on a heavy mahogany table nearly hidden by a huge rubber plant.

A house divided, Jessica reflected. Sam was master of his castle in almost everything—a harsh employer, a tough taskmaster on his ranch. But this room was Carrie's domain, and here his rough-hewn manner and drive for power were overshadowed. Here Carrie's righteousness and concern for propriety prevailed.

"I don't believe we've met, Miss Whittaker, though I've certainly heard of you." Hand outstretched, a slim man with soft brown hair advanced on Jessica. "I'm Clinton Carter." He indicated the woman beside him, who looked as though a strong gust of wind would dislodge her from her fragile hold on life. "My wife, Emma. We shouldn't have waited so long to greet the new teacher. Welcome to Hope Valley."

"Thank you." Jessica scrutinized him carefully, surprised by his courtly manner, his sensitive mouth, and his intelligent eyes. Clinton Carter owned the only other big ranch in the county, a cattle spread about twenty miles to the north, and she had expected the wealthy landowner to be more like Sam Blalock—loud, aggressive, intimidating. If Carter was any of those things, he disguised it well.

She turned to his wife, returning the woman's hesitant smile. Emma Carter had a pale face, faded blue eyes, and faintly red lips that owed what little color they had to artifice. She didn't look well, Jessica decided, but she seemed friendly enough.

Carrie didn't allow them any time for conversation. She rose from her chair and gave Jessica an accusing glance. "Now that we're all here," she said pointedly, "we can start dinner."

Like obedient children Jessica and Norval followed the others to the dining room. Mrs. Blalock had employed one of the neighbor women to help in the kitchen, and the dinner, already served in heaping platters in the middle of the lace-covered table, looked quite appetizing. One plus for the afternoon.

Apparently taking the view that her responsibility for arranging the day was over, Mrs. Blalock subsided into silence. Whether from lack of interest or lack of energy, Mrs. Carter also seemed content to leave the conversation to the men. Jessica concentrated on the dinner, only occasionally contributing a bright smile or a quiet comment. At times Norval arched a cynical eyebrow in her direction or gave her a slight wink, compelling her to attend to the present. Otherwise she much preferred retreating into her own world, where her thoughts and fantasies of Mark were far more vivid and engrossing than the discussion around her.

"If you ask me, they've got it too easy," Sam Blalock said in reply to Carter's observation on the worsening economic situation. The price of cattle had nose-dived while consumer goods had become more costly, and most ranch hands were feeling the pinch.

Sam stuffed a huge bite of steak into his mouth and waved his fork. "Give people too much prosperity, and they go soft. Hoover knew what he was doing. Americans don't want handouts. The way to get this country back on its feet is to help the businessmen put it there."

"As old Cal said, the business of America is business," Norval murmured sardonically.

"What's a smart-ass kid like you know about anything? Never worked a day in your life, just spent my money going to college. Ruined you."

"Certainly most people would prefer to work," Carter said smoothly, bypassing the interchange between father and son. "But work is hard to find. People are hungry right here in this valley, and there are thousands walking the roads, looking for work."

"There's work for them that wants it," Sam said, glaring at his guest from under his bushy eyebrows. "Most of the lazy bastards won't do an honest day's work. A dollar a day, that's what I pay, and I get plenty who'll take it without complaint."

"Surely that can't be the whole story," Jessica said, unable to remain entirely quiet. "Some men must be unable to find employment. One of my pupils fainted in school. She said her father had been out of work for months, and she hadn't had anything to eat for two days but a boiled potato. I just can't think any parent would willingly let his child go hungry."

Sam glared at her. "Probably out agitatin' instead of lookin' for work. Want to bring down the American system. Like them Hardys. Jeb Hardy never done a day's work in his life, and that litter he raised is just as bad."

Jessica's face flushed, and she opened her mouth to

make a hot reply. But before she could speak, Carter broke smoothly into the conversation.

"I don't know about all the Hardys, but one of them is sure willing to work. The oldest one, Mark, came by the ranch the other day. I didn't need anybody, but he seemed so earnest that I put him to work. And I certainly haven't regretted it. He does the work of five men."

Hardly breathing, Jessica carefully took a sip of water. So that was why Mark hadn't been by the schoolhouse. She had waited every afternoon, her spirits getting lower as the sun trailed down the sky. Where was he? Why didn't he send a message? She didn't know how he could send one, though. Alice was taking one of her periodic leaves of absence, and Jessica was left to her tortured imagination.

She imagined he was sick, that he had had been in an accident. All sorts of visions spun through her head in a kaleidoscope of fear. Strangely not once did she think he might be staying away of his own accord.

Norval raised a pale eyebrow. He and his father might be at odds in almost every other way, but they were united in their dislike of Mark Hardy. "Needs money, does he?" Norval sneered. "You'd never have thought it the way he bid at the box supper. Just like he was a gentleman instead of poor white trash." The smirk he gave Jessica was full of sly malice.

"I understand he outbid you." Mrs. Carter spoke suddenly, her voice sweet and matter-of-fact, but Jessica thought she caught an angry glint in the woman's eye.

Norval flushed. "Just because I didn't have the cash—"

"Caught with your pants down, as usual." Sam's tone was contemptuous. "And by the Hardy tribe!"

"That trash! How was I to know he had a dime on him? Apparently he's broke now."

Clinton Carter gave Norval a level glance. "He said his mother was sick. Something went wrong with the baby she was carrying, and he needed money for the doctor."

Sam snorted. "Another one for the litter. Can't expect anything else from a mongrel like Leah Hardy. Half-Indian she is, and shells 'em out like peas."

Emma Carter's voice was very soft. "I believe this one was stillborn, and Mrs. Hardy is very ill."

Something in the woman's tone caused Jessica to glance over at her. Was that pain in Emma's voice? She'd heard the Carters had no children.

Carrie Blalock resolutely changed the subject, apparently believing enough time had been spent on the Hardys' troubles. "Do you plan on attending the quilting bee next Tuesday, Emma?"

Emma nodded, and the conversation turned to routine valley concerns. Jessica blocked it all out, keeping her eyes carefully on her plate. So that was what had happened to Mark. His mother was still sick. She remembered Alice's anguished plea, and Mark's voice, a mixture of anxiety and anger. Her heart ached for him; it was all she could do to sit still as the conversation swirled around her.

Sam Blalock was apparently not yet ready to give up his diatribe about the Hardys. "Old man Hardy must have ten kids already," he said, spearing a biscuit. "He won't miss one—one less mouth to feed. He don't feed 'em much, but he must feed 'em something. Must get a little money from somewhere."

"Moonshine," Norval said.

His mother's head jerked up as though pulled by a string, and she fixed her sharp eyes on his calm face. "Moonshine?"

Norval's grin was close to a smirk. "Where do you think the whiskey comes from at the socials?"

"It's against the law!"

"Sure is," Norval said amiably. "But it goes down smooth enough, I'll say that for old Jeb."

Sam's face was suspiciously red, and Clinton was hiding a smile. Carrie sat rigidly upright in her chair.

"Whiskey has killed more people than bullets," she intoned, giving her son a venomous glance.

"That's because bullets don't drink," Norval replied.

"Talk like that is sinful! You'll get yourself in trouble one of these days."

He gave her a sly grin. "Probably not. *Virtuous* people get in trouble when they sin because they don't know how to do it correctly." The look he tossed his father was an obvious challenge. "That's why it's good to leave sinning to people like me who can handle it."

Jessica thought Sam's thunderous expression would have quelled almost anyone, but Norval merely smiled and regarded his father with serene interest.

For several minutes the only sound at the table was the clinking of forks, the rustle of napkins, and the creaking of wood as they all fidgeted in their chairs. Jessica had never been so glad to see a dinner end.

As at some unheard signal they all pushed back their chairs and wandered into the living room to recuperate. Mrs. Blalock's meals might be somewhat bland, but the atmosphere that accompanied them usually put a strain on digestion. Now there would be an obligatory hour of conversation before anyone could escape.

Jessica edged toward Clinton Carter, hoping to casually bring the conversation around to Mark, but her hopes were doomed as Carrie Blalock pulled him down on the sofa beside her and launched into a doleful discussion of the deterioration of the family in the modern world. The deepening Depression might help, Mrs. Blalock thought. Women would be a little more respectful to their bread-winning husbands. Mrs. Carter, after a word or two with Sam, sat quietly in her chair beside the hulking rancher.

Jessica wandered across the room to where Norval, having totally ignored his mother's indignant "Not on the Sabbath!" was putting a record on the gramophone.

"Want to reconsider?" he whispered, the Scottish brogue of Harry Lauder's voice covering his words.

"Reconsider what?" She had to grin at his conspiratorial manner. Norval was probably not to be trusted, but he could be amusing.

"Going out with me. I'll bet if I said I was going to take you for a ride, the folks would purr like kittens."

"I don't want to go for a ride," she said. "Besides, where would we go? You know your mother insists on everyone being here right after dinner."

"Aren't you forgetting the basic purpose of the ride? To get us both out of the house. Mother would certainly approve of our happy little tryst. What you do after we're out is your own business. As mine is mine." He gave her a measuring look. "Although, if I can offer a word of advice, I'd stay away from Mark Hardy."

She felt the color rush to her face. "What do you mean?"

"You know what I mean. I've seen him look at you, remember? And I've seen you look back. Oh, he's handsome enough, I suppose, in a ragamuffin sort of way, but—"

"If you have something to say, say it," she snapped.

He leaned over and whispered in her ear. "Remember this song? 'Last night I slept in a palace grand, and in my arms was my lady. Tonight she sleeps on the cold damp ground, in the arms of Gypsy Davy.'"

She pulled back as though he had burned her. "I suppose *you* know what you're talking about."

"Don't be a fool, Jessica. You've got it pretty good here—don't throw it away."

She had a cold, sinking feeling in the pit of her stomach as she looked into Norval's knowing eyes. Could he possibly have found out anything, or was he just taking a shot in the dark?

Her lips were dry, but she managed to keep her voice steady. "Why do you want me to go out with you, Norval? You must have something pretty important to do if you'll accept my company in order to get away."

She never knew what Norval might have replied, for at just that moment Clinton Carter rose to his feet. Glancing over at him, Jessica thought once again that he was somewhat unusual for a Hope Valley rancher. Obviously well educated, he projected a calm reserve that hinted at inner strength. And he had a gentle manner with his frail wife that pleased her.

"Emma and I must be going," he said, holding out a hand to assist his wife from her chair. "We're going to put a herd out on the upper range tomorrow, and I've got some things to attend to. Can't leave everything to the help."

"Can't trust anybody else to do anything if you're not there, that's for sure," Sam said, heaving himself to his feet.

Mrs. Blalock saw her guests to the door, and they parted with expressions of appreciation for the dinner and vows to see each other again soon. Then Carrie shut the door firmly behind them and walked back into the room. Jessica accepted that her chance to find out anything further about Mark was gone.

"Emma Carter sure looks poorly," Mrs. Blalock said, a note of satisfaction creeping into her voice as she sank back into her chair.

"Carter was stupid to marry her," her husband replied, settling farther into his own chair. "Just because she could play the piano! She always was sickly. Never could give him a son."

Jessica shot a quick look at Norval and saw the sardonic expression on his face. Obviously he wasn't a very successful son, though she wasn't sure why.

She felt she had to say something in the Carters' defense. Not to speak would imply agreement with Sam's crude assessment. "Perhaps he loved her."

Blalock's look was a mixture of amusement and disgust. "Love! Well, maybe so. But that's not the only stupid thing he did. Hiring Mark Hardy wasn't very bright."

"But he said Mark was a good worker," Jessica protested, ignoring Norval's knowing smile.

"Might be," Sam said doubtfully. "But he's a troublemaker. A born agitator. Best thing to do would be to run him out of the valley."

Jessica noted again the one subject on which father and son could agree. "He's a no-account," Norval said bitterly. "And thinks he's better than anybody else."

Jessica surveyed her three companions: Mrs. Blalock, with her rigid body and even more rigid ideas; Sam Blalock, whose raw aggressiveness matched his powerful body; and Norval . . . Who knew about Norval? She had the feeling that something sly and unwholesome moved under his suave surface.

Suddenly she felt that she was being smothered. She was surrounded, suffocated, by the inexorable will of the Blalocks. They were as relentless as a winter storm, a blizzard that had its own inhuman rules. You got out of the way, or you got buried.

At least she knew why Mark hadn't been back to the schoolhouse. His mother was still ill, and he was working for some desperately needed money. She wondered why she didn't feel betrayed by his failure to somehow get word to her. But maybe he trusted her to know that he would see her when he could. Maybe he, too, felt that the bond between them didn't really need words.

Her spirits began to lift. By thinking of him, she could invoke his presence, even here in the suffocating Blalock house. It was as though she were attached to him by a silver cord. The cord might stretch, and stretch some more, but it would never break. She loved him.

But what were they going to do?

5

"*Here. It's for you.*" Alice Hardy thrust out a grubby little hand.

"Why, thank you, Alice." Jessica took the note from the clutched fist, ignoring the resentment in the girl's voice. The paper was damp and soiled, but Jessica's hand trembled with eager anticipation as she accepted it. Could it be from Mark?

She hadn't seen him for several weeks, since the day they had made love, and in spite of a determined optimism she had to fight off occasional despair. He had been so interested in his lessons; wouldn't he have returned for those even if he had had second thoughts about the teacher? She tried to tell herself that only his mother's grave illness could possibly keep him so long from her side.

"It was sweet of you to bring it." She was proud of herself for managing to keep her voice steady.

The girl didn't reply. Her eyes, a startling cornflower blue, stared accusingly at Jessica, silently expressing the anger that smoldered in her thin body. Her rigid shoulders and set lips said as plainly as words that she didn't approve of Jessica, and that bringing the note wasn't her idea. As she turned back to her seat she twitched her meager hips slightly, just enough to emphasize her displeasure.

Jessica hid a tender smile. The girl was so pitifully vulnerable, and if her suspicions about the Hardy home were correct, Mark might very well be the only person Alice could count on. No wonder she was jealous.

Alice's problems slipped from her mind as she spread the note out on her desk, glancing at it surreptitiously when she hoped the eyes of the curious children were elsewhere. She willed her face to show nothing as she scanned the brief message scrawled in a firm, familiar hand.

Meet me after school.

There was no signature, no indication of where she should meet him, but her heart knew all the answers and beat wildly in response. She only hoped the flush she felt traveling up her neck to her cheeks wasn't visible to the students.

Never had a day dragged on so. Even Alice had lingered stubbornly, refusing to speak, measuring the teacher with reproachful, knowing eyes before finally slinking off into the trees. Several other students had loitered endlessly, as though aware that something unusual was happening, and she nearly had to remove Jeff Deeter bodily. But at last they were all gone. She was free to go to Mark.

She didn't bother with a wrap. The spring day was almost summerlike, and the wind was hot on her face as she hurried along the trail to the clearing beside the creek. She scrambled down the steep path and burst through the screen of willows, oblivious to the brambles that pulled at her dress.

He was waiting.

"Mark!" She barely managed a whisper. For a timeless moment she stood completely still, soaking in the sight of him outlined against the granite boulder. In his faded chambray work shirt and denim jeans, he looked almost a part of the weathered landscape. His brown eyes snapped with energy, and he seemed to be holding his breath. He opened his arms, and she started slowly toward him.

Then she began to run, spurred by the look of exultation on his angular face. She flung herself against him, and his arms closed around her, warm and protective, as she pressed her face to the hardness of his chest.

"Oh, Mark," she said again, a sob in her throat.

"I thought you'd never come!"

"I had to wait until—"

"I know, I know—oh, Jessica!" He tightened his hold on her supple body and buried his face in the fragrant cloud of her pale hair.

"Your hair smells like lemon." The words seemed choked out of him. She was dimly aware of his harsh breathing and felt the rise and fall of his chest against hers as she struggled for composure herself. He said something incoherent, then loosened his grip enough to pull away slightly and press his warm lips to hers.

A shock traveled the length of her body. The kiss went on and on, both questing and affirming, and she gave herself over wholly to the demand of his embrace. She felt feverish, a quivering bundle of need and desire, and she pressed closer to his body, aligning herself with his every rigid muscle and sinew.

The flame began deep inside her, then spread like liquid fire to all her bones and tissues.

"Jessica. Jessica." He said her name like a mantra, and she heard the desperate longing in the whispered word. Her knees would no longer support her, and she was held erect only by his strong arms. She moaned softly, and they melded together, sinking helplessly to the sun-warmed ground.

The wild delirium that swept them into the primeval stream of passion left no room for doubt or hesitancy. They were the only two people on earth, a man and a woman, linked by ageless longing. They fell into each other, merged, fused, until any boundary between them was but illusion, and she didn't know where her body ended and his began. And soon they moved rhythmically together toward the ultimate release.

When reason returned, they were lying side by side, breathing in gasps, flesh touching flesh all along the length of their bodies. The disengagement came as a kind of pain, an exquisite loneliness, as essences diverged, returning to their original places. But some quintessential part of each, she thought, remained with the other. They were inexorably linked at some dark, primordial level.

Eventually she sat up and straightened her dress, her eyes on Mark's face. "I've missed you so. You've been away so long."

He sighed, the harshness claiming his features heralding his own return to reality. "I know. I've missed you, too. I wanted to write, send a note by Alice, but . . ."

"Why didn't you?" she asked gently.

"I had no answers, only questions. There was so much I—" He stopped, finishing simply with "I didn't know what to say."

A sudden, inexplicable premonition sent a cold shiver down Jessica's back as she pondered his inarticulateness in the face of strong emotions. His failure to communicate with her at such a crucial time. She tried to shake off the chill.

"I heard your mother was very sick," she ventured.

"Yes." He bit off the word. "This time Pa nearly killed her."

She swallowed nervously at the bitterness in his tone. "But I understood it was childbirth, that there was trouble with the baby."

"There was. But there shouldn't have been a baby. Doc Alberson told him last time that Ma couldn't live through another pregnancy. But that didn't stop him. He said no doctor had a right to say what a man could do with his wife."

"But—but she's alive?"

"Barely." He snapped a stick angrily between his fingers. "Anyway," he finished, "I can't stay there anymore. I can't help Ma, and it's no good for me. The old man and I will kill each other if I stay."

"I heard you were working at the Carter ranch."

"That's why I didn't come to you sooner. God knows I wanted to, but I had to get enough money to pay the doctor." His mouth twisted in a mirthless smile. "Those in the medical profession work miracles, and we have to work miracles to pay them."

She lifted her hand and traced the lines around his mouth. There was nothing boyish about him now, she thought, outlining the hard set of his jaw with a gentle finger. "You're here now," she said. "That's what matters."

He captured her hand in his, kissed it gently, and placed it back in her lap as he held her eyes with his. He looked so solemn that she had another fierce surge of foreboding. Something in the set of his shoulders told her he had pulled away from her, mentally as well as physically.

"I have to talk to you, Jessica."

She waited, throat dry, every nerve tingling and alert.

"You know I love you."

"I love you, too."

"And you also know there's not a thing we can do about it!" His mood changed abruptly; he grasped her tightly by the shoulders and looked into her face as though he would devour her.

"Not now, maybe, but—"

"Not ever. Not as long as I stay in the valley. You know what they say. The mongrel, Mark Hardy."

She couldn't bear to see the pain in his eyes and averted her gaze. "You know *I* don't think that way."

"Everyone else does. Jessica, the stubbornness and stupidity in this place is beyond belief! No one has had a new idea in the last fifty years. And the servile mentality! All the dirt-poor farmers toadying to Blalock and Carter, even when it's against their own interests. I swear, it's medieval, the way they touch their caps and bow!"

"Mark . . ." Although she knew he was right, she was uneasy at the intensity in his voice, recalling Sam Blalock's assessment of him as an agitator. There had always been rich people and poor people, but what could anyone do about it? Mark was bound to get into trouble with his revolutionary talk.

As though he hadn't heard her feeble protest, he rushed on. "There's so much that could be done here in the valley. Look at the resources—timber, water, land—just waiting for a man with vision to develop them. This place doesn't have to be run by two rich, feudal cattle barons. There's enough for everyone."

Jessica was silent. Caught up in his visionary dream, he seemed to have forgotten her. Fear flashed through her—for him, not for her. He seemed to be in the grip of some purpose, something that was using him, not the other way around. He had, she thought uneasily, the look of saints and martyrs—or the communist agitators Blalock fulminated against. What, exactly, drove him so? She couldn't shake the notion that revenge was a large part of his motivation. She shivered.

Then the spell passed. Sighing, he loosened his grip on her shoulders and stared off into the distance as though it held the answer to their dilemma. "All that is pie in the sky, I guess. What they say about me is true. I haven't a dime. There's no way I could support a wife. Punching cows for a dollar a day—how could you live on that? Or moonshining with Pa—is that a life for an educated, intelligent woman?"

At the bitterness in his voice apprehension tightened her throat, and she spoke in a choked whisper. "I want to be with you."

"And you will be." He turned to her again, his brown eyes projecting a powerful, mesmerizing, almost physical force. "Knowing that you are mine is going to make it all possible."

"Make what possible?"

Driven by restless energy, he jumped up and strode about the small clearing, his eyes riveted to some future that she could not see. "I'm leaving Hope Valley, Jessica. I have to go. Here I'm nothing but a sniveling cur who takes handouts from men like Carter and Blalock. I know I can make something of myself outside."

"But your family?"

"My family." His mouth twisted. "A miserable tyrant and a passel of kids growing up to be just like him. The only one I care about seeing again is Ma, and maybe Alice." He paused, then said more gently, "There's nothing I can do for them by staying here. Try to step in on the latest emergency, that's all. The only way I can ever really help is by getting enough money so my ma doesn't have to live the way she does now. Don't you see? I have to go. For the future. And for both of us."

Jessica tried desperately to control the trembling that threatened to overcome her, but a cold, hard lump settled in the pit of her stomach, and she barely heard her own voice. "For both of us?"

He dropped to his knees beside her, cradling her head against his chest and stroking her long pale hair. "Oh, my darling, you're the most important reason. My reason for living. The reason I have to go. And I'll make myself worthy of you, I swear I will!"

"But where will you go? What will you do?" She pressed closer to his chest, her cheek touching flesh still moist from their recent lovemaking, feeling the soft hair tickle her skin. His warm, masculine scent enveloped her. At the moment it seemed the elixir of life, the only thing she could hold on to. He couldn't leave. She might never see him again.

If he were truly going, she would go with him. If she had to leave her job, follow him into the unknown, she was ready.

"Maybe I'll try Alaska," he said. "I hear things are just

starting up there. Great opportunities for anyone willing to work. I'm not sure yet where I'll go. But I'm sure of one thing." He squared his jaw in fierce determination. "Wherever I go, I'm going to make money. Lots of it."

All the pain and frustration of his life was in his voice, and she pressed even closer. "I'll go with you."

Slowly he pushed her away and looked down into her face, a soft, yearning smile on his lips. "No. I love you too much to put you through that. It's going to be a struggle, Jessica, and I couldn't stand to put you through it. I couldn't stand to be your husband and not be able to take care of you. But I'll be back for you. I'll come back with enough money to buy this damn valley. And then we'll be married."

His tone was so definite that she knew it was useless to argue. "I'll wait for you, Mark."

"Promise?"

He looked so vulnerable as he waited for her answer that her heart twisted with pain and infinite tenderness. She wanted to hold his head against her breast until he was at peace. But she knew instinctively that this man would never be at peace. A moment before he had been a harsh eagle, surveying his future with deadly resolve. Now he looked at her with the young, hopeful eyes of a boy.

"I promise." She answered him not only with words but with every atom of her being. She held his gaze, giving him her solemn vow. "I will wait for you."

A smile broke over his face, a smile like the sun lighting a craggy mountain peak, and he crushed her to him so tightly that she gasped for breath. An eternity later she pulled away and whispered in his ear, "When are you leaving?"

He took a long, hard breath. "Now."

She had thought she was prepared, but the word knifed through her. "But—"

"The longer I stay, the harder it will be to leave," he said firmly. "I've got everything I own with me. I'm going to walk to Hope, then hitch a ride."

"But how will you live? You haven't any money to—"

"I worked for Carter long enough to pay off Doc Alberson and get a small grubstake. I'll find work before that's gone. I'm young and strong"—he gave her a level, confident look—"and smarter than most. I'll make out."

Already she felt him slipping away. Although he still had his arms around her, she knew his mind had already forged ahead, judging, assessing, making future plans. Like a young eagle impatient with the nest, he was eager to try his wings.

She was already someone left behind.

He seemed to feel her misery. Cupping her chin in one hand, he smiled tenderly into her eyes. "Don't doubt me, Jessica. Don't ever doubt me. I'll come back for you. I plan to marry you. And I'm going to give Ma the comforts she deserves. Then we'll see what the yokels have to say about mongrel Mark Hardy."

As she read the resolve in his face, her misery lightened a fraction. She believed him. No matter how long it took, he would be back. And she would wait.

He lifted her to her feet, then traced the line of her profile with one finger as though he were etching her image into his heart. "I'd better go. I've got a long walk ahead of me."

Yes, she thought, he did indeed have a long, hard walk ahead of him. And as her heart broke he turned and loped up the trail, fading into the trees. He didn't look back. Perhaps if he had, he would not have been able to leave, she thought, straining for a last glimpse of him among the pines. She saw a flash of dark hair and broad shoulders. Then the forest enveloped him, closing around his figure as though he had never existed.

A crippling stab of fear lanced through her. Would she truly see him again? If her legs had not refused to move, she would have run up the trail after him, demanded that he take her with him. She wouldn't care about hardship as long as they were together.

Her shoulders sagged as she stared at the spot where he had disappeared. Of course, that might not be true. He might be right. She might care. She had no idea of true hardship, at least not the kind that was so familiar to Mark. She had always been protected until her father died, and even then she hadn't been truly deprived. As the schoolteacher, she was a presence in the community, living without frills, perhaps, but also without dire need, safe at a level above most of the people in the valley.

A stanza from the old song that had infuriated her when Norval sang it flashed through her mind, and she half smiled, in spite of her pain.

> *Last night I slept in a palace grand,*
> *My Lord's arms 'round his Lady,*
> *Tonight I'll sleep on the cold damp ground*
> *In the arms of Gypsy Davy.*

When she had heard that song as a child, she had always thought, rather flippantly, that the lady made the wrong choice. Now she wished she had the choice to make.

Shivering, she started back along the trail toward the schoolhouse, hugging her chest against the late-afternoon breeze. Had it grown colder?

Thank heaven it was the last week of school.

Jessica stared out at the row of pupils who stared back at her like gaping gophers. Immediately she felt ashamed of the thought. She was increasingly touchy and irritable. Certainly the children were better than gophers. They were simply unwilling and inattentive because they were already in the thrall of summer freedom.

And there were exceptions. Two of her students couldn't tear themselves away. Having reached the legal age, Jeff Deeter could have left school a month ago; it was

what everyone expected. Obviously, however, he preferred to sit in class. Even if it was only to spin fantasies
about the teacher—and Jessica had only to look at his avid
expression to know what those fantasies were—at least he
was there, and he had to be absorbing something.

And Alice. Alice Hardy had not missed a day of school
since Mark left more than two months ago, and she stuck
as close to Jessica as a shadow. Jessica didn't delude herself that the girl liked her. But every time she looked up
from her desk, those blue eyes were watching her, hood-
ed, unreadable.

Could she be making something out of nothing, reading things into Alice's behavior that were not there? She
had been frightened and irritable ever since Mark had
gone, snapping when there was no occasion, crying for no
apparent reason.

She glanced at Alice and met those enigmatic eyes.
They looked so much older than one would expect, and
Jessica reminded herself that they had probably already
seen more misery and anguish than she had seen in her
much longer life. She must remember that and control
her anxiety about the girl. Her feeling that Alice was spy-
ing on her, watching her every move, was probably due to
her own guilty conscience.

It wasn't that she regretted making love to Mark, although
it had gone against every value she had ever been taught.
She'd had no choice. The force that had swept them
together was preordained, as wild and remorseless as an
ocean tide. But now that Mark was gone, there were
times when she trembled at the enormity of what she had
done.

Maybe that was why she had been feeling so poorly lately, nauseated in the mornings, tired during the day. Or it
might have something to do with her periods. She had never
been regular, but it was unusual to skip a cycle completely.

Somewhere in the back of her mind a thought coiled
like a snake, ready to slither out into consciousness the

moment she relaxed control. Could the missed period mean something else? She knew almost nothing about such things; her mother had said she would explain everything on her wedding day.

An involuntary smile crossed her face. If her mother had explained it the way she explained the onset of her monthlies, she wasn't missing much. She remembered coming to her mother in embarrassment and terror, admitting finally that she was bleeding.

Her mother was just as embarrassed as she was. "That's the curse, dear. God's curse on women, for the sin of Eve. It means you're a woman, that's all." She had handed her a box of sanitary napkins, and that was that.

Her girlfriends had talked about it more, of course. She had heard you could become pregnant by sitting on a man's lap. Or from deep kissing. Now she realized it took more than that—took what she had done with Mark, in fact—but certainly you couldn't become pregnant by just making love twice, could you?

Could you?

Cold sweat shimmered on her forehead. It wasn't possible, of course. But if it were—if it were—then everything was lost. She would be fired immediately, and she would never get a teaching job anyplace else. Where would she go? What would she do?

Unconsciously she rubbed her hand lightly across her breasts. They had been feeling tender lately, seemed slightly swollen. Then she dropped her hand abruptly as she met Alice Hardy's knowing eyes. A deep blush spread up her throat and over her cheeks.

She stood abruptly. "Class is over for today."

There was a joyous shout as the herd of youngsters stampeded toward the door. Even Jeff Deeter followed the siren call of unexpected freedom.

"Bring your workbooks to correct tomorrow," she called to their backs. "Remember, only three more days of school."

She turned to see Alice standing silently by her desk, her eyes studiously on the floor. The girl seemed to want to say something but was apparently undecided as to how to begin.

"Yes, Alice?" The words came out more sharply than she had intended.

The girl's head snapped up. "Ma wants to know if you've heard from Mark," she blurted.

"Uh, why would I hear from Mark?" She had hoped that their relationship was a secret. But Alice had seen them in the clearing and evidently had put her own interpretation on the meeting. And either the girl—or Mark—had discussed her with his mother. It gave Jessica an uneasy feeling, as though she were suddenly naked.

Alice gave her a scornful look, telling her as clearly as words that her question had been ridiculous. "Have you heard?"

"No."

The girl shrugged, then stared insolently at Jessica's waist. Without another word she turned and marched out the door.

Shaking uncontrollably, Jessica sank back down at her desk and lowered her flushed face into her hands. How much longer could she deny the truth? Alice's expression had left no doubt as to what she suspected.

And Alice would know. There had been a morning or two when Jessica had to leave her desk to rush to the outhouse. She knew she was unusually pale. Alice had seen several babies born. She knew the signs. And she was watching Jessica like a small, determined hawk.

A sob racked her body, and for a moment she didn't think she could move under the weight of her sudden knowledge. She was pregnant; she could feel it.

Was there any way to find Mark? Marriage was the only solution now. She would lose her job as a matter of course. And she was under no illusions as to what Carrie Blalock would do when she found out. Kicking her out would be the least of it.

She couldn't teach; the only other possibilities were positions like waitress or maid, neither of which was readily available in the valley, and neither of which she could do while pregnant or with a small child.

So she would have to leave Hope Valley.

And go where? Jobs were nonexistent here and scarce everywhere else, now that the Great Depression was in full swing.

If only there were some way she could contact Mark. But she had heard nothing from him since he left. She didn't doubt that he would keep his promise and return to her, but that didn't help her now.

She rose shakily to her feet, holding the desk for support. How long did she have before her condition became obvious? Another month? Two? Even three or four? It didn't matter. Sooner or later she would be branded with the scarlet letter. Adulteress.

She raised her chin in a gesture of defiance. She still had a little time. She would think of something.

6

Jessica descended the stairs, her footsteps silent on the carpeted treads. After her bout of morning sickness it was an effort to leave her bedroom at all, but not to go down to breakfast would only add to Mrs. Blalock's growing suspicions. At dinner last night the woman's sharp eyes had never left her, and the wheels turning creakily in her narrow mind had been nearly audible.

At least school was out for the summer. It was a relief not to have to face the curious faces of her students—especially Alice, she thought, pushing open the door to the dining room.

She hesitated, her hand still on the doorknob, as the sound of voices came to her through the open door of the kitchen. An argument, judging from the angry tones. She began to edge backward into the hall.

Suddenly she froze, unable to move another step, as she made out several heated phrases. Sam and Carrie Blalock. And they were discussing her.

"I tell you I want that woman out of my house!"

"Now, Carrie . . ." Sam Blalock's voice carried like the

swing of a sledgehammer. "I don't think you've thought this through."

"What's to think through?" Jessica could almost see Mrs. Blalock straightening her stiff shoulders and thrusting out her narrow chin. "It's obvious she's pregnant. And who knows who the man is? She's no better than a—"

"True, true," her husband interrupted, his formerly strident voice taking on a soothing tone. "But what's to gain by kicking her out? I have a much better idea."

"She can't stay here. It's not right! I won't have Norval subjected to such—"

"Ah, yes, Norval. Our pristine, innocent son," Sam cut in, his voice hard and accusing. "At least we know he's not the man responsible, don't we?"

"What do you mean?" Carrie's voice wavered slightly.

"I mean your son doesn't care much for girls. Don't tell me you didn't know he has a male lover in Denver. Why do you think he spends so much time there? To think I have a—a pansy for a son!" There was nearly as much bewilderment as anger in his voice.

"Sam! You mustn't say things like that! You don't know!"

"Of course I know. And so do you." Blalock spoke so bitterly that Jessica shrank back farther into the hall, her heart beating a frenzied tattoo inside her chest. She should leave; it wasn't right to eavesdrop. But her feet felt like lead, and she couldn't move an inch.

"Our only son," Sam spat out. "Our heir. The man who will inherit the Blalock ranch. A fairy!"

Jessica heard wood squeak, and she knew he had sunk down heavily in a kitchen chair. "Do you realize we have no hope for a grandson? No one at all to carry on the Blalock name?"

"But—"

Sam continued as though his wife hadn't spoken. "That's all I ever worked for. The only reason I sweated to build this place into the biggest ranch in the county. To hand something down to my son and grandson, to have the name Blalock carried on. Well"—he sighed—"I've known for some time that that isn't going to happen. Not with Norval like he is. But now . . ."

Jessica's heart nearly stopped as she clung to the door frame and waited for Carrie's reply.

"What's that got to do with that hussy?"

"Hussy or not, she's pregnant. With a child who could be our grandchild."

"What! Are you out of your mind, Sam? That bastard she's carrying is *not* our grandchild!"

"No, it's not. But if she marries Norval, it will be. There will be someone to carry on the Blalock name. No one would ever have to know. I should think it might work out very well for both of them," he continued bitterly.

"But, Sam!" The outrage in Carrie's voice hit Jessica like a blow. "It was conceived in sin! A bastard! It won't really be our grandchild—not a child of our blood!"

"If you've taken a good look at Norval, you'll see we're not likely to have a grandchild of our blood," Sam said grimly. "This is as close as we're going to get, Carrie."

"I won't stand for it!"

"Yes, you will. It doesn't matter what you think of her. After the child is born, you can raise it, bring it up the way you want. She won't be in much of a position to protest. And she'll be getting a good deal, too. Better than she's a right to expect. A good home, security, and eventually her son will inherit. Can't think of anything against it."

"Norval's not likely to agree!"

"Of course he will." Sam's voice dripped cynicism. "You know our precious son. What better cover could he have for his—activities—than a wife and a child? If I know Norval, the minute I'm not here to keep a rein on him, he'll bring his lovers right to the ranch. But who would criticize a happily married man for having a few friends around?"

Jessica didn't hear Carrie's reply, as feeling inched back

into her legs and she crept silently away from the door. She was dazed, nearly unable to comprehend what she had heard. She felt as though she was going to faint, but she fought the weakness with every ounce of willpower she had. If she was to get out of this horrible trap, she had to keep a clear head.

At least this explained Norval. She remembered the uneasy feeling he had always aroused in her. She had known instinctively that he didn't like women. And it certainly explained the hostility between father and son. Sam Blalock was not the type to be tolerant of what he undoubtedly considered sin and deviance.

She put her hand on her stomach, swept with a physical wave of revulsion at what Sam was planning for her. Marriage to someone she didn't love to provide a cover for his homosexual activities and to secure a Blalock grandchild. A child for whom she would have to fight Carrie every inch of the way, with every card stacked against her.

She would rather starve. She would rather work the streets.

She took several deep breaths, trying to control her galloping pulse. Starving or working the streets *were* her alternatives. What to do when faced with two things equally horrible? There had to be an out. She had to think.

She heard the front door open and whirled around. Norval strode through, saw her in the darkened hall, and stopped to give her a quizzical look.

"You look like death warmed over. What are you doing lurking in the hall, Jessica?"

"I'm not lurking!"

He arched a delicately formed eyebrow, then glanced toward the kitchen, where Sam and Carrie still ranted. He smiled faintly. "Snooping, then?"

Before she could reply, Sam Blalock's voice boomed out. "That you, Norval? Get in here."

As Norval shrugged and turned to answer his father's summons, Jessica fled up the stairs and flung herself onto the bed. Her face sank into the goose-down comforter, but the room refused to stay still, swirling crazily around her until she clutched the mattress to keep from falling off. Her stomach was queasy, but whether from pregnancy or fear, she had no idea.

Finally she rose and walked to the window, staring unseeingly at the vast expanse of meadow and pastureland that stretched to the mountains that ringed the valley. That land was the reason Sam Blalock wanted her child—the huge, sprawling Blalock ranch.

She had no doubt that right now Sam was outlining his plan for an heir to Norval. How would Norval react? He wasn't in a position to oppose his father any more than she was. If Sam threatened to disinherit him, throw him off the ranch, Norval would acquiesce, no doubt about it. He loved the comfort of the ranch house, he loved the money, he loved the status of being heir apparent to a fortune and a huge ranch.

Oh, Mark, where are you? What am I to do? I've nowhere to go. I can't take care of our child. Yet I can't allow our baby to be brought up here in this stultifying atmosphere, shaped and molded by the narrow-minded Blalocks.

Her only answer was silence. Then she remembered a remark her father had been fond of repeating. When you're between a rock and a hard place, he had said, there's only one thing to do. Stall for time.

A couple of days later Jessica sat in a straight-backed chair, elbows propped on the oilcloth-covered table, cradling a teacup in her hands, as she watched Lydia Adams bustle about her cozy kitchen. With its wood-burning stove, pine-planked table, and bright chintz curtains on the windows, the room exuded a warmth and friendliness that soothed her. She bent her head to take a sip of the steaming tea, covertly surveying the woman from under lowered lashes. Lydia's cheeks were flushed from the stove, her red hair hugged her head in tight ringlets, and her plump white arms were bare. With a flourish she deposited a plate of cookies in front of her guest.

"I'm so glad you stopped by," she said breathlessly, pulling out a chair and sitting down opposite Jessica. "We don't see enough of you. I wondered whether you'd stay here during the school vacation. Not much going on for a young woman." Curiosity sparkled in her bright eyes.

"I—I had planned to," Jessica said carefully. "You know my folks are dead, and I haven't any relatives. There really isn't anyplace I call home."

"That's too bad," Lydia said, her blue eyes shining with sincerity. "Come over here as much as you like. It's a little lonesome now. Jimmy took off right after school was out—said he'd as soon starve where there's something going on as here in the valley." She chuckled, but there was worry in her expression.

Jessica took a deep breath. She knew that Jimmy had gone, leaving some extra room in the Adams house. It was part of the reason she was here. Of all the women in the valley Lydia seemed the most likely to sympathize with her plight. She was a good woman, always taking a loaf of bread to someone worse off than she, the first person to offer help when a child was sick. If Jessica could persuade Lydia to let her stay with her until the baby was born . . .

Lydia rambled on. "It's going to be a little different around here with just Jake and me. But we'll manage." For several minutes Lydia chatted, filling Jessica in on all the local gossip, until finally Jessica managed to jump in.

"Lydia, there's something I wanted to talk to you about."

"Why, sure." Her eyes narrowed. "You look pale. Is something wrong?"

"No . . . I wanted to visit, get to know you a little better.

I'm so busy during the school year, and now that I have a little time . . ."

"It does feel good to have some woman talk for a change," Lydia agreed. "Jake's fine, but there are some things he just doesn't understand."

Encouraged, Jessica smiled. "I know. What does a man know about—oh, cooking, children, clandestine lovers . . ."

Lydia threw back her head and laughed. "Well, you sure pick interesting topics! You won't find much of that sort of thing around Hope Valley!"

"Of course not. I just meant—"

Lydia's lips thinned. "Funny you should mention it, though. Jake and me was talking just the other day—his cousin's girl, it was, lives over in Oregon, she got herself in trouble and expected her folks to take her in. People don't seem to have any morals at all these days! Well, I can tell you, they wouldn't do it. Told her she got herself into that pickle, and she could get herself out of it."

"And—and you agree?"

"Well, you can't overlook something like that. It's against everything that's right. Looks bad for the whole family."

"But it seems so heartless."

Lydia sighed. "In a way, I guess. I wonder myself sometimes. . . . But I know Jake's right. He was real firm. He thought she might show up here, and he said I wasn't even to go to the door."

"But what will happen to her?"

"Well, I guess there's doctors. . . ."

"But that's illegal! And dangerous!" And impossible for Mark's child. She loved it already.

"Oh, there must be places for that kind. Anyway," Lydia said, shrugging off the problem and giving Jessica a wide smile, "that's sure something *we* don't have to worry about. I can't tell you how happy we all are to have you here, Jessica. Everybody says you're the best teacher we ever had. Somebody for the kids to look up to." Her round face beamed.

Numbly Jessica endured another half hour of chatter, then walked back across the field to the Blalocks'. She had, by what she hoped was discreet inquiry, learned that the state's home for unwed mothers had shut down for lack of funds. Lydia had represented her last hope. There was no use expecting anything from the other families of Hope Valley, or from any of the acquaintances of her parents. They had distanced themselves immediately after her father's suicide, as if the family's dishonor might somehow prove contagious. If Lydia wouldn't help, no one would.

The sun-warmed boulder was comforting to her back, and Jessica leaned against it, pushing away her problems and opening her mind to the sound of leaves swaying in the afternoon breeze and the creek gurgling ceaselessly over smooth stones. Outwardly the secluded clearing was just as it had been when she and Mark were here a lifetime ago. But inwardly she now shivered with loneliness. She had fled to this spot because she hoped it would bring her closer to Mark, but his essence eluded her.

In the week since she had overheard Sam and Carrie Blalock making plans for her, she had explored every avenue she could think of but hadn't come up with a thing. She was constantly on edge, strung as tight as the fiddle old Ben had played at the schoolhouse dance.

She seemed to be constantly holding her breath around the Blalocks—but nothing happened. No one spoke. Perhaps Norval looked at her more keenly, and maybe Mrs. Blalock was more remote than usual, but nothing was said. If she hadn't overheard them talking about her, she would have thought everything was normal. Her mind raced fruitlessly, like a squirrel in a cage, as she tried to come up with a plan that would allow her to remain unmarried until Mark returned for her.

At the sound of a step on the dried pine needles, she jerked around toward the steep bank, her heart in her

throat, hoping against all reason that it would be Mark.
Then she slumped back against the rock, weak with disappointment. The masculine form coming toward her was
definitely not Mark.

"Hello, Norval," she said coldly. "What are you doing
here?"

"Following you." He grinned and scrambled down the
bank, then lowered himself beside her, fastidiously brushing off some chaff that clung to his dun-colored trousers.
As always he looked cool and immaculate. "I've wondered
where you disappeared to every day."

She shrugged, turning her head away from him. "Well,
now you know."

"You don't seem exactly overjoyed to see me."

She detected an amused note in Norval's voice and
turned her head sharply toward him. "Should I be?"

"Well, you have a point there. I imagine there is someone else you'd much rather see." His gleaming white smile
reminded her of the bared teeth of a coyote. "We haven't
exactly been close friends, have we? Still, we do have a lot
in common."

"Really?" She put what ice she could muster into her
voice. "I can't think of what that could be."

His glance at her was frankly malicious. "Why, the best
wishes of dear old Dad, of course. The fond hopes of my
father. Your soon-to-be father-in-law."

Her chest seemed to freeze, and she had trouble
breathing, but she managed to keep her voice steady. "I'm
afraid I don't know what you're talking about."

"Of course you do." He reached over and picked up a
strand of her hair, twisting it idly between his fingers. "I
know now why you were skulking around in the hall, looking like you'd pass out at any minute. You overheard them
talking about us."

She didn't answer, and he nonchalantly continued.
"They put it to me pretty straight. Marriage—or they
turn off the money spigot. Decent of them to give me a

few days to work up to a proposal, don't you think?"

"And you let them order you around like that?" She didn't try to keep the contempt from her voice. "This is your life they're playing with, as well as mine. You can't really want to marry me."

"Oh, I don't know. It doesn't sound all that bad. I've always thought it might be nice to be a family man, but I never wanted what went with it." He made a little moue of distaste. "The physical side of marriage, shall we say. But with you—well, you'd hardly expect me to take up any husbandly duties, would you? Considering your situation."

Her face flamed with anger and embarrassment. "What kind of man are you!"

He threw back his head and laughed, a light, melodious laugh that was tinged with cynicism. "That's exactly what the old man has been asking for years!"

She leaned away from the boulder, spine rigid, her hands clenched tightly in her lap. But she no longer attempted to deny anything. "You must see it's impossible. You don't want me. And how could I live that way, with a husband in name only? One who is repulsed by me? And my child—what about that? How could I bring up a child in an atmosphere like that? Between your mother's Bible thumping and your father's narrow-mindedness and your—your—" She faltered, not wanting to be guilty of the same narrow-mindedness from which Sam was suffering.

"My sin against nature? You really are an innocent, Jessica." His eyes were bright with malice. "I think the real question is, what choice do you have?"

"I still have a couple of paychecks coming," she replied. "It's not much, but it will get me a room for a month or so, and—"

"You don't really think you'll get that money, do you?"

"Why not? I earned it, and—"

"And Pa is on the school board, and the school board writes the checks."

She took a deep breath, then answered quietly, "I

know. It looks bad. But something will turn up."

"Don't count on it." There was such bitterness in his reply that she gave him a sharp look. Was there more substance to Norval than she had thought?

"Nothing good happens around here," he continued, digging the heel of his boot into the ground. "Everything goes along just as the old man says it will. Think how easily he could have given me an allowance and sent me off to Denver. Everyone would have been happy. Me, because I could find a place where I belong, where I'm not an outcast. Him, because he wouldn't have to stand the sight of me. You, because you wouldn't be forced into a marriage you don't want. But no, he wants an heir. And so it shall come to pass."

"You're a grown man, Norval. You can do what you want, go where you want to."

He smiled lazily, his momentary lapse into sincerity abandoned. "Be reasonable, darling. May I call you darling, since we are soon to be so closely associated? The problem is, I like money, and I haven't the slightest idea how to get it on my own. Without working, that is. But the old man won't live forever. Someday I'll own the Blalock ranch. And when that happens, I'll know what to do with it. I know how to live. You won't see me doing all the grubby penny-pinching he does."

He glanced down at her clenched hands, a teasing smile on his face. "Come on. Would marriage to me be so bad? If you turn your head the other way when my friends are here, I'll see that you have money, clothes, that the kid gets what he needs."

"The marriage would be a mockery."

"Of course. What isn't? But you might not find it so bad."

"And if I don't marry you? If I can't live with that kind of hypocrisy?"

His expression lost its pleasantness; his eyes narrowed to slits, and his mouth lengthened to a thin line. For an instant she had a glimpse of what an older, even more cynical Norval would look like.

"You'd better make up your mind. I agreed to ask you. Make everything right and proper. If I tell them you said no, you'd better be prepared to get out." He raised an elegant eyebrow. "Considering everything, I doubt you'll find a better offer." His eyes went insolently to her waist.

The cold, hard lump in her chest expanded. How could she play for time? And what good would it do her? Sooner or later she was going to be out on the road, with an infant. With the Blalocks at least the baby would have food, shelter.

But her entire being rebelled. Mark would be back. She must hold on to that. He had promised, and she believed that promise implicitly. When he returned, he couldn't find her married to his enemy.

Norval rose slowly to his feet, then reached down to pull her up beside him. "We'd better get back to the house. Ma doesn't like to wait supper."

At the thought of one of Carrie's suppers queasiness enveloped her. It wasn't just the thought of food—it was the tense, gloomy atmosphere that hung over the house like the wings of a giant vulture. There was no light, no love, no laughter in that house.

Norval seemed to pick up on at least one of her thoughts. "When we're married, maybe you can take over the cooking."

She didn't answer.

Jessica awoke, groggy and exhausted, fighting remnants of dreams, forgetting for a moment where she was. Then reality surged in, and her first impulse was to put her head under the covers and shut everything out. Perhaps that way the day wouldn't arrive.

But no such luck. Through eyes reddened with crying she saw the sun streaming in the window, lying in yellow bands on the bare plank floor. It was late; she wondered why Mrs. Blalock hadn't called her for breakfast. Perhaps the woman had decided to starve her to death. She wouldn't put it past her.

Images of the previous evening, never entirely absent even as she slept, flooded through her, and she tightened her lips. She had to decide what she was going to do. The Blalocks had left no doubt as to what they expected of her.

It had been like a scene from a Dickens novel, she thought, overblown and melodramatic. The poor, miserable orphan surrounded by powerful, rapacious adults intent on bending her to their will. If she hadn't been so terrified, she would have found it funny.

After many fruitless efforts at prying the child's paternity from her tightly closed lips—a last-ditch hope for some promise of a decent "heir"? Jessica wondered bitterly—Sam Blalock had explained graphically what would happen to her if she refused to marry Norval, and how perfect everything would be if she consented. Carrie had merely sat in righteous indignation, her mouth a thin, tight line, but Jessica could almost hear what she was thinking. *Wait. Just you wait, girl. I'll teach you to be so high and mighty. You'll be sorry for the shame you brought to this house. And wait until I get my hands on your little bastard.*

Norval, of course, had positioned himself slightly outside the confrontation, watching the proceedings with a calm, knowing detachment. Would she ever really know what went on beneath that elegant, enigmatic exterior of his?

Eventually she had pleaded weariness and confusion and had escaped to bed, after promising to give them her answer today. She had already made up her mind. Today she would pack up what she could carry and start walking toward Hope. Beyond that she didn't dare think.

She heard a shout from the yard and pulled herself slowly from bed. She recognized Sam Blalock's indignant bellow and wondered who had incurred his displeasure so early in the morning.

After inching her legs from under the covers, she made her way to the bedroom window overlooking the front yard and gave the dusty expanse a cursory glance. Brown, struggling lawn. Tired yellow roses against a rail fence. A hitching post. She didn't see anything unusual. Just a man on a horse.

Pulling aside the curtain, she glanced at the stranger with faint curiosity. Then she drew in her breath sharply as she took a careful look at the lean form astride the large bay horse. True, he was just a man on a horse, but he was certainly an unusual man on a horse.

Her first impression was that he might have stepped out of the previous century—one of the crusty old mountain men around whom legends still flowed. With the immovability of a mountain, he sat easily in a worn western saddle, holding his massive frame, well over six feet, as stiff as a ramrod. From under a slouched, stained leather hat coarse black hair fell to his wide shoulders. A heavy beard covered his jaw, and what she could see of his skin was bronzed and weathered. He had a hawklike nose, and ice-blue eyes peered from under heavy black eyebrows.

Wild and uncivilized as he appeared, with his ragged clothes and insolent posture, he still radiated an undeniable aura of power and pride. Of danger, even. She surveyed him carefully. The denim pants were patched, the light blue shirt faded from countless washings. His horse was as weathered as its rider, the bay coat dusty and sweaty, the leather saddle patched and worn. Why did her eye pass over all that to concentrate on the man himself?

Perhaps it was the unbending way he sat his horse, his focused gaze, that gave him an undeniable air of dignity. Or the belligerent way his jaw jutted forward as he carelessly chewed on a wad of tobacco.

Or perhaps it was the rifle he cradled casually in one arm.

"What the hell are you doing on my property?" Blalock

shouted again.

Jessica moved a bit and was able to see Sam Blalock standing in the yard a few feet from the rider. He had apparently just stepped out the front door. His face red and mottled, his feet wide apart, he shook his fist at the rider.

"Git that pile of bones out of my yard, Hardy! I told you a long time ago not to show your face around here. I don't cotton to backwoods scum!"

Jessica gasped. Hardy! This must be Jebediah Hardy, Mark's father.

She clutched the windowsill and stared out at the two men. She had never seen Mark's father, but this man was exactly what she would have expected. The hard lines of his face, the proud, insolent carriage, the unkempt appearance. Her heart raced as she stared down into the dusty courtyard. What was he doing here? Everyone knew he and Sam Blalock were deadly enemies.

Could his appearance here have anything to do with her? Perhaps he brought news of Mark.

"I told you to get the hell off my ranch!"

Jeb Hardy gave him a long, disdainful look, then shot a mouthful of brown tobacco juice at Blalock's feet. The forceful stream kicked up a spurt of dust. "I'll go when I get what I came for."

Jessica swallowed at the dry, laconic tone, chilled by the menace in the harsh voice. In the lengthy silence that followed she heard clearly the click of a rifle bolt.

"What are you talking about? What did you come here for?" Jessica thought she heard a note of uncertainty in Blalock's voice, although he stood his ground.

"The girl. I've come for the girl." Almost casually Hardy raised the rifle until it was pointed at Blalock.

The two men stared at each other while at the window, hardly breathing, Jessica looked down at the tableau with a dry throat. Could he mean her? Could that frightening old man be here for her?

"What do you mean, you've come for the girl?" Blalock

broke the silence. "What's she to you?"

"I aim to take her home with me. Tell her to get ready."

"Are you crazy? Miss Whittaker is our boarder. This is kidnapping!"

"I don't reckon so. The chit belongs with us."

"What makes you think so?" Sam was recovering a little of his poise, and Jessica saw him reach furtively behind him. Carrie undoubtedly stood in the doorway, ready to hand him a pistol.

"She's in a family way, ain't she?" Hardy continued.

Blalock blinked in surprise. "So?"

"The Hardys take care of their own."

"Are you saying—do you mean—that mongrel son of yours . . ." Sam's voice trailed away as he stared at Hardy, his expression changing from pure outrage to angry understanding. Instinctively he stepped back toward the open doorway. In the sudden silence Jessica heard Norval's light laugh.

The mountain man's massive shoulders moved eloquently as he shifted the rifle a bit to cover Sam's retreating form. "My son's obviously got the brains of a jackrabbit and the prick of a bull. And that woman's no better than she should be. But she's our'n. She's carryin' my grandson. Get her out here."

Jessica had never realized her mind could work so quickly. Here was an out—but at what price? Under ordinary circumstances she would have been happy to live with Mark's family until his return. But this was no ordinary family. Still, they couldn't be too bad. After all, Jeb had come for her. That showed he had a sense of decency, of obligation. Besides, if it was too awful with the Hardys, she would hardly be much worse off than she was right now, and she could walk to Hope from there as easily as from the Blalocks'.

Breaking out of her paralysis, Jessica dressed hurriedly in a blouse and slacks, then threw some clothes and a few personal items into a bag. She couldn't carry anything more; if need be, she could return for the rest of her things later.

As she filled the bag she forced herself not to think too searchingly about what she was doing. From what she'd heard of Jeb Hardy, and from what she had just seen of him, he was no refuge a reasonable woman would ever choose. But at least he would get her away from the Blalocks. She could think of what to do later.

And she wouldn't be forced to marry anyone while Mark was away. It was that thought that finally decided her.

The men were still shouting as she rushed down the stairs. At least Sam was shouting. Jeb sat his horse like a granite boulder, his rifle and ice-hard eyes trained on Blalock. Carrie stood indecisively behind her husband, apparently too baffled and frightened to hand him the gun she held in her hand. Out of the corner of her eye, she saw Norval lounging in the doorway, the smirk on his face obscuring whatever ambivalence he might be feeling at the abrupt turn of events.

She burst from behind Sam, dragging her bag of clothing behind her. "Mr. Hardy!"

His expression didn't soften as she came toward him. Wordlessly he reached out his free hand and, catching her by the arm, swung her easily up behind him on the saddle. With a final, cold look at sputtering Sam Blalock he nudged his horse with a long leg, wheeled abruptly, and cantered out of the yard.

Jessica stared at the faded chambray shirt, watching his long muscles cord and relax with each step of the horse. He hadn't spoken since swinging her up behind the saddle; he was acting as though she didn't exist. She had tried talking, but he merely grunted, forestalling all attempts to question him or thank him for coming for her.

The hard jouncing of the horse forced her to clutch the rim of the saddle to keep from falling off. It would have been easier to hang on to his waist, but the thought of actually touching this remote man frightened her. She was totally unable to break through the wall of his silence. Cold dread encircled her chest in a tight band as she stared at the man's unyielding back. Had she impulsively jumped from a bad situation into a worse one?

She wished Jeb Hardy would give some indication that he was aware of her bouncing behind him, but apparently he thought that retrieving her from the Blalocks was all that was required of him. He stared stolidly ahead as they left the open pastures and turned off onto a trail leading into the forest. The lofty heads of pine and cedar met above them, blocking the sun, throwing the riders even deeper into silence and gloom.

It seemed they had traveled for miles, and Jessica's initial fright was giving way to indignation. He could behave a little less coldly. She hadn't asked him to come for her, but since he had, he could show a few manners. She wasn't going to let him get away with this silent treatment. She spoke firmly to his back.

"Thank you again for coming for me, Mr. Hardy."

He shrugged. "I didn't come for you. I came for my son's kid."

Stung by his reply, she didn't answer, and he continued grudgingly. "You got yourself into trouble. Your business. But the kid is Mark's. Hardys ain't beholden to other people. We take care of our own."

Anger flared in her at his callous words, but she forced herself to remain calm. "How did you know about the baby?"

"Alice blabbed," he said briefly. "She's like all women—can't keep her mouth shut. Said she saw you and Mark down by the creek, and you weren't studying. Said she was sure you were in a family way. Nothing to do but come and get you." His brusque tone and the shrug of his massive shoulders showed how little he had relished the prospect.

They rode silently once more after that, the forest

enveloping them in cool shadow. She had no idea how much farther they would go. It occurred to her she had never asked Mark exactly where his home was located. All she was sure of was that they were going farther and farther from any vestige of civilization.

The leather of the saddle bit into her legs, and the rhythmic jogging of the horse shook every bone in her body. But none of it was as bad as the apprehension that held her in its vise. It threatened to swamp her, and she tightened her grip on the saddle rim.

Deliberately, one finger at a time, she loosened her clenched hands. She would not give this sullen man the satisfaction of knowing she was frightened. From now on she was responsible not only for herself but for the child, and she had to be strong. This bully would find that she was not easily intimidated. Looked at logically, it was only reasonable that she should live with Mark's family, and she would make the best of it.

She relaxed a little as some of her anger ebbed away. She must remember one thing. No matter how horrible this man was, he had come for her when she needed him. He had deep family feeling. She had not been abandoned. He had come for her when she had no place to turn.

She smiled slightly, wondering if anyone had ever suffered such violently conflicting emotions. Blessed relief that she would not have to marry Norval, or survive as best she could on the streets. Uneasy at being under the protection of Mark's family until his return. Worry over when that blissful reunion would ever occur. And dreadful fear about her immediate future.

For what would Jeb Hardy's protection consist of? Her mind raced through what she had heard of the man. That he was brutal, cruel, contemptuous of normal values. For all his deep-rooted family feeling Alice's bruises must have come from those very hands that grasped the reins so competently.

Jessica thrust out her chin. He had better not try anything like that with her.

She jerked back to the present, alerted by the horse's change of gait as the animal left the trail and forded a small creek, splashing water on her legs. After the sweaty ride it felt cool and pleasant.

The horse scrambled up a steep bank, and Jessica realized, with a sinking heart, that they had arrived at the Hardy homestead. She glanced quickly around. Pine trees had been hacked back to form a small clearing, where a shack, haphazardly constructed of both logs and lumber, sprawled against the mountain that rose directly behind it. A stovepipe emerged from a tar-paper roof; small windows, some with glass, some boarded over, opened along one wall; two rickety steps led to a board-and-batten door.

No attempt had been made to fashion a yard—no grass, no flowers, nothing but wild brush that threatened to overwhelm the house. Remnants of tree stumps were scattered about, some topped with crude tables, others serving as hitching posts for horses. With indignant squawks chickens scampered away as they approached, and Jessica had an impression of several towheaded children staring at her with open mouths.

Jeb pulled on the reins, and the horse came to a stop, dropping its head to reach for a tuft of grass at its feet. Before it reached the morsel, Jeb gave the reins a vicious jerk, and the animal raised its head with weary resignation.

A woman came to the door, hastily drying her hands on her apron. From the distance Jessica had only an impression of a slightly built woman in a long, shapeless dress, her brown hair pulled back from her face to reveal high cheekbones and olive skin.

"Leah!" Jeb slid from his horse and threw the reins to one of the children. "Come here. I've brought Mark's woman."

As the woman walked slowly forward Jessica dismounted to stand beside Jeb. Her legs were numb, and every other muscle ached, but she held herself proudly erect, returning Leah Hardy's direct gaze.

She hadn't expected a woman like this. There was a presence about her, a serenity that armored her in spite of her shabby clothing.

Then a smile softened the stern expression on the older woman's face. Her features took on a look of sweet, almost childlike innocence as she reached for Jessica's hands. "Mark's girl," she said softly. Still holding Jessica's hands, she turned to her husband. "You didn't tell me."

Jeb shrugged. "Don't have to tell you everything. Supper ready? I'm hungry."

"In a minute." She turned back to Jessica. "I'll show you where to put your things."

Jessica followed the slender figure into the cabin, dragging her belongings behind her, too tired to lift the bag. They entered a small, windowless enclosure, and she put her bundle in a corner of the room, so exhausted she could hardly stand. It wasn't just the long ride; it was anxiety about what was to happen to her that sapped her strength. Her spirits plummeted further as she took in the narrow room furnished only with a cot and a pine dresser.

"You can share Alice's room. She's the only girl home now, and Mark fixed up this place for her." Leah's warm brown eyes met Jessica's. "I'll find another cot."

"Mrs. Hardy, I—"

The woman made a dismissive gesture with a slender hand that showed the effects of years of hard work. "My name is Leah. But," she said, dropping her eyes and smiling shyly, "you can call me Mom if you want."

As the woman left the room Jessica sat down heavily on the narrow cot. She could start to cry—or she could square her shoulders and get on with it. At least there was Leah. The woman exuded a calm strength that was catching. And whether she liked it or not, she was home.

7

Jessica straightened and pressed one hand against the small of her back, then bent again over the washboard. Her thin brown hands moving in the warm suds looked unfamiliar, not soft and white as they had been less than two years ago. So much had changed since she had come to live with the Hardys. Her lean body and tired back were the least of it.

She glanced at Justin sitting a few feet away in the shade of a pine, gleefully slapping at a beetle, and bitter-sweet pain knifed through her. She had endured much for her son, but he was worth it. Worth everything she'd had to endure. He was worth the resentment and rudeness she'd suffered at the hands of the Hardy children, who were confused at her intrusion and grudging of every morsel of food she consumed. He was worth the agony of his birth—eighteen hours in labor, with only Leah attending. Worth the first few months of constant fear, when he was so sickly she thought she might lose him. Worth the continual round of his care on top of all the other work she had to do. Jeb didn't believe in idle hands—women's idle hands, that is.

She searched the baby's chubby face for some resemblance to Mark, but he was a blond, rosy boy with snapping blue eyes and a quick, feisty temper.

Leah noticed her glance at the boy and smiled. "Mark was the only one of my children who had my black hair and brown eyes." She touched Jessica's shoulder and motioned her away from the washtub. "Let me finish. You look tired."

Jessica sighed and shook her head. Without Leah, who was unfailingly cheerful and sweetly serene, she never could have survived. Certainly the older woman was just as tired as she was.

"Leah!" Jeb's voice boomed from the cabin. "Bring me my shirt."

Without a word Leah moved to the clothesline and took down a patched chambray shirt, then started toward the house.

"Mom!" Jessica hissed. "Why do you wait on him like that? Why not let him get his own shirt?"

Leah looked at Jessica's indignant face, smiled, and continued walking toward the cabin door. It did no good to remonstrate, Jessica knew. Whatever Jeb wanted done, Leah did—quickly and silently.

For a moment she was almost angry with the older woman for being so passive. But she forced herself to remember the precariousness of Leah's existence with a man as rough as Jeb Hardy. Still, there seemed to be more to Leah's accommodating nature than a simple fear of violence. Yet what other hold could the rough-hewn mountain man possibly have on Leah's gentle spirit?

Jessica tried to shrug off the question and focus on her own situation. It was long past time she made her plans to leave here. She would have gone earlier, but where? And how? The country's economic picture was still bleak, and the isolation of the Hardy cabin made leaving more difficult than she had imagined. She would have to walk over ten miles to Hope, unless she was to "borrow" one of Jeb's horses. At least she had learned to ride better since she had been here.

Once more she forcibly shoved the problem aside as the two elder Hardys walked out of the cabin, Jeb in his clean shirt and worn jeans, Leah minus her apron and with her dark hair pulled severely back from her face. The style accentuated her strong cheekbones, reminding Jessica that the woman was half-Indian.

Ignoring Jessica, the huge man strode to where Justin sat playing in the dust, scooped him up, and tossed him high in the air, grinning at the infant's happy squeal.

"Hey, boy! Want to go to town with your grandpa?"

Jessica glared at Jeb, and there was frost in her voice. "I didn't say he could go."

Justin threw her a rebellious glance and pressed himself tightly against Jeb. He was a precocious child, but was he already learning to pit one adult against another? Jeb was clearly his idol, and for some reason Jeb was uncommonly kind to the child. The boy thrust his chubby hand into the old man's beard. "Go with Gramp."

Jessica stiffened. She and Jeb had been in constant conflict since her arrival, but it was worsening as Justin left infancy. Now Jeb glanced at her, his eyes frankly malicious. "The boy already knows a man don't pay much attention to women's nattering, don't you, boy?"

"Wivan." Justin imitated Jeb's tone so precisely that Jessica shuddered, fearful of his one day becoming a replica of Jeb himself. Why couldn't Mark be here to be the boy's role model?

"Nevertheless," she managed to say calmly, "he is my son, and I am responsible for—"

Jeb's glance was slyly triumphant as he cut her off. "Now, hold your horses. Ain't nobody tryin' to get the boy away from you. We're all goin' into town. We need supplies. I thought you women might need a few things, too."

Jessica whirled and strode toward the cabin, her slender shoulders rigid with indignation. How like the man to announce their departure without any warning at all.

"I'll need a few minutes to change," she called over her shoulder.

"Don't be too long. Can't wait forever." Jeb hoisted Justin onto his shoulders and ambled off toward the makeshift barn.

Jessica sank down on the cot in her tiny room and lowered her face to her hands, determined not to give in to tears. Although she had tried not to doubt him, she was beginning to believe Mark was never going to return. Still, she cried too much too often, and it didn't accomplish anything. She would talk to Leah and leave soon, making her way in the world as best she could. She knew from the tiny trickle of news that reached her that the Depression was deepening, but even standing on a breadline might be better than remaining here. For Justin soon *would* be old enough to absorb Jeb's attitudes, and anything was better than that.

She felt the soft touch of a hand on her hair and looked up to see Leah's shy, gentle smile. "Don't pay no attention to Jeb, honey. It's just his way."

Jessica straightened and forced a matching smile. Among the many survival tactics she had learned from Leah was that you might as well smile.

"When Mark comes back," the older woman continued, "everything will be all right. He'll take care of you, and he'll straighten out Justin. That boy is going to need a firm hand."

"When Mark comes back," Jessica echoed ruefully. "Maybe he's *not* coming back, ever. We haven't had one word from him. He might even be dead. Or maybe he's forgotten us." She hated to surrender to her despair, tried everything to avert it. She reminded herself of Mark's inability in the past to convey his deepest emotions. She told herself he was afraid to write, to be in touch, fearing any contact with her might weaken his resolve to stay away from her as long as he needed to. Still, the silence sometimes bred doubts, and those doubts sometimes clamored for airing.

"No." Leah's soft dark eyes gazed unseeingly into the distance. "Mark's not dead. I'd have known. And he'll be back when he can. He said he would." She squeezed Jessica's hand.

Jessica sagged against the cot. The thought of Mark's return was all that kept her going, and lately she was having a hard time holding on to that hope. It wasn't so much the grinding poverty that eroded her spirit, although that was bad enough. Worst of all was the way Jeb had taken over Justin, already attempting to imbue him with his own dislike for authority and his contemptuous attitude toward women. In time the boy could become an arrogant little monster.

"How can you stand it?" she whispered to Leah.

Leah shrugged and patted her shoulder. "It's harder when you're young. But everything passes. The thing to do is to keep going."

"Survival." Jessica's tone was bitter. She looked at Leah's worn, handsome face. Could the woman be more than forty? She looked to be near sixty. Jessica had heard Jeb tell the story of their marriage—of how he had been out riding and had seen the young girl standing outside the shack that was her home, had put her up on the back of his horse and ridden to find a preacher. Her family, left with only eleven children to feed, had been happy to see her go.

"How can that be enough?" Jessica persisted. "Jeb's a tyrant. Don't you ever want to yell at him? Defy him? Leave him?"

Again the slight smile. "There's good in him, too. Things aren't easy for him, either, scratching out a living. Besides, the Good Lord only gives us to bear what he knows we can bear. And he's my husband." She glanced down at the thin gold ring on her finger.

Jessica started to protest, then sighed. Where would

Leah go if she left? This was her life, and perhaps she showed a quiet strength in not rebelling against it. Perhaps her passivity indeed masked a deep instinct for survival.

"Come on now," Leah said, rising and handing Jessica a clean blouse. "Jeb don't like to wait." She started for the door, then paused. "Mark will be back. You'll see."

Jessica stripped and put on the blue cotton blouse and a black skirt that fell to midcalf. "Where's Alice? Isn't she going with us?"

Leah's usually serene face took on a worried expression. "I don't know where she went. She was here this morning."

Jessica shrugged. The girl was the only one of Jeb's brood left at home. Typhoid had claimed the two youngest nearly a year ago, and the older ones had simply drifted away. From the furtive way Alice was behaving, Jessica suspected she would be next.

They drove out of the trees, then rattled along the twisting road to Hope, the wagon wheels sending up a thin shower of dust, and Jessica steeled herself for what lay ahead. Although she longed for company, the trips to Hope were an ordeal as well. She had been there only a few times in the last two years, and she had no reason to expect this visit would be any different.

Jeb drew up in front of Hope Mercantile and strode inside, leaving the women to get down as best they could. Jessica, holding Justin tightly by the hand, followed Leah into the general store, ignoring the stares of the few people who watched them arrive.

Mr. Kincaid, a slightly built man nearing seventy, with sparse hair and a dour demeanor, observed them silently from behind the wooden counter.

"Here's a list of the things I need, Kincaid," Jeb said, shoving a wrinkled piece of paper at the storekeeper. "I'll pick it up in an hour or so." He turned and left, letting the screen door slam behind him.

Kincaid picked up the list. Leah must have written it, Jessica knew, since Jeb couldn't read or write. Then the shopkeeper turned to the two women. "Is there anything you ladies would like?" he asked courteously, his expression softening as he looked at Leah. "I haven't seen you for a while, Mrs. Hardy, Miss Whittaker." His eyes were kind, but he carefully didn't look at Justin, who peered with lively interest from behind Jessica's skirt.

"We don't get in too often," Leah said quietly. "I would like a few sewing supplies."

As Kincaid led the woman toward the threads and needles, Jessica moved deeper into the dimness of the store, holding Justin against her legs. She liked the cool of the huge room, the musty smell that came from bins of potatoes and barrels of wheat. Although Jeb usually bought primarily flour, sugar, and coffee, the store was stocked with nearly everything she could imagine—hardware, dry goods, groceries, notions.

The clanging bell signaled the front door opening, and Lydia Adams stepped in. The woman was at the counter before she noticed Jessica standing in the shadows.

"Oh!" Surprise, consternation, and perhaps pity mixed incongruously in her expression. "I—I didn't know you were here." Then, appearing to realize that something more was called for, she smiled uneasily and glanced surreptitiously at Justin. "How are you, Jessica?"

Jessica lifted her chin and met the woman's eyes squarely. "I'm fine, Lydia. How are you?"

"Oh, fine. Just fine." She glanced around as though seeking help. Finding none, she began backing toward the door. "Well, it was nice running into you."

"I'm sure." Jessica couldn't keep the irony from her tone, although she knew it really wasn't fair to judge Lydia too harshly. At least she spoke to her, which was more than half the people of Hope did. And who could blame the woman for being uncomfortable? What did one say to a former schoolteacher, keeper of the flame of morality, who had suddenly become a fallen woman? Relenting, she smiled warmly. "I'm glad I ran into you, too."

Kincaid called from behind the dry-goods counter. "Did you want something, Mrs. Adams? I'll be with you in a minute."

"Oh, no, no. It can wait until you're not so busy." She turned and went hastily out the door, where Jessica could see her whispering to Cam Beale. Mrs. Beale pursed her lips and looked at the storefront as though undecided, then turned and walked away with her friend. News of Jessica's presence would soon be all over Hope, and Mr. Kincaid probably wouldn't have any more customers until she left.

She turned to examine a row of cast-iron skillets hung along the far wall, letting Justin slip away to admire a barrel of oranges. She needed time to compose herself and be certain her spine was proud and straight.

The bell clanged again, but she didn't turn to see who came in. If someone wanted to speak to her, so be it, but she wouldn't embarrass whoever it was by making it necessary to greet her. Her body might have thinned, but her pride had grown enormously over the past couple of years.

"Miss Whittaker." There was genuine warmth in the deep masculine voice. "How are you?"

She turned and found herself gazing up at Clinton Carter. She hadn't seen him since that Sunday dinner at the Blalocks'—a dinner that now seemed part of a dimly remembered past.

Unlike her, he hadn't changed, she thought. His light brown hair was receding slightly over a high forehead, making his narrow face appear a tad longer. The harsh summer sun had darkened his skin very little; in fact, he looked unusually pale for a man who spent so much time outdoors. He wasn't too much taller than she, even with his high-heeled western boots, but his slender frame appeared strong and wiry in his freshly pressed denims and crisp western shirt.

And his eyes were as kind as she remembered. She hadn't noticed it before, but he was quite an attractive man.

He reached for her hand and held it in a strong grip. "I've often wondered how you were, Miss Whittaker. It's good to see you again."

At the obvious sincerity in his voice she smiled up at him, blinking as she fought an unreasonable urge to cry. She was proof against slights, but pure kindness was so unexpected that she nearly unraveled.

"Oh, I'm fine. I don't get to town much."

"You look a little thin." He frowned, his eyes going from her face down her slender body.

"Well, so do you."

He smiled, but his eyes held sadness. "I suppose you're right. I miss Emma. Perhaps you heard that my wife died a while back."

"No. I'm so sorry." Instinctively she reached out and placed her hand gently on his arm. He glanced down, and she hastily jerked it away.

"It wasn't wholly unexpected," he said slowly. "She had been unwell for some time. But—I had hoped. . . ." His voice trailed away, and he gave her a bright smile. "Is that your boy over there? He's sure a good-looking fellow. He must be nearly a year old now."

"A year and a half." So Clinton Carter knew all about her and Justin. It didn't really surprise her; she was probably a prime topic of local conversation. The difference was that he seemed genuinely interested. "Justin, come here," she said, beckoning to the toddler.

Justin peeked around a barrel just long enough to let her know he heard her, then turned his back. She bit her lip, unsure whether to go and get him or ignore his behavior.

Carter smiled. "It's the age, I'm told. Beginning to assert their independence."

"I suppose so."

They stood indecisively, then began chatting of impersonal matters. Clinton hoped Roosevelt's election would help the economy, and closing the banks had probably staved off anarchy, at least for a while, but he wasn't sure Congress should have given him such wide powers. Jessica was glad Frances Perkins had been appointed secretary of labor. It was a first for a woman, and perhaps she'd have a little more compassion for the workers.

They talked for over twenty minutes. Jessica was avid for conversation and news. Jeb had a radio, but it worked only sporadically, and usually they had to find things out by word of mouth.

Later, once they were home and Jessica was standing on the rickety porch looking up at the stars, she was still thinking of the conversation. It had been so long since anyone had treated her as an intelligent, worthwhile person. And Clinton Carter was an articulate, stimulating man. She hardly noticed when Leah drifted out onto the porch and came to stand beside her, until the older woman spoke.

"I saw you talking to Clint Carter today. He's a nice man."

"Yes. He mentioned that his wife died recently."

"They said he was real broke up about it. Lots of people couldn't see it—she always was sickly and couldn't give him the kids he wanted—but he always seemed to like her, from everything I heard. Of course, he's still a young man. . . ."

The conversation with Carter had aroused an urgency in Jessica for the companionship of educated, intellectual peers, a need that had lain dormant for several years, worsening since she had fled to the Hardys' backwoods retreat. She sighed, glancing from the stars to Leah's shadowed face. "You know, Mom, I can't stay here much longer. I'm strong now. Justin is healthy. I can probably find a job," she added with more certainty than was actually warranted.

Leah echoed her sigh. "I know it's hard for you here, but you won't be going to anything better. Can't you wait just a little longer? Until Justin is older? Until Mark returns?" she said quietly.

"No." She gripped the pole that supported the porch, oblivious to the splinters. She would die—or at least her spirit would—if she stayed much longer.

Leah was silent, then spoke so softly Jessica could barely hear her. "I'll miss you. But I'll help what I can."

A wave of tenderness for the woman rushed through Jessica. She had learned to know her, to love her. Leah was the only thing she would miss about this place. "I appreciate that, Mom. But what can you do?"

"Oh, I have a few dollars saved, but it won't take you far. And don't let Jeb know you're thinking of leaving. He'll never let you go."

"No? Why not?" It had never occurred to her that Jeb would be anything but happy to see her go.

"Because of Justin, of course. He's his grandson, kin. Mark's son," she added meaningfully. "He'll fight you for the boy."

"Well, he won't get him!" Nevertheless, Leah's words sent a chill down her back. She should have thought of that; Jeb had had a strong bond with Justin since the baby was born.

"You'll have to sneak away. He'll stop you if he can. And you'll have to go farther than Hope."

Jessica turned and wrapped her arms around Leah, surprised at how frail the woman felt. Perhaps it was only her spirit that made her seem so dauntless. "Don't worry, I'll go so far he'll never find me!"

Leah returned the hug. "Somehow you'll have to let me know where you are. Mark will want to know."

Jessica swallowed her retort. There was no use robbing Leah of hope, but as for herself, she would have to accept the truth. Mark was never coming back.

From that day on she began to be serious about her

plans, taking long, rambling walks after chores to be alone and sort out her options. Right now Jeb was often around the house, she reflected as she wandered down a trail that clung close to the creek bank, but in about a month he would begin hunting for winter food and could be counted on to be gone for several days at a time. She glanced back in the direction of the cabin, hidden around a bend in the stream. She would have to take a horse, what little money Leah had to spare, and get as far as she could before Jeb started looking for her. And somehow she would have to find a way to recompense the family, for they were already dirt poor, and despite the many problems attached to living with them, they had helped her when she was desperate, and she would always owe them for that.

The clatter of hooves against stones broke into her reverie, and she glanced up, startled, just as a horse and rider forded the stream a few yards ahead of her. She stiffened with surprise as she recognized the man. Clinton Carter. This was indeed unexpected; his ranch was at the far end of the valley.

He saw her at about the same time that she recognized him, and he cantered up beside her, then dismounted, dropping the reins so the animal could graze on the lush growth along the creek.

"Miss Whittaker! This *is* luck. I was just going to ride up to the house, and here you are." He swept off his broad-brimmed hat and smiled at her.

"Yes, here I am." She smiled back, sincerely glad to see him. Company was so rare that any visitor was welcome to break the monotony, but since their chat a few weeks ago Carter was especially so. "And here you are, too. You came all this way to see *me?*" With a shock she realized she was flirting a little, and she hastily smoothed out her expression. "What *does* bring you way out here in the sticks?"

He shifted his weight from one high-heeled boot to the

other, and although he still smiled, his eyes held a serious expression. "Jessica," he said slowly. "May I call you Jessica?" he interrupted himself. At her nod he continued. "I don't know any way to say this but to say it outright. I'm going to make a speech, and please don't say anything until I'm finished."

She began a reply, but he held up his hand. "Please, Jessica."

Puzzled, she watched him closely. He rolled his hat brim in his hands and frowned slightly, as though not entirely sure where to begin.

"Jessica," he said finally, "you know my wife died a while back. I loved her, and I miss her, but, well, I'm alone now. We never had any children, something I deeply regret. And you—well, I realized when I saw you in Hope the other day that things can't be easy for you. Or the boy. So I got to thinking . . . why shouldn't we help each other? Maybe it's too soon to be saying this—I know I'm not much of a prize, and I'm older than you—but you'd be well taken care of, have a good home, there would be security for you and the boy. . . ." Finally he trailed off.

Surprise widened her eyes, and she took a step backward. "Clinton—you're—you're not actually asking me to marry you?"

"Why not? It seems a good solution for both of us. I'm lonely, and I don't know anyone else I'd get along with as well as you. Justin is just a baby—he'll learn to think of me as his pa—and I've always wanted a son. I'd adopt him right and proper. And maybe someday we'd even have one of our own. I know I'm asking a lot. You're a beautiful woman. But things are hard even for beautiful women just now—maybe harder for you than for most."

Jessica turned away, hiding her face in her hands. This was incredible. She hardly knew this man. From everything she'd heard he was kind and honorable, just and fair. And in spite of being somewhat older than she, he was undeniably attractive. He would make some woman a good husband.

But that was all beside the point. She didn't love him. She loved Mark.

He put his hand gently on her shoulder, turning her toward him. "Think about it, Jessica."

"Oh, Clinton, there's nothing to think about. I don't love you. I hardly even know you. It wouldn't be fair—I would just be taking."

"I don't ask for love—at least not now. In time it may come to both of us. But I like you, I respect you, you're an intelligent, beautiful woman. And I think you like me all right, too. That's enough for now."

"Is it . . . is it that you pity me?" She could hardly force the words from between her trembling lips.

"Pity you?" He raised an eyebrow and gave her a crooked smile. "You'd be the one doing me a favor, if we're talking about favors. You'll be marrying a staid old rancher—not much excitement for a pretty girl."

Her lips twisted in a bitter smile. There would certainly be more excitement with Clinton than there was here with the Hardys. And she wasn't exactly a "pretty girl." She was a woman with an illegitimate child, and they both must know that his offer was more than generous. He was offering her and her child a life: respectability, comfort, security. Very few people would dare snub the wife of Clinton Carter, no matter what they thought of her. Better yet, he offered refuge from Jeb for both her and Justin. Jeb would think twice before trying to retrieve his grandson if he was adopted by one of the biggest ranchers in the county.

No, she thought, remembering Jeb's arrogance and pride, and how he had taken her from the Blalocks' at gunpoint. Maybe he wouldn't think twice. He would try to get Justin, but he wouldn't succeed. Already she knew that Clinton Carter was no Sam Blalock. If he offered protection, he would provide it, and not even Jeb Hardy would intimidate him.

But what was she thinking! Was she actually considering this bizarre offer? She had endured a lot to remain unmarried so that when Mark came home she would be free to love him.

Her shoulders sagged, and a lump rose in her throat. There hadn't been a word from Mark since he'd left. True, he had said he must return rich, and he obviously hadn't succeeded yet. But couldn't he at least have written a note, tried to send word by one of the itinerants wandering the roads?

Perhaps he was dead. Or in jail someplace. With his wild theories and enthusiasms and his penchant for angering the authorities, that was as likely as anything.

Whatever had happened, he was probably never coming back. By now Hope Valley and the people he had left behind were doubtless only dim memories, shadows in the past. And she had a son to think of. She had to look after Justin.

"Well?" He put his finger under her chin and forced her to meet his eyes. "Will you think about it? I really believe it would be a good solution for both of us."

When she was younger, more idealistic, she would have hotly scorned a marriage for security. Now it didn't seem half so bad, especially when the man offering it was pleasant, intelligent, and kind.

She took a deep breath, tilted her chin, and looked evenly into his eyes. "I don't have to think about it, Clinton. The answer is yes. And I promise I'll be a good wife to you."

Soberly he searched her face. Then he smiled and put his arm gently around her waist. "Well, then, let's go and get Justin."

Jessica glanced in the mirror, running her hand over the new lace dress Clinton had insisted on buying for her. It was a delicate cornflower blue with long, tight sleeves and a scarfed hem. She had thought something more practical would do just fine for the wedding, since only the minister and his wife were to be witnesses, but Clinton had insisted that she accept the extravagant gift. With her hair in a mass of curls on top of her head, a hint of mascara accentuating the black lashes around her deep blue eyes, she had to admit she was glad he had. She looked better than she had in the past two years.

Turning from the mirror, she glanced around the spacious bedroom that was to be hers and Clinton's from now on, and she tried to control the spasm of fear that weakened her knees. Everything had gone smoothly up until now. After a hasty explanation to Leah Hardy—Jeb, thank heaven, was away from the cabin—they had picked up Justin and taken him to the Carter ranch, gone swiftly to Boise to be married, then returned to Clinton's ranch house as man and wife.

While he stabled the horses and went to consult with his foreman on a few matters, she had taken a quick tour of the house and was awed in spite of herself. Perhaps her senses had been blunted by her time at the Hardy cabin, but this seemed almost a mansion. More than that, it was warm and welcoming, with polished hardwood floors, wide windows, and charmingly decorated rooms. It confirmed her first and only impression of Emma Carter; she would have liked the woman who had lived there, she decided.

She had strolled up the gracefully curving staircase, trailing her hand on the gleaming mahogany, and located the master bedroom. It offered such a contrast to her dark, tiny den at the Hardys'—and even to the stark, spartan room she had occupied at the Blalocks'—that she had paused in the doorway, drinking it in.

Her first impression had been of light pouring in through wide, organdy-curtained windows to play in wide bars on an Oriental rug of deep blues and glowing crimson. She had quickly averted her eyes from the bed, a large four-poster with an ornately carved headboard, and walked to a window to pull aside a curtain and look out over the lawn. A beautiful house. And hers now. She still couldn't believe it.

She wanted to go check on Justin, but she had just done so moments ago, and Karla, Clinton's stout Swedish cook, had taken him over happily. She didn't want to explain her urge to hold her son close right now, and she didn't want the woman to think that her competence was being questioned. She returned to stand at the window, so lost in thought that she wasn't aware of Clinton's presence until he put his hand lightly on her arm.

"Like it?"

She turned shyly to face him. "Oh, Clinton, it's beautiful."

He put his arms around her waist and pulled her briefly against him. They had eaten dinner in a restaurant, and it was now evening. Her wedding night. And a wedding night so different from what she had expected as a girl! This was more or less a marriage of convenience, she thought. Would Clinton even want her in his bed?

"If there's anything you want to change, just go ahead. It's your house."

"Oh, that's so nice of you. But really, everything looks perfect."

They stared at each other, ill at ease.

Finally Clinton broke the silence. "Jessica, about tonight . . . That is, you don't have to . . . ."

Her breath caught in her throat. The hope in Clinton's blue eyes told her what he wanted—and gave her her answer. "I promised I would be a good wife to you," she said softly.

Very gently he took her face between his hands, gazed into her eyes for a long moment, then kissed her, a tender kiss that seemed to demand no response.

Releasing her face, he removed the pins from her hair, letting it cascade around her shoulders. Then he slowly began to unfasten the buttons at the back of her dress.

When she offered no protest, he slipped the filmy garment over her shoulders, and it fell in a shimmering heap to the floor. His hands felt cool on her bare arms, and she shivered.

"I bought you some gowns," he said softly, pointing to the closet. "If you'd like to slip one on . . ."

She turned from his embrace and reached into the closet, blindly selecting a soft green satin nightgown, then ducked quickly into the bathroom, where she stood, hands on the washbasin, breathing deeply. When she came out a few minutes later, Clinton was waiting for her quietly, unthreateningly, in the bed.

Smiling his encouragement, he held out a hand, and she moved toward the bed, reached for him, and felt his warm, strong grip guiding her to his side.

"You are so beautiful," he murmured. And he lowered his head to find her lips. "Your hair shines like gold against the pillow."

She knew very soon that she need not have worried. Clinton's lovemaking was like himself—considerate, kind, and generous. He eased her into relaxation, slowly caressed and stroked her to languorous passion, then brought her finally to gentle satisfaction. When he sighed deeply, she knew that he had joined her in fulfillment.

Later they lay side by side, staring up at the ceiling, still holding hands, their bodies touching. His flesh, warm and moist, redolent of fresh air and soap, felt good against her skin. She didn't delude herself that she loved him already, but she liked him very much, and she enjoyed what they had just done together. She had heard that mutual caring and respect was the best basis for a marriage, anyway, not the wild, mindless ecstasy she had known with Mark. She never wanted to feel anything like that again. It was too excruciatingly painful.

He turned his head toward her and murmured in her ear. "Are you all right?"

"I'm fine," she whispered back.

"This is our life now," he said softly. "I'll try to make you happy. Do you have any regrets?"

She kissed him lightly on the cheek. "Oh, Clinton, not a one. Everything is fine. I promise to try to make you happy, too."

It was true, she realized. She didn't regret anything. Not loving Mark. Certainly not Justin. Not marrying Clinton. She might even find contentment with this excellent man. She was sad at losing Leah, who had watched her leave with tears in her fine brown eyes, knowing that, despite Jessica's wishes to keep in touch, their paths would not likely cross again. Not with Jeb's attitudes being what they were. It was the first time Jessica could remember having seen Leah cry. As for Mark, he was a shadow now, she thought fiercely, loved but lost, and he would recede even further into the past as she ventured into her new life.

Her husband was everything a woman could want—generous, kind, and, yes, a good lover. She was embarking upon a new life, and she would never look back.

SUMMER

8

His high-heeled boots clicked rhythmically on the linoleum of the kitchen floor, and he saw Jessica turn at the sound, her lightly tanned skin flushed a faint pink from the heat of the stove. She gave him a fond smile. Clinton's chest tightened, and he felt the familiar rush of tenderness and awe.

She was even more beautiful than she'd been ten years ago, he thought. Maturity had given her a poise and style that was yet somehow intrinsic, owing little to the clothing she purchased, at his insistence, from the best stores in Boise—when they had the coupons, that is. The blue linen man-tailored shirt she was wearing now and the fawn-colored slacks only served to accentuate her delicate femininity.

This morning she had pulled her hair into a loose knot on top of her head, leaving the back of her neck bare and vulnerable. Although his heart skipped a beat, his expression didn't change. Walking up behind her, he dropped a kiss on the nape of her neck and casually patted her luscious behind. Turning away, he sat down at the kitchen table and watched her graceful movements as she hastened to pour him a cup of coffee. It was part of their unspoken agreement—whether she realized it or not—that his actions never betrayed his unruly emotions.

"Where's Karla?" He glanced around the sunny kitchen, took a sip of coffee, and reached for the plate of bacon and eggs Jessica had placed in front of him. It occurred to him again how lucky they were to live on a ranch and butcher their own animals. Otherwise their breakfasts alone would use up a month's meat rations.

"She isn't feeling too well today," Jessica replied, sitting down across from him and reaching for the coffeepot. "She's still in bed."

"Too bad." He grinned at her, and her eyes crinkled with amusement. He realized she knew exactly what he was thinking. He was concerned about Karla's health, but he missed her cooking, too. In over ten years of marriage Jessica had never managed Karla's expertise at the stove, and it was a running joke between them.

"It's just a cold," Jessica assured him. "And worry, I suspect. They still haven't heard about her nephew. He's been missing in action for over a month now." She paused, suddenly nervous as she met Clinton's steady regard. "Why are you looking at me that way?"

"I like looking at you," he said quietly. Sometimes he thought he knew her every mood, her every mannerism. Yet even now, after so many years, he was aware that there were aspects of herself she had never shown him, some remote inner core that was forever closed to him. He couldn't complain. He knew her reticence wasn't deliberate. She was a good wife; she had certainly kept her part of the bargain. It wasn't her fault that he had fallen in love with her.

"Do you know you don't look a bit different from the day I married you?"

"I doubt that." She laughed, suddenly self-conscious. "But it's a nice thing to say to a woman on the wrong side of thirty." If she looked good, it was because life had been good to her over the past decade, she thought, smoothing a strand of pale gold hair away from her face and tucking it behind her ear. She loved ranch life. If only the war would end, she wouldn't have a single complaint. And sometimes days, even weeks, would go by, and she wouldn't once think of Mark.

She reached across the table to push a lock of hair from Clinton's forehead, then stopped in midgesture as the door banged open and a tall, skinny boy rocketed through the room and headed for the back door.

"Justin! Wait a minute. Where are you going?"

He paused in the doorway just long enough to make her wonder if he was going to respond at all, then turned reluctantly toward her, a scowl on his smooth face. As usual her heart ached with a combination of love and annoyance as she studied his adolescent visage: the clear blue eyes, regular features, and a mouth that appeared vulnerable no matter how hard he tried to keep it set in a harsh line. There was more of Jeb Hardy in him than either herself or Mark, she decided, in temperament as well as appearance. And he was at a painful, awkward age—not boy, not man, but an unhappy, uneasy mixture of both.

He stared at her, not moving from the door, and she said, "I asked where you were going. You haven't had breakfast, and you know your dad wanted you to help on the range today. There's cattle to be moved to the high pasture."

He shot Clinton a belligerent glance, and she wished she hadn't used the word *dad*. Although Clinton had adopted Justin when he was two years old, the boy persisted in calling him sir or Clinton when he was forced to call him anything at all.

"I was going over to Jeb's," Justin said grudgingly. "He needs help with one of the horses he's breaking. He says I've got a knack for it."

Jessica and Clinton exchanged a look over the boy's head. They had won the battle with Jeb—his arrogant effort to win custody of Justin had failed—but they had lost the war. As soon as Justin was old enough to get around on his own, he spent every minute he could with Jeb Hardy.

"I'd rather you stayed here today, son," Clinton said mildly. "As shorthanded as we are, I could use some help. Tim Kelly joined the army yesterday, and he was the last solid hand we had."

"But Tim's only seventeen!" Jessica shot Clinton an anguished glance, then looked at Justin. How much longer would this horror last? It was true the Allies were winning on many fronts now, and the Germans were in retreat, but they were fighting doggedly over every inch they gave up. And she'd heard an estimate that the Allies could lose a million men in a direct assault on Japan itself. It seemed hardly a month went by without word that someone she had known was dead. Thank God Justin was too young to serve. But if it went on much longer . . .

Justin slumped angrily down at the table. "I wish *I* could join the army. Then I'd be on my own! And why can't I drive the truck into town tonight?" he added, jumping from one grievance to another. "Why do I have to ride a horse when the pickup is right there?"

"Because you're too young to drive," Jessica said, just as Clinton replied, "You know gas is rationed."

"Not for you! You get all you want—this ranch is 'necessary to the war effort,'" he quoted with scorn. "Lucky for you."

"Justin! That will do. The gas is to be used only on ranch business," Jessica said firmly. "And you don't have a license to drive on public roads yet."

"Besides," Clinton added, "it wouldn't look right for you to be driving around while others are walking."

"Have some breakfast," Jessica coaxed.

"I'm not hungry." He jumped up from the table, and the door slamming behind his back added angry emphasis to his words.

Clinton's gaze met Jessica's, and he raised his eyebrows and smiled. "It's his age," he said soothingly. "All those hormones shooting through him—it's difficult on a boy."

She made herself return his smile, although she was still worried. If it was a difficult age for Justin, there had been a lot of them. From the minute he was born her son had been defiant, stubborn, resisting all authority except Jeb, his hero.

"Do you remember the first time you told me that?" she asked softly. "That it was a difficult age?"

"No. Oh yes," he said suddenly. "You and the boy were in old Kincaid's store. I hadn't seen you since that day at the Blalocks', and you were so changed. So tired, so haunted looking. But still so beautiful."

"A lot has happened since then," she said, reaching over and covering his hand with hers. "I wonder what Sam Blalock would think of things now. Roosevelt getting a fourth term. The war. Rationing."

"Maybe it's just as well he's dead," Clinton replied. "He wouldn't like what's happening to this country. And Carrie, right after him." He shook his head solemnly. "So many changes."

Suddenly he put down his fork and leaned toward her. "Jessica, I don't talk about things like this very often, but these years together—they've been good years for me. You told me on our wedding night that you had no regrets. Is that still true?"

She was silent a moment, her mind going back over the years. All in all she had no regrets. Her marriage to Clinton was solid, based on mutual respect and friendship. Even love of a sort. Certainly she was deeply fond of him, and he'd been so good to her. There hadn't been fireworks, but there hadn't been despair, either. Sometimes she missed teaching—or something that might engage her mind more fully—but she couldn't complain. Her life was secure and satisfying, and she had done her best to be everything a wife should be.

"No regrets," she said softly.

"I sometimes wonder if you need more to do," he said doubtfully.

"Clinton! Are you saying I'm lazy?" She gave him a playful swat.

Just as playfully he warded off the blow. "No! I just worry that you might be bored. You're so lively and so intelligent, you must feel stifled sometimes. Maybe we should try to entertain more."

"I'm fine," she said firmly, rising and clearing away the plates. Dinner parties weren't what she needed, but she had given up trying to become involved in the business aspects of the ranch. When Clinton had offered her protection, he'd meant it, and that included shielding her from concern about finances, management, or day-to-day problems of running the ranch.

A sharp knock rattled the screen, and Jessica turned to see Lydia Adams, their closest neighbor, standing outside the door. She set the dishes on the counter and hurried to invite her in.

"Lydia." She smiled, throwing open the screen. "I didn't expect to see you so early in the morning. Come in, come in. Have some coffee."

Her pleasure in seeing Lydia was genuine. They had long since made peace with each other. As though eager to make what amends she could, Lydia had been the first to welcome her as Clint's wife, and Jessica thought the woman was sincerely happy that she had found a haven.

Lydia sank into a chair, puffing slightly, and accepted the coffee. The years hadn't treated her too well, Jessica thought. Her hair was nearly entirely gray, and her plump white flesh had wrinkled under the daily assault of wind and sun. It was her spirit, though, that had suffered most. Her expression, even when she smiled, held a hint of sadness.

"Don't you two ever listen to the radio?" she demanded.

"Usually we do," Jessica said. In fact, she generally had

it on all day, avid for war news. "But a tube went out the other day, and we haven't gotten it fixed yet."

"And the phone line has been busy all morning," Lydia accused.

"Justin. I've told him time and again not to tie up the party line. I'm sorry." Jessica gave Lydia a swift glance. "You really must have been anxious to reach us. What's so important?"

Lydia paused, looked from Jessica to Clinton and back, then made her announcement. "The war's over."

"Over!" Coffee spilled from Clinton's cup onto the plank table, and Jessica could only stare, speechless, at Lydia.

"It came on the news early this morning," Lydia said. "The Germans surrendered. V-E day, they're calling it. Victory in Europe."

Jessica's hand flew to her heart. She could hardly comprehend the words. Later would come joy, elation, but now she felt only shock.

"But that's not the end of the war," Clinton protested. "What about the Japanese? They're still fighting, and damn hard, too. We're having to run them off every single island in the Pacific."

"It's as good as over. They can't hold out too long alone," Lydia said. "Now we're free of Germany, we'll bomb the Japs into a hole in the ground." Her usually soft voice was harsh with anger and pain, and Jessica gave her a sympathetic glance. Her son, Jim, had been one of the war's first casualties. When the Japanese bombed Pearl Harbor, he'd been aboard the battleship *Missouri,* and he was now at the bottom of the ocean with the rest of the crew.

Jessica managed to find her voice. "Oh, thank God," she breathed. Soon the men would be coming home, and Justin—Justin was reprieved.

Clinton frowned. "Not yet. Mark my words, there will be heavy casualties before the war is truly over."

"But at least the end is in sight," Jessica whispered. The end of the war. It seemed impossible. It was true that life was easier on the ranch than in the cities, where rationing was keenly felt. Here they had their own meat, their own butter, and they could skimp on sugar, shoes, and other goods without real hardship. But the spiritual toll had been heavy, and the tragic loss of so many young men difficult to bear. Everywhere you turned, you saw only the old, children, and women.

"We're all getting together at the schoolhouse tonight to celebrate," Lydia said, setting aside her empty cup and rising from her chair.

"We'll be there." Clinton escorted her to the door.

Then he returned to Jessica. Their eyes caught and held. Wordlessly they moved into each other's arms, and he held her tightly as she began to cry.

All that day Jessica went around the house in a daze. The phone rang repeatedly, with people anxious for news or just wanting to talk. Clinton had gone out to move the cattle; war or no war, ranch chores must be done. Justin was still with Jeb or out with his friends in town. Karla, on hearing the news, had rallied sufficiently to return to the kitchen, leaving Jessica with nothing pressing to do.

Finally she went outside and worked in her rose garden, lulled by the fragrance of the summer's first blooms and of moist earth burgeoning with life. Somewhere a bird sang vibrantly, as though it, too, welcomed the news. When Clinton returned, she brushed the soil from her knees and went into the house to take a quick shower. They would leave for the schoolhouse just after supper.

She glanced out the bedroom window and frowned slightly. A familiar car was turning into the driveway, a 1940 white Ford convertible. Her mouth twisted in a rueful smile. Trust Norval Blalock to have purchased one of the last automobiles manufactured before the war, and to have managed to keep it fueled and running.

But why was he coming here? They were on speaking terms, of course, but since his parents had died and Norval had inherited the ranch, he spent much more time in Denver than he did in Hope Valley.

She dressed hurriedly and went down the stairs just as Clinton opened the door to the visitors. Her eyebrows rose slightly as Norval came in and then turned to urge Alice Hardy through the door.

Jessica wasn't completely surprised to see the young woman with Norval. There had been gossip. Alice was really a pretty creature, she thought, with her cloud of pale hair and her delicate skin dramatizing her exceptionally large cornflower-blue eyes. Her furtive manner still suggested, though, that she was hanging on to life with her fingernails and might be pushed over the cliff at any unwary moment.

They exchanged pleasantries, Norval, as usual, slightly sardonic, Alice speaking only to reply to direct questions. Finally Norval broached the reason for his visit. He had some business he wanted to talk over with Clinton. His glance toward Jessica and Alice indicated the business was to be private.

Jessica didn't demur as the two men went into the study and closed the door. Ranch business was always private. If Clinton had one fault, she thought, it was his penchant to overprotect her. She had all the clothes, all the spending money, she wanted, but she had no idea of the actual financial situation of the Carter ranch.

Left alone, she and Alice gazed uncomfortably at each other. Finally Jessica spoke. "I haven't seen you for a while, Alice. Are you getting along all right?"

The girl tossed her head, and a little smirk curled her coral lips. "Oh yes, just fine."

Jessica sighed inwardly. For whatever reason Alice's resentment of her was evidently still alive and well. She wished she could advise the young woman about her involvement with Norval Blalock. Did she know what she was getting into or not? Yet there had always been a knowing look in Alice's eyes, even when she was a child, and she suspected there wasn't much that would surprise Alice.

"Where are you living now? At the Blalock ranch?" Immediately she wished she hadn't asked. As far as she knew, Norval and Alice weren't married, and although the war had somewhat relaxed the county's rigid morals, it still wasn't a polite question to ask.

It didn't seem to bother Alice. "Yes, I've been there awhile. Norval and me are getting married in a few days, you know." She held out her finger to display a huge diamond and slanted a triumphant smile at Jessica.

Jessica sighed. So Norval had seen the reason in Sam Blalock's plans for him. He had merely changed brides. Suddenly Alice didn't appear sophisticated at all. She was just a young girl dazzled by the thought of money such as she couldn't imagine. She might think she knew what marriage to Norval would be like, but Jessica doubted that she really did.

"Is that what you want, Alice?" she asked slowly.

Alice wiggled her finger, watching the diamond glinting in the light, but she didn't meet Jessica's eyes. "Why not?" She shrugged a thin shoulder. "It's better than being at Pa's. Or that rat hole in town I was living in before I moved."

Jessica knew the feeling of entrapment, remembered it well. Things had changed since her own desperate days, and jobs were more plentiful, but like many women, Alice was untrained, and she wouldn't earn much.

Jessica rose and walked to her desk, where she quickly wrote out a check, then handed it to Alice.

The girl's eyes widened. "What's this for? That's more money than I ever seen in my life!"

"It's for you—to get you out of here if you want to go. It will pay for business school, secretarial training. You're a smart girl, Alice. You don't have to settle for . . . what you're settling for."

The girl turned the check in her hand, glancing at Jessica, then at the closed study door, a puzzled frown on her pixielike face. "Why would you do this for me? I ain't never done anything for you."

Jessica smiled. "I don't know. Perhaps because I know what it feels like to be where you are now."

The pointed chin jutted out, and the blue eyes hardened. "I might just spend this, you know, and stay with Norval."

"That's your choice."

Alice opened her mouth to reply but closed it firmly as the men emerged from the study. Jessica saw her shove the check hastily into her pocket.

Clinton patted Norval on the shoulder. "It's settled, then. I hope you won't regret this, Norval."

Norval shrugged. "Not likely. I'm not my father."

"Will we see you at the schoolhouse tonight?"

Norval reached for Alice's hand and pulled her to her feet. "No, I don't think so. You celebrate for us. Some friends are coming in from Denver, and we'll be busy."

Alice shot Jessica a glance as the two said their goodbyes and went out the door.

Jessica watched them thoughtfully as they got into the automobile and roared away. Would Alice take the opportunity she had given her? She couldn't guess, but at least she had tried. She had somehow felt she owed it to the girl. Or, if not to Alice, to Leah—and, in a funny way, to Mark.

Clinton came up beside her and placed his hand on her shoulder. She turned her head to look up into his face. "What did Norval want?"

"Oh, nothing much," he said easily. "Ranch business. Ready for supper?"

∘ ∘ ∘

The celebration was already in full swing when Jessica and Clinton arrived at the schoolhouse. In fact, Jessica thought, glancing around at the loud, exuberant crowd spilling out onto the steps, the celebrating had likely been going on most of the day, judging by the appearance of almost all the men and some of the women. Jeb's moonshine? Probably. Although alcohol was legal, it was almost impossible to obtain. For months Southern Comfort had been the only libation available in the area liquor stores.

She pushed through the door with Clinton behind her, and Lydia immediately grabbed her by the hand. "Don't you look great!" she enthused. "Is that a new dress?"

Jessica glanced down at her sleeveless lace dress. "Not new. Just worked over a bit." She grinned at Lydia, who looked good herself in a green velveteen outfit that had also seen better days. "That music sure makes you want to dance, doesn't it?"

Lydia glanced at the corner where a group of high-school boys, their crew cuts accentuating their prominent ears and youthful faces, were pounding out a fast rhythm on horns, a drum, and a beat-up piano. "I don't know, I kinda miss old Ben. But I guess things change."

The simple comment summed up the tumult of memories overtaking Jessica as they chatted in the schoolroom, but there was little opportunity for more conversation as war-weary spirits bubbled over like a spring torrent loosed from winter ice. The walls of the schoolhouse vibrated with sound—music, shouts and cheers, and boots stomping happily on bare wooden floors. In twos and threes the men made frequent trips outside and returned even less able to fox-trot, two-step, or hazard a jitterbug.

Jessica was soon as caught up in the excitement as everyone else. The war was nearly over! The young men would be returning; life would be normal again. The bone-wearying years of the Depression, broken only by preparations for war, the years of worry and hardship as the Allies pushed the Axis painfully back in a bloody trail,

were finally behind them. A bacchanalia seemed eminent-
ly appropriate.

Finally Jessica, panting and perspiring, broke away
from the man currently herding her around the floor and
stepping on her feet, and collapsed on a chair in a relative-
ly quiet corner of the room.

Clinton witnessed her retreat and hurried to her side.
"Are you all right? Want to go home?"

"In a minute," she gasped, still laughing. "Right now I
don't have the energy to make it to the door."

He pulled up a chair and put his arm lightly on her
shoulders. "Anytime you like, we'll go." He grinned.
"Even if I have to drag you out."

"Hey, Clint!" Jake Adams staggered up beside them
and pounded Clinton merrily on the shoulder. He'd better be happy now, Jessica mused. Later tonight he'd catch
hell from Lydia for his frequent trips outside with "the
boys." "Have you heard the news?" he demanded.

Clinton grinned. "Yes, Jake, I've heard. The war's
over."

"No, not *that* news." Jake gave him a scornful, inebriat-
ed glance.

"What else?" Clinton asked cheerfully, humoring him.

"I just heard it in town. Everybody's talking about it.
And I got it straight, right from old Reilly—you know, the
real . . . realtor."

He was slurring his words and listing alarmingly to the
right. Clinton hastily shoved a chair under him, and he sat
down heavily.

"That vacant piece of land along the creek—the one
you use sometimes to corral your cows in—it's been
bought. And they're going to put a sawmill in!"

"A sawmill?" Clinton frowned thoughtfully. "I hadn't
heard. That *is* news."

"Nah, that's not the news." Jake paused, as though trying to recall exactly what the news had been.

"Yes, Jake?" Jessica encouraged. "What is the news?"

"The *news* is who bought it!" Jake's expression glowed with triumph, and he brought his hand down heavily on his knee.

"Who bought it, Jake?" Clinton asked, smiling.

"Hardy! Mark Hardy bought it!"

Jessica froze. Everything seemed to become very still, and strange details imprinted themselves on her mind. She saw drumsticks rise and fall, a horn put to a mouth, lips open and close, but she heard nothing. The group around her seemed to gyrate in silence, bodies cavorting in grotesque dances, shapes fading away and returning without a sound.

Then the walls of the schoolhouse began turning, spinning, faster and faster, until she was swirling in a vortex, her chair the only unmoving object as everything revolved around her. Then sound returned, a horrific blast that nearly knocked her to the floor.

She felt Clinton's shocked eyes on her and made a supreme effort to control her expression, although her lips were stiff and she knew all the blood had drained from her face.

The tension seemed to penetrate even Jake's sodden brain. He stumbled to his feet and gazed blearily around. "Where's Lydia? Better be going . . ."

Clinton rose and put his arm around Jessica, pulling her smoothly to her feet. "I think it's time we went home."

She nodded numbly. The initial shock was subsiding, and her mind began working again, clicking along like the second hand on a watch. Mark had bought a piece of land in the valley and was starting a sawmill. If he could afford the land and the start-up costs for a mill, he was not only coming home, he was coming home rich.

Just as he had promised he would.

Even in the warmth of Clinton's sheltering embrace she shivered. That wasn't all Mark had promised.

9

Amber's velvet nose, soft as thistledown, nuzzled Jessica's bare arm, and she stroked the horse absently, her gaze on the panorama spread before her. Rolling hills, brown now in August's heat except where streams cut lines of vivid green through them, stretched to where the mountains rose, pale and blue, in the distance. Everywhere, as far as she could see, was Carter ranchland.

Raising her arm to slide back her wide-brimmed hat and wipe the perspiration from her forehead, she turned to Clinton, who was standing beside her on the knoll. They had just dismounted after pushing several dozen head of cattle through a draw and up the side of the mountain.

"That's the last of them. I hope they're smart enough to stay up there where the feed is better."

He shrugged and grinned at her. "Don't count on it. Not many things dumber than a cow." His expression softened. "Are you all right? That was a hard bit of riding."

Jessica smiled and turned to Amber, running her hand along the animal's smooth flank. "I'm fine. Amber's breathing a little hard, though. This kind of work isn't easy for a horse her age." The mare, basking in her affection, snorted and nibbled at her hand.

Clinton grunted, but Jessica didn't miss the fondness in his eyes. He, too, was sentimental about Amber. "You should try out another horse. Amber must be nearly fourteen."

"I know. But you gave me Amber that first summer. I'd feel like a traitor if I abandoned her now."

Traitor. She wished she hadn't used that word. A glance at Clinton's face confirmed his usual calm good temper. But these past few months she had felt as though she were creeping through a mine field, where any misstep might cause an explosion. How much longer could they avoid discussing Mark's imminent arrival in Hope Valley?

He placed his hand on her shoulder, squeezing slightly. "I wish you didn't have to do this, Jessica. It's too much for you, working like a cowhand. But the men should be coming home anytime now. If we can keep going awhile longer, I'll be able to hire some help."

"I don't mind." She didn't. In fact, she rather liked the exertion. It kept her mind off other things. Japan had surrendered two weeks ago, just a few days after the United States dropped some kind of horrible new bomb on a city called Hiroshima and another on Nagasaki, and now the war was truly over. There was a feeling of optimism throughout the States at the end of this war to end all wars.

Jessica, though, found herself thinking more about Mark's rumored arrival than about the fact that the other men would soon be returning. For weeks a crew headed by a brawny red-haired stranger named Cullen MacDougal had been preparing the site for the sawmill. The town was rife with speculation about him, about the men he was recruiting, and about the machinery he was sliding smoothly into place. He had snapped up the first ablebodied men to return to the valley, offering wages higher than the cattlemen were prepared to pay. But Mark

Hardy himself had not yet arrived.

"Ready to go?" Clinton picked up the reins of his horse, a blocky bay named Scotch that was grazing a few feet away, and turned expectantly to Jessica. "Karla should have supper ready by the time we get home."

She didn't move, her gaze still focused thoughtfully on the horizon. Her uneasiness was growing, deepening the chasm between her and her husband and making honest conversation more difficult the longer she postponed it. She took a deep breath. "Clinton, what—what do you think about the sawmill?"

"The sawmill?" His voice was carefully noncommittal. "It will mean change in the valley, that's for sure."

"For the better? There will be jobs for everyone, I suppose."

"Yes. And good wages."

"What did they say about it at the cattlemen's meeting last night?"

"Oh, the usual reactionary complaints. They're scared, of course. High wages at the mill mean we'll have to pay more. And there will be shorter hours. There's even talk of a union." He smiled bleakly, and dried grass crackled under his heels as he shifted from one foot to the other. "I guess you could say they were a little stirred up."

"Where will the logs come from? All the land around here is for grazing."

"*Has* been." He gestured toward the mountains. "That's all public land—Forest Service land. We only lease it. Hardy must have worked out a deal for the timber."

There—Mark had been mentioned. She steeled herself. "Clinton . . . about Mark . . . We've got to talk about it."

She thought he was going to shrug her off again, but after a slight hesitation he replied, "Yes, I suppose we must."

"I *did* love him," she said softly. "You know that. After all, there's Justin. But it was a long time ago. Things change. I've changed. When I agreed to marry you, it wasn't only to get out of an intolerable situation. I liked you, was attracted to you. . . ."

He didn't respond, and she rushed on. "These years with you have been good. I—I came to feel more for you than just liking. I'm . . . I'm deeply fond of you."

A shadow of pain crossed his face, and she stumbled on. "Not just fond. More than that. No one could have been as good to me as you have. Kind, gentle, generous. I just wanted you to know you don't have to worry about Mark coming back."

He smiled, a smile of such sweetness and sadness that her breath caught in her throat. "I don't worry, Jessica. I know you. You're an honorable woman, a loyal woman. You keep your promises. Otherwise I—I wouldn't love you as I do."

She reached for his hand. He seldom spoke of his love for her, as if he didn't want to burden her with it, and now it nearly broke her heart. She had known it, of course, but since she could not match the intensity of his feelings, it remained almost an unspoken secret between them. But in a different way, a special way, she did love him. How could she not?

"I do love you, Clint. I really do. You know that, don't you?"

His eyes were infinitely sad, and she knew he was aware of the different nature of her love. "We have a good marriage, Jessica. I know it's precious to both of us." He took her chin in his hand and looked deeply into her eyes. She felt as though he was laying bare a vulnerable part of himself that she had never seen before. "I trust you," he said softly. "You won't betray me."

He kissed her gently, and then they silently mounted their horses and cantered toward home. Her feelings were a jumble. It didn't matter that Mark would be here soon, she repeated to herself. After all, he'd left over a dozen years ago! That part of her life was over. Her marriage to a wonderful, gentle man was rock solid and secure.

*   *   *

Jessica dropped the novel she had been trying to read for the past half hour and let it slide from her lap to the floor. Leaning back in the comfortable overstuffed armchair, she closed her eyes and sighed wearily. For days she had felt as though she were living in a vacuum, waiting for the proverbial other shoe to drop. True, the ranch had seen some activity lately. A few of the hands they had employed before the war had returned to the valley, and two had come back to work for Clinton. Three, however, had taken jobs with the new sawmill.

Logs now filled the millpond; the first board was to be cut next week. But the new owner had not yet put in an appearance in the valley, and to her consternation, Jessica was finding herself more than a little edgy.

The shrilling of the phone jarred her from her irritable thoughts, and she reached over to the small stand and took it from the hook. "Hello."

"Jessica! He's here!"

Her pulse raced and her heart did several flip-flops, but she responded calmly. "Hi, Lydia. Who's here?"

"Mark Hardy, of course! Jake thought he saw him driving through town this morning in a limousine as long as Main Street! Then Billy, who cuts Mrs. Craddock's lawn, said he saw a huge car pull up in front of the old Townsend mansion, the one that's been vacant for years, and that—"

"Lydia, hold on. Are you sure it's Mark? Where is he now?"

"Well, *I* don't know. I certainly don't keep track of his every move," Lydia replied more righteously than truthfully. "But I suppose he went out to see his mother. Etta Jensen phoned and said he was seen driving out of town along that old dirt road that leads past the Hardys' homestead. Jessica—Jessica?"

"I'll call you back," Jessica murmured, gently replacing

the phone. There were goose bumps all along her arms. So he was here. Naturally he would go to see Leah, and then . . .

She jumped from the chair and paced about the living room, giving vent to the agitation that wouldn't allow her to sit still. Her throat felt dry, her chest tight. Perhaps she was just borrowing trouble. Maybe he wouldn't try to see her at all. Leah would certainly tell him she was married, if he didn't already know. Perhaps they would meet in time, at a party, a neighborhood gathering, exchange a few words, and that would be that. Mark had been gone for years without a word; it wasn't likely she had been enshrined in his heart all that time.

When Clinton came in from work, they had a quiet supper. Justin had asked permission to eat with a friend, and the atmosphere was unusually peaceful. She wondered if Clinton knew Mark had arrived. Probably— everyone else in town did. But if so, he gave no indication.

After supper they read for a while, although Jessica could not have said what was on the page. Twice the phone rang, but the calls were for Clinton, and Jessica's heart, after jumping into her throat each time, subsided. Finally they went on up the gracefully curving staircase to bed.

Clinton gave her a quiet kiss, then turned away. In a few minutes she was aware of his even breathing, but it was a long time before sleep came to her. Wide-eyed, she stared at the ceiling, telling herself how ridiculous she was being. Even if Mark did try to see her, she didn't have to agree.

It was midmorning the next day when the doorbell rang. Justin was out. Clinton was riding several miles away on the north range. Karla was in the kitchen. Jessica went to the door.

She let out her breath in a combination of disappointment and relief when she saw Billy, a towheaded, freckled-faced boy of about nine, standing on the doorstep. Had she really expected Mark?

"Hello, Billy." She smiled down at the youngster.

He thrust out grubby fingers and shoved an envelope into her hand. "Here. He said to give you this."

Involuntarily her fingers curled around the envelope; her heart nearly stopped beating. "Who told you to bring this?"

"Mr. Hardy. He saw me mowing the lawn next to the Townsend place—he just moved in there—and said I was to bring this to you. Put it right in your hand." His blue eyes were both solemn and curious.

Before she could question him further, he scurried down the steps. She watched him jump onto his bike and careen down the driveway. Then she walked slowly back into the house, the note clutched in her moist fist.

Only when she was in her bedroom with the door shut did she unfold it. Already she knew what it would say, and she was not mistaken. Firm, powerful strokes marched across white paper.

Meet me this afternoon.

The arrogance of the summons filled her with fierce anger. No salutation, no signature, no apology, no explanation. And no mention of where she was to meet him. He was assuming that she would know. She clenched her teeth and crumpled the note into a tiny ball, threw it toward the wastebasket, then retrieved it and tore it into tiny bits. It wasn't only his arrogance in assuming that she would know where to meet him that angered her; it was her own reaction. He was right: She did know.

But she certainly wouldn't go. How could he even suggest such a thing?

Of course, it was inevitable that they meet sometime. Might it not be better to see him privately, say whatever needed saying, where they would be safe from prying eyes? Memories in Hope Valley were long, and nearly everyone in town knew her story. Justin's father might have been a mystery before she went to live with the Hardys, but after that, the paternity of her child was common knowledge.

She glanced at her watch. It was several miles to the secluded glade by the schoolhouse where they had first made love. She wasn't even sure the little clearing was there anymore. She could drive, of course, but someone might see her.

The trail across the mountain was much more direct. She could ride over, and no one would be the wiser. When she got back, she would tell Clinton, of course, explain that she had thought it best to meet Mark privately.

It took her only a few minutes to dress in riding clothes and saddle Amber. She would be there in plenty of time to see Mark and return home before dark.

She draped Amber's reins loosely around a willow branch and slipped along the trail overgrown with brush and pine seedlings. What would Mark say? she wondered for the hundredth time. Would he look the same? She would be as cool as she could be, formal, if possible, to let him know that there was absolutely nothing between them anymore. Assuming, of course, that that unlikelihood was among his reasons for this clandestine meeting.

In spite of imagining the scene time and again since leaving the ranch, she froze at her first sight of Mark. It had been so long. So terribly long.

She could only stare, immobilized by the fierce emotions that lashed through her. He had changed so much—and yet he hadn't changed at all. He stood in the clearing with his back to the boulder, erect and unyielding as a desert prince, impatient eyes scanning the surrounding willow screen. Except for his eyes he was still as a statue, but he appeared intensely, vibrantly alive. His youthful body had filled out, and now he had the broad, powerful shoulders, the confident stance, of maturity. His hair was about the same length as before, but now it was stylishly cut instead of hacked off at his collar's edge.

The contours of his face had hardened, she saw. The

vulnerable, idealistic boy was gone, replaced by a square-jawed, hawk-faced man with deep-set brown eyes that blazed with restless energy. A thought flashed through her mind: he wasn't used to waiting.

She hesitated, and although she didn't think she had made a sound, his head swung around in her direction. "Jessica?" His voice was deep, stirring, accustomed to command.

Slowly she came out of the undergrowth and walked toward him. He was dressed differently than when she had last seen him—no tattered denim for this Mark. He wore an obviously expensive ivory shirt, sleeves rolled and neck open to accentuate the deep bronze of his skin. His dark twill pants were tailored to fit his narrow hips and long, lean legs to perfection. Highly polished western boots were his only concession to the uniform of the county.

She glanced down at her own outfit, glad that she had selected the simple elegance of a silk shirt and fawn riding pants. It gave her confidence—a confidence she suspected she was going to need as she met his eyes.

Slowly, as though gliding through honey, they moved toward each other, then stopped about three feet apart. He limped slightly, she noticed, her heart filling with an aching tenderness.

"It's been a long time," he said quietly. She would have believed he was perfectly under control if she hadn't noticed his hands were clenched tightly at his side.

"Yes, it has." She wondered how she was able to match his cool, noncommittal tone when her heart was slamming against her chest like a sledgehammer.

"I understand you're married," he said politely.

"Yes," she agreed again.

"You didn't wait long."

This time there was cold anger in his voice. Her head snapped up, and all the pent-up fury of the years surged to the fore. Utterly forgotten was her resolve to be distant, formal, polite. "You could have written. I prayed that you would. But not a word, not a note!" Her icy tone matched his.

"I—I— Oh, hell, what was I supposed to say?" His control snapped, and he pounded his thigh with a clenched fist, for a moment reminding Jessica of his long-ago youthful frustration with attempting to express his deepest emotions. "I told you I'd be back for you as soon as I could care for you, support you! As soon as I could come back as somebody, not a backwoods bum!"

"Over a decade?" she exploded. "I was supposed to wait for years and years without a single, solitary word from you? You could have been married, in jail, dead—anything!"

"You didn't wait a decade to find yourself a new man, Jessica." He took a deep breath, then continued in a hard tone. "And you found quite a rich one at that, didn't you. You may have jumped from the frying pan, but you didn't exactly land in the fire, did you?"

Anger at the injustice of his attack made it almost impossible to speak, but she managed a swift retort through stiff lips. "I don't have to listen to this! If you know all about my marriage to Clinton, you must also know why I married him."

"My son," he said quietly. Abruptly his anger seemed to drain away, and a look of pain flooded into his deep brown eyes. He sighed, shook his head as though clearing it of unwelcome thoughts, then moved toward her. He placed his hand on her arm, seemingly oblivious to the tremor his touch induced in her, and led her to the boulder. "Let's sit down, Jessica," he said tiredly.

The clover, protected by the trees and nourished by the river, was still green and lush, and the fragrance of crushed mint rose to envelop her as she settled herself beside Mark. With his anger seemingly burned out there was a brooding, desperate look about him that reminded her of the old Mark.

"What happened, Jessica?" he asked softly. "Tell me everything."

She studied her hands, loosely clasped in front of her,

as she wondered whether she could possibly recount for him everything that had occurred since he had left. The desperate fear, the dark despair, the sweet joy of Justin. The finding of a refuge with Clinton. Haltingly she began, and when she had finally finished, he sighed, closed his eyes, and leaned his dark head back against the gray boulder.

"If I had known you were pregnant . . ." The words seemed torn from him in anguish. Then he sighed again and seemed deep in thought. Finally he spoke. "At the time it seemed my life depended on leaving. I had to get away, make money, and then come back for you." His mouth twisted in a parody of a smile. "It never occurred to me that . . ." Again he paused. "I guess it never occurred to me that *you* would change."

"I waited, I hoped," she said softly. "But it was so long. . . ."

He smiled, a mirthless smile, and she sensed he was reliving the years he had been gone. "It wasn't easy out there. But with hard work and a lot of luck I was beginning to do all right. I thought I'd gradually be able to stockpile some cash and come back, but then the war came along."

"You were in the fighting?" Immediately she thought of his limp. And immediately she wondered why he hadn't notified her that he was going overseas.

As if reading her mind, he said ruefully, "I wanted to write, but I didn't want you to worry more than I figured you already were." He gave a mirthless laugh. "Anyway, I was lucky. I got shot early and was sent back stateside. And once I recovered, I found the main chance." He paused. "A lot of people made a lot of money out of this war, Jessica. I was one of them. And now—now I'm in a position to change things."

She caught a flash of the old idealism, and the fury that had fueled it. She shivered slightly. "What do you want to change?"

His lips tightened. "What Hope Valley needs is an

alternative to cattle ranching. My mill will provide employment—and pride—to the men the old cattle barons have been running over for years."

"Well, the 'old barons' aren't going to just sit still while you—"

He threw back his head and laughed. "I never thought they would." Suddenly he grew serious, and he turned to look at her. "But you, Jessica. I never thought I'd find you on that side of the fence." Frowning thoughtfully, as if reviewing the reasons for her unwilling defection to the enemy camp, he said, "Well, I won't move too fast until you're free."

A cold cloud of anxiety swirled around her, coalescing in the pit of her stomach. "Free?"

He leaned toward her. He brushed the hair back from her averted face, traced her cheek with one finger, then cupped her chin in his hand, forcing her eyes to meet his. "Divorced. We love each other," he said quietly. "I'm as sure of that as I was the day I left here. Something happened to us—something I suppose neither of us wanted, but something rare, unique. When I first saw you standing in the doorway of the schoolhouse with the sun making a halo around your hair, I knew you were the only one for me."

"But—but things have changed." Her throat was so dry, she could hardly force out the words.

She never should have allowed this situation to develop, she thought in a panic. It was wrong even being here. His lips were so close; she felt his heat, caught his musky scent. More than her mind remembered; his essence was imprinted on her very soul. Everything that had happened since he left fell away, unimportant, nonexistent. There were only the two of them in the entire world. . . .

Desperately she jerked away from his hand, fighting for her life. "It's too late! I'm a married woman now, Mark. I can't forget my vows."

He smiled lazily, placing his hand behind her neck and holding her a scant few inches from his lips. "You made another vow before that. A vow to a man you loved. A man you still love."

She felt impaled on misery, twisting, turning, desperate for rescue but equally desperate to get even closer to Mark. This couldn't be happening! She wasn't a young girl anymore, pummeled by wild emotion. She was an adult. A wife. A mother. She had values, obligations—loyalty, fidelity.

"Mark, you've got to understand!" she cried. "You were gone so long. And Clinton took me in when I had no place to turn. He's made a home for me and Justin, and he's been kind and good and—"

"Do you love him?" His lips curled, as though he knew the answer.

"Mark, I—I—"

"Have you forgotten what love is, Jessica? Have you forgotten the passion, the need to belong to one person, one person alone? What we had happens only once in a lifetime, and we can have it again. Don't throw it away."

"*You* threw it away!" She was nearly sobbing. "If you knew how desperate I was. Even a note—"

"Yes, yes, I admit I was proud, Jessica, too proud to let you know how things were with me until I could come back a success. And I was afraid, too. Afraid if I heard from you, I wouldn't be able to stay away. Then, when I was discharged from the service and started my cost-plus business, the money finally started rolling in. I could see all my dreams coming true. Returning here, a power in the community, and claiming you."

Something in his voice made her give him a sharp glance. "Which means more to you, Mark? Your revenge in returning to Hope Valley a conquering hero, showing everyone your success? Or me?"

"Oh, Jessica!" He caught her against his chest, and she felt his heart thudding in a deep, powerful cadence. "How can you even ask that? I wouldn't have returned at all if it hadn't been for you! We belong together. And you know it."

She pulled away as much as she could bear to. Once they had belonged together, but the river of time had branched between them, carrying them in different directions. Yet every iota of her being still yearned for him. She no longer needed to wonder how she would feel on seeing him again. It was more than passion, more than desire. She was transported back to a time when her soul had merged with Mark's, and she realized it had never been completely her own since. On some elemental level they belonged together still.

But she mustn't give in to her urges and desires. She must exercise restraint, responsibility. Clinton trusted her. She was his wife. That meant something.

For the first time anxiety flickered in Mark's eyes. "You can get a Nevada divorce, and we can be married immediately."

She raised her chin and spoke firmly, even though her lips trembled. "I can't."

With a low oath he clasped her to him so tightly she could hardly breathe, and his lips roved frantically over her hair, her cheeks, finally finding and claiming her lips. Molten fire poured through her every vein, as her arms, oblivious to the commands of her mind, went around his back, caressing the powerful muscles, moving up to his neck. Her fingers tangled in his dark hair, pulling his mouth even closer to hers. She was aflame, out of control. Right at that moment, if it had meant her life, she could not have resisted his kisses.

Time ceased to exist. Years and maturity fell away like autumn leaves, and they were once again two young lovers in a secluded grove, glorying in the passion they had discovered one warm spring afternoon.

She fell back on the warm grass, every nerve singing under his touch. She was conscious of nothing but him, his hands in her hair, on her face, unbuttoning her shirt, slipping it from her shoulders. She shivered, both from the feel of the breeze on her bare skin and from the frantic kisses that followed the breeze. Soon their other clothes lay in a jumbled heap beside them, and free of all restraints, they came together.

Their bodies remembered. Every surge of ecstasy, every exquisite movement, was familiar and precious. As inevitably, as inexorably, as the tide, they flowed together, merging in a whirlpool of passion, their essences intermingling in a burst of fulfillment.

Afterward he lay atop her, breathing raggedly, his lips on the moist, heated skin at the hollow of her throat. She welcomed his weight, the feel of his heart thudding against her own exquisitely sensitive skin. She didn't want to move. She wanted nothing to disturb this perfect world the two of them alone inhabited.

But the breeze was suddenly cooler on her skin, and she glanced up as the sun dropped below the jagged horizon. Reluctantly she shifted. Mark slid off her and propped his head on his hand, looking down into her face with dark eyes still glowing with passion.

"Was I too heavy?" he asked.

"No." Tears of love stung her eyes. Still enveloped in his warmth and adoration, she knew that soon she would be swamped with guilt and regrets. She reached up and brushed his lips with hers. "But it's late. I have to be going."

"Going where?" His eyes darkened.

"Why, home, of course." She gave him a startled glance. "I—I don't know how this happened, Mark. I didn't mean it to, but—"

"It happened because we love each other. We're meant for each other," he said calmly. "You know that."

"There won't be a divorce. I can't do that to my husband," she said, sitting up abruptly. At his sardonic look she felt her cheeks burn. "I can't say I wish this hadn't happened—I'm not that strong. But we can't let it mean more than a fond remembrance of what once was. Our time together is over, Mark. I wish it were different, but it isn't. Clinton hasn't done a single thing to justify my betrayal."

He stared at her, his eyes so dark they were almost black. "Making love to me just now—that was a betrayal? Jessica, the only real betrayal here would be pretending that what we just shared was simply some 'fond remembrance'! What about *our* love—can you go on betraying that?"

She returned his angry stare, knowing she had to be strong. She shouldn't have allowed her emotions to sway her judgment as they had. Her only excuse was that she had loved Mark so long, and seeing him again had swept her into a confusing maelstrom of long-ago need and frustrated desire.

If Clinton ever discovered what she had done, it would hurt him horribly. But he need not know. She could protect him that much. And somehow she would make it up to him. If, on the other hand, she left him for Mark, it would destroy him. Perhaps if he hadn't been so kind, so generous, so trusting . . . But the ties that bound her to Clinton—loyalty, respect, gratitude, and even love—were strong.

"I wish you'd leave the valley," she said abruptly, desperately. "You say you came for me, and surely you can see that that's impossible."

He gave her a grim smile. "Impossible? You can still say that after what's just happened? We both know you love me. You're simply afraid to rock your boat, risk your respectability."

"That's not fair! I certainly risked it—no, tossed it away—for you many years ago!"

"And then there's that—Justin," he acknowledged.

"Justin! Certainly you're not thinking of—"

"I want to see him, talk to him. Let him know his real father."

"Clinton has been his real father," she retorted. "You were nowhere in sight."

"Well, I am now. And I can open doors for the boy, give him a glimpse of a world beyond this place. Not even the mighty Clinton Carter can offer him that. I'll expect to see him, Jessica," he said firmly. "Soon."

Knees weak, hands trembling, she rose and dressed quickly. Brushing the leaves from her pants, she turned to face him. "Good-bye, Mark."

He grasped her hand and pulled her fiercely toward him. "When will I see you again?"

"You won't. At least not like this. It's better if we stay away from each other," she said dully.

Her entire being ached with despair. And there was really nothing else to say. Mark had come home. She loved him still. And there was nothing she could honorably do about it. Turning away, she walked slowly down the trail.

Silently, his face a bleak, stiff mask, Mark watched her go. It took his every ounce of self-control to keep from bounding after her, forcing her to admit what he had always known—that they could never say good-bye.

Fierce anger welled up inside him, tightening his jaw. This could not be the end of his dreams. At the thought a vast emptiness opened inside him, as all the years without Jessica flashed through his mind. The torturous early years, when he went to bed dog tired every night with an ache in his heart that threatened to annihilate him. The desperation when he looked for work, any work, only to be turned away. The brushes with the establishment until he finally learned to use the system to his advantage. Always, everything, for the day when he could return to her.

And then the war, the shrapnel in his hip that threatened to sideline him for good. The struggle to recover, then to retool his business for war production. And then the money was finally flowing in, more than he had ever expected, bringing him closer and closer to his goal: Jessica.

He clenched his jaw so hard that his teeth ached as her slender form disappeared into the trees. The sawmill he was starting in Hope Valley was just one of a number of highly profitable enterprises. But could he really give up, relinquish Jessica? His heart became a cold, hard lump of pain at the prospect.

Yet she was tied to another man now.

If he'd written, or sent word, would she have waited? He'd held fast to his love. It hadn't crossed his mind that she would ever doubt him.

Fists clenched, eyes staring at nothing, he left the clearing and stalked to his car parked on the road several hundred feet away.

One skirmish was lost, he decided. But the battle wasn't over.

10

Clinton switched off the ignition in the automobile they had bought just the week before in Boise and turned to face Jessica, a troubled frown on his face.

"Are you feeling better? I don't want to insist, but it will look strange if you don't come with me. Everyone in the county has been invited."

She turned away from him to look at the Townsend mansion, resplendent in new paint and a refurbished roof, partially to look at what Mark had done to the old place and partially to hide her expression from her husband. Although she had prepared Justin for his meeting with his real father, she had not accompanied him, and she hadn't seen Mark since they had made love several weeks before. Staying out of his sight hadn't been easy. He had made a determined assault—calls, just showing up where he thought she would be, but she had managed to elude him. Luckily, she thought. Missing him was once more a constant ache in her heart, and seeing him face-to-face might topple the edifice of control she had so painstakingly built.

She wasn't sure what Clinton suspected. He was invariably kind, although sometimes she caught a speculative look in his eyes. How she longed to confess, to assuage the guilt that ate at her like a vulture. But she knew how cowardly that would be. The guilt was hers; she couldn't break her husband's heart in a spasm of contrition.

"I'm feeling much better," she replied. A headache had been all she could think of to avoid Mark's open-house party, but it was no solution. Sooner or later she would have to see him. After all, they lived in the same community, and they would be thrown together from time to time no matter how hard she tried to avoid him.

Clinton touched her lightly on the shoulder, then went around the car to open her door. Side by side they walked up the front path recently bordered with roses and a riot of dahlias. The entry also had been updated. Two slender marble columns flanked a wide white door that sported narrow leaded-glass windows on either side. As Clinton raised the ornate knocker Jessica considered the contrast to the Hardys' shack deep in the woods. Did Mark consider it often, too?

Etta Jensen, a thin, wiry woman with a quick smile and pale blue eyes full of curiosity, apparently had been pressed into service. She opened the door and directed them down the hall.

"Just go on in, Jessica, Clinton. Mr. Hardy's in the living room with everybody else."

Jessica bit back a cynical smile. Mr. Hardy. Like many others, Etta Jensen had once been accustomed to calling Mark "one of the Hardy litter." It was interesting what money could do to one's perception of a man.

As they went down the hall, passing several open doors, she had an overall impression of designer elegance—an oil painting here, a beveled mirror there.

The high-ceiling living room was spacious and beautiful. Windows along one wall were draped in a rich blue-green brocade that was echoed in the vast Oriental carpet on the polished hardwood floor. An enormous fireplace with a marble mantel dominated another wall. The furnishings were plush and expensive looking, and a dozen or so people were scattered among them like brightly colored seashells on a sun-washed beach.

She took a deep breath, arranged her face into a pleasant expression, and stepped into the room. She saw him immediately, of course. How could she not? He stood out from the others like a magnificent raven in a flock of sparrows. Dressed in dark trousers, a superbly fitted jacket, and a maroon silk tie, he was lounging against the mantel, a glass held negligently in one strong, bronzed hand. He raised his dark head and looked across the room and caught her eyes. Flint striking flint.

Taking his time, he moved to greet them. Was that triumph in his eyes? she wondered. Certainly he had a lot to be proud of. Not many people could have made the impact on Hope that he had. In only a few short months he'd become the town's leading employer, owner of the one real mansion in town, and a personage to be courted and visited by prominent people from all over the state. Had he arranged this reception in order to gloat? Or to force Jessica to see him?

Hand outstretched, he advanced toward them. "Clinton. Jessica." His voice came from deep in his chest, projecting warmth and heartiness. "Glad you could make it. I don't see nearly enough of old friends." His glance at Jessica made her want to turn around and run, but she didn't lower her eyes.

"We're happy you asked us," Clinton replied. "Mostly I just see you at the cattlemen's meetings. They're always a little confrontational, I'm afraid. It helps to put things on a social basis."

Mark's lips curved in a smile. "I hope so. I certainly don't mean to put anyone out of business. There's room in Hope Valley for both lumbering and cattle, I should think. I hope you can persuade some of your colleagues of that."

Clinton shook his head ruefully. "I guess even *I'm* not

completely convinced of that. We've used the public land to supplement our ranches for years, and it's been a real boon. Cutting the trees, making logging roads—it's bound to change the county."

"And force you to pay higher wages," Mark said lightly but meaningfully.

"Your crews fenced off a spring that we've used for years," Clint replied, his voice still mild.

"If the cows can't drink there, they'll move on," Mark replied. "The spot is perfect for a resort I'm thinking of building."

Clinton's face flushed. "That's public land. You can't build there."

"I had most of this county surveyed recently," Mark replied, "and I found some surprises for all of us. That particular tract is surrounded by forest land but privately owned. I bought it from young Garrotson just the other day."

Clinton stared, speechless, and Jessica rushed into the breach. "I hope we're not going to talk business all day. I'd love to see what you've done to the house."

Mark took her arm. "I'd be delighted to give you the tour. Clint, help yourself to some refreshments. I'll have your lovely wife back in a few minutes."

Jessica opened her mouth to protest that her husband should join them, but aside from digging in her heels and screaming, she didn't see how she could elude Mark's possessive grip. She gave Clinton a supplicating glance, but Mark eased her out the door and into a small study before she could regain her composure.

"Well," he said, backing her up against the wall, one arm propped behind her shoulder. "Alone at last."

He wasn't touching her, but he was so close that any movement of hers would have brought them into physical contact. Even if his body hadn't been positioned so, she would have been held immobile by the energy he radiated. Still, she managed to speak.

"Mark, I don't know what you hope to accomplish by this. You must know by now that I don't want to see you."

"No, I don't know that at all." His lips were so close. Too close. "I know that you've been devilishly clever at hiding from me. But that's over now. We're going to have this out."

She studied his set expression. He was so near, she could feel the heat of his body. Her senses reeled, and her legs felt as though they would give up the struggle to support her any minute now. But her mind was made up. She couldn't undo the past, but she could be positive it didn't repeat itself.

She tried to duck under his arm, but he raised his other hand to imprison her. She lifted her chin and faced him defiantly. "There's nothing to discuss. We made a serious mistake. It would probably be easier for both of us if we didn't see each other at all, but that might be impossible in a small community. So we might run into each other on occasion, but I'd appreciate it if you'd please leave me alone."

Agony flared deep in his eyes, and he moved an inch closer. She edged back against the wall.

"Mom asked about you the other day," he said softly.

"How is Leah?" That was another thing she felt guilty about. She loved Leah, but after she went to live with Clinton, she saw very little of the woman. It had seemed easier, all around. Although the older woman had never indicated it by word or look, Jessica knew that Leah felt she belonged with Mark.

"She's about the same. A little older, of course, but she seems indestructible. I've tried to convince her to come here and live with me, but she won't." His mouth twisted in anger. "She says Jeb is her husband—she won't leave him. You women seem to be singing the same tune."

Under his anger she detected his frustrated longing, and it took all her courage to refrain from putting her arms around him and easing his pain. But she couldn't buy happiness—his or hers—at the expense of an innocent person.

As though he sensed her softening, he leaned toward her. "Are you sure, Jessica? Won't you change your mind? You and I were bonded forever from the moment we met. I know I'll always love you, and I'm positive you feel the same way. Don't try to deny it."

"I don't deny it." Her shoulders slumped, but she met his eyes. "But there are such things as honor, integrity—"

"Words!" he spat.

"Our words have to mean something. Otherwise we're no better than animals," she said firmly.

He searched her eyes for an endless moment. Then the fire seemed to go from his, and his skin paled under the bronze.

"Is everything all right?" Clinton's even voice came from the open doorway, and Jessica gathered all her resources, then turned to him with a smile. "Yes. Everything's fine, Clint. We were just coming back to the party."

Had her husband seen Mark's stricken expression, her flushed cheeks? If he had, he spoke smoothly nonetheless.

"Mark, I haven't had a chance to thank you for what you're arranging for Justin. I've never seen him so excited—especially over school. I guess the idea of being grown up enough to leave home and go away to school is pretty thrilling for a boy his age. It's making a different kid of him."

Mark took a deep breath. His lips tightened, and he clenched his hands. Then he managed to give Clinton a smile. "I think a private school will be best for him. He's bright but impulsive. He needs direction. This school is highly recommended. It will give him a good start on college."

Clinton shook his head. "I'm not sure he wants to go to college. Last I heard he planned on following the rodeo circuit."

Mark gave him a challenging look. "The boy will take over my enterprises one day. He can't do it without college. He's young, and he'll come around."

Jessica half expected Clinton to object. Legally Justin was his son, and over the years he had done a great deal for the boy. Yet in the few weeks since they'd met, Mark had become Justin's hero, alienating him still further from Clinton's love.

Clinton shrugged and said generously, "Perhaps you'll have better luck with him than I've had." He put his hand on Jessica's back and guided her toward the door. "I think we should be going, and you'll want to get back to your guests. Some of them were becoming a little rest—"

He broke off at the sound of shouting coming from the other room, and they all turned and stared at the man who stumbled in and glared angrily from the doorway.

Jessica recognized Leland Patrick, a rancher from just across the county line, although he looked quite a bit the worse for wear. His clothing was rumpled, his faded red hair disheveled, and he held on to the doorway as though it might get away from him.

"Mark Hardy, you bastard!" His words were slurred, but it didn't detract from their venom.

Jessica gasped. Mark's eyes narrowed, but he didn't move. Clinton walked quickly toward the intruder. "Now, Lee, you're drunk. Come on, sit down." He gently maneuvered the man toward a chair.

Patrick shook Clinton's hand off his arm and staggered on into the room, his face mottled with anger. "Communist! You should be run out of the county! What's this I hear about you starting up a union?"

Mark eyed the man as a dedicated biologist might examine a particularly interesting specimen. "There's been talk of organizing the mill workers. I'm not doing it, but I'm certainly not standing in their way. What business is it of yours?"

"It's un-American. It will ruin the American worker. It—"

"It will force you to raise your starvation wages and set decent hours," Mark said coolly. "Now, I don't like to seem inhospitable, but I suggest you might be more comfortable somewhere else. Like out of my house."

The look he gave Patrick was so deadly that Jessica was relieved when her husband turned the man around and steered him from the room.

Mark gave a short bark of laughter. "It seems the good people of Hope are united. They all want me out of here." His glance was savage, cutting her as surely as a knife. "All right, Jessica, you've convinced me. You don't have to stay a prisoner in your house to avoid me. I won't bother you again."

She wanted to say something that would take the anguished anger from his eyes, but there was really nothing left to say. She had convinced Mark that it was over between them—and she would have to learn to live with the pain that got sharper with every breath she took.

It was ten o'clock on a crisp blue morning that harbingered autumn. Jessica wandered aimlessly about the house, pausing to run her hand over a buffet that Karla had already dusted, then up to her bedroom, where the bed was made as meticulously as ever. She was thrilled the war was over, but with the return of the hired hands she was relegated to housework—housework Karla managed efficiently and jealously. Justin was always out and about when he wasn't in school, and Clinton seemed busier than ever.

She meandered back downstairs, reflecting once again that, for all of having lived on a ranch for years, she had very little idea of what was involved in managing one. That process was off-limits to her. Clinton, always so indulgent, didn't believe a woman should be involved in financial concerns. In some ways, she realized, women were treated much like children.

She was becoming increasingly restless, bored not only with the loss of physical activity but with the lack of mental stimulation. Also, she needed something to keep her mind off Mark. The image of his anguish amid the wealth he had dreamed of had haunted her since his open house a couple of weeks ago.

The study door was closed, a sure sign that Clinton was within. She tapped lightly, then walked into the room. He looked up from his desk and gave her a smile, but he looked a little abstracted, she thought, as though her interruption wasn't entirely welcome.

"Problems?" she asked, leaning one hip on his desk and gazing at the papers fanned before him.

"Nothing to worry about," he replied, reaching over and taking her hand. "What are you up to on such a glorious morning?"

She hesitated, then plunged into what was on her mind. "Clinton, I've been thinking. Now that I'm not working on the ranch, I've got a lot of time to fill. How about teaching me the business? I mean, there must be things I could do to help you, things you don't have to be personally involved in."

He chuckled, rose from the desk, and moved up behind her, rubbing her neck and shoulders. "It's all very dull, dear. Nothing to concern yourself about."

"But you spend so much time in here. Is there something going on? Are we losing money, or having problems with prices?"

He laughed softly, lifted her hair from the nape of her neck, and dropped a soft kiss on the exposed spot. "Now, whatever gave you that idea? We're doing fine."

"But I've heard that some of the other ranchers are worried about Mark's sawmill, and having to pay higher wages."

"Many of them always did pay too little. We've paid a good wage from the beginning. Nothing to worry about." He squeezed her shoulders and edged her gently toward the door. "Look, dear, if you're bored, why don't you think about redecorating the house? You did without for so many years. The stores must be full of new products now, and you can run wild." He raised his hand as she started to reply. "Don't worry! We can afford it."

Dismissed, she continued her aimless ramble about the house. Should she redecorate? The problem was, she loved the old house just as it was—the spacious rooms, the hardwood floors, the warm colors and furnishings that fit so unobtrusively into the whole.

Maybe the kitchen. She entered Karla's domain. The heavy, graying woman looked up as she approached.

"Hello, Jessica. What would you and the mister like for dinner tonight?"

At least she could choose the menus. "How about that salmon steak you do so well?"

Karla frowned, her round face flushed from the heat of the stove. "I suppose . . . But a nice roast might go well, too, since it's started to get cooler."

Jessica smiled to herself; she only *thought* she chose the menus. "Whatever you think. I've been wondering, Karla. Would you like a new kitchen?"

"Why would I want a new kitchen?" Karla stepped back from the wood-burning cookstove, put her hands on her substantial hips, and looked around the large room. "Nothing cooks like wood. The mister got me an electric stove before you came, but I had him take it right out. This is fine for me."

Jessica backed out of the room and headed for the barn. Was she more sensitive than usual, or was she really completely unnecessary? Becoming more and more superfluous to her rapidly growing son, denied the chance to learn about ranch management, shielded from the everyday household chores. Why hadn't she noticed it before?

She opened the door and stepped into the warm, humid stable, inhaling the mingled odor of hay and horseflesh.

Perhaps she'd ride over to see Lydia. Amber wouldn't reject her, and Lydia was always ready for a gossip.

Her friend welcomed her warmly, put on the teakettle, and pulled out a chair from the kitchen table.

"I'm glad you could come over. I don't see nearly enough of you. Are you all right? You look a little peaked."

Jessica settled herself in the chair. Peaked was one way to put it. She'd lost weight recently, and there were circles under her eyes that didn't go away with a night's sleep. Trust Lydia's inquisitive eyes to dredge out any secret.

"It's the weather," she offered. "It's been too warm. I'm glad fall is coming."

Lydia nodded. "That's one thing we can be sure of— the weather changing. It don't scare anybody. Now, the things Mark Hardy is doing—that's what's scaring folks."

She might have known Lydia would want to gossip about Mark. Why should she be any different from the rest? Mark's name was on every tongue, it seemed, along with talk of all the changes he was bringing to Hope Valley. Was that the reason she had come—to hear Mark's name and find out what he was doing?

"Don't tell me he's thought of something else to stir people up."

Perhaps her voice wasn't as neutral as she wanted it to be. Lydia gave her a sharp glance, then settled down in a chair opposite her. "I'll say. He's picked a good one this time. You know that acreage between Hope and the Blalock ranch? He's bought it, and he's going to put up houses."

"Houses! But it's just a small piece of land. How can he put houses on it?"

"Well, the houses ain't very big. And I understand they're going to be closer to each other than hairs on a dog."

"Who on earth would buy them?"

"Oh, mill workers, ranch hands, retired people—word is he'll get plenty of takers."

Jessica was silent, thinking over this news. The sawmill was one thing; it provided employment, but it didn't completely change the character of the valley. But a development! More people, more children meant a bigger school, more roads, more social services. Who would pay for them?

Property taxes, she realized. The ranchers would have to pay. And the entire makeup of the county would change. The land itself would change. She hated the thought of it.

She was still contemplating Mark's new venture when she rode back to the Carter ranch. The day was nearly gone. She would just have time to unsaddle Amber and present herself for supper.

She was running lightly up the front path when she caught sight of someone sitting on the stairs to the veranda. She stopped abruptly. Alice Hardy. What on earth was she doing here? Her first thought was that Mark must have sent her, and her pulse pounded erratically before she realized how unlikely that was.

Her cornflower-blue eyes somber, Alice watched her approach and rose to her feet only when Jessica was within a few steps of the veranda.

"Hello, Jessica." There was something set and stubborn about her small, coral-colored mouth, a surliness that was as much a part of Alice as her cotton-candy hair and her pale, translucent skin.

"Why are you sitting out here? Didn't anyone invite you in?"

"Oh, sure." She bobbed her head in the direction of the door. "But I thought I'd wait here, since it's you I need to see."

Jessica sank down on the step and patted the space beside her. "Well, sit down. Tell me all about it." She hadn't seen Alice since that day she had arrived with Norval and she had given her a check to facilitate her escape. Evidently she hadn't taken advantage of it.

"No need to sit." Alice opened her purse and thrust a piece of paper toward her. "Here's a check. I spent yours, getting my tuition paid, but then Mark came back."

Puzzled, Jessica glanced at the check. It was exactly the amount she had originally given Alice, and it was signed by Mark Hardy.

"I don't understand. That was a gift, not a loan." Frowning, she held the check out to the girl.

Alice shook her head. "Mark says to give it back. Hardys take care of their own."

Stunned, Jessica stood speechless as Alice wheeled around and walked briskly away. Having the check returned in such a manner by Mark was almost like a slap in the face.

Hardys take care of their own. The words rang in her ears. Jeb had said them when he whisked her away from the Blalocks. This time Mark had said them, brusquely reminding her that she was now one of the "others."

Well, that was as it should be, wasn't it? She had convinced him there was no future for them together, and at last he was being reasonable. But why did it have to hurt so much?

11

"Justin, have you been drinking?" Mark's voice lashed out at his son. Justin dropped his gaze to the floor and managed to look both defiant and miserable. How young and vulnerable he was, Mark thought, walking over to the boy and draping his arm lightly around his thin shoulders. Fourteen, an insecure age.

He had missed so much of Justin's childhood. He was trying to make up for it now. Justin had his own room in the mansion, which he could use anytime Jessica gave him permission. And now that he had a driver's license, Mark had gotten him his own car, a snappy red convertible that was much too fast for Jessica's tastes.

Mark glanced at the mirror in his bedroom suite that reflected both himself and Justin. The boy didn't favor either him or Jessica, he thought. Jeb Hardy's features were stamped on the young visage: the thick shock of brownish hair, the shrewd, pale blue eyes. His grandfather's cragginess was only slightly softened in the boy's chin and mouth.

He'd also inherited Jeb's disdain for appearances, Mark thought with a wry inward smile. Justin seemed content to wear the same jeans and shirt for days. Tonight, in spite of the fact that Mark had asked him to dress up a little for the visitors, there wasn't much evidence that he had done so.

Mark tousled his hair in an affectionate gesture, though his tone was stern. "Will you answer me, please?"

Justin continued to study the floor. "Nah," he finally said. "Not really drinking. I had a beer or two before I came over."

"A beer or two," Mark repeated. "Then you won't be able to drive your car for a week." Ignoring Justin's outraged protests, he took a brush from his dresser and neatened his son's hair. The boy had ignored Clinton's suggestion that he get a crew cut like all the other boys, and he kept his hair long. "There, you look great. Shall we go on down? They should be here any minute."

"You're just like Mom," Justin growled, but he followed along docilely enough. Mark sensed that in spite of his grousing Justin loved him—perhaps almost as much as he loved the boy.

Etta Jensen had already shepherded the visitors into the living room, and Mark paused in the doorway long enough to survey the two people seated on the love seat in front of the fireplace. He couldn't repress a surge of pride—he'd come a long way from his backwoods roots to warrant such company. Alton Parks was only a state senator now but was almost certain to become a United States senator at the next election. His political network, his affable personality—and his money—would ensure it. And he was eagerly courting Mark.

He glanced at the young woman sitting beside him. Alton's daughter. Dressed in a green satin sheath, with her expertly coiffed dark hair piled high and her makeup impeccable, she looked as elegant as a long-stemmed rose. During his frequent trips to Boise he had spent considerable time ducking her less than subtle advances.

Mark's heart contracted in his chest, and pain lanced

through him. He clenched his jaw, then made a determined effort to relax. Was he going to keep comparing
every woman he saw with Jessica for the rest of his life?
She didn't want him, and he'd be damned if he'd beg anymore. It was about time he caught one of the many
women who persisted in throwing themselves at him.

As he and Justin entered the room Alton Parks rose to
his feet. A man of perhaps fifty, he was short and slender
with a leonine head and huge dark eyes that assessed
everything with a shrewdness Mark was careful not to
underestimate. He was a power in Idaho, and the fact that
he was here in Mark's living room meant that Mark was a
power, too.

"Mark," he said genially, holding out his hand. "How
are you? Aren't you tired yet of holing up here in this little
backwater? When are you coming back to Boise?" Before
Mark could reply, Parks gestured to the girl who was
observing the exchange with a quiet smile. "Amanda
insisted on coming along. There must be some attraction
here—usually she's bored to death with my company and
my friends." His arched eyebrow and insinuating smile
told Mark he knew exactly what the attraction was.

Amanda smiled lazily, her green eyes meeting Mark's
in an intimate glance that made him slightly uneasy. "Why
shouldn't I come? Mark and I are old friends."

Mark would hardly have gone that far. He knew her,
had often traveled in the same crowd. He had even taken
her out to dinner a few times. She had made her interest
in him known, but he had successfully evaded it. Jessica
had filled every corner of his heart.

She still did, he thought. But he was going to have to
learn to live without her. For a moment bitterness
engulfed him, leaving a sour taste in his mouth. Would she
care if he became interested in someone else? He'd been
devastated when he learned of her marriage. Or would
she shrug it off, glad to be rid of him?

He smiled at Amanda, perhaps more warmly than he

should have, and put his hand on Justin's shoulder. "This is my son, Justin."

Justin mumbled something, and Parks looked at him, eyebrows raised. "You've been keeping something from us, Mark. I didn't know you had ever been married."

Mark just looked at him, and the older man flushed slightly.

"Good to meet you, Justin."

Mark poured the adults sherry and Justin a Coke, and they all settled in to casual conversation. Yes, the winter did seem exceptionally long and cold this year. Was the United Nations doomed to failure, just like the old League of Nations, or had humankind actually learned something? Joe Louis appeared unbeatable, but wasn't he getting a little slower? This next fight might tell the tale. Justin took no part in the talk, his assessing blue eyes going from one adult face to the other, his expression a careful blank. Finally Etta Jensen called them in to dinner.

Amanda, seated across the table from Mark, seemed determined to give him the full benefit of her amazing green eyes. Her cleavage, too, he decided, watching the candlelight dance on her smooth skin. The indulged daughter of a filthy-rich father, the polished product of elite boarding schools, she was the kind of woman he had once considered completely out of his reach. Of course, he had never wanted to reach—Jessica had filled his heart for years. Now he had only to put out his hand. Amanda was beautiful and intelligent—and ambitious.

It was after dinner, when they were sitting in the living room sipping coffee from Mark's new gold-rimmed Lenox china cups, that Senator Parks brought up what was on his mind. As was characteristic of the man, he did it in a roundabout way.

"You surely have a nice place here, Mark. And the val-ley—it's idyllic. So rural, so unspoiled. Great place to retire. But you're not ready for that, are you?" He didn't wait for an answer. "There can't be much scope for a man here, not a man like you. Your major financial interests aren't even here. Have you ever thought of making Boise your headquarters?"

Mark grinned. "There's enough challenge here right now to satisfy me. Breaking the political stranglehold of these ranchers may take a little time."

"What's to fill the vacuum once you succeed?"

Mark frowned. "I'm still a bit of an idealist, I guess, but I hope we'll see some real democracy around here. There's talent aplenty in the workers—brains, ambition. They just need a chance."

"And someone to lead them." Parks's brown eyes danced with amusement. "I figure that's where you come in."

"I've never thought much about politics," Mark said slowly. "Not for me, personally, that is."

"It's where the power is. And you'll need power to accomplish your goals." Parks's shrewd eyes looked straight into Mark's. "My organization—my friends—can help you get it, if you help us. You're young, you're intelligent, you've got drive and energy. That's a very attractive combination. And you have a good power base here. You could start small, run for state representative."

"What's in it for you?"

"We think you agree with us on what this country needs. Economic progress. Incentive for investment. This is a pretty hidebound state—cattle raising, sheep raising, hardly any industry at all. You've made a good start with your mill, but we have a chance to pull this place into the twentieth century. Sure, we'll make a lot of money, but so will everyone else."

Mark rose to his feet and lounged against the mantel. "It's something to think about. But I have to tell you, I'm not likely to get any votes around here. Not with my background."

"About the same as Abe Lincoln's, I'd say." Parks grinned. "Sure, you'll have the old-timers against you, but there's new people coming in all the time. I think you'd make it."

Mark was silent, considering the scenario. An invitation from Alton Parks to run for political office meant he'd have a machine behind him. In time he would be even more of a mover and shaker than he was now. His money already gave him power, but with political office he would have a real chance to make a difference. He could see that everyone had suitable housing, medical attention, job security. No one would ever have to live as he had lived.

"Think it over," Parks said genially. "Now, why don't you show Amanda around the place? I want a chance to get acquainted with young Justin here."

Realizing that he had been deftly maneuvered, Mark graciously complied. There were worse things—many worse things—than showing Amanda Parks around his home.

They ended up on the small enclosed balcony that opened out from the dining room. Amanda peered through the frosty glass at what in summer was the rose garden. Now snow lay in drifts under the amber light that shone from the window and the paler light of the icy moon. The thin barrier of glass couldn't keep out all the cold. Her bare arms shimmered in the moonlight, and Mark slipped off his jacket.

"Here," he said, draping it over her shoulders. "Just looking at that snow is enough to freeze you to death."

Somehow she managed to snuggle against him as she slid into the coat. He wasn't sure how she got there, but suddenly she was standing in the curve of his arm, leaning against his chest. A faint fragrance from her shining hair wafted up to him. She felt good. Soft, feminine. A purely physical response swept over him, followed by a wave of anger. It could have been—should have been—Jessica standing here beside him.

"It may look cold, but it's beautiful," Amanda whispered softly. She turned until she was gazing up into his face, her body pressed against his. "Don't you get lonely here by yourself, Mark? Don't you want . . . company?" Her lips were only a breath away.

He restrained a sharp retort. He was beginning to understand. Alton Parks's offer didn't come without strings. Both the senator and his daughter knew a rising star when they saw one. The strongest criticism Mark had heard about Parks was that he was an elitist, a member of the upper crust, out of touch with the common people. That perception could certainly be defused if he had a son-in-law like Mark, who was definitely one of the common people.

So they wanted to use him. Well, that was all right. He could use them, too.

"It's lonely sometimes," he admitted. He didn't add that he was used to loneliness, that for years he had preferred dreams of Jessica to any woman available to him. But, he reminded himself bitterly, that dream was over. What they had known together meant so little to her that she could throw it away, bind herself to a husband she didn't love because it was the safe, respectable thing to do. The Jessica he had known when he was young—the one who had thrown all caution to the winds for the sake of a few hours in his arms—was gone. And he might as well get used to the idea.

"It doesn't have to be lonely," Amanda said softly. She tilted her head—she was almost as tall as he was—and kissed him softly on the lips.

Something inside Mark went very still. Something died. Hope, perhaps. Youth. Certainly his dream of a lifetime with Jessica.

He wasn't young any longer, and he wanted a home, a family. Even his son was legally Clinton's. He would like children to fill his house with the laughter that had been sorely missing from his life. Amanda Parks was young, beautiful, intelligent—really quite desirable.

Best of all, he didn't love her.

He could, he supposed, go through the motions of courtship, but she had already made her feelings quite apparent. Weariness descended on him, a vast desolation that drained him of everything but a desire to get things settled. He put his arms around Amanda and pulled her close, then found her willing lips. Drawing back slightly, he looked into her emerald eyes.

"Will you marry me, Amanda?"

The minute he said the words he wished he could retract them. But it was too late, and he was too weary. He was on a bobsled ride of his own making, and he saw no way to get off until the bottom of the run.

"Oh, Mark." Her eyes glittered with excitement. "Certainly I'll marry you. Let's go tell Dad!"

She raised her silky arms and clasped them around his neck to give him a sizzling kiss. Then she grasped his arm and began propelling him back into the main part of the house. "Oh, darling, I've dreamed of this since I first saw you at the Hawkinses' party! Sometimes you just know immediately when something's right, don't you?"

She had no idea how much her words pained him.

Mark took a deep breath and let himself be pulled along. What did it matter? Amanda would make a perfectly adequate wife. He couldn't spend a lifetime mooning about Jessica.

Alton Parks broke off in the middle of something he was saying to Justin and surveyed the couple entering the room. One eyebrow went up as he saw his daughter's flushed face, noticed she was grasping Mark's hand. Then a broad smile broke over his countenance. No wonder, Mark thought, glancing at Amanda. She looked like someone who had just won at Wimbledon—flushed, tousled, but triumphant.

It didn't take long for her to relay the happy news. Mark stood silently by her side, only inclining his head briefly and accepting the older man's congratulations. Parks didn't seem particularly surprised, Mark thought.

But why should he be? He'd practically offered his daughter on a silver platter.

He glanced at Justin, and cold tendrils of apprehension wrapped around his heart. The boy looked nearly shell-shocked. Why hadn't he thought of that? This was no way for him to hear such news. Justin was just getting to know his father, to trust him, and he must feel as though he was being shoved aside. Even though Jessica and Clinton undoubtedly had done the best they could, life couldn't have been easy for a boy known to be illegimate. Classmates could be cruel—Mark knew just how cruel. Justin already showed his deep-seated resentments—toward Jessica, toward Clinton. Would this marriage bring further pain to the troubled boy?

And how would Jessica take the news her son would surely bring her? A sheen of sweat broke out on his forehead. Although he had impulsively wished to hurt her as she had hurt him, the thought of causing her additional anguish made him wince.

Justin didn't bring Jessica the news. She read of it a week later in the *Idaho Statesman.*

The announcement leaped out at her like an arrow from a bow. She felt as though someone had actually struck her a physical blow to the chest. She gripped the paper with frozen fingers and stared, her mind a blank.

Then she took in the picture of the bride-to-be. She was young, dark-haired, expensively dressed, and beautiful. Senator Alton Parks was pleased to announce the engagement of his daughter, Amanda, to businessman Mark Hardy. An accompanying article mentioned that Mr. Hardy was planning to run for the legislature, and that the couple would make their home in Boise, although Mr. Hardy planned to remain personally involved with his interests in Hope Valley.

Jessica let the paper flutter slowly to the floor. Her

head felt as though it were bursting, her body a shell with not a single sensation. Then the pain flooded in, and she doubled over, rocking in her chair, and a low moan came from her lips. How could Mark do this to her?

Finally she was able to lean down and retrieve the paper. She read the society-page article again, slowly, forcing herself to think rationally. Why shouldn't Mark marry? Had she expected him to spend his life mourning her? If so, she was completely selfish, as well as unrealistic. He was too vital, too passionate, too much a man to settle for an insubstantial dream.

He had given her every chance, and she had made it clear she would never leave Clinton. She couldn't. Oh, God, she really couldn't, although she longed to do just that. It was much better this way. Mark would be married, and he would be living miles away in Boise. She wouldn't have to worry about running into him, and she could settle back into her uneventful life. It would really be best for everyone.

So why did she feel as though her heart were being torn in two?

A shadow fell across the rug, and she glanced up to see her son standing in the doorway. For a second she forgot her own grief. Justin was so tall; he would be as tall as Mark one day, and right now his expression reminded her of the young Mark—bewildered, confused, and defiant.

"Hello, Justin," she said quietly. "I wasn't expecting you home so early."

He didn't reply, and she saw him gulp, as though uncertain what to say. He must have seen the paper, too. Her own reaction was pushed into the background as she realized this might have been a shock to him, too.

"Did you know that Mark is getting married?"

Anger flushed his adolescent face—masking a spasm of pain. "Yeah."

"I'm sure it won't make a bit of difference between the two of you. Come here, sweetheart."

Justin approached slowly, dragging every step. She rose from the chair and ran her hand over his hair, then kissed him on the cheek, steeling herself not to care whether he flinched away. "Boise isn't that far away."

"Who cares about Mark? I just came in to tell you I want to go to boarding school."

She looked at him in surprise. At first Justin had been ecstatic about the prospect of going away to school, but then he had changed his mind. He would be too far from his friends and, she dared hope, her and Clinton. Now his chin jutted out in a perfect imitation of his grandfather Jeb.

"I thought you didn't want to go," she said mildly. "You told me you liked the kids at your high school. And I thought you liked living at home and seeing Mark at his house."

"Nah. I want a change."

He stared at her, and she knew he was unwilling or unable to discuss what had changed his mind. It didn't take much figuring out, though. Justin was hurt and confused and wanted to be away from both the parents who had caused him so much pain.

Her heart heaved in her chest. Her relationship with Justin had actually improved since Mark had taken him under his wing. He spent lots of his free time with Mark, but he wasn't as resentful when he was at home.

Perhaps because of his early bonding with Jeb, Justin had never warmed up to Clinton. Yet since Mark had returned and shown such an interest in him, he was behaving almost like a normal adolescent—infuriating, volatile, but basically sound. Now he looked at her with near hatred, as though she were the cause of all his problems.

"Certainly you may go to boarding school if you wish," she replied. "Although your father and I will miss you very much." He said nothing. "What about holidays? Where will you go then? Here, or to Mark? You won't want to stay at the school during Christmas."

JOIN THE
TIMELESS ROMANCE READER SERVICE AND GET FOUR OF TODAY'S MOST EXCITING HISTORICAL ROMANCES FREE, WITHOUT OBLIGATION!

Imagine getting today's very best historical romances sent directly to your home – at a total savings of at least $2.00 a month. Now you can be among the first to be swept away by the latest from Candace Camp, Constance O'Banyon, Patricia Hagan, Parris Afton Bonds or Susan Wiggs. You get all that – and that's just the beginning.

PREVIEW AT HOME WITHOUT OBLIGATION AND SAVE.

Each month, you'll receive four new romances to preview without obligation for 10 days. You'll pay the low subscriber price of just $4.00 per title – a total savings of at least $2.00 a month!

Postage and handling is absolutely free and there is no minimum number of books you must buy. You may cancel your subscription at any time with no obligation.

GET YOUR FOUR FREE BOOKS TODAY ($20.49 VALUE)

FILL IN THE ORDER FORM BELOW NOW!

YES! *I want to join the Timeless Romance Reader Service. Please send me my 4 FREE HarperMonogram historical romances. Then each month send me 4 new historical romances to preview without obligation for 10 days. I'll pay the low subscription price of $4.00 for every book I choose to keep — a total savings of at least $2.00 each month — and home delivery is free! I understand that I may return any title within 10 days without obligation and I may cancel this subscription at any time without obligation. There is no minimum number of books to purchase.*

NAME_____

ADDRESS _____

CITY_____STATE____ZIP_____

TELEPHONE_____

SIGNATURE _____

(If under 18 parent or guardian must sign. Program, price, terms, and conditions subject to cancellation and change. Orders subject to acceptance by HarperMonogram.)

GET
4
FREE
BOOKS
(A $20.49 VALUE)

"I haven't decided yet," he said, turning away.

The pain she had felt on learning of Mark's marriage now dulled to a deep, pervasive ache. Was Justin to be completely lost to her, too?

"Do you mind being alone tonight?" Clinton turned toward her from the doorway, his lips pursed and his brow furrowed in a frown. "I'd ask you along, but it's just politics—pretty dull for a woman. We're trying to come up with someone to run against Mark Hardy in the election."

Jessica hid her flinch as she glanced up from her sewing. "I thought I'd mentioned that some of the wives would be coming over here to visit while you men take care of the problems of the world." She paused. "So, do you have any idea who can beat Mark?"

He shrugged, walked back into the room, and lowered his head to drop a kiss on her hair. "I doubt if anyone can. But we can't allow him to just waltz in unopposed."

"I suppose not." She lifted her face and accepted his gentle kiss. "Don't be too late, dear. The radio says a storm's coming in. The road may be treacherous."

When Clinton was gone, she continued with her embroidery, watching the bright colors become a delicate pattern. Her lips twisted in a derisive smile. Not exactly an activity of earthshaking proportions, but it filled the time. Time that seemed to hang heavier now that Mark's disruptive presence was gone. He was now married and running for lieutenant governor, which everyone seemed to think was just a step before he made a play for the top prize. She had hoped that with his absence she would be able to forget about him, but his name still seemed to be on everyone's lips.

Lydia Adams was the first to arrive. She hung up her coat, then settled herself heavily in a chair and took her mending out of a canvas bag still dusted with snow. They had hardly had a chance to exchange a word before Etta

Jensen came in, followed closely by Cam Beale. Soon the four women were grouped around a small table under a warm yellow light, briskly plying their needles and talking aimlessly.

It felt comfortable, Jessica thought, and safe, as they chatted and laughed, nibbled on cookies, and took occasional sips of steaming tea. For how many generations, she wondered, had women busied themselves like this, taking comfort in each other, doing their housewifely tasks, while the men were off somewhere deciding their lives?

Lydia broke into her thoughts. "Jake said the cattlemen are going to try to find somebody to run against Mark tonight. Do they have anybody in mind?"

Jessica lifted her head. "Didn't Jake go?"

Lydia squirmed a little, but her voice was firm. "No, he don't really belong there. He's not a cattleman, although he's worked for some. He likes his job at the mill. And he plans on voting for Mark."

Jessica's eyes widened in surprise. "He does? But he knows what Mark stands for. There will be tacky little houses all over this place. The way of life we know will be gone."

"Jake says scenery don't mean much if you don't have money," Lydia commented.

"What about Norval Blalock? Which side is he on?" Cam interjected.

Jessica grinned. "The side that gives him the most money. He spends it faster than he gets it. That ranch of his is going downhill fast. Old Sam must be turning over in his grave."

"Not to mention Carrie," Etta snickered. "But it's a shame, in a way. The Blalocks used to wield a lot of power, but not all of it was bad."

Jessica's thoughts flashed back to the time the Blalocks had tried to exercise their power over *her,* and she had a hard time agreeing with Etta's assessment. Yet she understood the woman's meaning. The cattlemen who had carved their empires from the land had once represented the best of an independent way of life that now seemed to be all but fading away. Their deep, patient partnership with the land was being replaced by the worship of the almighty dollar—and the quicker the buck, the better. She suspected that even Sam Blalock had loved every inch of his land, every boulder, every blade of grass. And that respectful relationship of man with his environment was not to be tossed away lightly.

She herself had come to love the Carter ranch and, by extension, the entire Hope Valley. Over the years the land had seeped into her very being—the ebb and flow of the seasons, the stark majesty of the mountains, the gentle swell of the pastures with the creeks cutting through them like blue ribbons. She felt a kinship with the wildlife, too—the elk and deer that occasionally competed with the cattle for forage, the coyotes that bayed mournfully at the moon on crisp winter nights. All these things had become as much a part of her as her own breath. She hated to see even a part of that world bulldozed under.

"Maybe we should get a little more involved in politics," she said slowly.

Etta's eyes opened wide. "I don't know about that. What would we do? Mr. Jensen knows all about things like that, and he always tells me who to vote for."

Lydia snorted. "Women's suffrage just gave your hubby one more vote, huh?"

"You never do what Jake tells you to do?" Etta retorted, stung by the criticism.

Now Lydia laughed, a huge laugh that shook her ample frame. "Not often."

Cam looked at Jessica. "Seriously, I don't know why we should get involved. The men are doing as much as they can. And I agree with what they're doing. Don't you?"

Jessica considered. It wasn't that she didn't agree with what they were doing; she didn't *know* what they were doing. Only what Clinton let drop in passing comments.

But perhaps the other women were right. She trusted Clinton's judgment, and she knew he would do everything he could to protect the land from being despoiled.

"I guess so," she said slowly. "Still, it's our children's future. . . ."

"Speaking of children," Lydia said, glad to get the conversation back on a topic that interested her, "how's Justin doing in that fancy school?"

Jessica winced. Not well, if the truth were known. He was, in fact, close to being expelled, but Mark had intervened, and the boy had promised to try to raise his grades.

"I guess he could be doing a little better," she admitted. "He doesn't seem to be academically inclined."

Etta chuckled. "That's one way of putting it. But don't worry about him. Every boy has to sow his wild oats."

"I wish Mark hadn't given him that car," Jessica said almost to herself. More than a year later it was still a sore spot with her. "He drives too fast, and I heard—there was a rumor—that he sometimes takes a drink. Not that I believe it, of course."

Lydia reached over and covered her hand with hers. "They're all a worry, aren't they? Sometimes I think about what Jim would have been like now, if he hadn't—hadn't given his life for his country. Young men are so impulsive."

The pain in the woman's voice was still raw, and the other women remained respectfully silent, concentrating on the needles going in and out of their sewing.

Jessica stabbed savagely at the linen place mat she was making, pricking her finger and drawing a faint trace of blood. Lydia had more to grieve for than she did, and yet she endured. But was that all they could hope for—endurance? There had to be something more they could do. Something more to life.

12

"You're so beautiful," Clinton murmured, holding Jessica's new full-length coat so that she could slip her arms into the silky lining. "I swear, you don't look a day older than when I married you."

Jessica smiled and leaned back against his chest, tilting her head so that it rested on his shoulder. His warmth was comforting in its familiarity.

"Thank you, dear. If anything can make a fortieth birthday bearable, it's hearing that."

"I mean it," he insisted. "You were beautiful then, of course, but just a girl. Now you're a woman—elegant, assured. I'll be the proudest man in the restaurant tonight—in the state, for that matter."

Twisting slightly, she gave him a quick kiss on the cheek. "We'd better get started."

She walked ahead of him down the steps that led from the veranda, holding her coat tight against the chill March wind that blew down from the snowfields on Packer Mountain. It was a two-hour drive to Boise, where Clinton had made reservations at the most expensive restaurant in town, insisting nothing less would do for her birthday. He'd planned an intimate celebration—dinner, dancing, then an overnight stay at the Hotel Boise. She was looking forward to it.

Settling back in the car seat, she studied Clinton's profile as he negotiated the curves of the narrow road. He was so familiar, so dear, that she rarely *saw* him, even when she looked at him. He had aged in the last year or two, she thought sadly. His light brown hair had turned snowy, and his skin had lost some of its tension. Well, time didn't stand still. Impelled by a feeling of deep fondness and vague regret, she reached across the space between them and put her hand over his.

By the time they arrived, the restaurant was crowded with well-dressed people. The buzz of conversation, the clink of silverware against china, the soft lights gave the room a festive atmosphere.

Jessica was aware of eyes following them as they were escorted to their table. She usually wasn't too interested in clothes, but now she was glad she had come to Boise the week before to shop. Her velvet gown was cut low in front to show just a hint of cleavage and flared from the hips in a soft swirl that ended at midcalf. The saleswoman at the Mode had assured her it was the latest style and that it went well with the high-heeled silver sandals she wore. Lydia had helped her with her hair; it was piled on top of her head in a heavy golden mass with a tendril or two coiling down. She knew she must look all right as she saw heads turn and a little murmur accompany their progress.

When they were seated, she took a minute to gaze around the room. She'd been here a few times before, and she loved the feeling of plush luxury that surrounded her—the tables topped with crisp white linen, the fine china and crystal flatware sparkling under the ornate chandelier that hung from the high ceiling. If you had to be forty, it was a good place to celebrate the occasion.

When the waiter, attentive and competent, had taken their order, she leaned across the table toward Clinton.

"This is a real treat. I love this old place. But those prices—haven't they gone up since the last time we came here? Are you sure we can afford it?"

Clinton chuckled. "The Depression is over, Jessica. Just relax and have fun. We can afford it. Sometimes I wish I could persuade you to spend a little more on yourself. You deserve it."

"I suppose for some of us the Depression will never be over," she said softly. "It seeped into our bones. Besides, I have everything I need."

"And everything you want?"

The question seemed somewhat pointed. There were times when she couldn't fight the dark moods that seemed to come from nowhere, times when she wondered about the choices she had made. She tried to keep those moods from Clinton, and she laughed now. "And everything I want, too. How could I complain? My goodness, the price of this meal would keep the Martinez family in food for a week."

His expression clouded slightly, and his lips tightened. "The Martinez family. You spend a lot of time with them. I'm not sure I completely approve of what your women's group is doing in that community. You're over there nearly every day, helping them fill out forms, taking them groceries, getting the kids outfitted for school."

Jessica shifted uneasily in her chair. She knew Clinton was concerned about her interest in the poorer people in the community. It wasn't that he was an ungenerous man—anything but. She suspected, though, that he somehow considered her too delicate for exposure to hardship. She wished she could convince him that he needn't worry. She would hate to give up the informal social work—it made her feel needed. After her impulsive suggestion to her women friends a couple of years ago that they somehow get involved in local politics, things had gradually snowballed. They were organized now—the Women's Club—and they found plenty to do. Helping the Mexican workers who moved in to help with the harvest was just one of their activities.

"Are you telling me to stop?" she asked quietly, her eyes meeting his across the table.

He sighed. "No, of course not. It's up to you how you spend your spare time."

They were silent a moment, neither wanting to pursue a subject rife with potential discord. Would she stop if he told her to? Jessica wondered. The club's projects gave her a sense of purpose that she had lacked for a long time. She was lucky he wasn't going to force the issue.

An excited buzz rippled through the diners, and Jessica shifted her gaze away from Clinton. Several couples, obviously a party, paused at the door, then paraded on through the entrance. All the flamboyant crowd needed was a band to announce them, Jessica thought wryly. Then she recognized two of them, and her heart started hammering in her chest, as she followed their progress into the room.

A tall, assured woman wearing a strapless silver dress that seemed held up by little more than a wish led the way. Amanda, Jessica said silently, feeling her cheeks burn. Striding behind her, not even bothering to glance at the whispering people who lined their way, came Mark, tall and lean and every bit as handsome as she remembered. Without making the slightest effort, he dominated the room. Her mind flashed back to that evening when he had invaded the school dance to purchase her box supper. He'd had the same commanding presence even then. Jessica didn't recognize the two couples who tagged along after them, but they looked vaguely familiar.

She glanced away quickly, not wanting to be caught staring. Besides, if they chanced to look her way, she was afraid her emotions would be too clearly stamped on her face. Clinton, she saw, was watching their progress, too, his thoughts unreadable.

Unwillingly but unable to help herself, she glanced again at the group. They were being seated at a table by a window, and there was much ado about holding out chairs, draping shawls. She was reminded of a group of monkeys chattering and jockeying for position. Mark stood apart from them all somehow, his expression closed, an invisible wall encircling his erect body.

Suddenly, as though aware of her scrutiny, he raised his head, and his dark eyes met hers. She felt the thrust of his glance right down to her toes. Her mouth felt dry, her throat tight. It was almost impossible to pull her gaze away; it was as though he were physically compelling her to remain locked to his dark eyes. He inclined his head slightly in acknowledgment, and she did the same.

Finally she managed to look back at Clinton. Had he been aware of that moment when she had been emotionally linked with Mark? If so, nothing in his expression indicated it.

It had been at least two years since she had seen Mark. He looked a little older, somehow weary. But maybe she was imagining that. After all, what did he have to be unhappy about? He was wildly wealthy, his wife was undeniably beautiful, and his political career was advancing like a tank. Everything he touched made money. He had even diversified in Hope. He not only owned the mill, but one housing development was completed and all the units sold.

Clinton's voice was barely audible above the babble around them. "I heard he bought the old Patterson farm the other day," he said to Jessica as he nodded his own greeting to Mark.

She'd heard it, too. The old folks had refused to sell, but they had died a few months ago, and the son had quickly sold out. Mark seemed to be buying up everything in sight.

"I'm surprised he hasn't offered to buy our ranch," Jessica offered.

Clinton smiled—a bit grimly, she thought. "Oh, he has."

"He has!" Her head jerked up, and she met her husband's eyes. "What did you say?"

"I said no, of course. You don't have to ask that, Jessica. I'd never sell a foot of the ranch."

"I'm glad. Very glad. I don't know what I'd do if we ever sold out. I love that place!"

"I know that." For a moment his eyes seemed to bore into hers with great solemnity. "I know the ranch will be safe with you." Before she could respond, he brushed aside the moment of gravity. "But enough of such serious talk on your birthday!" he said. "Let's leave Mark Hardy to his entourage and enjoy this delicious meal."

But despite his efforts the festiveness had gone from the occasion. Jessica managed to keep her eyes away from Mark, but there was no way she could blot out her awareness of his presence. Was he really as jaded and alone as he appeared? She hated what he was doing to the countryside in Hope Valley, but she could never stretch that hatred to include the man himself.

Clinton made a sound so light that Jessica almost missed it. She gave him a quick glance. As usual his expression was calm, but she thought his skin looked a little gray.

"Is something the matter?"

He smiled apologetically and shrugged. "No, not really. I just find I'm suddenly a little tired. Will you mind terribly if we don't go on to the club for the dance? I hate to disappoint you, but—"

"I don't mind at all," she replied. "But are you sure you're all right? Do you want to go right on up to the room?"

"It's so early to go to bed. If you don't mind driving, why don't we just head on home. There's no reason to stay overnight if we're not going to make an evening of it. But I will definitely give you a rain check on dancing till dawn."

"That's fine with me." They finished their coffee and left the restaurant, tacitly agreeing to forgo greeting Mark.

It would have been awkward with all those people there.

Soon they were driving along the narrow, twisting road that led to the ranch. Although she had looked forward to the evening, it was true that Jessica didn't mind leaving. Mark's arrival had certainly put a damper on the celebration. She only hoped that she was the one feeling the strain, not Clinton.

She had worried about his ashen appearance, but he had seemed to rally in the fresh air. He had been working hard enough to be tired, as he'd said, and when they arrived at the ranch house, he kissed her good night, once again promised her a future night on the town, and went immediately to bed.

She lingered awhile downstairs, not yet ready for sleep. She was standing at the desk in the living room, riffling through some mail she hadn't had time to look at before, when she sensed someone standing in the doorway. She turned quickly, then relaxed as she recognized her son.

"Justin, you startled me." She smiled a welcome. "What are you doing home? I thought you were at school. The term isn't over for another three months or so, isn't it? Is this some kind of holiday?"

Her tall, handsome son walked into the room. He'd changed a lot since he started private school. His hair was styled, not simply cut. His clothes, paid for by Mark over Clinton's protests, were expensive and well tailored. But the basic Justin—challenging yet achingly vulnerable— was still there. God, she loved him so, but he was such a problem.

This time, to her surprise, he hugged her lightly around the shoulders and gave her a quick kiss. He wants something, she thought, then hated herself for being so cynical.

"It's not a holiday—I've decided to quit that school," he said, moving away from her and slumping down in the chair beside the desk.

"Quit? But you'll graduate in three months!"

"Not likely." He glanced up quickly, then looked away. Furtively, she thought.

"Justin, has something happened?"

"Old Pryor got a hair up his nose," Justin replied, edging deeper into the chair. "You'll be hearing about it, I'm sure. He says if I can't abide by the rules, I can't stay there." He grinned an engaging grin to show her how ridiculous the whole thing was. "It's a dumb place, anyway. I thought I'd stay here with you."

"Oh, Justin, what will Mark say? Have you talked to him? He's so set on your getting the best preparation for college." She twisted her hands together and began pacing the room.

Justin watched her with cool eyes. "Why should he say anything? He didn't even finish high school. And look how well he's done for himself."

Frowning, she faced her son. "Justin, times were very different when Mark was your age. You have a choice. Well, perhaps two choices," she amended. "You can always go to Mark and ask to stay with him. But if you live here, you have to finish high school. You can finish out the term at the local school, I imagine, and get your diploma, but you must go."

Justin was silent, apparently thinking over the ultimatum. Then he jumped up from the chair and grinned at her. "Okay, Mom, school it is. Is my room fixed up? I'm ready to hit the sack."

"Justin, wait!" she called as he headed out the door. "What did you do to make them kick you out of school?"

Apparently he didn't hear, or if he did, he chose not to reply. Jessica sank down in the chair and rested her head in her hand. She supposed she'd hear the exact details from the school officials soon enough. It would doubtless be more of the same she'd heard before. Since Mark's marriage the boy had reverted to the old, uncontrollable Justin. He rarely visited his father, seemingly angry with Mark and uncomfortable around Amanda.

Damn Mark! She had always done the best she could for Justin. But it never seemed to be enough.

The next morning produced one of those soft, balmy March days that seemed to conspire to cloud one's judgment, Jessica thought, leaning against the corral railing and watching Amber nibble at the hay she had just thrown her. You know it isn't yet spring, but with the sun warm on your face, the smell of new green life pushing up through the cold earth, the gurgle of freshets coursing down the brown hillsides to become a roar when they reach the swollen creek, you tend to believe the frost and snow is really behind you.

Amber left her feed and came up to Jessica, sticking her nose through the corral bars and nuzzling her hand. The horse was glad the worst of the winter was over, too, Jessica thought. It must be hard on old bones. She had another horse that she rode now—Leader, a brown gelding with intelligence and spirit—but Amber would always be her first love.

"I thought I'd find you out here." Clinton's voice at her elbow was soft and amused. "You should have a coat on. This weather can change like lightning."

She turned quickly. "Clint! I didn't hear you coming. How are you feeling? Are you sure you should be out here?" He had been sleeping when she left their room, and she had slipped out quietly, hoping not to disturb him.

He laughed and propped his elbows on the railing. "You're worse than Karla. I couldn't get out the door without a breakfast that would stuff a horse. If I were sick, it would have killed me off." He put his hand on her shoulder. "I'm fine. I was just tired."

She scrutinized his face, then smiled. "You're looking fine. I suppose you know that Justin is home."

"So Karla told me." His mouth twisted in a wry grimace. "She also said he left early, off to visit some friends of his."

"Yes. He drove over to Hope." Jessica had hoped to have a long conversation with Justin about his future, but his early departure had squelched that.

Clinton glanced up at the clear blue sky in which a hawk wheeled lazily. "I've got the entire morning free. Why don't we go for a ride? Make up for cutting your birthday celebration short."

It seemed a marvelous idea. Soon the two were cantering out the pole gate toward an open meadow. Leader, living up to his name, was a few steps ahead of Dusty, Clinton's big roan.

Jessica closed her eyes and turned her face toward the sun, basking in the warmth, her body adjusting effortlessly to the smooth rhythm of Leader's stride. When they reached the meadow that bordered the creek, she nudged the horse, and he broke into a gallop. The breeze flattened her shirt against her chest and blew her long hair out behind her. Exhilarated by the speed, she urged Leader on, then, breathless and excited, drew up by a little waterfall and waited for Clinton to canter up beside her.

They rode all morning, never leaving Carter land, then finally turned their horses toward home. If there was anything that could make her forget her moments of vague depression, it was riding the ranch, Jessica decided. A horse warm and responsive beneath her, the burgeoning of spring all around. She loved each season, saw beauty in every changing aspect of the land, but spring filled her with such exuberance that she wanted to run and shout. It made every problem seem ephemeral.

They were about half a mile from the ranch house when she spotted a car parked in front of the veranda. Squinting against the sun, she recognized it, and her pulse quickened. There was only one automobile like it in the valley—the old beat-up black sedan of Doc Alberson. Folks liked to joke that the old man had a hard time making the adjustment from horse and buggy to automobile, so he kept as close to the buggy as he could.

But what was Doc Alberson doing here now? She spurred her horse into a gallop. Could something have happened to Justin?

They neared the veranda, and Clinton slid from his horse, reaching for Leader's reins. "I'll tie up the horses and join you—you go on in."

She ran lightly up the steps, thinking that her apprehension was probably ridiculous. Doc Alberson dropped in occasionally. There didn't have to be an emergency. But it was midday; he should be busy with his calls.

She opened the front door, and the doctor rose quickly from a chair.

"Hello, Jessica. Hope you don't mind my just barging in. Karla plunked me in a chair here to wait for you."

"Why, of course, it's fine. You know that." She strode quickly across the room and took his hand. "I'm always glad to see you."

"Clinton around?"

She frowned slightly. "He'll be here in a few minutes. Did you want to see him?"

Doc Alberson shifted uneasily. He was a short, bald man with unremarkable features, but his eyes were bright and alert. He was showing every one of his advanced years, Jessica thought. She remembered the doctor from her younger days; he had been middle-aged then. It seemed he had always been a part of her life. Although he hadn't been present at Justin's birth, he had arrived soon after, dispensing comfort and optimism as much as anything else.

What was it with her lately? Why was she becoming morbidly aware of everyone's mortality, including her own?

Doc Alberson was probably eighty, she decided, and still putting in a full day—and often a full night as well. There were other doctors in the valley now, doctors said to be more advanced, better educated, but there were few who could be counted on to drive miles on a winter night to look in on a sick child. He still had a flourishing practice. No wonder he looked tired.

He hesitated, then patted her gently on the shoulder. "No reason Clinton shouldn't be here, I guess. Still, it was you I wanted to see."

Puzzled, she motioned him back into his chair, then perched on a sofa across from him. "This isn't a social call, then?"

He shook his head. "Well, partly, partly not. I wanted to bring you the news myself. Thought you would want to know right away."

A hundred thoughts raced through her head, but she sat patiently. Another one of the doctor's well-known idiosyncrasies was his indirectness in coming to the point.

"I remember a long time ago," he said slowly, "you and Leah Hardy were friends."

Leah. The name sent a little shock through her. It had been such a long time since she had seen the woman who once had meant so much to her. She ran into her infrequently in Hope, but Leah refused all invitations to visit, and Jessica didn't feel comfortable visiting the cabin, where she might run into a disgruntled Jeb—or even Mark.

"Yes, friends," she said quietly. It would take more than absence to change the way she felt about Leah. "Is something the matter? Is she sick?"

He sighed heavily, and his old shoulders sagged. "Leah is dead. I thought you should know—that you'd want to hear it from me before the grapevine gets it."

"Dead?" A heaviness settled on her, a numbness that made it impossible to move. Even her voice felt heavy. "Leah is dead?"

"Yes. I just came from there," Doc Alberson said, holding both knees with blue-veined hands.

Jessica rose very slowly and walked to the window,

where she gazed unseeingly at the beautiful spring day. When she could speak, she said softly, "How did it happen?"

"My death certificate will say influenza, going into pneumonia. The real cause? Overwork, too many children, neglect—you name it."

"There will be a funeral, of course."

"Yes. I'm sending the hearse out for her. Jeb will come in with it to make the arrangements."

"Jeb." Her voice held bitterness. "I'm almost surprised he'd go to the trouble."

The doctor shot her a quick glance, then shook his head. "Don't jump to conclusions, Jessica. People are strange critters—I've learned that, if nothing else, in my life. When I left, Jeb was holding her in his arms, and he was crying."

"He should be," she gritted.

"Yes. Well, I know how you feel. You didn't have much of a time there. And there's a lot to be said against Jeb. Still, I think he loved her."

She turned from the window. "Thank you for coming to tell me."

"Well, I thought I should." He looked down at his hands. "She wanted you to know something," he said reluctantly. At her raised eyebrows he continued. "She was nearly gone when I got there. But she rallied a couple of times. Near the last she mentioned your name. Yours and Mark's." Now he was definitely not meeting her eyes. "She said to tell you both she loved you."

The silence lengthened. Jessica glanced down at her hands, surprised to see them clenched into fists.

"Mark wanted her to go and live with him," she said slowly. "She wouldn't."

"No. She said her place was with Jeb." He shook his head, then got slowly to his feet. "Well, I'd best be going. Say hello to Clinton for me."

She walked to the door with the doctor, then returned

to the living room and sank slowly into a chair before her legs gave way. Despite their long separation she loved Leah, and hearing of her death made her feel as though the breath had been punched out of her.

Again she was back in that little clearing, poverty-stricken and desperate. Leah was always there, serene, optimistic, making her almost believe that everything would turn out well in the end. At times she had thought the older woman weak, spineless, passive, but now she wondered if her strength hadn't surpassed that of anyone she knew. She had lived life as it was dealt her, smiling, uncomplaining.

And that life had been anything but easy. The rest of the country had climbed out of the Depression, even if it had taken a war to do it, but the Hardys' life hadn't changed. Mark had tried to build them a new house, and when Jeb refused, his son had proposed a new kitchen, indoor plumbing. Jeb's response had been quoted with amusement throughout the valley. "Ain't nobody going to crap inside *my* house!"

But it was more than just Leah that Jessica grieved for—it was for herself as well. With Leah's death an era had ended, forcibly reminding Jessica that she herself was no longer a young woman for whom in time all things were possible. Now Leah had dropped into the abyss and no one stood between Jessica and the cliff's edge.

13

Jessica sat gingerly in a wing chair in the living room of the old Townsend mansion and looked across at Mark. He was slouched on the sofa in an attitude of dejection, his lips tight, his deep brown eyes rimmed with red. She knew hers were, too.

Although well attended, Leah's funeral had been simple, costing no more than Jeb could pay for, and Mark had had to content himself with ordering the huge spray of roses that covered his mother's casket. At the graveside service he and his father had barely spoken to each other. Jeb had not returned with the others to Mark's home, nor had Mark made any move to go with him. Obviously the bitterness between the two men still ran deep.

Now the other mourners had gone, leaving plenty of food and condolences, and since Mark had asked her to stay, the two of them were alone in the big house.

"Thank you for staying, Jessica," Mark said heavily, leaning his head back against the emerald velvet upholstery of the couch and closing his eyes. "I needed someone to talk to—someone who loved her as much I did."

She quelled an impulse to reach out and smooth the

lines from his forehead. Instead she twisted in her seat and looked down at her hands, a little self-conscious at being alone with him. "Clinton wanted to come, but he hasn't been feeling too well for the past few days. A touch of the flu, I guess." She raised her eyes to his face, and a rush of sympathy engulfed her as she saw the sadness in his expression. "I thought Amanda would be here."

He grimaced and turned his face toward the fire. The flames threw red slashes across his craggy face and deepened the harsh shadows under his jutting cheekbones. "That was a going-away party for her at the restaurant the other night. She's on her way to Greece with some friends. There's no way to contact her until she gets there."

"I'm sorry."

"Don't be. She would have come to the funeral, but only because it would look strange not to. She and Mom never quite hit it off." A cynical smile curved his lips, indicating, Jessica supposed, that his remark was an understatement of the relationship that had really existed between his wife and his mother.

Suddenly his eyes met hers with such directness that she felt his glance like a physical touch. "Mom always thought it should be you and me."

She swallowed painfully. If only it could have been. But life hadn't worked out that way. "I hadn't seen Leah for a long time. I feel terrible about it—I had no idea she was in such poor health."

A muscle twitched in his cheek as he clenched his jaw. "She was always frail. It was her spirit that was strong. Without her encouragement, her support, I never could have gotten away from home, could never have become what I am today."

His lips twitched in a rueful smile. "Whatever that is. Sometimes I wonder just what I *have* become. It seems so long ago now, the days when I thought everything would be all right if only I could accumulate some money, some power. That I could have what I wanted. That I could change things."

His gaze swept over her face, lingering on her lips, and she winced at the pain in his eyes. "That's why I asked you to stay a few minutes," he continued. "Now that Mom's gone, you're my only link with the past. I didn't want to be alone just now, and you're the only one who really knows about the old days. About what she was like then."

"I'm glad you . . . think of me as a friend."

"Well, you're that, too," he said, almost smiling for the first time that afternoon. He rose abruptly and stalked to the fireplace, leaning one elbow against the mantel as he gazed down at her. Though the grief in his eyes made him appear slightly haggard, worn, he looked distinguished, urbane, in his soft gray suit, his polished black shoes, his subdued silk tie. His hair, once so unruly, was now brushed firmly back from his high forehead, and it was showing wings of gray. His skin was deeply tanned, and he still exuded a restless energy, a sense of purposefulness, that was nearly palpable. His essence—vital, masculine— permeated the room.

Awareness of him as a man rushed through her, and her cheeks colored. In spite of all the changes in both of them, Mark was still Mark, and he still affected her.

"How are things with you, Jessica?" he asked, his voice suddenly wistful.

"About the same. The ranching life never changes much."

"Are you happy?"

"I'm . . . busy." She glanced away from his intense gaze. "Besides caring for Clinton and Justin, I do some volunteer work."

He raised a dark eyebrow. "I've heard a few things about your ladies' group. Sounds like you could cause businessmen like me a lot of trouble."

She smiled. "Not too much, I imagine. Clinton isn't sure he approves, either, but I need something to do."

"Yes." He nodded agreement. "You're too intelligent to be stuck as a ranch wife forever. I always wondered how you stood it. But I suppose Justin takes up some of the slack."

"You knew Justin quit school, I suppose."

"Oh yes." With an exasperated sigh he moved away from the fireplace and paced a few steps on the plush carpet, running a hand through his hair. "The dean called. They just can't handle the boy. He was disrupting everyone else, they say. I guess I blame myself. I knew he was upset by my marriage, and perhaps I should have tried harder to establish some kind of communication. But he didn't get along with Amanda, and he didn't want to live in Boise."

"I'm sure you've done the best you could. We all have."

"Well, I'm thinking of a change, now that Mom's gone," Mark replied. "Something like that makes you zero in on the basics. I left here, among other reasons"—his eyes shot fire in her direction—"because Amanda didn't want to live in Hope. But she's home so seldom, what with her yachting friends in Greece and her skiing friends in Switzerland, that it really doesn't matter where I live. I'll keep the place in Boise, but I'm coming back to Hope."

Her heart went still inside her chest as she realized the implications of his announcement. She would be bound to run into him again, be ever more solidly under his spell. Her mouth felt dry, her lips numb, but she forced herself to echo his words. "Back to Hope?"

"I need to be closer to Justin," he said. She wondered if he was aware that he was clenching and unclenching his hands. "It's late, I know, but I want to try to be a real father to him. If I live here, where I can be available when he needs me, perhaps we can still salvage something."

He met her eyes. She couldn't look away. What about her and Mark? Was there anything to be salvaged? She should get up this very minute and run for the door. Her feelings were too turbulent for casual friendship. His were, too. They both knew it.

Then it was too late. Perhaps it always had been too late. In one huge stride he was beside her, dropping to his knees beside her chair. With a moan he buried his head in her lap, and his arms went around her, pulling her against him. She barely heard his muffled words. "My God—Jessica, Jessica!" It was a prayer, a desperate litany.

Of its own accord her hand stole out to stroke his hair. It felt springy under her touch, and she dug her fingers in deeper. As her caress traveled down his neck, traced the rough texture of his jaw, she shivered at the feel of his skin beneath her fingers—warm, alive, sensual.

A shiver convulsed his body, and then he sprang to his feet, scooping her up in his arms.

"Mark!"

"I want you in my bed," he said grimly. "You belong there. Do you realize we've never been together in a bed?"

As he strode through the living room and carried her up the broad staircase, she nestled against his shoulder, all ambivalence swept away by the force of their mutual need. It was wrong. Everyone would say so. They were both married, and they were about to commit a sin. But which was the greater sin? Mark was her first love, and she had never given him up in her heart.

Debating was useless now. She was on fire, and the world had shrunk once more to just her and Mark and their endless, relentless, unquenchable love. He kicked open a door and placed her reverently on the bed. If fate exacted a price for this, she would pay it. But for now he was all she wanted in the world.

His lovemaking was fierce, demanding, interspersed with moments so tender that tears welled in her eyes. She responded with all the force of her being. Only when both were exhausted did they lay side by side, moist skin touching moist skin, breathing heavily as they slowly returned to earth.

The firestorm had subsided, and she was able to speak,

though shakily. "Oh, Mark, I love you so. What are we going to do?"

"I love you, too. I always have." He raised himself on one elbow and kissed her mouth, then drew back a few inches so that he could see her face. "We're going to get married. Be together. This time I won't take no for an answer."

If only it were that simple. "We can't," she said softly. "You're married—I'm married."

"We'll both soon be divorced," he said firmly. "Jessica, you can't continue with this misplaced loyalty. Don't you think Clinton deserves a wife who loves him? I know Amanda will find a better husband. Things have gone from bad to worse with us, and it's mostly my fault. I didn't love her; I never should have married her."

"Why did you?"

"Rebound, I guess. I'm ashamed to admit it, but I think my main motive was to hurt you. Then I hoped she would help me forget you. But when I saw you in the restaurant, I knew I was kidding myself. Did you ever think of me?"

"All the time," she said, tracing his lips with the tip of her index finger. "We've made a terrible mess of things, haven't we?"

"It's a mess that can be fixed," he said firmly. "You have to agree, darling. What good is this? You miserable, me miserable, and certainly Clinton and Amanda can't be too happy."

"I don't know. . . ." But how wonderful if she could convince herself that that was true. "I just don't want to hurt anyone."

He pulled her against his chest and kissed her on the lips, a kiss that demanded and promised everything. "You can't still say that—not after what we just did! This kind of love doesn't happen often, Jessica. Not many people ever experience our kind of bond. We belong to each other, and you're going to have to admit it. The true crime is in denying our destiny."

She put her hand on his chest, ruffling the moist hair. She felt his heart pounding strongly and rhythmically; it filled her with confidence and determination. "I'll talk to Clinton."

Under her hand his heart seemed to stop, then thudded more furiously than ever. "When?"

"Tonight."

It was dusk when she pulled up into her yard and parked in the driveway. Clinton would wonder why she had been so long. Could she possibly jump directly into the subject? *Sorry I'm late. By the way, I'm planning to leave you.* It would be such a shock to him. Was there some way to prepare him, to soften the blow?

Would it really be such a shock? she wondered. How much did he already know? They had lived together for years, the two of them, always skirting around her feelings for Mark. If you didn't mention it, it didn't exist. But Clinton was an intelligent, sensitive man. How much had she hurt him already?

She tried to think of something—anything—he had done or not done, anything that would justify the blow she was about to give him. But there was nothing, of course. If there had been, doubtless she would have seized on it long ago. No, she would be hurting him in a way he of all men didn't deserve, and she would have to bear the full weight of the guilt.

She squinted thoughtfully at the house as she eased her car into the garage. Lights blazed from every window. That was unusual. Had Justin brought some friends home?

She reached for the door just as it swung open in front of her. Karla, her plump face blotchy and her eyes red, threw herself into her arms.

"Jessica! Where have you been?" the woman sobbed.

She staggered back under the larger woman's assault,

then put her hands on her shoulders to look into her eyes, apprehension sharpening her voice. "Karla, what's wrong?"

The woman was nearly hysterical and couldn't seem to answer. Frowning, Jessica gently moved out of her clutches and glanced up the stairs just as Doc Alberson began a slow descent.

Her heart seemed to freeze in her chest. The old man's face was pale, and he moved slowly and carefully as though he were exhausted, as though he had fought a great battle—and lost. A dark premonition swept through her.

She hurried forward, meeting him at the bottom of the stairs. He raised his head and saw her, then rubbed his hand over his eyes. "I'm very sorry, Jessica. There was nothing I could do."

"Not—not Clinton!" she gasped.

He nodded. "He went quickly. By the time Karla called me, it was already too late." He saw her face and added hastily, "There was nothing you could have done, Jessica, even if you had been here. It was his heart."

"His heart! I didn't know—"

"He didn't want you to worry."

She pushed past him and rushed up the stairs. Moving with uncharacteristic speed, Doc Alberson caught up with her at the door to the bedroom. He took her hands and held them at her side, then moved her head against his chest. She held herself rigidly; then slowly the tears began.

"It's all right," the old man said. "Go ahead and cry. We'll go in and see him in a minute, but just cry now. Cry. He was a good man, an excellent man," the doctor crooned.

Yes, he was. A man far better than she deserved. And while this fine man, her husband, had lain dying she had been making love to Mark.

Any dreams she had had of being with Mark were dead

now, as dead as Clinton Carter. This guilt she could never overcome.

"Do you feel up to going in now?"

She nodded, and Doc Alberson opened the door. She crept toward the bed, not sure what she expected to see. But Clinton lay there looking peaceful, his dear face calm and gentle. Had it always been a mask for his real emotions? Had she ever really known this man who had taken her and her son into his home and into his heart? She prayed that at least he was finally at peace.

"Did he . . . say anything?" she asked the doctor, her heart breaking at the thought that he might have suffered.

Karla had come up behind them, and she said simply, "He called your name."

Jessica motioned the man ahead of her into the study, then closed the door behind them. It was less than a week after Clinton's funeral, but there were business matters that could not be ignored. Phillip Angle, Clinton's attorney, was a tall, spare man with a deceptively casual appearance. He was wearing rumpled pants, a tweed jacket, and a slightly wrinkled tie. Jessica suspected that his unkempt appearance was carefully cultivated; juries in the county distrusted lawyers who appeared too fashionable. She wasn't misled by his folksy demeanor, either. His reputation was that of a man with a keen intellect and uncompromising integrity.

"Thanks for coming all the way out here. I could have come to your office," she said, seating herself behind the desk where Clinton had so often sat to work on the ranch accounts. She motioned to a comfortable chair across from her. "I know how busy you are."

"No trouble," he said, sitting down and propping his briefcase on his knees. "Let me tell you how sorry I am about your husband, Mrs. Carter. Clinton was a friend as well as a client."

"Thank you." In the days since Clinton's death she was

learning more and more about her husband, and though sad, it was also oddly gratifying, making her feel closer to him than his modest reserve had sometimes allowed. In his quiet, unostentatious way, her husband had been known in a far wider circle than she had imagined. She'd had calls of condolence from the statehouse and various ranching organizations, as well as a steady stream of neighbors and friends. She and Clinton had lived quietly, unpretentiously, but she was learning that her husband had been a power in the community.

"I don't know how much you know about Clinton's business affairs," Angle said, snapping open his briefcase and pulling out a sheaf of papers. "In many ways he was of the old school—he believed in shielding his wife from financial matters. I told him he was perhaps overprotective, since you would someday have to cope with the business."

"Is the ranch in trouble?" She leaned forward, her eyes searching his. "Clinton never talked about it—I guess he didn't trust my business sense—but sometimes I thought he seemed a little worried."

"Nothing like that." The attorney smiled. "As for trusting you—he trusted you implicitly. We discussed that at length when he made his will."

She was silent as Angle laid the papers out in front of her on the desk.

"The details are all here, but I can sum it up for you quickly. You are the sole heir of his estate. He left everything to you rather than dividing it between you and Justin because he knew you would cherish the ranch and pass it on to Justin intact in your own time. The Carter ranch is now yours, and it's completely unencumbered."

He gave her a satisfied glance. "Mrs. Carter, you are now the richest woman in the county. Actually, maybe one of the richest in the state."

Her eyes widened, and she stared back at him, not quite taking in what she had heard. The richest woman in the county?

"You really didn't know, did you?" he said, faintly bemused. They had always lived so simply; Clinton had never denied her anything, but she had always debated before she made a major purchase—could they afford it? This was hard to grasp.

"You mean I own the Carter ranch, free and clear?"

"As well as several others, including the Blalock ranch," he said dryly.

"The Blalock ranch! But that belongs to Norval!"

"Not since he came to your husband to borrow money on it to keep up his rather expensive life-style. At first Clinton only had a mortgage, but Norval couldn't keep up the payments. Then he sold it outright to your husband, on the condition that he be allowed to live there when he wasn't in Denver. That ranch has been in your husband's control for several years."

That hardly seemed possible. Wouldn't she have known? Then she remembered the day Norval had come to see Clinton, and the secrecy of their discussion in the study while she and Alice waited in the living room. She caught her lip between her teeth. All these revelations about Clinton stunned her. How many facets of himself he had concealed!

She continued to stare at the attorney. "He never discussed business with me," she said slowly, "never let me participate in the management. I know very little about it."

"I told him that was a mistake," Angle said firmly. "He insisted he didn't want to worry you—that you'd had enough worries to contend with in your life. He said that if the time ever came when you'd have to take charge, you could do it." He lifted an eyebrow, obviously in disagreement with Clinton's assessment. "But of course you'll want a manager. You can certainly afford one, and I know some very good people."

She stood up and gave him a level glance. "No. That won't be necessary."

"But you've no experience in—"

"You can start me off, tell me what I have to do first. I'll make an appointment with the bankers tomorrow. It may take me some time to sort things out, to understand just what's involved, but I intend to manage the ranch myself."

"But there are other enterprises as well—"

"Those too."

He opened his mouth to protest, then closed it as he met her determined gaze. "Very well. I'll leave these papers with you, and—"

"I'll call you as soon as I've looked them over. Thank you for coming." She hesitated. "Mr. Angle, you say you were Clinton's friend. I hope you'll be mine." She held out her hand.

He looked at her thoughtfully, then smiled and shook the proffered hand. "Of course. I'll do everything I can."

She waited until she heard his car start, then she sat back down behind Clinton's battered old desk. It was hard to assimilate everything she had just heard. It would be harder still to shoulder the responsibility for Clinton's beloved ranch. In this way, though, she vowed to honor his memory and prove herself worthy of his generous trust in her. She would do whatever it took, and she would do it right.

She lowered her head into her hands. But, oh Lord, why hadn't he given her at least a hint or two along the way? It wasn't distrust. If he hadn't trusted her, he wouldn't have left everything in her hands. She guessed it was just his old-fashioned need to protect her. When he first asked her to marry him that day in the woods so many years ago, he promised to take care of her. He'd certainly done that—and more.

But now she had to take care of herself. Herself and her son. She raised her head and glanced at the papers in front of her, symbols of a new life. In spite of her grief, which was very real, she felt almost exhilarated.

Looking back, she realized that she had never truly been free or independent. Her parents had protected and controlled her while they lived. After they died, her new community had told her how a schoolteacher should live. Her love for Mark had been a brief fling at independence, but she'd soon been a prisoner of her pregnancy and of poverty, of Jeb's rigid ideas about women. Then she'd become Clinton's girl wife, indulged but never independent. Of course, she had contributed to her dependence; with Clinton it had been safe and comfortable.

But now, for the first time in her life, she could chart her own course. A woman of property, an important woman, with the means to change things she didn't like. The thought was almost heady.

A spasm of aching regret tightened her lips. How much sadness had led to this independence. All the affluence in the world couldn't make up for the loss of a fine, decent man. And that Mark was lost, too. She couldn't start a new life on the basis of guilt and betrayal.

She had seen him only briefly the afternoon of Clinton's funeral. And remembering that she had been lying in his arms while Clinton was calling out for her, dying, she had told Mark that it was best that they didn't see each other again.

He hadn't taken the decision well, she thought, rising from the desk and gazing, unseeing, out the window. Bitterness seemed to be an integral part of his personality now. He'd had some pretty harsh things to say to her. But she would not be moved from her resolve.

She was really alone now. She leaned her head briefly against the windowpane, then lifted her chin and returned to the desk. Independent, alone—maybe they were always one and the same.

If one good thing could be said to have come from all of this, it was that Justin finally seemed to be straightening out his life. When he learned that Amanda would not be coming to Hope to live with Mark, he had accepted Mark's invitation to move into the old mansion for a while at least, and he seemed to be quite content with returning to the local high school. She missed him, but she was glad he was happy.

For a moment she thought again about the past. The Blalocks, rigid and righteous and domineering. The austerity of life with Jeb and Leah Hardy. Clinton, kind and gentle and—controlling. She had floated with the current, she thought, for nearly half her life. It was time she learned to swim.

She sighed, then straightened her shoulders and shrugged off everything except what was right in front of her. She didn't delude herself: learning to manage an operation as large as the Carter estate wouldn't be easy or mastered in a few days. But despite her apprehension she anticipated the challenge.

As for Mark, she would have to accept that their lives would not converge again. Their love was part of the past she must leave behind. She would have to see him occasionally, to talk about Justin, but that was all; they would never be intimate again. The thought of Clinton's agonized face would always come between them.

AUTUMN

14

Jessica, on her way out the door, caught sight of herself in the hall mirror and hesitated. She knew she'd changed in the last few months, but it was almost a shock to see how much. Her hair, always pale, was now bleached nearly white by the sun, and her skin was deeply tanned, making her deep blue eyes appear almost indigo. Clinton had always insisted she wear a hat out of doors to protect her delicate complexion, but she'd long since given up the practice, finding she loved the caress of the summer sun on her bare skin and the feel of the wind whipping through her hair, which she now wore shoulder length and loose. She looked fit, she decided, looking critically at her reflection. Fit and neat. But that was about all that could be said for her.

She had changed her style of attire, too, eschewing the soft, feminine fabrics of the dresses and trousers she had worn before. Now she slipped jeans on over her long legs and usually wore a lightweight chambray shirt.

Lydia had laughed and told her that for a newly wealthy woman, she was going in the wrong direction. Jessica had retorted lightly that she didn't have to dress to impress anyone or redo the house or buy a new car. She loved the house the way it was, and her present automobile was quite serviceable. Besides, she was much too busy learning the ranching business to give much thought to trivial luxuries. Since Clinton's death her days had been filled with endless meetings—bankers, accountants, attorneys—and when she could break away from all that, she had the day-to-day operation of the ranch to supervise.

Frowning, she spun away from the mirror and continued on out the door. That was turning out to be more difficult than she had expected. The foreman, Ken Hoskins, had been with Clinton for years, and she was finding out he didn't like change—especially change instigated by a woman.

She stepped into the yard and glanced around. Later in the day the midsummer sun would turn the grounds and pastures into an oven, but now the air was still fresh and cool and carried the delicate scent of ripening fruit from the orchard behind the house. The birds—blackbirds, wrens, finches—were darting through the branches of the old elm trees, raising their voices in a cacophony of song, although they, too, would be quiescent in the heat of the afternoon.

She narrowed her eyes, glancing toward the corrals, where a couple hundred steers munched on hay and occasionally let out low, indignant bellows. Where were the cattle trucks she had asked Ken to order for this morning? They should have been here by now.

She walked on and found the foreman lounging on the corral rail, gazing at the sea of cattle. Ken Hoskins was a short, grizzled man in his sixties, with sparse brown hair bleached gold by the sun. His wind-weathered skin was the color of deep coffee; his bowlegged stance gave evidence of long years on a horse.

At her approach he shot a stream of tobacco juice from his mouth, turned, doffed his wide-brimmed western hat, and gave her a tight smile. "Morning, Miz Carter."

"Good morning, Ken." She would always be Mrs. Carter to him, she supposed, although the foreman had used Clinton's first name. It was not so much politeness, she suspected, as a means of distancing himself from her. "Aren't the cattle trucks here yet? I hoped we could get the main bunch into the sale yard by early afternoon."

"Well, no, they ain't here."

"Why not? I told you to call them a couple of days ago. That should have given them plenty of time."

He shifted his weight from one high-heeled boot to the other. "This really ain't the best time to sell, Miz Carter. Clinton wouldn't have sent this bunch in until fall."

"I know that," she said crisply. "Ordinarily that would be the best thing to do. But our grass is way down this year, and I want to get rid of a few steers now before they lose any weight and before we have to start feeding—" She broke off. Ken knew all that. They'd had this very conversation a few days ago. She gave him a sharp look. "You *did* order the trucks, didn't you?"

He glanced down at the ground, then back at Jessica, insolence in every line of his lean body. "I know you're trying, ma'am, but you need help. A little advice. A woman can't run a ranch like this, not by herself. Clint would've bought a little hay and—"

"You didn't order the trucks." Anger laced her voice, and she stiffened, glaring at the stubborn features of the man in front of her. This wasn't the first time Ken Hoskins had questioned her judgment, but it was his most direct defiance. She'd been challenged in many ways and by many people since she took over the operation of the ranch, but Hoskins was the most recalcitrant. In his mind a woman belonged in the kitchen or the bedroom—she certainly didn't belong near the corrals, giving orders to men.

"No, I didn't order them," he admitted. "I knew when you thought about it, you'd see I was right." He smiled, a conciliatory smile that invited her to relax and let someone who knew what he was doing make the decisions.

Out of the corner of her eye she saw that they were no longer alone. Several of the other ranch hands, sensing excitement and a break in routine, were drifting up, ostensibly busy but well within earshot. She nearly wavered. Maybe Hoskins *was* right. He certainly had more experience than she did. But prices were high just now—if they could get their cattle in first, they'd make a good profit.

But that wasn't the issue. She set her jaw and gave Hoskins an icy stare, ignoring the little tremor that ran down her spine. It didn't matter who was right and who was wrong in this particular instance. Of course she would make mistakes; she was still learning. Her biggest mistake, though, the one she wouldn't be able to recover from, would be to let Hoskins win this test of wills.

She made a swift decision. Even if she forced him to call the trucks, it wouldn't be the end of it; he would continue his harassment on every issue that came up. The truth was that Hoskins would never acknowledge her as his boss. She took a deep breath.

"Ken, you're fired."

His mouth dropped open, showing teeth stained with tobacco. His face paled under his deep tan. For a moment he didn't move. Then he glanced around at the circle of men who had moved in closer. There was curiosity, interest, on every face, but no indication of active support. Sweat broke out on his forehead as he again faced Jessica.

"You can't fire me, ma'am." His eyes challenged her. "I've worked here for years. Clinton would never have let me go!"

"Clinton isn't running the ranch now. I am. You can't seem to accept that. You have defied every one of my orders." She faced him squarely, legs apart, hands on her hips. "I'll see that you have a good pension, enough to live on. You can still live in the foreman's cottage, if you like. But you're not working for me anymore."

Rage and incredulity struggled for prominence in Hoskins's expression as he took in her determined stance. Then his pale eyes searched the group of men. When none of them would meet his gaze, he swung back to Jessica.

"You won't last a year!"

"Maybe. Maybe not. But you won't last the day. I'll have your check ready in a few minutes." She turned to one of the men who was leaning on the corral railing, a grin on his face. He was one of the last men hired, younger than many of the others and, with luck, less antagonistic toward working for a woman.

"Dell, order the trucks."

"Yes, ma'am!" He shot Hoskins an amused glance, then strode quickly away toward the bunkhouse.

Jessica wheeled around, ignoring the muttered oath that followed her. She hated to fire Hoskins—it was the first time she had terminated anyone's services—but he had been a thorn in her side, a constant irritant, and it had to be done if she were ever to establish her authority.

She was at her desk in the study, writing out Hoskins's final paycheck, when she heard the hum of an engine and then the sound of wheels cutting into the gravel of the driveway. She raised her head, then heard Karla's heavy footsteps moving toward the door. She returned her attention to the task at hand. It seemed she was always getting uninvited visitors now—strangers or slight acquaintances eager to sell her something or enlist her help in some worthy cause. She could wait to see who this one was.

"She's in the study? I'll just go on in, Karla."

She recognized the suave, familiar voice, completely without an Idaho accent, and glanced toward the open door of the study. It was early for Norval to be up and around. It was the talk of the county that on his infrequent trips from Denver to the old Blalock place, he usually slept half the day and wasn't seen about much before nightfall. She wondered what he wanted. Could he be worried about his future? She had no plans to alter the arrangement he had made with Clinton.

"Jessica, hello." He posed in the doorway, as elegant, as poised, as ever, and Jessica gave him a warm smile. Over the years her attitude toward Norval had softened from disapproval and wary hostility to acceptance. Whatever else Norval was, he was witty and clever, and while not, perhaps, exactly a friend, he was something more than an acquaintance. Was she getting sentimental in her old age? she wondered ruefully. She rose from behind the desk and moved forward to give him her hand.

He pressed it, then made a big production of looking her over. "That's an interesting new style, Jessica. Jeans, man-tailored shirt. And no makeup?" He grinned, his familiar, mocking grin. "If you keep it up, I may be interested in you myself."

"I doubt I'll ever be *that* masculine," she retorted.

He shook his head sadly. "No, probably not. Too bad. In some ways you and I are alike, Jessica."

She smiled. "I can't think of many."

"Of course you can. We're both different, you and I. We don't fit the mold. They don't know what to make of us. How many women do you think could take over a ranch and run it the way you have?"

"Perhaps any who got the chance," she said dryly.

"Don't you believe it. You're a natural leader. That women's group of yours is giving old Mark fits. Every time he tries to uproot a tree for one of his crackerbox houses, somebody's there chaining herself to the trunk!"

"That's a bit of an exaggeration." She sat back down behind her desk, unable to repress a grin. It was true her group had become quite active, and more and more people were beginning to take them seriously.

"Not much of an exaggeration." He eased himself into a chair across from her, carefully crossing his long legs so that his knife-sharp trousers crease was preserved, and grinned. "They're saying you're communists, you know, a bunch of troublemakers standing in the way of capitalistic progress."

She threw back her head and laughed. "Well, that's certainly one thing I'm not. But what brings you here, Norval? I thought you were in Denver."

"I came back last week. I thought I'd stay for the summer, but I've changed my mind." He rose abruptly, paced a few steps, then sat back down and leaned toward her across the desk, his habitual mocking expression gone. "I don't belong here, Jessica. I never have, and I never will. I'm not one of them, and I don't want to be. You probably know that when Clinton bought the ranch, we agreed I'd hang on to the ranch house and a couple of acres around it. But I want to sell that, too."

She drew a deep breath as her eyes searched his face. She was a little short on cash just now—one of the reasons she had wanted to sell some cattle. Much of her wealth was tied up in land. Also, she had very little use for another house. But Norval's eyes held hers, pleading. She gave an exasperated sigh. "Norval, why don't you get a job?"

Now he threw back his head and laughed. "Can't. It would ruin my life-style. Besides, there's no market demand for my talents."

She had to laugh with him. "How much do you want for it?"

"Well, old Mark offered me twice what it was worth. But I don't want to sell to him." His expression darkened, and he seemed to be looking back into the past. Then he shrugged, named a reasonable figure, and Jessica nodded. "Then I'm off to Denver for good, and out of your hair."

Later she stood in the doorway and watched him drive away, unaccountably depressed. She'd never thought she would be sorry to see Norval go—he was so unprincipled, so unlike everything she thought a man should be. He had taken the heritage Sam had left him and frittered it away, and when he had spent this last money, she had no idea where he would get more.

But he had been a part of her life for so long that his absence would leave a hole in it. She would miss his cynicism, his refusal to bend to the rigid moral code of those around him. In some ways she wished she were more like him.

She jerked her thoughts away from that heresy. One had to have a code to live by, and she had hers. It had caused her deep pain, cruel sacrifice—it had cost her Mark—but in the end it was worth it. She was now a strong, independent woman, a woman who could look at herself in the mirror and be unashamed.

Why did Mark want that house of Norval's? Was it an obsession to buy up everything in the entire valley?

She had run into Mark a few times at meetings and such, but their greetings had been brief and guarded. Maybe he was even grateful for her decision. She heard from Justin, who always came to stay with her when Amanda arrived, that his wife made occasional trips to Hope and that Mark was sometimes in Boise, so apparently they were not separated.

She glanced at the corrals and saw Hoskins walking toward the house. He would want his check. She moved inside to pick it up, but for several moments she just stood there, staring at the desk, unseeing.

Where had all the possibilities gone? The pattern of her life was set now. She couldn't avoid the thought: She was middle-aged. There would be few surprises from now on. She would devote herself to the ranch, and to Justin when he would allow it, and consider herself fortunate.

Eventually her feelings for Mark were bound to fade to a soft, sweet memory, their love half remembered like a song that floats just out of reach in the back of your mind. She would think of him in his house a few miles away, and her heart would not ache. Someday that would happen.

"Do you want me to get it?" Lydia glanced toward the ringing phone, then at Jessica, who was leaning back in an armchair, ensconced in pillows, her bare feet propped up on an ottoman. It had been a difficult day; she had spent hours riding with Dell scouring the far range for strays, and she was exhausted.

"Please." She wiggled her toes luxuriously and gave Lydia a grateful glance.

Lydia moved toward the phone, calling over her shoulder, "You shouldn't spend so much time riding—that's what you've got hired hands for."

Jessica closed her eyes. "I know." She'd tried to explain to Lydia that she loved the riding and would give up almost everything else first. It brought her close to the heart of the Carter ranch—the sounds, the smells, the beauties of the earth. It renewed her spirit, even if it did sometimes exhaust her body. Lydia, though, would never understand, and she had given up trying to articulate the almost mystical connection she felt.

Something in the tone of Lydia's voice caused her to open her eyes and glance at the woman. Her stomach did a slow flip-flop. Lydia's usually ruddy face was drained of color, and she glanced nervously at Jessica, then murmured something so low it was impossible to understand. Sudden uneasiness prickled Jessica's skin. Lydia was holding the phone as though it were a snake that might bite her at any minute.

"Who is it?" she asked, straightening in her chair.

Lydia replaced the phone gingerly, then moved reluctantly toward Jessica. "I'm sorry, Jess. My God, I'm so sorry!"

Jessica simply stared at her, unable to breathe. She saw the tears in Lydia's eyes as her friend leaned over and grasped her hand, squeezing it fiercely. "There's been an accident."

An accident. An accident. The words ricocheted in her mind.

"It's Justin," Lydia said. The words hung between them, heavy, incomprehensible.

Finally Jessica forced a question through stiff lips. "How—how bad?"

"It's bad." Lydia swallowed. "He's—he's dead."

Dead. The room spun around her, and she gripped the arms of her chair. A low moan started deep in her body; she clutched her stomach. Not Justin. An image of her son as she'd just recently seen him flashed through her mind: so vital, so full of enthusiasm. All that energy couldn't just be snuffed out, as though it had never been. He was just now coming into his own. It wasn't possible that he'd never have a chance to be a man.

Lydia pulled her against her shoulder and rocked her silently, cushioning her sobbing friend against her ample bosom. "Nothing helps now, I know. I still remember Jimmy, all the time, every day. But the worst will pass eventually. Just hold on, Jessica, hold on," she crooned.

It was several minutes before Jessica could stop sobbing enough to ask, "How—how did it happen? Where is he?"

"His car went off the bridge outside of Hope. A rancher found him. He took him to the hospital, but . . . he never made it. That was Doc Alberson on the phone. He's coming right over."

"Where's . . . Mark?" she whispered.

Their son was dead. Was he never to be there when she needed him? Numbness seemed to claim her body, seeping into every muscle, until her limbs felt too heavy to move. She tried to concentrate on Lydia's voice, which seemed to come from a great distance.

"They're trying to find him, to notify him. I guess he's on a trip someplace. Here, let me help you lie down."

She allowed Lydia to lead her to the couch and ease her onto the velvet cushions. One horrible thought reverberated through her mind: Justin was dead. His troubled life was over before it had even begun. And now she was truly alone.

By the time Doc Alberson arrived, she had regained

some semblance of control, and she refused the medication he offered, insisting that he take her to her son. Reluctantly he agreed, and with Lydia holding tight to her hand, she went to the hospital and saw her son for the last time.

Later, looking back over those months after Justin's death, she was never able to see any single event clearly. She lived in a miasma of grief, going through the necessary motions, making the proper arrangements. There was the funeral in Hope and, coinciding with the first fall of autumn leaves, the burial in the same churchyard that already held Leah and Clinton. There was Mark's face, a bitter mask of pain as they laid their son to rest, and then, like the walking wounded, went their separate ways. There were the days alone when she tried to cope by working harder, riding longer. But when the first snow fell, she was forced to spend more time indoors.

Lydia came by daily, bringing a casserole, trying to interest her in the valley's gossip, and Karla, though suffering badly now with arthritis, made tempting dinners, which usually remained uneaten. It would undoubtedly get better—everyone assured her it would—but for now day blended into indistinguishable day, little remarked, unremembered.

She sat now in her living room, staring at the fire that blazed in the hearth. Dell had started it, she believed, as he had every night since the storms had begun in earnest. It was strange she didn't feel warmer, she thought, watching the flames lick voraciously at the dry pine logs. The house was tight enough, although she could see the snow falling beyond the window. Somehow she had to shake herself out of this lethargy, but right now she couldn't think of a good enough reason to make the effort.

She continued to stare unseeingly into the fire. One scene stood out from the others in the gray mist that surrounded her. It had been a few weeks ago, when she had gone to Hope to do some infrequent shopping. She was standing near the curb ready to get into her car when suddenly she looked up. Mark was standing directly in front of her.

"Hello, Jessica." His tone was diffident, and he looked more haggard than she had ever seen him. He had lost weight since she had last seen him at the funeral.

"Hello, Mark." She knew her voice was dull and listless, and she saw in Mark's eyes that he was as shocked at her appearance as she was at his.

"I was out to the ranch to see you yesterday."

"Karla said you had come by. I was out riding." She hadn't been. She had seen him come to the door and retreated to her room, unable to face him just yet. Her emotions were too raw.

"I had something I wanted to tell you."

She glanced at his face, seeing the hard set of his jaw, the stony expression in his eyes. For an instant compassion flickered through her. His grief might almost equal hers. Then she closed her heart. How could it? He'd had only a few years with Justin. She had known and loved him from the cradle to the grave. "Yes?" She hoped her expression was as noncommittal as her voice.

"I'm leaving Hope."

The announcement came as a shock. "Oh. You're moving to your house in Boise?"

He stared into the distance. "A little farther than that, I think. Now that Justin's gone, there's no reason for me to stay here. MacDougal's been running the mill all along, except for management decisions, and I can make those decisions just as well from anyplace in the world."

"You're leaving Idaho?" She was surprised at the sudden flash of pain that lanced through her lethargy. "I thought you were going to run for governor next time around."

"Not just now. Maybe later. Maybe never. I think I'll take some time to myself, enjoy a little of the money I've made." His dark eyes moved carefully over her face, as though memorizing each separate feature. She couldn't guess at what was going on behind those enigmatic eyes. "Amanda has been wanting to see the world—what little of it she hasn't already seen." His laugh was completely without humor. "She's always wanted me to go with her, and now I think I will." His lips tightened, and a tiny muscle pulsed in his jaw. "I probably won't see you again, Jessica, at least for a while."

Not see him again? She hardly ever saw him now. Their only contact for months, years even, had been through Justin, and now there wouldn't even be that. Mark's absence certainly wouldn't leave an obvious hole in the fabric of her life. Yet the thought of his leaving brought raw pain.

"I hope you'll enjoy traveling," she said politely. "Are you leaving soon?" *Don't leave, Mark, don't leave me. Even if I can't have you, I need you close.*

"Tomorrow. It was lucky that I ran into you today. I would have hated to leave without saying good-bye."

Good-byes are what you're best at, she thought fleetingly. But she smiled carefully. She had no reason to be bitter. Mark had asked her to be with him; it was she who knew it was impossible.

He put his hands on her shoulders and turned her to face him squarely, his eyes holding hers as though he would delve into her heart. Then he let out his breath in a long, ragged sigh, shrugged, and released her. "Well, I guess I'd better be going."

Silently, frozen to the spot, she watched him walk away. She knew she would remember this last glimpse of him forever. His head was bare, and his dark hair, liberally streaked with gray, blew in the chill wind. His black jacket fit perfectly across his broad shoulders, his lean legs were encased in expertly tailored pants. He looked successful, important, a man of power and substance. Which he was, she reminded herself. She must be imagining the aura of dejection that surrounded him.

If he had turned one more time, if he had looked back,

had asked her once more to marry him, would she have done so? It was possible. A part of her yearned after his tall figure as he walked away for what might well be the last time.

But the impulse passed, and she was once again in control of her emotions. She had made the only decision she could—the decision that was best for both of them. Perhaps they could be excused the wild surrender to passion when they were young, the cathartic times they had succumbed to fierce emotion upon their reunion. But now they were older, mature. They knew right from wrong.

Now, overcome by a sudden agitation, Jessica rose from her chair and paced briefly about the room. Any activity was better than just sitting here, giving in to self-pity. So what if she was now truly alone? So were a lot of others. And she still had a lot to live for. There was the ranch. There was the women's group, which was becoming more politically active every day. There were friends.

The doorbell rang, and she paused in her recitation, waiting to see if Karla would answer it. Then she glanced at her watch. It was well past ten, and Karla had gone to bed. She supposed she would have to go to the door, although she didn't really want to see anyone this late at night. What were they doing here at this hour, anyway? She should have heard a car drive up, but perhaps she wouldn't have above the sound of the wind that was whipping around the sides of the house and pounding the windows with snow.

Sighing, she went to the front entry, switched on the outside light, and threw open the door. Whoever it was should have called first. There was nothing wrong with the telephone.

Her eyes widened with astonishment as she took in the slight figure standing on the veranda. An unfamiliar young woman stared solemnly, almost fearfully, back at her. She couldn't see much of her visitor; the girl's pinched face peered out from under a woolen cap, and she held a long, oversized jacket tightly about her body, but Jessica guessed she was about fifteen or sixteen.

The visitor continued to stare wordlessly, and Jessica recovered her manners. "Uh . . . hello—" The girl offered no name. "Won't you come in?" She stepped back from the door and motioned the girl inside. "You must be frozen."

The girl walked silently into the room, her wary eyes never leaving Jessica. Jessica had the impression of a person on the edge of a cliff, hanging on with her fingernails. She led her into the living room, keeping up a line of pleasantries as she studied the girl. She hadn't seen her before; she was almost sure of it. She knew most of the young people in the county, at least by sight.

The girl pulled off her cap, letting a flood of chestnut hair cascade around her shoulders, and then held her hands toward the fire. They were red with cold, and again Jessica wondered where she had come from.

"You're a cake of ice," she said briskly. "How long have you been out in this weather?"

"Not long. I walked here from the bus line."

Jessica hid her surprise. There was no local bus service. The girl must have been on the interstate bus that passed at least three miles from the ranch house.

"Let me take your coat." She took the bulky garment, stiff with snow, and tossed it over a chair, then turned back to her visitor. Her eyes widened. The girl was painfully thin, with narrow shoulders, delicate hands, and a very pretty face. But that wasn't what made Jessica gasp with astonishment.

She was also very, very pregnant.

Getting to the bottom of the mystery could wait, Jessica thought, noticing that the girl was swaying on her feet with exhaustion. Gently she led her to a couch and urged her to removed her wet shoes and warm her toes.

"I'll get you something hot to drink," she offered.

She started to move toward the door, but the girl's hand on her arm halted her. "Mrs. Carter? You don't know me, but I'm Debbie."

Just Debbie. She probably wouldn't get a last name out of her, Jessica realized, if the girl was what she thought she was—a runaway desperate for shelter.

"I hate to bother you like this, but I'm really up against it."

There was no sign of a wedding ring on the girl's hand; she was desperate for help, any help. Jessica should call the welfare department to arrange assistance for her, and she would in the morning. But for now she would offer what comfort she could.

"Your . . . parents don't want the baby?" she ventured.

Debbie's laugh was harsh, too harsh for a person of her age, Jessica thought sadly. She'd supposed times had changed since she had faced the same situation this girl appeared to be in, but apparently they hadn't changed all that much if Debbie was seeking sanctuary with a stranger.

"I haven't seen my parents for years," the girl said dully. "I've been on my own—except for the baby's father. . . ." She faltered.

"You lived with the baby's father, then? Where is he now? Can he help?" Jessica gently probed.

Debbie's gaze met hers squarely, and she raised her chin. "I didn't exactly live with him. He saw me when he could get away from his folks. He said we'd be married, but he still had school, and he didn't have any money of his own yet. But he told me about you, and he said that if I ever needed anything and couldn't reach him, I could come to you. I didn't think I would . . . but I found out I was knocked up . . . and now that he's dead . . ."

Jessica couldn't tear her eyes away from the girl's face as the mystery began to clear. Had it been only a few months ago she had told herself that the pattern of her life was set, that there would be no more surprises?

"Who is the baby's father?" she asked softly, already knowing what she would hear.

Debbie gave her a surprised glance. "Why, Justin, of course. Your son."

15

Jessica had fallen in love twice in her life: first with Mark, and again when she took the squalling, red-faced baby in her arms and held her against her chest. She took one look at the large, unfocused eyes with the sweeping dark lashes, the delicately pointed chin, the well-shaped head, and she was forever lost.

Doc Alberson, his face gray with weariness, motioned her away from Debbie's bedside. He had given the girl a sedative, and already her eyes were closing, her pale hands loosening their frantic grip on the wrinkled sheets. Jessica supposed that as births go, it had been an easy one, but she also knew that even the easiest birth was an ordeal for a woman.

"She'll sleep for a while," Alberson said, moving ahead of Jessica into the next room and lowering himself gingerly into a chair. "Wish I could, but I'd best start home soon. These old bones are getting too brittle for this late-night work." He smiled—a little forlornly, Jessica thought.

She gave him a fond glance. "Nonsense. You wouldn't know what to do with yourself if we didn't call you out in the middle of the night. It makes you feel needed."

"If I were needed any more, I'd be dead. Besides, there *are* hospitals," he said gruffly.

"She absolutely refused to go to one. Insisted on having the baby here, with just you and me. She's a secretive little thing." Jessica frowned. "She's lived with me nearly two months, and I still can't believe I know so little about her. Not where she lived or who her folks are." She shook off the puzzle and gave him a brilliant smile. "Anyway, I appreciate your coming."

He grinned. Then his pale old eyes darkened with remembrance. "Least I could do. Never quite made it to you the night Justin was born. Always felt bad about it, but I guess you and Leah managed. Shouldn't have been any news to her, as many as she had of her own."

Jessica gazed down at the small bundle squirming in her lap. She had already cleaned the baby, wrapped her in a soft blanket, and now she held a bottle to the little lips. They were shaped like flower petals, she thought. And they refused to have anything to do with the rubber nipple she tried to insert between them.

"She's not hungry yet," the doctor said, smiling at her effort. "When she is, her mother's breast is just the thing."

Jessica shook her head. Debbie had steadfastly refused to agree to breast-feed, and Jessica knew her well enough now to realize that she was unlikely to change her mind. Debbie was frail—she looked like a stiff wind might blow her away—but she had a will of iron.

Jessica looked down at the baby. Poor little tyke. Her father dead, a mother who didn't seem interested in her. Still, that might very well change when Debbie actually got a look at her daughter, held her in her arms. . . .

A chill went down her spine, and she couldn't suppress a shiver. Debbie might be more than interested; she might even take her baby away. And already, only a few minutes after the birth, Jessica wasn't sure she could bear the loss.

Doc Alberson opened up his scuffed black bag and

took out several sheets of paper. "What's her name? Might as well get this thing filled out."

Jessica hesitated. That was one of the myriad topics Debbie had refused to discuss. It was as though by not talking about her pregnancy, she hoped it would go away. By not mentioning the baby, it might somehow vanish.

"Maureen," she said suddenly. "I'll call her Maureen."

The old man smiled and raised an eyebrow. "Last name?" He shot her a quick glance, his pen poised.

"Carter," she replied firmly.

Frowning, he put his pen down on the table beside his chair. "Are you sure, Jessica? You could be letting yourself in for some legal hassles."

"I don't see how. Debbie won't tell me her last name, and she's shown no interest at all in the child. You're the only one who knows anything at all about the baby's history."

"You could have found out who she is. You could have gone to the authorities. Young women don't simply vanish without *somebody* looking for them."

Possibly she could have tried harder to find out the facts, but she had been afraid that any such move would have sent the poor girl scuttling back out into the night. She explained the situation to the doctor. "She said if I did anything like that, she would run away. She said her parents didn't care what happened to her, that she hadn't seen them for years. That nobody would even notice she was gone. I didn't want to risk frightening her back into harm's way. Who knows what would have happened to her and the child if she'd fled?"

He sighed. "All right. Maybe that's all true. And maybe I'm doing something illegal, but at my age I don't suppose one little infraction will really matter. Besides, it won't be the first time I've stretched things a bit if they needed it. Who do we put down for the father?"

"Justin Carter."

He paused. "Are you sure you want to do that? You don't really know for sure. And it could cause you trouble later on."

"I don't see how."

"Inheritance, for one. You might not be too worried about that, but it looks to me like you've got the kid on your hands, and she's going to grow up, start asking questions. You might want to think about what you'll tell her."

"But this is my grandchild." She stopped, suddenly uncertain. She was Mark's grandchild, too. This child was an unexpected gift, and she wanted her desperately. That someone could someday challenge her right to little Maureen sent chills down her spine. Jeb Hardy had fought for Justin. And Mark had actually succeeded in claiming the boy's affections. If and when Maureen was grown enough to need answers, she would tell her the truth. But until that need arose . . .

Alberson stared at her unblinkingly, and she raised her chin. "Unknown. For the father, put down unknown."

During the next few days Jessica rarely slept except in short snatches, always alert for Maureen's cry. Karla tried to help, but her arthritis had really slowed her down, and Debbie was recovering very slowly. Jessica should have felt exhausted, but she didn't. She felt exhilarated, full of energy.

She tried several times to discuss the future with Debbie. The girl seemed uninterested, turning her head to stare blankly out the window when Jessica brought Maureen to her. She began to feel uneasy as the girl's sullen silence continued. Perhaps there was more wrong with Debbie than the aftermath of having a baby. Should she get professional help for the girl?

Doc Alberson came by for a few minutes each day. Debbie was getting along fine physically, he said, but he was worried about her outlook. She didn't seem interested in much of anything. Sometimes, though, that happened to young mothers. Given time, she might snap out of it.

Just as Jessica had nearly decided to call in a specialist, Debbie decided to get out of bed. Her appetite returned, and although she drifted about the house like a ghost, Jessica began to relax. It wasn't unusual for a woman to be depressed after childbirth, and Debbie seemed to be gradually coming out of it. Perhaps now was the time for a talk.

Debbie was sitting in a deep chair in the living room, absentmindedly staring at the fire. Jessica sat down opposite her, having just tucked Maureen in. The baby was finally managing to sleep through the night.

Jessica surveyed Debbie keenly. The young woman looked less and less like a waif each day. She was glad to see her out of her nightgown and robe and actually dressed. The girl had arrived with only the clothes on her back, but Jessica had shopped, and now her visitor wore well-fitted jeans and a warm turtleneck sweater. Her dark hair had regained its gloss, and she had it caught firmly in a ponytail, accentuating the delicate bones of her face. She had even put on some makeup, and she no longer looked as though a slight breeze might blow her away.

"Debbie," Jessica said, reaching for the girl's hand, "we're going to have to talk."

The girl turned toward Jessica, but she didn't respond. Jessica was encouraged, though; she didn't draw her hand away.

"You seem to be feeling better. Don't you think it's time you got to know Maureen? Spent some time with her?"

Debbie shrugged her narrow shoulders. "You mean, take care of her? You're doing a pretty good job, if you ask me." She paused. "And you don't seem to mind it a bit. Do you?" she asked with uncharacteristic solicitousness.

Jessica sighed. "No, of course I don't mind. I love Maureen. But I'm not her mother. Debbie, you've never told me where you lived before you came here, how you lived, who your people are, but I don't think we can put it off any longer. There's Maureen's future to consider."

Debbie remained stubbornly silent, and Jessica took a deep breath. "And she is my grandchild. Justin's baby. I don't want to lose her." She looked straight at Debbie, who was looking down at her hands, now nicely polished in a light coral shade she had obviously found on Jessica's dresser. "Debbie, I'd like you and Maureen to live with me."

Debbie raised her eyes and gave her an enigmatic glance. Jessica didn't know what she had expected—surprise, gratitude, maybe even resentment—but Debbie's voice was uninflected. "You really do love her, don't you?"

"I really do," Jessica replied softly. "And I love you, too, Debbie—or could if you'd give me a chance. If you would open up just a little. I think it would work out extremely well for the three of us. I'm alone. You two need a place to live. I'd be happy to have you."

Debbie was silent, her gaze returning to her hands. Finally she replied, "You're a good person, Jessica."

"Does that mean you'll do it?"

"It means I'll consider it. I'll let you know in the morning."

In spite of Maureen's new sleep habits Jessica spent a restless night. She had brought the crib to a room next to hers, and once she thought she heard a disturbance. Worried about the baby, she eased out of bed and crept to the door. Debbie was standing over the crib, looking down at her sleeping child.

It was a hopeful sign, Jessica thought, inching, unseen, back to her room. The young woman wasn't as indifferent to her child as she seemed. She was an extremely reserved person, but there must be emotion somewhere under her cool facade. After all, she had loved Justin; she knew it from the slight tremor in her voice when she said his name. She must want what was best for her daughter.

To Jessica's mind the best would be for the two of them to stay with her. She had no idea what kind of a life Debbie had led, but she suspected it wasn't easy and would only be worse if she were on her own with a baby.

How had she and Justin met? she wondered for the hundredth time. Had he really loved her? Wanted to marry her once he was out of school and able to work to support her? Her heart ached that now he would never answer those questions, never realize his dreams, whatever they might have been.

Her heart constricted again at the thought of losing Maureen, too. She had no legal right to her, and she suspected Debbie was quite capable of simply vanishing with her, never to be heard from again. And the thought of that sweet baby, Justin's baby, facing hardship, crying, hungry, possibly neglected, was almost more than she could bear.

She would be exceedingly persuasive when she talked to Debbie tomorrow. There was no reason she could see that Debbie wouldn't want to stay. It was in her best interest as well as the child's.

She busied herself in the morning taking care of Maureen's needs, tickled her under the chin, then put her back in her crib and went down the stairs. The aroma of coffee greeted her, and she walked into the kitchen to the welcome sight of Karla at the stove.

"Feeling better this morning?" She poured some coffee and took it to the table.

Karla shrugged. "It comes and it goes. No getting rid of arthritis. What would you like for breakfast?"

"I think I'll wait for Debbie." She paid no attention to Karla's sour look. For the past week the girl had been coming down to breakfast, and Jessica had enjoyed having someone at the table with her, even someone as uncommunicative as Debbie. This morning she was especially eager to see the girl, to hear she had decided to stay permanently.

She had nearly drained the coffeepot when she glanced at the clock above the range. It was after nine, late even for Debbie, who in her own words was a "night person."

"I think I'll just go up and see if everything is all right," she said, ignoring Karla's sniff. Debbie might have endeared herself to Jessica, but Karla had never warmed to the girl.

Jessica tapped on the bedroom door. When there was no reply, she pushed it open.

The minute she entered the room she sensed what had happened. Her heart fell, and she clenched her fists at her sides, willing herself to remain calm. The room was neat, the bed made. She glanced around, but she knew what she would see. The clothes she had purchased for Debbie were gone, the toiletries cleared from the dresser.

Her heart pounding, she sprinted down the hall and peered into Maureen's room. She took a deep, relieved breath; the baby was still there. Closing the door softly, she walked more slowly back to Debbie's empty room.

She entered and looked around again. Then she saw the note, white against the polished maple. Walking slowly to the dresser, she picked up the single sheet of paper and read the scrawled message.

You're a good woman, Mrs. Carter. I wouldn't leave my baby with you if I didn't know that, even if you are rich. She's much better off with you than where I'm going. Don't try to find me. If you do find me, I'll leave again and take her with me. There was no signature, but there was one more sentence, a scribbled afterthought. *I took a hundred dollars from your desk.*

Jessica let the paper drop slowly to the floor. When she saw Debbie bending over Maureen's crib last night, she had thought that the girl was beginning to take an interest in her baby. Instead she had been saying good-bye.

Where could she have gone in the middle of the night? Perhaps she had called some unknown person to pick her up and take her away. Or perhaps she had walked to the highway and flagged down a bus.

Poor, pitiful girl. She rested her head briefly against the mirror, her eyes closed. Debbie had vanished into the night, disappearing in the same way she had come. Perhaps she had planned to all along; maybe she had deliberately avoided becoming attached to her baby. Perhaps she had loved the child enough to leave her to what she thought would be a better life than any she herself could give her. Jessica's heart ached when she thought of the pain such a decision must cost a young mother.

She would never know for sure, of course—more of life's questions to be left forever unanswered. But, she decided, when Maureen grew up and asked about her mother, that is what she would tell her. She loved you so much she wanted a better life for you.

She would search for Debbie, of course. She couldn't just allow her to fade away, as though she had never existed. But she wasn't optimistic about finding her. She knew nothing about her, and the girl was undoubtedly an expert at melting into a crowd. Still, she would try. Debbie should know that *someone* in the world cared about her. And Jessica felt she owed it to Justin as well. And to Justin and Debbie's child.

Going back into the nursery, she lifted the sleeping baby from the crib and held her tightly against her chest. Her adored grandchild.

Her second chance.

16

"The meeting will come to order." Lester Jensen, glasses low on his long nose, appearing uncomfortable in a two-piece suit, and county commissioner since the last election, gazed out over the crowd and banged the gavel that he clutched in his callused hand. "You all know what we're here for."

There were solemn nods, murmurs of assent, and Lydia leaned over and touched Jessica lightly on the arm. "Looks like we got a good crowd," she whispered.

Jessica glanced around the meeting room of the new county courthouse and agreed. The Adamses, the Beales, Doc Alberson, even old Ira Kincaid had hobbled in. Was the man immortal? There were a lot of new faces, too, younger faces, people she recognized but didn't really know. A public meeting didn't usually draw such a crowd, but this one had been discussed for weeks, engendering unusual emotion. Jessica had fought at a lot of these meetings, but not often was the issue so clearly delineated—housing development versus land conservation. Depending on which side you were on, it was greedy money grubbers tearing up the land or a bunch of woolly-headed do-gooders standing in the way of economic progress.

Lester Jensen coughed importantly. "This is a meeting to see how you all feel about that new development Hardy Enterprises plans to put on the old Snyder place. He's requested a permit, and some people in town"—he threw Jessica a dark glance—"mainly the Women's Club, have protested. So we're going to hear both sides."

"Where's Hardy?" someone called from the back. "Ain't he here to tell us what he's got in mind?"

Cullen MacDougal stood up. He hadn't changed much, Jessica thought, since he'd come to Hope years ago to ramrod Mark's sawmill venture. Now he handled all Mark's interests in the county, although Jessica suspected Mark always knew exactly what was going on. His red hair was speckled with white now, and he had a slight paunch, but he hadn't lost his air of authority.

"Mr. Hardy can't be here. He's asked me to tell you what he has in mind, explain what the benefits will be for the county."

Jessica rose and faced MacDougal. "We all know what the so-called benefits will be, Cullen. More people, more crowding, more land taken out of production. In fact, I can't see that anyone here will benefit except Hardy Enterprises."

There were murmurs of agreement, a boo or two, as Cullen faced her with a smooth smile. "Let's talk a little about that land taken out of production, Mrs. Carter. It's squarely between your home ranch and the Blalock ranch—which is yours, too. I understand you've used it for years to trail your cattle from one range to the other. But it's not public land, you know. The Snyders sold it to Mr. Hardy."

She lifted her chin and regarded him with cold eyes. "It's no secret that the strip of land is handy for me. But I can always drive my herds around it. The real loss will be to the people of Hope and to the wildlife on the land now. The grass will become concrete. The stream will be forced into a culvert. It's almost the last stand for the lynx and the red-tailed fox."

Cullen met her eyes, and his lip curled. "You seem to

care more about wildlife than you do about people. But then, *you* don't have to worry about making a living, Mrs. Carter. The development will bring jobs to Hope, provide homes for some who are living in subhuman conditions. Bring in taxes for the county."

"And money to Mark Hardy."

"Yes, that too. Is there anything wrong with making money? Your cattle are bringing a good price now, I understand. That land is useless as it is; we want to put it to use."

"Human use isn't the only use for land! Don't the other inhabitants of this planet deserve something? Must there be a house on every vacant acre?"

"Or a cow?" he challenged.

Jensen rattled his gavel. "Jessica, Cullen, this here is a meeting for everybody. I'd like to hear some other views."

Lydia sprang to her feet, and Jessica half listened to her impassioned speech. She knew every word, anyway; they had worked on it together. Lydia must be nearly sixty now, she thought; she herself was fifty-two. Lydia had slimmed down, wore a tailored shirtdress with sensible heels, and her hair was tightly permed. Jessica knew that other parts of America were in turmoil, with civil-rights sit-ins and rumors about trouble in Vietnam, but here in Hope they still clung to the fifties, in dress and style of living. Lydia might have stepped directly out of the pages of the *Ladies' Home Journal.*

After Lydia spoke, the meeting became general. Everyone had a definite opinion; it seemed there were no fence sitters here, Jessica thought, listening to one neighbor after another voice their views.

"Do you think we've made an impression?" Lydia whispered in her ear.

"Hard to say," Jessica whispered back. "I don't know where Jensen himself stands. His wife works for Mark—or did."

"But she's a member of our club."

"I know." Jessica sighed. She understood the ambivalence of some of the people. Jobs were at stake, and yet none of them wanted to trade their sleepy little village of Hope for the bustle and frenzy of urban living. "If Mark were here to speak for himself, I think he'd win. But some of the people resent his absentee ownership. He's only been back once in the last couple of years."

"Why do you suppose he doesn't come back more often?"

"Why should he?" Jessica shrugged. "His mother is dead, he doesn't get along with his father—and his money comes in regularly wherever he is."

"Don't be too hard on him. I think he really cares about this county. But when you were brought up poor like he was, maybe money becomes the most important thing there is."

Jessica knew there was some truth in her friend's remark. After all, the Depression had permanently affected her, making it almost impossible for her to spend a dime foolishly. And Mark had spent his entire youth in bleak, grinding poverty.

Her gaze swept the crowd. "A lot of people would agree with him. But how much will it take to make him feel secure? He's already bought up most of the county."

The meeting finally ground to a halt, and after Jensen had promised a decision in a week, Lydia and Jessica stepped out into the night air. As Lydia called good nights Jessica stood on the step and took a deep breath, nearly oblivious to the people swirling around her like autumn leaves in a brisk wind.

The stars were out in the deep velvet of the summer sky, so thick she could hardly make out the constellations. It had been unseasonably warm today, but now the breeze was pleasant, laden with smells of midsummer: fresh-cut hay, roses, scent of pine—all combining with the faint scent of gasoline. The roar of departing motors drowned out the night sounds—the scurryings in the brush, or the occasional flutter of nocturnal wings—but she thought she heard the far-off bark of a coyote.

She was engulfed by a momentary sadness so acute that she clutched her chest. This was all so ephemeral, so fragile, this last little outpost of a way of life that was changing daily. Housing, industry, new businesses sprang up like mushrooms virtually overnight. Not all Mark's, either. She felt that she and the other ranchers were under siege, desperately battling to keep out the encroaching barbarians.

She smiled slightly, remembering a long-ago conversation with her prize pupil: Mark Hardy. Just who *were* the barbarians, they'd debated. She was one of very few people who thought of the population advancing on Hope Valley as barbarians. She had been told often enough that she was trying to stave off civilization, standing in the way of progress.

Well, she would stand in the way of progress as long as she could.

She said good-bye to Lydia and hopped into her pickup to begin the long ride home. As soon as she was away from the town streetlights, darkness enveloped her. The road to the ranch was still unpaved, and gravel spun under her wheels, plinking against the metal fenders. She was alone in the night, but the country darkness greeted her like an old, familiar friend.

She saw the lights of the ranch when she was still a few miles away and, as always, she let out a sigh. It was still there. And everything she loved was in it.

She drove up to the driveway and parked the truck. Dell would take care of it, and she was eager to see Maureen. The girl was ten now, and old enough to stay by herself occasionally, but Jessica never liked to leave her alone long. She had felt better about it when Karla was there, even though the old woman had rarely left her room. But last year Karla, so crippled with arthritis that she could barely get up and down the stairs, had gone to live with her sister. Various women now came in to cook and clean, but Jessica no longer had anyone living in.

She ran lightly up the veranda steps. The door opened before she got there, and Maureen hurled herself at her like a little tornado.

"Hey! You're late!"

"No, I'm not." Jessica squeezed the girl to her, then pulled back to look into her face. As always, her heart clenched tightly, and she felt love so strong it was almost pain.

The child was so beautiful. She had long black hair almost the exact color of Mark's, and even at this age her resemblance to Leah was remarkable. If Jessica had ever had the slightest doubt that Justin was Maureen's father, it had evaporated at the sight of the girl's huge, almond-shaped eyes fringed by heavy black lashes. Her cheek-bones were high, revealing her Indian heritage, and her mouth was wide and full. Perhaps she would go through an awkward stage, Jessica thought, although so far she showed no signs of it, but there was no question that ultimately she would be a beauty.

Her emotions, as she gave the girl another hug, were tumultuous. Her grandchild, and the center of her life. But how long could she keep her wrapped in innocence and love? She had had no difficulty adopting her, and so far Maureen was blissfully uncurious about her background. All she knew was that her mother had come to Jessica for help, and then, in order to give her a better life, had vanished. She seemed to have no wish to delve deeper—who her father was, for instance.

If she asked whether Jessica knew, she would certainly tell her, but the prospect sent a cold chill down her back. Where Maureen was concerned, she was a coward. There were no secrets in the town, and Justin's relationship to Mark Hardy was widely known. If Maureen knew who her father was, she would soon know who her grandfather was. And Jessica didn't want that at all. Maureen was her treasure, and she meant to keep her safe from the troubling conflict Justin had suffered.

Obviously she couldn't keep the secret forever. But she would remain silent as long as she could.

Maureen took her hand and pulled her into the room. Her deep brown eyes were shining with excitement. "Guess what I did while you were gone?"

"Made cookies?" Jessica asked, laughing. It was a joke between them that Maureen's cooking skills were no better than Jessica's, which were pedestrian at best.

"No!" Maureen grinned at her. "I rode Tiger!"

Jessica's heart did a little flop, but she kept her voice steady. "Tiger is much too wild for you, and too headstrong. You have your own horse."

"Oh, Lady Jess, I can't ride Ozzie! She's so slow, she can't get out of her own way. Tiger is great! He goes like the wind!"

Uneasy but unwilling to dampen Maureen's excitement, she gazed steadily at the girl. "Who saddled Tiger for you?" When she found out, the man would be down the road before he knew it.

"I saddled him myself," Maureen said proudly, throwing out her little chest. "I'm not a baby!"

"No, you're certainly not," Jessica agreed, ruffling the girl's long dark hair. She was, in fact, extremely precocious and had already caused her grandmother a few sleepless nights. She was also competent and truthful. If she said she could handle Tiger, she probably could. "Have you had supper?"

"I had a hot dog, and some of that chocolate cake Aunt Lydia brought by. Hungry? I'll put another one on to boil." She skipped on ahead to the kitchen, and Jessica followed more slowly. Maureen was like a flame, she thought, vital, energetic, and fairly leaping with excitement.

As Mark had been. The thought came unexpectedly, and she felt suddenly old.

She sat down at the kitchen table and watched Maureen drop a frankfurter into a pot of boiling water. So far it was her biggest culinary accomplishment, and Jessica was willing to eat anything she didn't have to cook herself. With a serious, dedicated expression Maureen speared the wiener, placed it on a bun, and slathered it with mustard, then put it with a flourish in front of Jessica. Then she sat back, her chin propped in a brown, grubby little hand.

"You look nice tonight," she said.

Jessica glanced down at her expensive jeans and hand-tooled western boots. Her tailored shirt was of soft sea-green silk, and her hair, whose pale color camouflaged whatever gray was there, was caught at the back of her neck with a silk scarf.

Lydia constantly pressured her about her wardrobe. She was one of the richest women in the county; why wasn't she also one of the best dressed? Jessica always put her off with a joking remark. She liked her functional, easy attire, and it suited her lean frame. Besides, she had too much to think about without worrying over the latest fashions—which she found a bit weird, anyway.

Would Maureen someday become fashion conscious? she wondered. At ten, the child was happy to run around in jeans, although her teacher had once sent home a note saying dresses might be more appropriate. When Maureen had groused, Jessica had been glad to use her influence on the school board to pump for greater comfort and flexibility in girls' wear.

She listened as Maureen prattled on about her day. She knew she should go into the study and take care of the pile of paperwork that seemed to grow higher each day. Still, she lingered, sipping hot tea and watching the expressions play across Maureen's face. How fortunate she was, Jessica reflected. Life had taken much from her, but it had left her a delightful prize—her granddaughter.

A granddaughter who didn't know their real relationship, she thought uneasily as she listened to Maureen's artless chatter. How long could she keep her innocent of the potentially disturbing truth? Someday the girl was bound to hear rumors, innuendos. She would have to tell her before she discovered it by herself.

17

Day slid imperceptibly into day, year into year, and Jessica told herself she was content. The changes in her life were so gradual that she scarcely noticed them happening. But as she stood at the veranda railing gazing at the valley where cattle had roamed when she first came to Hope, she could not help regretting that the vista that had once appeared so pristine was now crisscrossed with roads and dotted with houses, the pines and firs replaced by the sedate poplars or stately elms favored in the new developments.

Her battles against the encroaching projects had been frequent and fierce, and many of them she had lost. It was like trying to hold back the tide. But at least she could congratulate herself on a partial triumph. The Carter ranch was surrounded, besieged by progress, as some liked to call the burgeoning development, but it was still a working cattle ranch, the largest in the county. And it would remain that way as long as she had a breath left in her body.

Still, Jessica was a realist, and she was aware of both her strengths and her weaknesses. She knew she had become an astute businesswoman, a power in the county, but when economics collided with preservation, higher employment with virgin timber or meadowland, the community usually opted for jobs.

Mark Hardy gave them those jobs, she acknowledged. Although he rarely came to Hope anymore, his presence was felt. He was the guiding force behind the booming economy. He ran the sawmill and his real-estate company through Cullen MacDougal—and he ran them for a handsome profit. Many of the hillsides she could see from her veranda were denuded of trees, and condos dotted the creek bank where they had once made love. The old schoolhouse itself had become a quaint tourist attraction. But all the acres of the Carter ranch remained intact.

She heard the purr of a motor and glanced down the road. Her part of the road that ran from Hope to the ranch was still unpaved, and behind the brow of the hill she saw a puffy beige cloud rise into the azure sky. Then over the crest came the little blue convertible trailing its billowing tail of dust.

As usual, the presence of her granddaughter pushed all vague regrets from her mind. She hurried down the steps and waited for Maureen to turn into the driveway.

In a splash of gravel Maureen swung the roadster up in front of Jessica, hit the brakes, and killed the engine. The top of the convertible was down, as it usually was except in the most inclement weather, and Maureen's flawless complexion was covered with a thin sheen of dust. It certainly didn't dim her beauty or vitality, Jessica thought as the girl rested her arm on the door and leaned toward her, a bright smile on her face.

She had been right when she had assessed Maureen's potential for unusual beauty; at sixteen, the girl was stunning. Her thick dark hair fell around her wide shoulders as she opened the door and swung her feet out onto the gravel. She wore a pair of skimpy shorts that made her legs seem endless, and her halter top revealed strong bare arms and shoulders. She had none of Jessica's delicacy;

she was more like a Valkyrie. Her skin was tanned to the shade of creamy coffee, and her eyes, a rich brown, were fringed by long lashes of sooty black. High cheekbones, sleek nose, full, generous mouth—all her features fit into a perfect, harmonious whole.

Yet she had more than beauty. She possessed that indefinable spark, that mysterious current of energy, that could lift even the mundane into the blazingly spectacular. Leah had possessed it, Jessica thought, although it hadn't shone as fiercely in her gentle personality. Mark had it, too. In him it burned as a bright, unquenchable flame. Now Maureen.

Her heart seemed to twist in her chest. God, how she loved the girl. For years she had poured her every emotion into her. Lydia had once teased that she was acting like a frustrated old maid, and that she should spend some of that passion on the masculine sex, but Jessica had merely laughed. That part of her life was over. Maureen satisfied her need to love and be loved.

"Hi, Lady Jess." Maureen flung an arm around Jessica, and they skipped up the stairs together. As usual, Jessica was incredulous at how tall the girl had become. She already topped Jessica by a couple of inches.

At the top of the steps Maureen dropped a quick kiss on Jessica's cheek. "You should have come with me. It's a great day for tennis, and there was this new man at the court. He was really cute, and just about your age—"

Jessica held up her hand to stop the flow of words. "Whoa, girl. I've got a question for you. Weren't you driving a little fast just now? And haven't I told you I'm not interested in meeting any men?"

Maureen put her arm around Jessica's waist, and they walked into the house together. "That's two questions," she observed. "First, I wasn't exceeding the speed limit." Her dark eyes searched Jessica's face, and she frowned slightly. "Don't worry about me. I know how you feel about speeding—what happened to your son. I promise, I'm very careful."

Jessica knew that was true. Maureen liked speed, but she wasn't careless, as Justin had often been. Her innate concern for Jessica's feelings kept her foot from pushing too heavily on the gas. Jessica had suffered many nights of soul-searching before she gave Maureen the convertible she had her heart set on. Finally she had realized she couldn't warp Maureen's life with her own fears. The girl seemed completely confident and fearless, and she hoped to keep her that way.

"Now," Maureen said with a wide grin, "let's get back to why you refuse to meet any men."

Jessica's mouth turned up slightly at the corners. Maureen could be as determined as she was, and the girl had decided that Jessica needed a man.

"Maureen, I'm your grandmother!"

"So?" The girl's dark eyes sparkled. "You aren't dead. I know that for a fact, in spite of the way it looks sometimes!"

"No, I'm not. I keep busy, and I have friends who—"

"You need someone to stir you up a bit—and I'm not talking about your women friends!"

"I don't much like this conversation," Jessica said primly.

"And you're real classy looking, too," Maureen continued, ignoring her comment. "I'll bet you could snag just about anybody you wanted." Her eyes narrowed, and she surveyed Jessica thoughtfully. "When you get dressed up, there's no one who can touch you. Why you always wear those jeans and shirts, and why you don't do something with your hair, I'll never know."

Jessica's hand went to her hair, the subject of Maureen's strongest concerns. She was used to Maureen's prodding her to look more fashionable, and she occasionally bought something the girl suggested, but she absolutely refused to let her meddle with her hairstyle. In a life where almost everything shifted, her hair was one of the few things that seemed nearly impervious to change. It was still thick and a pale, glowing gold, the few strands of gray blending in enough to be nearly invisible.

Maureen continued with her pet subject. "How many years have you been a widow, anyway? It's unnatural. You must have some physical needs that—"

"Maureen!"

"Okay, okay, so you don't want to talk about it. I don't know how your generation managed to reproduce!" Maureen's glance managed to combine both exasperation and mischievousness. "Did anyone ever tell you you're just a bit old-fashioned? We're in the sixties, for heaven's sake! There's nothing wrong with talking about sex."

"Contrary to what you seem to think, your age group didn't invent sex," Jessica said dryly. "And I trust, at your age, that all you're doing is talking about it. Now, why don't you wash some of that dust off your face and we'll have lunch."

"Are you starving? I thought I'd take Tiger out for a run first. I haven't been on him for a couple of days, and you know he gets antsy if he isn't exercised. Why don't you come with me?"

"That's a great idea. I'll slip into my riding boots while you're changing and saddling up."

When she neared the barn a few minutes later, she had to hide a smile. There was no way that Dell would let Maureen saddle her own horse. He spoiled the girl almost as much as Jessica did. Both Tiger and Leader, fully saddled and bridled, waited by the gate, the jingle of bits revealing their impatience to be off and running.

She glanced at the man talking to Maureen, realizing that it wasn't Dell. He was taller, leaner—different. Probably the new hand Dell had mentioned hiring. Jessica hadn't met him yet.

Was it just her recent discussion about the lack of men in her life that made the stranger appear so virile? Suddenly every nerve was on the alert.

Surprised at her reaction, she surveyed him carefully. Probably in his early thirties. His broad-brimmed hat was pushed back on his head, revealing a shock of blond hair and strong, even features. Low-slung jeans fit tightly around his narrow hips, she noticed, and his shirt sleeves were rolled high on his arms, revealing tanned, muscular flesh. Primal masculinity radiated from him. It made her slightly uneasy.

He stepped toward her and took off his hat with a sweeping gesture. Had he sensed her reaction? Did she imagine a bit of mockery in his deep blue eyes?

"Brad Costain, ma'am. Your foreman told me to get these horses saddled up for you ladies."

"Thank you," she replied, continuing her close examination. She had long ago learned to rely on Dell, her foreman ever since she had fired Hoskins. Had he made a mistake this time? There was something about Brad Costain—something untamed, dangerous, even—that stirred her anxiety.

He moved with the grace of a wild animal, and he was probably just as unpredictable. She had seen his type before—a restless drifter, always searching. He would probably stay for one paycheck and be on his way. She was suddenly aware that her mouth was dry and her chest felt tight. She gave herself a mental shake. She realized why she had thought him dangerous. He was incredibly sexy.

She couldn't possibly be thinking what she was thinking—that it would be exciting to see just how sexy he was. She was being ridiculous. He wasn't a youngster, but he was much too young for her.

But was she too old for him? She must have imagined that his hand lingered on her leg as he gave her a quick boost into the saddle. Forget it, she told herself. You're becoming a silly old woman.

It was easy enough to forget; it had been just a momentary flash of sexual speculation. Thoughts of Brad Costain faded as, side by side, she and Maureen rode over the ranch meadows and then started up the steeper terrain toward the forest.

Jessica soaked in the sights and sounds of the summer

day. The smell of crushed clover and bluegrass gave way to the brisk fragrance of pine as they climbed higher. She flinched slightly at the scream of a hawk that wheeled high in the azure sky, then dived on some unsuspecting victim. The squeak of the leather saddles, the jingle of bridles, the rhythm of the horse's gait, nearly mesmerized her. She took a deep breath and tilted her head back to let the breeze play over her face.

Although she and Maureen exchanged occasional comments, her mind drifted to a familiar subject. How much did her granddaughter suspect or know about her background? The concern was always present, never acknowledged. Jessica, having decided years ago to wait until Maureen sought information, still hadn't discussed much about her birth with her. And the longer she waited, the harder it became to bring it up. How could she explain her long silence? Maureen didn't ask, and that in itself was strange. Had she heard gossip and come to her own conclusions?

It didn't seem too likely to Jessica. Her own story was known to the older residents of the county, but it was old news now, its potential for spicy gossip gone. It would take a malicious person to seek out Maureen specifically to tell her that Jessica had long ago had a child out of wedlock. As for Justin being the girl's father, Jessica didn't think anyone but Doc Alberson actually knew that, although there might well have been speculation. But even that was long ago.

Tears welled in her eyes at the thought of Justin.

"Is something wrong, Lady Jess?"

She blinked and smiled tenderly at Maureen. "Not really. Sometimes I think of Justin and . . ."

Maureen's eyes clouded with sympathy, and she leaned over to pat Jessica's hand. Then, as if to cheer her, she shouted, "Race you to the top of the hill!"

Jessica spurred Leader into a fast gallop. Maureen's instinct had been right—she needed movement. The wind whipped through her hair, and she exulted in the speed. Whatever her problems were, she always felt better with a strong horse under her and the ground skimming by.

Maureen, slightly ahead, reined at the top of the hill. Both she and Tiger were panting from the exertion. The girl's cheek were red, and her eyes sparkled with excitement.

A warm glow spread through Jessica, a feeling of pride and affection, as she looked first at Maureen, then at the Carter ranch spread below them. Her granddaughter loved it as much as she did. As long as she had the ranch and Maureen's love, she had everything she needed.

She ignored the cold little prickle of fear, the thought that both could be in jeopardy. In both cases Mark was the danger. One misstep, one disastrous year, and the ranch might fall to his brand of progress. True, she was wealthy, but her wealth was tied up in land. She needed a considerable cash flow. So far she had always had it, had averted trouble, but the price of cattle could plummet at any time.

And if Maureen ever found out that Jessica had kept the truth from her for all these years—especially that a man as powerful and wealthy as Mark was her grandfather—would she feel she had been betrayed?

It must have been near midnight when Jessica gave up any hope of sleeping. She slipped from her bed and padded softly to the open window. Why had Maureen had to bring up her need for physical love? Or, rather, why had she been so unusually susceptible to the suggestion? She had managed very well over the years, having discovered that when her body became too demanding, she could assuage the desire by becoming involved in other things. The thought of an affair had always been abhorrent to her. She told herself she needed love, commitment, before she became physically intimate.

Over the years there had been men who offered both,

but she had always been wary. Men were betrayers, leaving when you needed them most. Besides, she never expected to reach the heights she had reached with Mark, nor achieve the gentle satisfaction she had known with Clinton.

She pushed aside the gauzy curtain and peered out into the darkness. She could almost feel the land breathing. There was no moon, but a few stars relieved the blackness. A soft breeze wafted through the open window, bringing the scent of moist earth and roses from her garden below. She was assailed by a sudden, poignant yearning. Throwing back her head, she closed her eyes and raised her hands to her breasts, feeling their smoothness, their heaviness, running her fingers over the tautness of her nipples.

She swallowed painfully. Damn these feelings. Time took so much—why couldn't it have taken this aching need also?

Suddenly her eyes narrowed, focused. Down by the corral a light glowed faintly. She held her breath as she made out a shadowy form. Someone was standing there, looking up at the house, a cigarette in his hand.

She knew it was too far for him to hear her harsh intake of breath, but she made herself breathe shallowly. The light made a tiny arc as it was flung to the ground, then vanished as it was apparently ground into the dust by the heel of a western boot. After a couple of seconds a match flared, revealing the strong features of a man as he tilted his head to draw on another cigarette. The illumination didn't last long, but she knew immediately who stood there. Brad Costain. She had known it even before he struck the match.

As though he sensed her presence, he raised his head and looked directly at the window. It jolted her. She felt a connection between them, an invisible rope of desire. Could he see her outlined in the window, or did he merely feel her unwavering regard?

She let the curtain fall and stepped back hastily. She was trembling. What was happening to her? For years she had curbed every sexual impulse, every errant desire, and now she was panting like an animal in heat. It was the discussion with Maureen that had opened this abyss. She had managed for years to keep the lid on her emotions, but the girl had started her thinking again. Thinking of Mark. Thinking of Clinton. Thinking of passion.

Well, thinking never hurt anybody. She'd sensed the moment she saw him that Brad was a sexy devil, but she was a mature woman and no longer prone to roller-coaster emotions, impulsive actions. During the past few years she had left more and more of the day-to-day operation of the ranch to Dell, and there was no reason she even had to see Brad Costain again. No reason at all.

She turned back to her bed and slipped under the cool sheets. The man was a drifter anyway. He might even be gone by morning.

He wasn't. The sun had already topped the eastern peaks and was flooding into her room when Jessica awoke from a drugged sleep. She slipped out of bed and padded across the floor to the window to look out over the ranch. It was a ritual with her—this early-morning assessment of the coming day.

The breeze through the open window lifted the curtain gently, and she stood back a little, gazing out over the yard and corrals. She saw him instantly; he was in the corral. He had a rope on a horse and was coaxing it around and around the enclosure. His hat was pushed back on his head, and the sun glinted on his bare, bronzed arms. Through the light chambray shirt she could see the muscles of his broad back contract as he put the horse through its paces. Two magnificent animals, she thought.

Her head was much clearer this morning. The sharp yearning that had assaulted her last night had subsided, although she still was aware of a vague ache in her body. It was a reasonable reaction, she told herself. It had been quite a while since a man had held her in his arms. She had managed to push her natural need for physical affection to the back of her mind, but Maureen's remarks had forced the longing out of hiding. And if she could judge at all by appearances, Brad Costain was a walking pleasure machine!

Suddenly, as though aware he was being observed, he turned and looked directly toward the window. Startled, she stared back. She wondered if she could be seen, but she didn't dare retreat lest the movement call attention to her presence. Even from this distance she saw a slow grin break over his face. He raised his hand and gave her a mock salute, then turned back to the horse.

Shaken, and angry with herself for the reaction, she dressed quickly and ran downstairs to breakfast. Since Karla was no longer there, the meal now consisted of cold cereal, toast, and cups of black coffee, but she still enjoyed starting the day with Maureen sitting across from her. The girl's vivacity was sure to assuage her ridiculous restlessness, her urge to look out every window to see if Brad was nearby.

Maureen was there ahead of her. She looked up from her bowl of cereal and waved a spoon. "Morning, sleepyhead." Her magnificent eyes narrowed. "You look a little bedraggled. Did you sleep all right?"

"Not bad." Jessica filled a cup with hot, steaming coffee and sank down in a chair across from Maureen. "What do you have planned for today?" Since the school term was over, Maureen was managing to fill her time with tennis, friends, running, and riding horses. Today, though, Jessica would welcome the girl's company.

"A bunch of us are going over to Sharon's place," Maureen replied. "She's got a new Beatles record I'm dying to hear."

Jessica smiled. "That shouldn't take all day. I was wondering if you might like to drive into Boise and shop a bit."

Shopping was one activity that usually diverted Maureen from any other plans.

But now she frowned. "Gee, Lady Jess, I'd like to. But could we make it another day? I was just about to tell you—Sharon's brother is coming home from college today. You know Andy. He's been writing to Sharon about the Vietnam war and how terrible it is. He was even in Washington, D.C., when they had that peace march a few months ago at the Lincoln Memorial. Sharon's awfully scared—she doesn't know when he'll have to go."

Sharon was Maureen's best friend, and her brother was a hero to both girls. Jessica and shopping were obviously outclassed. "They won't draft him while he's in college," Jessica assured her. "So, what will you three do with your afternoon?"

"Well, there's a march today. . . ."

Maureen glanced away, and Jessica was immediately alert. It wasn't that she disapproved of the growing peace movement; she was simply concerned for Maureen's safety. Peace marches were occasionally anything but peaceful, and Jessica also suspected that the FBI was there, taking names. She hated the idea of a government dossier on Maureen.

"A lot of the kids are going to Boise with him. . . ."

"And you plan to go, too. You know I'd rather you didn't. Be very, very careful, Maureen."

Maureen raised her clear brown eyes to Jessica's. So like Mark, Jessica thought—the young, idealistic Mark whose memory still struck in the dark of the night. "Someone has to go," the girl said.

The war was like a dark, malevolent cloud over the country. Even in Boise protests were becoming larger and more frequent. Jessica sighed. Had she really been naive enough to believe that World War II—the War, as she and her friends had called it—would actually end all wars, that the United Nations would provide peaceful solutions to international conflicts of interest? Korea should have taught them something. And now this horror, tearing everything apart, pitting citizen against government, parent against child, friend against friend.

She rose and dropped a soft kiss on the girl's hair. "Don't be too late."

After Maureen had gone, she wandered about the house, restless, unable to settle down to anything. Why had this unwelcome need struck just now? Doubtless it had been simmering a long time, and Brad was merely the catalyst. But what was there about Brad Costain that triggered her dormant desires? She had seen handsome men before, and she'd never felt an urge like this.

Her mouth curved in a dry smile. Despite what she'd told Maureen it probably *was* something in the air. The new permissiveness of the sixties. All the old taboos were falling by the wayside. Lord, if she had become pregnant in a moral climate such as this, how different her life might have been! She had even heard of "commune" living, where no one married and paternity of the children was moot—even to the mother!

If she wanted a man now, she supposed there was nothing shameful about taking him. She was independent, her own woman. She should be able to take pleasure where she found it—as men had always done.

There was a sharp knock on the kitchen door, and she turned toward it. Brad Costain stood on the step. Her heart did a quick flip-flop. Think of the devil . . .

He looked somewhat diffident, rolling the brim of his hat in both bronzed hands, a boyish smile on his lean face. His pose might even have fooled her, if it hadn't been for his eyes. There was nothing boyish about the look in his eyes. It sent hot blood up her throat, suffusing her cheeks with color.

"Yes?"

"I didn't mean to disturb you, ma'am. I just wondered if you'd like to ride today. It's so beautiful out. I could have Leader saddled in a minute."

She walked toward the door and gazed at him through

the screen. His eyes were bold, bold and sure, even though his tone was completely respectful.

"I hadn't thought of it. I don't generally ride alone. And Maureen's gone for the day."

"I know. I saw her drive off."

Her gaze sharpened. So he was sure enough of himself to come right to the door. Then again, why shouldn't he be confident? He must be used to his effect on women.

"It really isn't a good idea to ride alone, anyway," he said softly. "If you like, I could go with you. Just to be sure you're safe."

She hesitated. What did she really know about this man? Dell had hired him, and Dell usually checked his people well, so Brad Costain wasn't likely to be an ax murderer. No, his only danger to her was one that she might welcome.

"All right." Her voice sounded much calmer than she felt. "I'll be out in a few minutes."

If she had expected Brad to make a crude pass at her, she was mistaken. They rode side by side, speaking only occasionally. But the silence, she thought, was more eloquent than words would have been. She was strung as taut as a lasso around the neck of a bucking steer. She was aware of his every movement, his jeans tight and straining across his muscular thighs, his well-shaped brown hands lightly holding the reins, his bronzed forearms bare beneath his rolled-up shirt sleeves. When he glanced at her, his smoky blue eyes were admiring, heated.

When they returned to the corral, he moved to help her from the horse, his hands spanning her waist, his touch burning through her light shirt as she slid through his grasp to put both feet on the ground.

Breathless, she turned away to hide the flare of passion in her eyes. When she looked at him again, he was a decorous foot or so away.

"I'll just unsaddle now."

"Yes." She watched him lead the horses away, knowing

they had arrived at some understanding, one that didn't need words. He was here, he was virile, he was available. What did she want to do about it?

Retreating to her bedroom, she paused in front of the mirror and took a long look. What did he see in her? She was attractive, but she wasn't a young girl. Was he interested in the fact that she was wealthy, powerful? Did he see her as soft and ripe and ready for picking? Or had the same impersonal, inexplicable force that had seized her captured him also?

And what did she see in him? She wasn't particularly interested in him as a person; she hadn't the slightest idea whether he was even educated, intelligent. He simply radiated a force that made her want to get up close and warm her hands. For years she had been freezing.

The phone rang, and she picked it up, her mind still on Brad. She greeted Lydia and listened absently before her friend finally caught her attention.

"I said, what are you doing today?" Lydia sounded faintly exasperated. "Do you want to have lunch?"

It seemed a good idea to get her mind off her dilemma. She agreed to meet the woman at an unpretentious little restaurant in Hope. A huge hamburger, french fries, and a hefty portion of Lydia's usual bounty of gossip ought to do the trick.

Today, though, Lydia was interested in picking up a few morsels herself. She settled cozily into the booth, took a bit of hamburger, then zeroed right in. "I understand you hired Brad Costain."

"Do you know him?"

"I've heard of him. And I've seen him." A conspiratorial smile dimpled her round cheeks. "He's too sexy to live. Better watch yourself, Jessica."

"He's young enough to be my son!" she protested weakly.

"Well, you can't hold that against him."

Jessica gazed thoughtfully at Lydia's cheerful face.

They had all changed so much. Could this be the same Lydia Adams who would have refused her a place to live when she was pregnant with Justin? She had long since forgiven Lydia; rather, she realized there was nothing to forgive. Lydia had reacted as every person of "good" morals had at the time. It was she who had been the transgressor. But had they all changed so much that she could casually take Brad Costain as a lover?

Lydia waited, eyes alight, but when confidences were not forthcoming, she changed the subject.

"Guess what I read the other day."

"You've been at those tabloids again, haven't you. And you're going to tell me, aren't you, no matter what I guess?" Jessica teased.

"There was a big article about Mark."

Jessica smiled. Hearing his name no longer sent unbearable spasms of pain and desire through her. She had read several years ago that he was divorced, and at the time she had toyed with the idea of getting in touch with him. After all, passions had cooled, and she had been Clinton's widow almost as long as she had been his wife. Perhaps a card or a letter from an old friend . . .

Then she had wondered if Mark would try to contact her. When he didn't, she realized that he, too, must feel that the past was best left to the past. She supposed she wouldn't even know him anymore. The young, idealistic man she had loved was long gone, replaced by the hard, driving captain of industry she so often read about. Someone she no longer wanted to know.

"What company has he gobbled up this time?"

"Oh, Jessica, that wasn't it at all. It seems he was on this Greek island with a Hollywood starlet, and some photographer got too close, and—"

"And Mark decked him?"

"Yes! But there was a great picture of him, anyway," she enthused.

"He seems right at home with the jet set."

"I guess so. Etta Jensen said she heard he's coming back to Boise for a few days."

"Not to Hope?" It was true. Her heart didn't even skip a beat as she thought of Mark's possible visit.

"She didn't think so. You know, he's always kept that old house, and she's lived and worked in it so long, she thinks it's hers! But she said he didn't send word that he wanted it put in shape, so I guess he won't be here."

"Why Boise now?"

"Jake thinks it's because of the elections. There's talk again of his running for governor, and he would want to be here awhile before the elections, I suppose."

"Yes, it probably would be hard to run Idaho from the French Riviera," Jessica said dryly.

"Now, be fair, Jess. He's not there that much—just vacations. He spends a lot of time in the state."

"I guess he does." She picked up a french fry, dipped it in ketchup, and popped it into her mouth.

Sometimes she wished he would spend less. That way maybe she could eliminate once and for all the residual fear that one day Maureen would find out Mark Hardy was her grandfather and blame Jessica for not telling her about her heritage. The girl never displayed any curiosity in the matter—perhaps she sensed Jessica's reluctance to talk about it—so the fear was faint. But because of history, because of Justin, the fear was real: that Mark would somehow take Maureen's affections from her.

As Jessica slid from the saddle Brad Costain caught her in his arms. They had been riding daily for the past three weeks, and for the first time he didn't immediately let her go and step away. Instead he pressed her hard against his lean body.

Startled, but as fascinated as a bird by a snake, she stared up into his face. He leaned over her, and his mouth found hers. Even in her confusion she recognized the hard, searing kiss for what it was—a declaration of sexual intent.

She had been waiting for something like this for weeks, unsure how she would react. Love wasn't part of the equation; all she felt was physical desire, a fierce voracity that urged her to match the demand in his kiss.

The knowledge placed her on the razor edge of decision. Her sensual nature had been quiescent so long. With Mark she had known blazing, incendiary passion. With Clinton she had found a slower-burning satisfaction. Now, in the autumn of her life, the fire still smoldered. Was she meant to simply smother it entirely? Or was this her last chance to fan the glorious flames, build a fire that would blaze until it burned itself out. Leaving what? Regrets? Emptiness? Did it matter? She moved back a fraction of an inch and met his eyes.

Then she took his hand and led him toward the house.

Jessica stretched lazily, glancing at the pillow that still held the imprint of Brad's head, and smiled to herself. It had been a beautiful, dizzying night. They had drunk of each other as though they could never get enough. And then, sated, they had both known it was over. The fire that had raged so inexplicably was now reduced to harmless ashes.

She had tousled his hair gently. He was a dear boy, and she would cherish the moments they had had.

He had rolled over onto his elbows and looked into her face. "I guess I'd better go."

"Yes, I suppose so. It's nearly dawn."

"I mean," he had said, uncomfortable, "really go. I've been thinking of getting over into Oregon before winter comes. . . ."

"You don't have to leave."

"I think I'd better. Not that it wasn't—that you weren't—it's just that . . ."

"I think that's a good idea," she had said gently. "I'll

always remember you, Brad." And she *would* remember the way he had made her body sing.

"Yeah . . ." He had glanced away, embarrassed with words, and she had simply smiled. Whatever had been between them had little to do with words.

Perhaps her ravening hunger for him had been a belated surge of the life force within her.

After he had crept out of the house, she had turned over and snuggled down into her pillow, feeling warm and serene. She could accept it now, without sorrow: that part of her life was over. She would concentrate on Maureen, on her community activities, and on overseeing the Carter enterprises. And she would slip gently, uneventfully into her winter years.

She turned uneasily, vaguely aware of something familiar in that smooth, tranquil assessment. Hadn't she thought once before that life held no more surprises?

WINTER

18

Brad had been gone a few days, and Jessica was finally getting her hormones under control again. An obsession took a lot out of one, she thought wryly, and a recovery period was required.

When she saw the rider half a mile away, she thought at first it might be Brad, and her fingers tightened around Leader's reins. Their union had been so perfectly timed, complete with a prompt and amicable parting, she hoped he hadn't returned to rehash it. As the rider neared, though, she saw how wrong that impression had been. This person was not over twenty, with a sparse beard, long hair, and scruffy jeans. It looked as if it had been a while since he'd had enough to eat, too.

Leader danced impatiently as she waited near the corrals and watched the boy ride toward her over the uneven terrain. It wasn't often that anyone trespassed on Carter land.

When he was closer, she decided that at least there was nothing threatening about him. His horse looked more prepossessing than he did. He rode up and surveyed her with anxious eyes.

"Mrs. Carter? Jessica Carter?"

"That's me."

"I was just riding up to the house to see you. Lucky I ran into you here."

Lucky for who? she wondered. "What did you want to see me about?" She didn't recognize him, but that didn't mean much. These days there were a lot of young people wandering the county, sleeping in the woods, eating where they could. They called it freedom; she'd always called it poverty. This one looked skinny enough to blow away. Perhaps all he wanted was a handout.

"I got a message for you from Jeb Hardy," he said.

Her eyes widened with surprise. What did Jeb Hardy want of her? She hadn't heard of the man for years, not since Leah had died. Although she supposed he must have surfaced occasionally for supplies, she had never seen him. For all she'd known he might even have been dead—although probably she would have heard about that through the grapevine.

"A message from Jeb?" she echoed. "Who are you?" She gave the young man a stern look, uncertain of his veracity.

He shrugged. "My name's Ben Dale. But that don't matter. I was just passing through the county and stopped in at Jeb's for a couple of days. He gave me this horse if I'd come and get you."

She glanced at the animal, a sleek, shiny roan gelding. That accounted for its looking better than its rider. Jeb had always treated his horses well. It was hard to believe he would just give it away in return for the delivery of a message, but something in the boy's tone made her think he was telling the truth. Her eyes narrowed. "Why didn't he come himself? Or call?"

"I didn't steal it, if that's what you're thinking." Anger flashed in the pale eyes. "I wasn't at his place long, but I sure didn't see no telephone. And I reckon he couldn't come himself—he's feeling poorly."

"What does he want?"

"He didn't say. All I had to do was tell you to come."
He reined his horse and trotted off, leaving Jessica to stare
thoughtfully after him.

She took a deep, uneven breath. Even though it had
been years since she had seen Jeb, he still had the power to
upset her. Anger bubbled up inside her at the insolence of
his message. The old man hadn't changed; he was as arrogant and autocratic as ever. He thought all he had to do
was summon her, and she would come running. After all
he'd done—to her, to Leah, to the rest of his family. As far
as she was concerned, he could wait until hell froze over.

He must really want to see her badly. It was no surprise
that he was still without a phone; Jeb had never had any
use for modern technology. She knew he couldn't read or
write, so he would have been unable to reach her by letter. Still, how alone he must be if the only way he could
get a message to her was to pay a wandering hippie with
one of his horses. If it had been anyone else, she would
have felt sorry for him.

But Jebediah Hardy? He had made life hell for her
during the two years she had lived there. A tyrant. True,
he had had even less money than most during the Depression, but that shouldn't have precluded simple human
kindness. Pressing her lips together, she wheeled her
horse. Somehow she didn't feel like going on with her
ride.

What had Leah seen in Jeb? Was it merely habit that
had bound her to him? Mark had given her the opportunity to leave, and she had refused. Had she stayed all that
time purely from a sense of duty, or had she sensed a kernel of something in him that was invisible to everyone
else? He was a hard, cruel man.

But he did have his own warped sense of ethics. Her
mind flashed back to her first sight of him sitting astride his
horse in the Blalocks' yard. She'd almost thought him a sav-
ior. A man of granite, an unyielding boulder of a man come

to do what his rigid pride told him he had to do. *Hardys take care of their own.* She could almost hear his voice.

She had to give him that. When she had had nowhere else to turn, he had come for her. There had been times when she'd almost wished he hadn't, but because of him she had had food, shelter, a place to give birth to Justin.

She supposed it wouldn't hurt just to drive out and see what he wanted.

It was late afternoon by the time she finished a few chores and hopped into her pickup to drive to the Hardy cabin. The sun was peeking through the trees, throwing long shadows on the road, and bugs were beginning to dive-bomb her windshield. It was a much shorter trip than she remembered. The road was paved now, and she was in an automobile. The last time she'd made the trip she had been bouncing along in a wagon.

She almost missed the dirt trail just wide enough for her vehicle that led from the pavement into a grove of trees. Turning abruptly, she maneuvered the trail to the ramshackle bridge crossing the same creek Jeb had forded with his horse when she had her first sight of the place. She drove over it, holding her breath as the boards bowed under the weight of her pickup, and got her first look in years at the rustic homestead that had once dominated her life.

From its appearance the clearing might have been deep in the wilderness instead of a few hundred yards from a paved road. It was still hemmed in by a stand of old-growth trees that gave it a feeling of eerie isolation. She knew the area was surrounded by housing developments, but if she hadn't known, she never would have guessed.

The cabin hadn't changed much, either, although she'd heard that Mark had put on a new roof and a porch while his mother was alive. The structure was a little more weathered, there was more trash in the yard than there had been when Leah was alive, but it was still the same old shack. She pulled up in the yard and jumped from the pickup, trying to ignore the uneasy feeling that she was literally stepping back into her past.

In one way she and Jeb were alike, she thought, an ironic smile curving her lips. Neither believed in the blind beneficence of progress. He had kept his homesite immune from it, as she had her ranch, each an oasis in a desert of impersonal change.

Why wasn't Jeb out here to meet her if he was so anxious to see her? He must have heard the truck pull up. Gingerly she picked her way along the familiar path, still strewn with pine needles that crackled under her feet, and stepped up onto the rickety porch.

"Jeb?" She knocked smartly on the door, then more gently as it trembled under her assault. She didn't want to knock it down.

A faint voice answered, and she pushed open the door, wincing at the creak of rusty hinges as she stepped into the room.

"Jeb?" A wave of nausea hit her as she inhaled the stale air, the rancid cooking odors. It was dark, too, the grimy windows letting in a light so dim she could barely make out the form lying on a cot by the wall. She strode to a window and opened it wide, took a deep breath to steady herself, then walked over to the cot.

She hardly recognized the emaciated man as Jeb Hardy. He must be nearly ninety, of course, but that didn't entirely account for the haggard appearance of his once hawklike features. Under the blankets she made out the outline of a gaunt frame, and the hand he lifted briefly looked almost skeletal.

"Jessica. Come closer."

His voice retained its commanding authority, she thought as she reluctantly approached his bed. "Jeb, how are you?" Her voice quavered.

He snorted. "How do I look? I'm dyin', girl. Don't ask fool questions."

"But what's wrong? Have you seen a doctor?"

He ignored the question. "There's something I want you to do."

In spite of his brusque tone there was a flicker of pleading in his eyes. The Jeb Hardy she had known had been a proud man, a man who would die before he asked anyone a favor. True, he hadn't couched his request in the form of a favor—it was more a command—but he was begging just the same.

"You need a doctor."

He made a dismissive noise. "Doctors! Only one I trust is Doc Alberson, and he's put himself out to pasture. The rest of 'em don't know anything."

"I'll get someone to come in," she said quickly. "Someone to take care of you. A nurse. You need help. You can't stay here alone like this."

He raised his hand imperiously. "Didn't you hear me? Ears clogged up? I'm dyin'. And I don't want no mealy-mouthed woman doggin' my last days." He was silent so long that Jessica nearly prompted him. Then, in a voice she had to bend to hear, he whispered, "I want my son."

"Your son! Mark?"

"They all left me, every one of 'em," he said bitterly. "Maybe I wasn't always right. I know Mark always blamed me about his mother. But I done the best I could."

Jessica almost protested, but she closed her mouth. In his lights, perhaps he had.

"Where's Alice? Maybe she could help." And maybe she couldn't, she thought, remembering the blue marks that had sometimes appeared on the girl's white skin.

"I want Mark," he said stubbornly. "My firstborn. The only whelp with guts I had. It ain't right to die with bad blood between a man and his boy," Jeb continued, his voice becoming weaker. "I want you to go get Mark for me. Bring him here. I want to make my peace with him."

"Me! I can't do that. I haven't seen him for years, and I don't even know for sure where he is."

His bony hand snaked out and caught her wrist in a surprisingly strong grip. "Bring him here."

"I'll write a letter for you," she offered, moved in spite of herself by the desperation in the old man's eyes.

"He won't come on account of no letter. Last time I saw Mark he told me he hoped I rotted in hell—and I told him the same thing." She couldn't believe the chuckle that issued from the old man's throat. "Only way to get him here is to persuade him. Only person that can do that is you."

"Not me." Gently she tugged her wrist loose from his grasp. "I haven't even talked to him in years. And the last time I did we had a fight. Why on earth do you think he would listen to me?"

Jeb turned his head toward her and met her eyes. He didn't say a word, but she understood the eloquent message.

"Some things don't change," he finally said.

She tore her gaze away and looked around the tiny room. Mark had been born here, had lived here until he was a young man. For better or for worse Jeb had played a large part in forming his character. He had helped make Mark what he was. And, she thought, sinking down into a chair beside the bed and lowering her head into her hands, the old man was right. Some things don't change. She still loved him.

The enormity of the realization hit her like a slap in the face. For how many years had she deluded herself into believing that what she felt for Mark was over, burned out? That fierce affinity for him hadn't cooled; it had merely gone underground, where it had simmered like molten lava, ready to erupt at any moment. Here in this shack where she had waited for him to come back to her, here where she had borne his son, here where she had finally despaired and given up, she couldn't hide from the truth. She loved Mark Hardy. Still. Always.

The room seemed to swim around her. It was too late. Fate had taken away her last chance for happiness with him. But she owed it to the old man in the bed to find Mark for him. And she owed it to Mark. She knew how bitter he was. Still, if he could reconcile with his father before he died, it might save him even more bitter self-recrimination in the future.

She reached over to squeeze the bony hand that now lay on the blanket like a broken bird. "All right. I don't know exactly how I'll find him, or what I can say to convince him. But I'll find him. And I'll try."

She had to bend down to hear the faint whisper. "Hurry."

Jessica sat in the reception area of Hardy Enterprises and tried not to feel intimidated by the luxurious surroundings. She was no stranger to wealth, but for the first time she realized how simple her way of life was compared with that of the truly rich. She and Maureen enjoyed a good, comfortable living, but essentially little had changed since she married Clinton. She often shopped from the catalog, and a high-fashion show she saw once on television sent her into gales of laughter.

She raised her chin, refusing to feel inferior. After all, it required only money and a hired decorator to come up with the pale green walls splashed by expensive oil paintings, the couches of soft off-white leather, the lush sea-green carpeting so thick that she wondered if she would sink in it up to her knees. And money alone did not confer superiority.

She glanced at the receptionist, an ice-cold blonde with perfect features who wore an emerald silk dress by Christian Dior, and then down at her slender hands placed casually in her lap. When she had dressed this morning, she'd thought she looked fine. Her tailored pants were of soft, fine wool in a color that matched her hair. Even Maureen admitted she still had the figure for them. Her shirt was a delicate blue silk the color of her eyes. It peeped through the raw silk jacket that she thought gave her a casually elegant look. She'd pulled her hair back smoothly and tied it with a vibrant blue scarf, and she had even donned a pair of gold hoop earrings. Now, looking at Mark's receptionist, she suddenly felt like the Little Match Girl.

The receptionist had sent her name on to the secretary, and as she waited for a summons she thought back over the last two days. Everything had gone so fast. Mark had been unexpectedly easy to locate. She'd gone to see Cullen MacDougal, who told her the date Mark was arriving from Europe. All she had to do was come to Boise that day and sit in his office until he showed up.

She'd considered making an appointment but decided against it. Mark might refuse to see her if he had time to think about it. At the very least he would be well prepared, all his defenses in perfect order. She had a feeling that she would need every advantage if she was going to be able to convince him to see his father.

Doubt assailed her again. Was it even any of her business? Then Jeb's pleading eyes flashed before her, she heard his whispered "Hurry," and she tightened her lips with determination.

She raised her head as a door opened and a woman stepped into the room. "Mrs. Carter?"

Jessica rose, surveying the woman as she did so. Not as spectacular as the receptionist, but she had an air of competent authority that served her just as well. She wore a navy-blue suit and dark pumps, and her gray hair was cut short, giving her a sleek, efficient appearance.

"I'm Jessica Carter."

"I'm Mrs. Hazelton, Mr. Hardy's personal secretary." The woman gave her a keen look. "He asked me to bring you right in." Without waiting for Jessica's reply, she turned and led the way down a hall bordered on both sides by offices. All filled with people working for Mark, Jessica knew. In fact, the six-story structure housed nothing but various Hardy enterprises.

"Go right on in." Mrs. Hazelton opened a door and motioned her inside.

Jessica was aware of the soft click of the door closing behind her, of the faint tick of a clock from somewhere in the huge room. Her throat felt tight, her mouth dry. For an endless moment she stood there, her eyes riveted to the man behind the mammoth desk. His back was to a floor-to-ceiling bank of windows, so his face was partially in shadow. The chiaroscuro accentuated the harsh features, the hawklike nose, the deep lines around a firm mouth. He had changed so much, she thought, sudden tenderness welling up inside her as she remembered the vulnerable young man he had once been. There was nothing vulnerable about the mature Mark Hardy. His dark hair was liberally streaked with white, adding to his aura of authority, and his face appeared to have been blasted clear of any emotion, leaving only a cool, expressionless mask.

He rose and came around the desk, his iron features breaking into a polite smile, and extended his hand. "Jessica. This *is* a surprise. When Mrs. Hazelton said you were here, I thought she must be mistaken. What can I do for you?"

His voice was as devoid of warmth as his expression, and Jessica cringed. She had allowed herself to hope that after all this time they might meet as friends. Or even enemies. But they were meeting as strangers. She sighed inwardly. That, of course, was what they were now.

He motioned her toward a chair, and when she had sunk down into its soft cushions, he seated himself across from her, crossing his long legs and leaning back. The chrome-and-glass table between them might as well have been the earth, she thought. Had she really fantasized that they might rekindle something? It was patently ridiculous, and she nearly blushed at the memory.

"You're looking well," he said, his expression softening slightly. "How are things in Hope?"

"That's what I wanted to talk to you about."

His mouth curved in a sardonic grin. "No 'How are you, Mark, how's it going'?"

"There's something I have to tell you."

She saw one heavy eyebrow arch slightly, and she plunged right in before she lost her nerve. She had gone over this conversation many times in her mind—how she would lead up to it, how she would prepare him—but now that she was here, she found herself stating it baldly. "Jeb wants to see you."

His expression didn't change. He merely stared at her as though she had commented on the weather.

"He's very sick," she hurried on. "He wants to see you before he dies."

"That bad?" His expression showed how little he cared. "What's wrong with him—besides meanness and old age?"

"I don't know, but he can't last long. He wanted you to hurry."

"You're wasting your time, Jessica," he said coldly. "I don't know how Jeb got you to do this—as I recall, you and he weren't exactly buddies—but as far as I'm concerned, I don't have a father."

"He's an old man. Surely you can make allowances now—"

"Is that all it takes to erase unforgivable behavior? Age? The passing of time?" He jerked himself up from the chair and strode to the window, turning his back to Jessica as he gazed out over the mist that blanketed the city.

He spoke so quietly that she had to strain to catch the words. "I used to think of him as an ogre, you know. We were all afraid of him. All the rest of them managed to get away—just drifted off to live like he did, I suppose. For the longest time I couldn't leave. I couldn't run out on Mom. Then, finally, I saw I had no choice. For her, for myself, I had to get away and make something of myself so I could take care of her." He was silent for a moment.

"But, of course, you know all that." The bitterness in his voice intensified. "And then, when I could have taken care of her, gotten her away from all that misery, she wouldn't go. She might be alive now if she had come with me. That bastard as good as killed her."

Impulsively Jessica jumped up from the chair and moved to stand beside him, placing her hand on his sleeve. "You don't mean that, Mark."

He turned toward her, and for a moment she saw such stark pain in his eyes that she shrank back. Then it was gone, and his expression was mocking. "Well, I'm willing to concede that he didn't shoot her, if that's what you mean."

"Mark, I think he's changed. I think he's sorry that—"

Mark threw back his head and laughed, a laugh with absolutely no humor at all. "Sorry? You mean he's having one of those deathbed conversions? I really don't believe in those, Jessica. And even if it's true, what's it to me? So he's scared of death. He damn well should be."

Jessica was silent. Mark's hatred of his father was too deeply ingrained—and too justified, she admitted—to yield to a few moments' pleading by her. She had suspected that her efforts would be fruitless, but she had had to try.

Mark looked down into her face. "Why did you come, Jessica? Surely you remember how I felt about him. I haven't seen him or spoken to him since Mom's funeral, and that's the way I plan on keeping it."

"I suppose I knew that," she said slowly. "But when I actually saw him lying there in bed, helpless, wanting only to see his son before he died, I had to try. But not just for him. For you."

"For me?" A dark eyebrow shot up in obvious disbelief.

"Mark, bitterness eats away at the soul. Soon Jeb will be dead. If you should ever change your mind"—she ignored his snort of disbelief—"it will be forever too late. Isn't it better to make your peace now than to chance regrets later?"

"My life is full of regrets," he said lightly. "Why worry about one more?"

"You admit then there's a possibility—"

"Not at all. I will never understand why Mom didn't leave when she had the chance."

"But she didn't leave! Something must have held her with him. Something more than fear."

He sighed. "Possibly. Who can understand women? I know there were times when I wanted to kill him, especially when he did everything he could to keep me tied there. She tried to justify his behavior, make excuses for him. She said it was his code. A man's family stayed with him. I know it was a blow to him when I left."

"If you won't see him for his sake, or your sake, why not see him for Leah's sake," she said softly. "I know she would have wanted that. She used to dream of the time you'd come back. She never doubted you would."

He turned toward her, a sardonic expression on his face, but his voice was softer. "So you know what Leah would have wanted, do you? How perceptive of you."

Despite his sarcasm she saw the chink in his armor. His mother. "You can doubt me if you will, but Leah was a gentle woman. A loving woman. She wouldn't want her son and his father to be enemies to the death."

He half lifted his hand, as though to touch her, then let it fall to his side. "You're also very persuasive. Why do you care?"

Because I can't bear to see that bitterness in your eyes. She couldn't say that, though. She was partially responsible for that bitterness herself. Perhaps, in Mark's eyes, more so than his father.

"I've been thinking about him," she said softly, "ever since I talked to him a couple of days ago. It was a shock to me when I went to live with him and Leah, a hardship, but I can't forget he didn't have to take me in. He did it because he believes in family."

"Yeah, he needs someone around to beat up on," he said dryly.

She sensed capitulation and pressed her advantage.

"He only wants an hour of your time. You could drive up tomorrow and come right back."

He stared silently out the window, then turned again to face her. She thought he looked pale under his tan. "All right. Perhaps you're right, and Mom would have wanted it. I guess I can spare an hour or two. But don't expect a lovefest."

"Thank you, Mark."

"Do you want to stay and have lunch? It's a little early, but—" He glanced at his watch.

"Oh no," she said hastily, backing away. That glance at his watch convinced her: he wanted her out of his office. Simple politeness may have required that he issue the casual invitation, but she knew he would be relieved when she declined. "I have a million things to do before I leave town. And I have to get back to the ranch early."

He smiled thinly. "I know. The clarion call of duty. Well, perhaps I'll see you around, Jessica."

"Yes. Of course." She quickly backed out the door. She glanced up just as it closed in front of her, and she had one last look at his face.

Her head spun crazily, and she felt weak with disappointment. He had actually seemed anxious to get rid of her. Well, what else could she expect? Just because she'd had an attack of nostalgia, had allowed herself to dream that he might be glad to see her, might even want to resume a friendship, didn't mean he would feel the same way. She had spent her life in the tiny backwater of Hope; perhaps she had lost track of the real world.

But he was worldly, sophisticated, a mover and shaker. He had known dozens of beautiful women, and from the things she had read he had known them well! The country boy she had loved, the eager young man with the hunger in his heart and the ambition in his soul, was as far removed from the present man as fire from ice.

The analogy was apt, she thought. The young Mark had been all fire and intensity, passion and need. The man she had just talked to had a casing of ice around his heart.

*   *   *

Mark turned back to the window and waited until he saw Jessica exit the building and walk to her car. An old-model Mercedes. He smiled briefly. It was about what he would expect her to drive.

He sighed, a deep emptiness in his chest, as he watched her pull out into traffic and disappear around the corner. If he hadn't known better, he would have thought he was trembling. He clenched his hand, then held it in front of him, relieved to see that it was steady.

When Mrs. Hazelton had told him who was waiting in his outer office, he couldn't believe it. The few times he had seen Jessica over the last several years, they had met as adversaries over lumbering and whatnot, but he hadn't been able to think of any project he had pending right now that would have raised her hackles.

Perhaps—the thought had sent warmth shooting through his veins—perhaps she just wanted to see him. When he had divorced Amanda years ago, he had wondered if Jessica would get in touch. He had even thought of calling her. Then he remembered how they had parted, and he knew it wasn't a good idea. He wasn't a glutton for punishment.

Her first words had disabused him of any foolish ideas, he thought, his lips twisting in a self-mocking smile. She had come as a do-gooder, in the clutches of what she saw as her duty. Trying to arrange a reconciliation with the old man, for God's sake. Jeb really must have done a number on her.

But, God, she was still so beautiful. Different, of course, from the fresh-faced young woman he had fallen in love with, but her figure was still lithe and slender, her features even more dramatic now that the years had pared them to their essentials. And her eyes. Nothing at all had changed in those vibrant blue eyes.

He'd seen her startled look when he'd impulsively

asked her to lunch. Her reaction had been like a slap in the face. Obviously she couldn't wait to get away from him. He'd considered asking if he could see her, too, when he went up to see Jeb, but now he was glad he hadn't. He didn't think he could take another of her polite refusals without exploding.

He wheeled around and sat back down at his desk. He shouldn't have agreed to see the old man. Work had piled up here, and there were deals pending that required his decision. As for the way the sight of Jessica had hit him like a hammer—he must be getting senile.

He pushed the papers away and lowered his head into his hands, more depressed than he'd been in years. What did he care about deals, about how many more dollars he made? All his life money had been his driving force, fueled, he knew, by his recollections of poverty, his memory of enduring the sneers of Hope Valley's fine residents. But what did he really have to show for all that drive? A divorce. No children since Justin had died. No one who really cared.

He shook his head impatiently. Self-pity wasn't his style. He'd drive to Hope tomorrow, see the old man, then finish up some work and take off for Rhodes. Or maybe he'd join the Jacksons on their yacht in the Caribbean.

People who said money wasn't everything usually didn't have much of it.

19

Mark pulled up in front of the dilapidated shack and sat for a few minutes in his luxurious sedan, hands gripping the steering wheel, looking thoughtfully around the clearing. It seemed so small, almost like a stage setting. His automobile dominated the space, reducing even the cabin of his youth to insignificance.

He was surprised at the turbulence of his emotions. He had thought he was long beyond the point where the sight of the place could affect him at all. He'd agreed to see Jeb, figuring he would drive up, do whatever was necessary to shut the old man up, and then get back to his world. He hadn't expected the sharp pangs of misery, the flood of memories the old place evoked. Not all of them bad, he admitted. He could almost believe his mother would come around the corner of the cabin, a welcoming smile on her face. And he could almost imagine seeing the ghost of his own youth, energetic, eager, burning with ambition.

It was strange to realize that he had never seen Jessica here. How many times she must have stood under that very tree, run up those rickety steps, called Justin from playing too near the creek. How many times she must have gazed toward the road, hoping he'd return. And what a bitter young man he had been when he had accused her of not waiting for him. My God, when he thought about what she had gone through …

He shook his head angrily. Could that burning in his eyes be unshed tears? He must be losing it. All that had happened ages ago. A line from a half-remembered play flashed through his mind: *But that was in another country, and besides, the wench is dead.* What he had to do now was see the old man and make some arrangements for his care. He didn't plan on any heartfelt reconciliation, but he couldn't let even a dog exist like this.

He slid from the vehicle and walked the few steps to the porch, taking the stairs gingerly in case they collapsed under his weight. He shoved open the door. Not locked, of course. There wouldn't be anything to steal here. Any self-respecting burglar would know that at a glance. And any from around here would also know that Jeb kept a shotgun under his bed.

"Who's there?" The voice whipped across the tiny cabin, surprisingly strong and unmistakably Jeb's.

"It's Mark." He moved farther into the gloom. The room was smaller than he remembered, too, but he knew memory played tricks on people. The musty smell, though, the clutter, was new. Leah would never have allowed such disorder. His eyes, adjusting to the dim light, picked out the recumbent form on the cot in the corner, and he walked toward it, pressing his lips into a thin, hard line. For an instant he felt as though he were a young boy, reluctantly approaching punishment.

He stood above the bed looking down at the man who had caused him such misery in his youth. Shock held him speechless. This was no frightening ogre; this was a sick old man. His face was eroded into sharp peaks and gullies; his skin looked like parchment. But his eyes, picking up the glint of a ray of sun from the open window, were as fierce as a hawk's. Mark decided he'd better not write the old man off just yet.

"Took you long enough," Jeb grumbled.

Mark bit back a retort. There had been very little force behind Jeb's ungracious remark. And he certainly hadn't expected to be greeted with enthusiasm. Gratitude was foreign to the old man. Demands had always been Jeb's style, and Mark didn't expect him to change at this late date.

"You sent word you wanted to see me," he said mildly.

Jeb was silent, and Mark shrugged, appreciating the old man's inner struggle. To admit he had wanted to see him would take every ounce of courage he had. To ease the moment he looked around the room, then back at his father.

"How long have you been sick?"

"I've been poorly for a year or so," the old man said. "Only the last couple of months I've had a problem cooking or keeping the place up. Anyway," he said, pulling himself up on the pillow until he was nearly in a sitting position and glaring at Mark, "I'm not sick. I'm just old. Never thought it would happen to me."

"You need care. I'll see about a nursing home for—"

"One more word like that, and I'll horsewhip you. I aim to die in my own home."

From anyone else in Jeb's condition it would have seemed an idle threat, but with Jeb you couldn't be sure, Mark thought, half smiling. "Someone to come in then."

Jeb was silent. Then he gave a deep sigh that moved the blankets over his bony chest. "I never thought I'd end up depending on strangers. Had a passel of kids. Always figured Leah would be here—she was so much younger than me."

"She might have been here if you hadn't worked her to death," Mark said dryly. His tone didn't hold the outrage it once might have. Seeing the old man in such straits— the man who had always seemed a dynamo of power and energy—effectively spiked the worst of his anger.

The expected explosion of rage from Jeb didn't materialize, either. He was silent; then he clutched nervously at the blanket and spoke in a whisper. "She always loved you best. Yet she helped you get away. I never understood it. You'd think she'd have wanted to keep you here. Like I did."

His tone was so wistful that Mark looked at him in surprise. He started to speak, but the old man held up his hand. "Let me finish. I ain't never going to get this said if I don't say it now. I surely hated it when you left."

"Nobody to help with the work," Mark said, bitter remembrance in his voice.

"Yeah, that too. But that weren't all of it. I was raised to think a son was supposed to help his father. 'Specially his firstborn. Why else do you have 'em? But you always hated everything about this place, couldn't wait to get away. It wasn't just wantin' money, either. I could have understood that. But you hated everything I stood for."

"I—" Mark shrugged. "You are what you are. I finally accepted that. But I could never forgive the way you treated Mom."

Jeb stared unseeingly into space. "She was a good woman," he whispered. "I really loved that woman."

"What!" Now Mark did explode. He clenched his hands to keep from pounding a fist through the rickety headboard. "You loved her? You worked her to death, had a dozen kids when you knew she was delicate—you even hit her!"

"Yeah, I was wrong about hitting her. Sometimes things just built up, and I went crazy. No excuse—I know that now."

Mark took a deep, shuddering breath. "What do you want? You say you don't want a doctor, you don't want help. Why did you call me here?"

"I don't want to die with bad blood between us," the old man said. "You blame me for your ma—maybe you're right. I can't do nothin' about it now. But I want you to know I loved her." He was silent, his mouth working. Then the words came out reluctantly. "And, damn it, I loved you, too."

Mark stared down at him, his first impulse to shout at the old hypocrite fading under Jeb's unwavering regard. His father had never said he loved him. If he'd ever told Leah he loved her, Mark had never heard it. Yet she, somehow, must have known. Was that the reason she wouldn't leave?

"I don't expect no love in return," Jeb continued. "Maybe I don't deserve it. But I wanted to tell you that before I died. I wanted you to know."

Mark's expression softened. Unaware that he was moving, he reached down and touched the old man's hand. It felt like paper, hot and dry and thin. With his other hand he pulled up a chair and sat down by the bed. "You'll get better," he said, suddenly embarrassed, knowing he was lying. "You'll be up and around in no time."

"No," Jeb said, his fingers tightening around Mark's. "And it don't bother me none. I'm older now than a man has a right to be. I can die, now I've told you."

Mark looked at the harsh old face. How much useless hatred had he expended on the man? Jessica was right; bitterness ate at the soul like acid. He'd never forget the misery Jeb had put him through or the way he'd treated Leah, but it didn't have to be a malignant force within him anymore, shaping his actions and his emotions. He could accept that Jeb was a product of his time, of his upbringing, and that it was useless to wish he had been something else.

He grinned and pressed the old man's hand. "There's another way to look at things. If you hadn't been such a bastard, maybe I never would have gotten out of Hope. I'm pretty successful now. Maybe I owe it all to you."

Jeb grinned back, and his watery eyes snapped. "Successful, hell. I've kept up with you, boy. No son, no wife—what's all that money got you?"

"The same thing not having money got you, I guess. We're both alone."

"Nope. Not quite. I got you," Jeb retorted.

Mark started to protest, then he threw back his head and laughed. It was the first time he could ever remember laughing around the old man. If Jeb had him, it was a pretty tenuous possession. But even so, he was right—that was more than Mark had.

"What about the others?" he asked. "Have you gotten in touch with any of them?"

"How?" Jeb snorted. "Only one that ever wrote a line after they left was Alice. And that was years ago. Said she was married and living someplace on the coast. Do you know where she is?"

"I've heard from her from time to time," Mark said. "She's got a husband, a couple of kids. She seems happy enough."

"I sure miss Justin," Jeb said weakly. "A boy after my own heart."

Mark was silent for several seconds, trying to control the lump in his throat. The thought of Justin was as painful as it had ever been. The boy had been a handful, a problem, but he surely missed him. Here, at least, was something he and Jeb could agree on.

He stood up abruptly and paced about the tiny room, glancing now and again at the man who watched him with an expression combining hope and belligerence. What could he do? Finally he returned to the bedside, a scowl on his face.

"I don't care what you want. I can't leave you here like this. You refuse to go to a nursing home?"

"You damn well got that right!"

"Then I'm going to hire someone to come in days and take care of you, clean up this place." He glanced around the cluttered room, then back at his father. "A practical nurse—someone to cook for you, clean you up."

He waited for the explosion, but it didn't come. "That's right nice of you, son. Anyway, it don't much matter. I can die now." He closed his eyes, and for a second Mark wondered if he was already gone.

"And—and I'll come by once in a while."

Now, why had he promised that? Wasn't his duty done if he arranged for someone to care for the old reprobate?

"I—I'd like that fine." The old lips barely moved.

Mark nodded abruptly and strode from the room. He despised sentimentality. The wrongs the old man had done couldn't be erased just because he was weak and helpless and needed someone now. But was he really so altruistic in saying he'd return and arranging for care? Didn't he need the old man just a little himself, if only to remind him of where he had come from?

If Jeb expected complete forgiveness, a heart-to-heart reconciliation, he was in for a surprise. This was as far as Mark could go. But Jeb was right. He shouldn't die without having tried to make his peace with his son. And Mark would be a monster if he didn't give a little. He could meet him halfway. He couldn't say he loved the old man, but for the first time in years he didn't hate him.

He drove back into town and swung by the old Townsend mansion. It had been years since he had been there, even for a visit, but it should be in good repair. Etta Jensen and her husband still lived there rent free in return for keeping it up. He walked quickly up the path to the front door and rang the bell.

Etta Jensen opened it so quickly, he suspected she had heard him drive up. She dried her hand on her apron, then thrust it forward. "Mr. Hardy! I declare, it's been years! Why didn't you let me know you was coming! I'd have got things ready. But your room's made up, your—"

"That's all right, Etta," he said soothingly, breaking into her flow of words. "I'm not staying. I just wanted to use the phone. And to talk to you."

"Why, of course." She smoothed her gray hair in a nervous motion, then ushered him into the living room. "There's the phone—but I expect you remember."

"First, do you know anyone who needs a job looking after somebody?" She herself was much too frail to handle a big man like Jeb.

"For your pa?"

"Yes. But how did you know?"

Her shrewd eyes narrowed with her grin. "No secrets 'round here. Somebody saw Jessica Carter drive out there the other day. Then my boy who works for Cullen Mac-Dougal said she was there asking about you. Didn't take much figuring."

He shook his head in wry amusement. The county grapevine was alive and well. "I need someone to go in, clean out the place, do some cooking."

"My cousin Ezra's got a boy. Big, husky kid, and he cooked at a diner a couple of months. I'll take care of it, if you want me to."

"Thanks." Mark picked up the phone and called a local doctor, who agreed, after considerable persuasion and the promise of a hefty fee, to look in on Jeb and arrange for a practical nurse. Then he stood up and held out his hand to Mrs. Jensen. There was nothing more he could do now; he would drive back to Boise and call his travel agent. He had agreed to see Jeb once in a while—not to camp on his doorstep. And he wanted to get out of here before he bumped into Jessica.

He drove slowly through town, noting the changes. They were surprisingly few, considering the way everything all around was being developed. Ahead of him to the right was the old general store Ira Kincaid used to run. The weathered sign that proclaimed HOPE MERCANTILE still hung above the door. Kincaid was long dead, of course, but the outside of the store hadn't changed a great deal.

Perhaps it was seeing his father that had put him in a nostalgic mood. For the first time in years he remembered that he had never returned the book of law by Blackstone that he had stolen years ago. The present owner would probably be astounded if he went in to pay for it now. But impulsively he pulled to the curb and cut the motor.

The door banged behind him with the same jangle of bells he remembered from years ago. He glanced around the interior. The place had been renovated, but it retained the look of a bygone era. Items never to be found in a modern department store dotted the walls and counters—kerosene lamps, harnesses, butter churns.

When a tall, impeccably groomed woman in a long skirt came toward him to ask whether he was interested in a particular period, he realized what had happened. He was in an antique shop.

His momentary impulse had been a mistake. He felt embarrassed. "I was just admiring that butter churn," he said easily, pointing toward the window.

"It's a beautiful piece," she acknowledged, and they walked toward the window just as an automobile pulled up at the curb. He recognized the old-model Mercedes, and his pulse quickened as he saw two women step out and walk together up the sidewalk.

Jessica. He hadn't expected to see her today. He'd definitely decided he wasn't going to call at the ranch. One old wound was enough for one day. When his chest tightened at the sight of her moving up the street, her long hair loose along her back, her incredible legs striding smoothly along, he knew he'd been right. He'd just stay inside here until she was out of sight.

He glanced at the young woman beside her and frowned slightly. She was taller than Jessica, a little broader across the shoulders, with a narrow waist and thick dark hair that bounced when she walked. When she'd gotten out of the car, she'd turned toward him for a moment, and he'd caught a glimpse of her features. Young. Beautiful.

But there was something else about her that tantalized him. He had the strong feeling that he had seen her before. Something in the bones of her face, the upward tilt of her eyes, was hauntingly familiar.

He closed his eyes and concentrated on bringing her

features into focus in his mind. Dark-winged eyebrows over deep brown eyes. Flawless skin the color of heavy cream. A wide mouth that curved in a familiar smile. Something kept dancing on the edges of his consciousness, refusing to be classified.

He turned to the woman beside him, breaking into her enthusiastic comments about the churn. "Do you know those two women walking up the street?"

She gave him a glance full of curiosity. "You mean Mrs. Carter?"

"Yes, that's the name." He kept his voice deliberately casual. "Who is that with her?"

The woman looked out the window again. "Oh, that's Maureen, her granddaughter." Then, as though she had spoken too freely with a complete stranger, she tightened her lips and gave him a keen glance.

Catching sight of her guarded look, he spoke quickly and, he hoped, reassuringly. "Yes. Jessica Carter, that's it. I thought I recognized her. But I didn't know she had a granddaughter."

"Well, she's adopted," the woman said. "Maybe that's why you hadn't heard. I wasn't here at the time, but I understand somebody left the little bundle on her doorstep."

Those eyes. The tilt of the head. Suddenly he had it. He sucked in his breath, and sweat sprang out on his forehead. He knew now who the girl resembled—Leah. Black anger coursed through him, rising like bile in his throat, and he swore softly. How dare Jessica keep such knowledge from him? Left on her doorstep, indeed. He would bet his life that the young girl with Jessica was truly her granddaughter. Which meant she must be Justin's child.

He didn't know how it had happened, or how she had managed to keep the paternity a secret, but the resemblance was too strong to be denied. That girl, Maureen, looked just like his mother. She really *was* Jessica's granddaughter.

And his.

All these years—all these lonely years since Justin's death—he had actually had a granddaughter he knew nothing about. A part of himself. A part of Leah. A part that Jessica had hidden from him.

Gradually he became aware that the woman beside him was looking at him with a mixture of curiosity and concern. She put her hand lightly on his arm.

"Is everything all right? You look a little pale. Do you want to sit down?"

"It's nothing." He ran a hand across his forehead and gave her a quick forced smile. "I don't think I'm interested in the churn right now, though."

"I can put it away for you. If you change your mind—"

"Thank you." He was almost out the door, and he threw the words over his shoulder. "But that won't be necessary."

All this time he had thought himself alone in the world. And it hadn't been true. Now, in spite of Jessica's duplicity, he had discovered the truth. He had a granddaughter—and he wasn't going to lose her.

Jessica tried to concentrate on Maureen's cheerful chatter as the two women entered the sporting-goods store and strolled over to the counter, but it was difficult. Twice already she'd asked the girl to repeat a comment, and she'd received a puzzled glance in return. She'd been restless all day, and when Maureen had suggested a quick trip to town to pick up the new tennis racket she had ordered, Jessica had been happy to agree. Anything was preferable to hanging around the house wondering whether Mark had actually gone to see his father. And whether, out of courtesy, he might even stop by the Carter ranch to report on the visit.

While Maureen stood at the counter talking to the clerk, Jessica leafed idly through some tennis skirts at the front of the store. Maureen might be a while; the clerk was a boy she went to high school with, and Jessica suspected the girl was trying out her flirting technique. She picked up a skirt and held it to the light. Should she give in to Maureen's insistence that she take tennis lessons? She had long ago resolved that she would never use her age as an excuse not to do something, but could you really become a passable player if you didn't start when you were young?

She glanced out the window, and her heart seemed to leap into her throat. She felt like a deer caught in headlights, afraid to run, afraid to stand still. Striding down the street, looking like a thunderstorm about to burst, was Mark. And he was coming this way. She threw a quick look at Maureen. How much longer could she hope it would take the girl to conclude the transaction? She shouldn't have chanced having her in town today. If Mark saw her, especially with Jessica, she didn't doubt that he would immediately leap to the correct conclusion. Maureen looked more like Leah every day.

Perhaps she could head him off and avoid the discovery. Her heart raced as she saw the angry expression on his face. "Take your time," she called to Maureen. "I'm going to run down to the bookstore. I'll meet you back here in half an hour or so."

Maureen laughed and raised a hand in acknowledgment, then turned back to the clerk. Jessica heard a giggle, saw the boy blush, and let out her breath in relief.

She darted out the door. She didn't doubt Mark had seen her enter the store and that he planned to confront her, perhaps in anger over his visit to Jeb; his approach was too purposeful for a random walk. But if she could intercept him before he got here, perhaps she could keep him from seeing Maureen.

"Mark," she said breathlessly, hurrying up to him. "What a surprise. Imagine seeing you here. I supposed you'd just stop in to see your father and drive on back to Boise. There can't be much that's exciting for you in Hope. Have you already been out to see Jeb?" She knew she was speaking too quickly, but she couldn't stop herself.

"I imagine seeing me here *is* a surprise, Jessica." His cold eyes raked her face.

Her stomach contracted, and she knew what his enemies must feel when they faced him. She had seen those eyes spark with passion, she had seen them warm with love, she had seen them filled with loss and pain. She had even seen them bright with anger, but never had she seen them so cold and implacable. It sent an icy chill through her.

"You've taken great care that I shouldn't find out, haven't you?" he demanded.

He knew! The chill became near paralysis. "I—I don't know what you mean," she stammered, playing for time. He had obviously seen—and recognized—Maureen. Could she convince him he was mistaken?

He snorted impatiently. "Don't be coy, Jessica. It doesn't become you. You know very well what I mean."

She tried to reply, but her voice stuck in her throat. Mark appraised her, and she was reminded of a predator surveying its trembling prey.

"I shouldn't be surprised, I guess," he said softly, his eyes glittering. "You *are* a great one for family. Think of all the trouble you went to to reunite me with my father. Undoubtedly you were going to get around to introducing me to my granddaughter—someday. Perhaps on *my* deathbed?"

She stared back, mesmerized by the icy anger in his eyes, and ran her tongue over her dry lips. "What do you mean?"

"Is that all you can say? 'What do you mean?' I think you know what I mean, Jessica. You used to be much quicker with the snappy retort. But I'll go along with this new shy, demure act. I *mean* that the girl I saw go into that store with you is my granddaughter."

"That's a pretty wild comment," she said desperately. "Why would you think a thing like that?"

He reached out and grabbed her wrist, pulling her so close to him that she felt the heat from his body. His eyes were only inches from hers, and she didn't like what she saw in them.

"Isn't she?" he demanded.

Briefly she considered lying; there was really no way Mark could prove anything, thanks to old Doc Alberson, who had advised her not to put Justin's name on the birth certificate. But the damage was done, anyway. No matter what she said, Mark knew the truth. Worse, if he decided he wanted Maureen, she doubted there was much she could do to keep the girl.

She dropped her gaze miserably to the ground. "Yes, she is your granddaughter," she whispered through dry lips.

Mark's grip loosened on her arm, and he glanced up the street. Turning her head, she saw Maureen emerge from the store and glance questioningly around.

"Please," she whispered. "Please. Can't we talk somewhere? I can't tell her just now. ..."

He gave her a dark, enigmatic glance, then looked again at the girl. The lines around his mouth deepened. "So she doesn't know," he murmured, almost to himself. "Eight o'clock," he said to Jessica, "at Clanahan's."

Rubbing her wrist, she watched him turn and stride back down the street. Then she arranged her face into a welcoming smile and turned back to Maureen.

Why hadn't she told the girl when she was younger? Her silence was now a weapon, and she had given it to Mark. Now everything would come out. Maureen would know that Jessica hadn't merely adopted her—she was truly her grandmother. She would never trust her again, a woman who had kept the truth from her all these years.

Her entire body felt numb. Her hands were tingling with cold, even though the temperature was in the eighties. Mutely she watched Maureen, who was half skipping toward her, a wide smile on her lovely face. How soon would it be before she saw anger and disappointment there? How soon before she lost her?

20

The steady purr of the engine sounded like a dirge in her ears as Jessica drove toward Clanahan's Bar on the outskirts of Hope. Her earlier panic was at least partially under control, but she still shivered a little as she thought about the coming confrontation. She took several deep breaths and was glad to see that her hands were steady on the wheel. Perhaps this showdown had had to come sometime, and now that it had, she was determined to face it with resolve and determination. She had never backed down from a fight, and this was one she had to win.

It was still early; dusk had just fallen over the expanse of sagebrush, but the lights of the bar provided a beacon as she drove toward it. Mark had chosen the site well, she thought, a wry smile on her lips. Clanahan's, shabby and isolated, frequented by truck drivers and married men out on illicit assignations, was well known in the community as the place for clandestine meetings. Whether by design or accident, the parking lot was in the back, hidden from view from the highway.

She pulled into it and glanced around, reluctant to face the coming scene. Mark's sedan was parked there, along with a half-dozen other automobiles, but the place wasn't nearly as crowded as it would be later in the evening. Dinner hour was over; the evening crowd had not yet arrived. This was about as private as you could get in a public place.

She wondered briefly why Mark had chosen a public place to meet. Then she remembered that the last times they had met privately, the situation had boiled over into passion. Of course, that was no longer a factor. Judging from his recent demeanor, he was more than immune to her by now, even if she couldn't claim that the feeling was mutual.

She took a deep breath, gathering her courage, elevated her chin, and stepped out onto the hardtop. The insistent beat of country music seeped out to the parking lot, then faded away into the fast-deepening night. At least it wasn't "Eleanor Rigby." She was getting a little tired of the omnipresent Beatles, even though Maureen would consider that attitude heresy.

She opened the door and peered into the dimness. The bar to the left had a few customers; the dining room to the right was empty.

One of the figures at the bar eased off his stool and walked toward her. The minute he moved she recognized the broad shoulders, the tall elegant form, of Mark. He held a drink in his hand and motioned to the bartender as he moved toward her. "I'm taking this to the dining room. Please bring the lady a—Jessica?"

"White wine," she supplied.

She moved stiffly ahead of him toward a table in the far corner of the room. The glass of wine was placed in front of her, the bartender retreated, and she and Mark were alone. The music seeped softly into the room, less strident, but still loud enough to cover their conversation from any possible listeners.

She ignored the glass. The gesture was Mark's way of taking control of the situation from the beginning. She was on the defensive but she hoped it didn't show too clearly.

A thin smile curved his lips. In the dimness of the room

his eyes were in shadow, but she felt their intensity. His tone, though, was mild. "You were drinking white wine the night I saw you at the Hotel Boise."

Stunned, for a moment she nearly forgot why they were here, that he was the enemy. "That's a long time to remember."

One eyebrow shot up, and he gave her a mocking smile. "Oh, I remember a lot of things. I even remember a time when I thought you an honest, guileless woman."

Her chin came up, and she felt the heat coloring her cheeks. No matter what her mistakes in the past, she was not going to submit to bullying.

"All right, perhaps I should have told you about Maureen, but I just couldn't. I knew what you'd do, that you'd want her. Please try to understand. After I lost Clinton and Justin"—and, she almost added, you—"she was all I had left. You had everything you wanted. But Maureen was everything for me."

"Everything I wanted?" His laugh grated. "You seem to forget that I lost Justin, too. He was my son—my only child—just as he was yours. You had no right to keep the knowledge of his daughter from me."

"It was for her sake as much as mine," she countered. "I didn't want her confused, vacillating, unsure of her loyalties. It was bad enough that her mother had abandoned her. This way she didn't have to feel like an obligation to anyone. She's had security, she's had love."

He leaned forward, and the intensity in his expression made her shrink back against her chair. "Jessica, I might be willing to forget what's happened. I'm not vindictive. But I want justice. You've had her all these years—now I want a chance."

"No!"

"Yes," he said, his expression implacable. "Think what I can do for her. Things that you can't do. I'm sure your life is fine for you, but she's young, Jessica. With me in her life she can sample the best. See the world. Attend the finest schools. Gain entrée to the highest social levels."

"The highest social levels! You mean those barracudas you run with? Those superficial, greedy—"

"Surely she's entitled to more than a backwater like Hope. I can give her the world."

"I don't care for your values, Mark," she said coldly. She was seething inside, but she forced herself to remain calm. "And Maureen is quite happy here on the ranch."

"Because she's never seen anything else. And if she stays here, she never will. She'll get through some college nearby—you'll see to that—then marry some rancher or other. I can give the girl a chance to follow her dreams, however large they are."

"Dreams of the jet set, the restless rich, people with no integrity, no goals but their own comfort and amusement?"

"You're stereotyping, Jessica. You know better than that. Not everyone shares your views about hiding from the twentieth century. And what's wrong with a little fun? Fabulous clothes, great vacations—what girl hasn't dreamed of those things?"

Jessica clenched her hands and took a long, tremulous breath.

How could she fight a Pied Piper? Maureen was a sweet, levelheaded girl. She had values—kindness, generosity, sensitivity, concern for the land, compassion for those less fortunate—and yes, she had dreams. And she certainly had a mind of her own. Take those peace marches Jessica worried so about. With her friends and her sports and her healthy, energetic life-style, Maureen was happy, active, involved. But wouldn't the life-style Mark could dangle in front of her turn the head of any sixteen-year-old girl, no matter how levelheaded? The glamour, the glitter might be irresistible.

"I don't think I'm being selfish in wanting what's best for her," she said simply.

"What's best for her—or for you? In spite of what you think, Jessica, my life isn't an endless round of conspicuous consumption. I work damned hard, and I provide the grease that keeps the wheels of this country turning. For instance, I and men like me keep the economy rolling so that you can get a good price for your beef—and hang on to your sacred ranch!"

She sighed and leaned back against the seat, consciously relaxing her rigid shoulders. "Arguing won't get us anywhere, Mark. Even if you had all the logic in the world on your side, I still couldn't give up Maureen. Please don't ask me to."

"You wouldn't be 'giving her up.' She could spend time with both of us."

He looked at her set face and smiled, a cool, predator's smile. "You made a mistake, didn't you, Jessica? You didn't tell Maureen who her father was, or that she had a grandfather, and now you're afraid that when she finds out, she'll turn against you. You're more worried about that than my distasteful life-style."

She didn't answer; she didn't have to. She knew he could read the terror in her face.

"Didn't you ever think she'd want to know?" he continued. "You could have explained it all when she was young, and she'd have accepted it readily. Now you don't know what her reaction might be to a woman who's lied to her all these years. Why didn't you tell her?"

Her eyes searched his face for a trace of softness, but she saw only the ferocity of a bird of prey. Was this the same man she had known in her youth? A man she would have died for? The man whose child she had borne against such intimidating odds? It couldn't be. If he had ever harbored a trace of tenderness for her, it had long since burned out. Only recently had she finally realized that she still loved him—loved him with a fervor and intensity that had been dormant for years. She'd even allowed herself to fantasize that they might be able to salvage something of their old intimacy. But all that was clearly in the distant past as far as he was concerned. She had to fight for the one thing left to her—Maureen.

"Why didn't I tell her?" she echoed. "Because I was afraid of exactly what is happening now. That if you knew about her, you'd try to take her away."

"Hasn't she ever asked questions?"

"No. She seems quite happy to leave everything the way it is."

"Don't you find that a little unusual?"

She was silent, and his lips tightened. "I want to see her, Jessica. You and I can debate this as much as we please, but the decision should be hers. She should know the truth."

At the muffled sound that escaped her lips, his eyes narrowed. "If you don't arrange for me to see her, I'll find a way. Don't you think it would be better coming from you? It may be late"—his mouth curved in a humorless smile—"but it's the only way you can hope to salvage anything."

She straightened in her chair and lifted her chin in defiance. "What makes you think she'd believe anything you say? What if I deny it?"

"So it's war to the finish, then? All right, I tried. I'll be coming out to the ranch tomorrow afternoon. And I intend to see her and tell her just who I am and who she is. And then I will invite her to come and live with me."

The rough-hewn chair on the veranda of the ranch house was precisely positioned so that Jessica faced the stark, untamed visage of Packer Mountain as she waited for the sun to dive behind its rock-capped peak. By shifting slightly she could see the line of condominiums faintly visible to the east. She took some comfort in the fact that they were not on Carter land.

Mark would soon be here. She had better stop daydreaming about the past and think about what she was going to do. Everything that was dear to her could well turn to ashes tonight. Perhaps she should have warned Maureen, but she hadn't. And tonight might be the last time her granddaughter would ever look at her with trust and love.

She heard the drone of the powerful motor and stiffened in her chair. Then Mark's sedan topped the brow of the hill and eased smoothly into the driveway. The door opened, and Mark stepped out and glanced around the ranch. His suit fit his tall frame flawlessly; his silvery hair was perfectly styled. He looked distinguished, powerful, a man used to getting what he wanted. He hadn't yet seen her sitting on the veranda. She rose slowly and walked to meet him.

"Hello, Mark."

He hesitated. "Hello, Jessica."

"You haven't changed your mind?"

"No."

She turned and walked ahead of him into the house, her steps slow and measured.

Mark, following her, thought that she looked like a woman on her way to her execution. There was something so vulnerable about her narrow shoulders, held so stiffly, the sweet curve of her back. Damn! He had never wanted to hurt her, but didn't he have a right to know his own granddaughter?

He tore his gaze away, vaguely noting his surroundings as he followed her into the living room. He'd been in here a few times when he worked for Clinton, and he couldn't see any great changes. Everything appeared comfortably worn and lovingly cared for, from the faded Persian rug on the floor to the highly polished cherrywood furniture. It spoke of stability, he thought, of security, and for a moment he hesitated.

He was here to shatter that stability, and he was sorry about that. He couldn't hate Jessica for what she'd done. Hate her? Hell, he still loved her. But he deserved some consideration also.

His chest tightened as she turned to him. He'd never seen her face so white. She looked almost . . . old. The realization hit him with the force of a sledgehammer. Not Jessica. Not the beautiful young woman with hair like a field of ripe wheat. Never.

"I'll tell Maureen to come on down," she said softly.

So she was leaving it entirely up to him. She hadn't said a word to the girl. Well, so be it.

His lips tightened with anger. He'd faced worse challenges, times when the stakes were high. What could be so difficult about telling a girl you were her grandfather? Offering her the kind of life any young woman would dream of?

He had only a few minutes to pace, head down, hands clasped behind him, before he heard quick footsteps, and he lifted his head to see Maureen running lightly down the stairs. Behind her, moving more sedately, came Jessica. For an instant he nearly relented. She moved like a woman in a trance.

The two women reached the bottom of the stairs, and Jessica took Maureen's hand, pulling her along to the spot where Mark stood gravely watching them.

"Mark, this is my granddaughter. Maureen," she said gently, "I would like you to meet Mark Hardy." If Mark hadn't been listening so intently, he might not have heard the catch in her voice.

Maureen put out her hand, her magnificent brown eyes bright with curiosity. "I've heard a lot about you, Mr. Hardy. But then, who hasn't? Even though Lady Jess has seemed a bit touchy since she said you were coming, you don't look like anyone to be wary of." Her generous lips curved in a mischievous smile as she gave him the youthfully blunt appraisal.

"I hope not," he said smoothly. "And I hope you've heard a few *good* things about me." That glimpse he'd had of her yesterday hadn't done her justice. She was brimming with girlish beauty, intelligence shone from her wide-spaced eyes, and energy sparkled in her entire face. A face so like his mother's.

"Well," she said slowly, "I hadn't heard that you were

so good-looking." She grinned at Jessica. "You've been holding out on me."

"That's enough, Maureen," Jessica said tartly. "Mark has some things he'd like to say to you. Perhaps we'd all better sit down."

Mark lowered his frame into a soft chair and gazed across at the two women. Maureen sat on the couch, her bare arms folded across her chest. Jessica perched on the arm of the couch, her hand placed protectively on Maureen's shoulder. They didn't look much alike, he thought, except in their mannerisms, but there the similarities were pronounced: the proud tilt of the head, the steady regard in the eyes. Those alone bespoke their closeness.

How could Jessica manage to appear so elegant in her simple outfit? he wondered. She wore a tailored silk shirt and a long denim skirt, yet he'd seen women in designer clothes that cost thousands of dollars who couldn't touch her. Her glorious hair was loose but swept back from her face, accentuating her eyes and the clear, sweet curve of her cheek. Did she wear lipstick, or was her mouth naturally that fresh, soft coral?

He was almost overcome by a rush of tenderness. Hers was not a young face. All the nonessentials had been scoured away by time, leaving the enduring dramatic beauty.

For much too long he couldn't say a word. He had to handle this just right—or risk seeing neither of these women again.

Jessica, he had to accept, his heart constricting in his chest, was lost to him. She had made it clear she didn't wish to see him again. She had never tried to get in touch with him even when both he and she were free, and she had rushed out of his office the one time she had come to him. But he still had a chance with their granddaughter. When she learned of their relationship, that Jessica had kept it secret all these years, what would she do? Would she feel betrayed, angry with Jessica? Or could she turn that anger on him, as the messenger bearing the truth?

"Are you staying long in Hope, Mr. Hardy?" Maureen's voice was polite, but she couldn't hide the curiosity in her eyes.

"Well, that rather depends on you," he replied.

"Me? I don't understand." She shot a look at Jessica, then back at Mark.

He saw Jessica close her eyes, and her lips moved slightly, almost as though she were praying. But he refused to let it deter him. He opened his mouth.

And suddenly he couldn't do it. He couldn't shatter Jessica's life by dropping this bombshell on Maureen. He couldn't see her shrink when Maureen turned to her, asking why she hadn't been told. It was really quite simple. He couldn't bear to break her heart again.

Maybe there was another way. He thought quickly, desperately. Maybe he could convince Maureen that he was altruistic enough to want to pay for her education, introduce her to his friends, even have her live in his home . . . because he had been born in Hope and—and wanted to help someone.

He knew it was a ridiculous idea before he opened his mouth, but he had to say something. "I guess you know that I'm rather a wealthy man," he said. Jessica started, her eyes opening wide, as he continued. "I was born in Hope, and I've always wanted to help some young person. I'm completely alone, have nothing to do with my money. I would consider it an honor to, say, take you under my wing, see that you get to the right schools, travel, have the opportunity to—"

"You can't be serious!" Maureen broke in. "Why would you do that for me? It doesn't make sense. You don't even know me."

He wavered. Now, if ever, was the time. He could still tell her who he was, that he was willing to do anything, turn his life upside down, inside out, to have his granddaughter by his side.

He saw Jessica lean forward slightly. Her lips were parted; she seemed to be holding her breath, waiting for him to speak and destroy her world. Suddenly he was reminded of the last time he had gone deer hunting. The animal had stood there, seeming to know it was in his sights, paralyzed by fear but somehow resigned. He'd lowered his rifle; he hadn't hunted again.

"Why you? I—I knew Justin, your grandmother's son," he said lamely. "I was prepared to—to help him along, be his mentor. I guess I thought perhaps I might do the same for"—he nearly slipped—"her granddaughter."

Maureen's expression told him how bizarre his explanation sounded to her. "What exactly are you proposing, Mr. Hardy?" she asked cautiously. "A scholarship of some sort?"

"Oh, I'd enroll you in whatever school you liked. But also you could, say, travel with me to some very lovely parts of the world, where you'd meet all kinds of fascinating people. I could help you do whatever you wanted to do in life." He broke off, conscious of how odd all this must sound if he didn't reveal his relationship to her. What girl in her right mind would accept such an offer from a stranger? Doubtless the only reason she wasn't convinced he was a dirty old man was that her grandmother was there and offering no protest.

Maureen's almond-shaped eyes narrowed. "You mean, leave Lady Jess?"

"Well, part of the time, perhaps," he floundered. "Naturally you could visit—"

She rose slowly, her gaze boring into his, and tilted her lovely chin. "I don't know exactly what's going on here, but I'm not in the least interested in leaving Lady Jess. I appreciate your goodwill, but I really have everything I want right here. Good night, Mr. Hardy," she said to him. "I'll be in my room, Lady Jess," she added.

Mark and Jessica watched silently as Maureen headed up the stairs. A sheen of sweat bathed his forehead, and he felt a vast emptiness that he had experienced only once before. When he had walked away from Jessica that last time years ago, after they had made love, and she had told him that even though Clinton was dead, they couldn't be together.

Damn them both!

Jessica, appearing pale and shaky, rose and came slowly toward him. She put out her hand. "Thank you, Mark," she whispered.

He shrugged, ignoring her hand. "You were right. She's much better off here with you. No use upsetting her at this late date."

"You gave her up. You didn't have to."

"Yes. Well, I'm good at that." His lips twisted into a grim smile, and he rose and turned toward the door.

"Mark, where are you going? Can't we talk?"

"About what?" He didn't turn around. His couldn't afford to. If he just kept walking, maybe he could make it to the door and out of her sight without making a complete fool of himself. "We have nothing more to say, Jessica. You have your precious granddaughter. I won't interfere in your life again. I'll leave Hope in the morning. There's no reason for me to come back."

He thought she called out something, but he closed the door and strode out to his automobile. Slamming the car door viciously, he turned the ignition, then gunned the engine, spinning gravel as he roared out of the driveway. He'd get out of this hick town first thing in the morning. Returning to the past was always a mistake.

Jessica stood in the living room, hands helplessly at her sides, wide eyes staring at the door closed with such finality, until the sound of the motor faded away.

She shook her head to clear away the haze. She should be relieved that the confrontation was over and that for some inexplicable reason Mark had changed his mind. Why did she feel so numb, so bewildered, so bereft? Why did she feel like rushing out into the night after him?

She took a long, quavering breath and sank down slowly onto the couch. She could hardly believe it; the danger was past. Mark would be gone from Hope in the morning, and she wouldn't have to worry again about his taking Maureen away from her. Moreover, he had done a kind and generous thing, had sacrificed all claim on the girl. Now she wouldn't have to face Maureen's accusing eyes. All she had to do was forget this entire evening.

Which, of course, she couldn't do. She leaned her head back against the velvet upholstery and closed her eyes. Tears stung behind her eyelids. She had been so frightened at the prospect of losing Maureen that she had ignored the fact that Mark was right about one thing. She tried to push the thought away, to deny its truth, but it was impossible. She had been terribly wrong all these years, unfair to her own granddaughter. Mark had been generous enough to give her another chance to redeem herself. She could no longer deny the obvious: Maureen deserved to know who she was.

If Mark could be generous, so could she, she thought, sitting up straight and clenching her hands in her lap. If she lost the girl by doing what she had to do, it would be her own fault. She had lied all these years, but she couldn't continue the charade. She had been selfish; she had wronged Maureen, and she had no alternative but to make things right if she could. What Maureen would do when she knew the truth, she couldn't foresee. But Mark's actions tonight had convinced her it had to be done.

She thrust aside the thought of how much pain his renunciation must have cost him. Rising slowly from the couch, she put out a hand to steady herself. All of a sudden, facing the inevitability of loss, she felt her age deep in every bone. She placed one foot on the stairs and slowly began her ascent.

When she reached the landing at the top, she hesitated a moment, listening for any sound that might give her a clue to Maureen's mood. There was nothing but the soft sound of the Beatles coming from Maureen's open door. Something monotonous about a yellow submarine. She paused on the threshold, glancing automatically around the pleasant room.

It was neat but not obsessively so, with a furry sheepskin rug on the floor and life-size photos of the Beatles covering the walls. Maureen was sprawled on her bed, her dark head propped on a pillow. When Jessica entered, she swung her legs to the floor and gave her an inquisitive glance.

"Has he gone?"

"Yes."

"That was certainly weird," Maureen said. "Imagine just coming in here and asking me to leave with him! It's so weird, in fact," she said, her keen eyes on Jessica's face, "that I just can't help wondering what's really going on here."

Jessica moved to a chair by the side of the bed and sat down quickly before her knees gave way beneath her. Those deep brown eyes held hers relentlessly. No more dissembling.

"You've never asked me anything about your parents," she said slowly.

Maureen's face became very still. The record ended, leaving a sudden, heavy silence, as her eyes searched Jessica's face. A board squeaked somewhere down the hall; a gust of wind rattled the window. Finally the girl spoke softly, carefully.

"You always said you didn't know, that my mother wandered in out of a storm one night and left as soon as I was born. I assumed you didn't know who my father was."

"That was true—of your mother." Jessica swallowed a huge, painful lump in her throat.

"What are you trying to tell me?"

"I—I knew your father, too. He . . . he was Justin, my son. You are my real granddaughter, not adopted. And the man you just met—Mark Hardy—is your grandfather."

The words seemed to echo around the room, gaining a life of their own, almost as though they had not come from her lips. She watched Maureen's face. There was shock, amazement—what else? Now she would know whether she had lost the girl or not. Whether autumn was over and winter had come.

21

"*You—you're my real grandmother? My honest-*to-gosh, flesh-and-blood real grandmother?" Maureen's voice was so low, Jessica could hardly hear her. She nodded miserably. She couldn't begin to decipher the emotion that blazed across the girl's face, leaving her skin so pale under the light tan that Jessica wondered if she might even faint. She sat as motionless as a statue on the edge of the bed, her lips slightly parted, her dark eyes enormous.

"I'm sorry," Jessica whispered. "So sorry. I always meant to tell you."

"My own grandmother!" Maureen catapulted from the edge of the bed directly into Jessica's embrace. Her firm young arms closed around the woman's slender back, squeezing her so hard that Jessica gasped for breath.

For an instant she was frozen with surprise. Then, slowly, as though gathering in a fragile flower that might break with the slightest pressure, Jessica put her arms around Maureen and pulled her even closer to her breast. Could the girl feel the frantic hammering of her heart, the relief that was turning every muscle to water? With a muffled sob she buried her face in the fragrance of the girl's hair, then moved one trembling hand to softly stroke the flawless texture of her cheek. She tried to speak, but her throat was choked with emotion.

They clung together wordlessly as Jessica stroked the girl's back and crooned nonsense syllables as she had done when Maureen had needed comforting as a child. Finally Maureen pulled away, tossed back her mane of dark hair, and gazed incredulously at Jessica. "No kidding? You're my very own grandmother?"

Jessica's laugh was shaky, but it was a laugh. "Your very own."

Maureen's eyes narrowed. "Why didn't you tell me before?"

This was the moment she had dreaded, the moment when so much hung in the balance. But she had gone too far to pull back now. There could be nothing but honesty between them. "It's a long story. I—I was afraid of a lot of things. Afraid I might lose you if the truth were known. I kept waiting for you to ask, but you never did. I guess I deluded myself that you really weren't interested."

"No, I was interested. But I was afraid to ask," Maureen murmured. "Of course I've wondered. I've made up stories, fantasized, but you always seemed so edgy every time the subject came up that I thought—well, you'll laugh when you hear what I thought."

"Try me."

The silence lengthened. Maureen moistened her full lips with her pink tongue, then whispered, "I hoped maybe I was really your daughter. Maybe that was the reason you wouldn't talk about it."

Jessica gasped, and Maureen refused to meet her eyes, going doggedly on.

"Well, would that have been so impossible? You said my mother wandered in out of a storm and left right after I was born. She's never been heard of since. That's not really a very likely story—much too convenient. Why, out of all the people in Hope, did she come to you? Why did she leave me with you, a stranger? It made much more sense to think that maybe you—maybe you just had a love affair and couldn't admit it."

"Maureen, I was over forty years old when you were born!"

"Well, it wouldn't have been impossible. . . ."

Jessica shook her head, both amused and incredulous at Maureen's fantasy. "Your mother! And I thought nothing was going on in that little head of yours."

Maureen scooted back to take her former place on the bed, but she kept her hand in Jessica's, excitement and bewilderment competing in her mobile features. "Anyway, you're my grandmother. So we really *are* related. That's just super. But I still don't understand . . . I don't understand anything. Did you say that Mark Hardy is my grandfather?" At Jessica's nod Maureen whooped, deducing correctly, "So you *did* have an illicit love affair, Lady Jess!"

Jessica was so dizzy—giddy—with relief that she wasn't even embarrassed. She stroked Maureen's hand, swallowed the lump in her throat, and managed a soft whisper. "You don't hate me, then? Hate me for keeping the truth from you?"

Maureen shot her an incredulous glance, then raised Jessica's hand to her lips and placed a soft kiss on the fingers. "Really, Lady Jess! I'll never understand your generation! All that secretiveness, when it's so much easier to tell the truth. Why should I suddenly hate you when I've loved you all these years? Suddenly finding out you're my real grandmother doesn't change anything—except it *is* great to know more about my history, and to know we're really related." She faced Jessica, her warm brown eyes as stern as they could ever be. "However, since you really *did* have this love affair, don't you think you might as well tell me the whole story?"

Jessica lifted her hand in a supplicating gesture, hoping even now to be spared revealing the details. But Maureen frowned, and Jessica sighed and capitulated. The girl had a right to know everything, and the truth was long overdue.

She began to speak, trying with her words to make Maureen feel the past as she had lived it: the harsh morality of the times, the poverty, the wonder and beauty of Mark. She described the trap the Blalocks had offered, her ambivalence when Jeb Hardy came riding up to the ranch for her, Justin's birth, and her despair when she decided that Mark would never return. She told her how Clinton had rescued her, and how she had finally come to love him. Maureen sat frozen, her eyes never leaving her face, as she told of Mark's eventual return, his abrupt departure, Clinton's death, then Justin's, and finally how she had rejoiced when she was allowed a new beginning when Maureen's mother drifted in and left her with her grandchild.

Jessica's voice trailed away, leaving a heavy silence. She was vaguely aware of the wind playing with the curtain at the open window, the first pale rays of the moon flowing softly across the floor. A night bird called from somewhere in the darkness. She held her breath, waiting—for absolution, for understanding, for rejection, for anything but silence.

"So it was true about my mother," Maureen finally said. "She left me. . . ."

"Because she loved you. Never doubt that. I never have. She was only a child herself, lost and bewildered, the man she loved dead. She knew she couldn't care for you. She knew you would have love and security with me. It was an act of selfless love."

Again Maureen was silent, and Jessica's uneasiness increased. Then, as though she had assimilated it all, the girl flashed her familiar, mischievous smile, and her eyes danced. "Wow! That's quite a story!"

Jessica let out the breath she didn't realize she had been holding. "I've been afraid to tell you for so long. Afraid you would disapprove, think less of me."

Maureen jumped up from the bed and hugged her fiercely, then drew back to look into her worried eyes. "Oh, Lady Jess. How ridiculous can you get? That's the most romantic thing I've ever heard. Star-crossed lovers and everything . . ."

She pursed her lips thoughtfully. "There's one thing I don't understand, though. You say you and this Mark Hardy have loved each other for years—"

"I've loved him for years," Jessica corrected. "He got over it long ago."

"How do you know?"

"Well, it's obvious. There are the beautiful women I've read about, the fabulous life he's led. All so glamorous and glittering. Besides, he would have said something. . . ." Jessica floundered.

"Like you did?" Maureen shrugged impatiently. "Honestly! And to think that handsome man is my grandfather! Is that why he offered to do all those things for me?"

"Yes," Jessica admitted. "And he is the other big reason I kept your heritage secret. From everyone. I knew if Mark ever found out about you, he would try to take you away from me."

"How did he find out?"

"He saw you yesterday and realized at once that you strongly resembled his mother. He put two and two together and figured out who you must be. Justin's daughter. He threatened to tell you who you were, and I knew—I thought—you would never trust me again."

Maureen thrust out her lower lip and nibbled thoughtfully, her gaze fixed on something unseen in the distance. Her magnificent eyes narrowed. "But he didn't tell me. He came off looking a bit of a fool, which must hurt a man like that a lot, but he didn't tell me."

"No, he didn't."

"Doesn't that tell you something?" Maureen swung her attention sharply back to Jessica.

"I'm grateful to him," Jessica stammered. "It was a kind

thing to do. Maybe, though, he thought he would alienate you if he tattled. Maybe he thought it would backfire."

"Oh!" Maureen raked her hands through her hair and then flung them upward, rolling her eyes. "I don't know what I'm going to do with you!"

"Anyway," Jessica said, "it's over now. He's leaving Hope in the morning, and we can settle down again."

"And never see him again? I'll never see my grandfather again?" Maureen's eyes bored into Jessica, and her lips tightened.

A thrill of fear shot up Jessica's spine. "Aren't you happy here?" she pleaded.

"That has absolutely nothing to do with it. I've never seen such a stubborn person in all my life! Open your eyes! He didn't tell me who he was because he knew it would hurt *you*. That's obvious. You should get down there immediately and tell him how you feel!"

"I couldn't possibly!"

Maureen gave her a long, hard look, and Jessica wondered if the girl's disappointment in her was finally surfacing. Maureen turned away and walked into the bathroom. Jessica heard the splash of water, and in a minute a silent, stormy Maureen rushed out. Jessica stared as she slipped into a pair of slacks and threw a jacket over her shoulders, wiggled into some boots, and reached for her purse lying on the dresser. She was almost out the door before Jessica found her voice.

"Maureen! Where are you going?"

"I'm going to see my grandfather!"

The words echoed in the room long after Jessica heard the front door slam and an engine come briskly to life, then the scatter of gravel as Maureen's convertible took the curve of the driveway. She was going much too fast; she would have to speak to her.

Then she realized it was possible Maureen would never submit to her admonitions again. Her throat hurt. She was completely unable to rise from the chair. Every muscle felt like lead, pulling her down, as she stared unseeingly at the floor. Her eyes stung, but she couldn't cry. If she did, she might never be able to stop.

She had gambled, and she had lost. Maureen was going to see her grandfather, and she might never be back. She knew how persuasive Mark could be. And once Maureen had time to think about her grandmother's deceptions and everything they had cost her . . . Suddenly her resolve melted and the sobs came, huge, racking, shaking her slender body as a dog shakes a rat. In spasm after spasm they came, and she was powerless to halt the flood. What did it matter? What did anything matter now?

Finally the storm passed, leaving her trembling and weak. She rose from the chair and, half in a trance, moved from room to room in the old house, touching polished wood, running her hand along worn upholstery, as though the touch of things familiar could soothe her shattered life. The house was usually so comforting, so warm, enfolding her like a cozy blanket. Now it was full of ghosts that whispered to her as she drifted along. Clinton, Leah, Justin—they called softly to her from the shadows.

Was she losing her mind? Why not? she thought, her lips twisting in a humorless grin. She'd lost everything else. The thought stopped her in her tracks, and she straightened her shoulders and lifted her chin. Talk about self-pity! She'd had joy in her life, as well as heartbreak, and she wasn't just going to roll over and play dead.

As usual, action seemed the best medicine. She slipped into her riding clothes and made her way out to the stable. The moon was high enough now to bathe the landscape in silver, and she had no trouble making her way to the corral. Leader's soft whinny floated out to meet her, and she lifted her head and took a deep, healing breath of the night air. There was still the land.

The warm, familiar smell of hay and horseflesh enveloped her as she entered the barn and quickly saddled Leader. She hadn't ridden him much lately; he was getting old—older than she in horse years. Tonight, though, it seemed appropriate that they ride the Carter ranch together. He seemed to sense her mood, nuzzling her arm with his velvety nose as she led him out into the open and pulled herself up into the saddle.

Leader settled into a slow, leisurely walk as they passed through the meadow and began the climb into the hills. She didn't need to guide him; he followed the trail they had ridden so many times before, and leaving the reins slack on his neck, she absorbed the beauty around her. The moon was full, a huge silver orb still low in the eastern sky, and it flooded the landscape with light. Each tree, each rock, seemed etched in silver, interspaced with lush shadow. The delicate leaves of the aspen shivered along the trail like a cascade of silver coins. The white clover brushed against her legs, ghostlike in the moonlight. She had no goal, no destination, no intention but to immerse herself in the spirit of the healing land.

As she rode along, jouncing to the rhythm of the horse, all of her life seemed to spread itself out around her in an intricate tapestry. Time took on a strange aspect, not the linear progression she had always imagined. All the events of her life seemed to coexist. She could feel herself back in the schoolhouse, with Mark's face as clear to her now as it had been when she was twenty years old. Norval was there, too, witty, tragic Norval who had been branded by other people's expectations. Sam Blalock, Carrie Blalock—they stared at her from the darkness, indignant and judgmental but somehow pitiful as they fought for the heir they craved. Leah walked silently beside her, kindness and generosity in her luminous brown eyes, strength and endurance in the tilt of her proud chin. Clinton, Justin—they were all here, their spirits inseparable from the land.

She searched for a pattern, but all she saw was an endless ebb and flow. People came; they went. She was joyous; she was sad. And all the while the land abided. Who was it who had written that the unexamined life is not worth living? She wasn't sure she agreed. In examining her own life, she was absolutely sure that tonight was the nadir of her existence; better to be less introspective.

She gave herself a little shake. Leader was puffing, his sides heaving, and she realized the steep mountain terrain was too much for the old horse. She tugged gently on the reins, turning him around in the trail, and they moved slowly back to the ranch.

Her spirits rose once she was ensconced in the familiarity of the living room; she seemed to have left the ghosts and shadows behind in the mountains, and her usual optimism buoyed her up. She had gone through bad times before and survived; she would survive this.

Gradually she realized that there was no use at all sitting here passively and bemoaning the loss of Mark and Maureen. She had a decision to make. It seemed as though everyone she loved was lost to her. Mark planned on leaving forever in the morning. Maureen's last words, *I'm going to see my grandfather*, rang in her ears.

She could, she supposed, react like some of the Victorian ladies she had read about and retreat from the world. She could drift silently around the house, a pale wraith, or even take to her bed. Her eyebrows rose in wry amusement. People would be very sorry for her—if they remembered her existence.

Or she could fight for what she wanted.

She glanced at the clock. It was close to midnight. If Maureen had found Mark, she had been with him for hours. What were they talking about? What decisions had they made? Maureen had seemed so sure that Mark loved her, but Maureen didn't know what had gone on between them over the years. She was young and romantic, still living in a dreamworld where everything turned out right.

No, she couldn't hope that Mark still loved her, but of one thing she was as sure as that the sun would come up in the morning. She loved him.

Excitement trickled through her lethargy, and her heart began to beat a little faster. Perhaps now was the time for truth for everyone. She had told Maureen of her heritage, and she might as well go all the way and tell Mark she still loved him. He had been generous to her, trying to spare her further heartbreak. That must mean something. On the other hand, he might not care at all. But the record should be set straight.

But it was nearly midnight—not the time to go bursting into a man's room, unsure of welcome. She would drive to Hope first thing in the morning. In the meantime perhaps she should try to get some sleep, although she doubted that she would achieve even partial oblivion.

She had risen from the chair and started toward the stairway when she heard the sound of a motor. Her breath caught in her throat; her heart did a dizzying flip-flop. Had Maureen come back? The drive was private, and she couldn't think of anyone else who would be using it so late at night.

She forced herself to stay away from the window. If it was not Maureen, she didn't know how she could bear it. She pressed her hand against her chest and waited; she would soon know.

The automobile stopped, and a flurry of feet came up onto the veranda. She stared at the door, hardly breathing. It burst open, and she raised her hand to her mouth, stifling a tiny gasp. Not Maureen, but Mark, stood outlined in the doorway, his broad shoulders nearly filling the space. Before she could do or say anything, he came into the room, literally pushed by her granddaughter.

He smiled a little sheepishly. He was so handsome, she thought, and so huge. His lean, rangy frame dwarfed her own and made the living room feel ridiculouly small.

"Jessica, I hate to disturb you at this hour of the night, but—"

He seemed unable to finish the sentence, and Jessica, gathering every one of her resources, answered calmly. "That's quite all right. I—"

Maureen pushed impatiently in front of him and grabbed Jessica by the hand, pulling her toward Mark. "I've about had it with you two," she announced, her dark eyes flashing. "Isn't it time you stopped this silly pretending? You've both admitted to me that you love each other. Why can't you unbend and admit it to each other?"

"Maureen!" Jessica gasped. Maureen had pulled her so close to Mark that she could hear his breathing, feel its warmth on her lips.

Maureen ignored her protest. She stood a few feet away from both of them, her hands on her hips, her eyes swiveling from one face to the other, then settled accusingly on Jessica. "When you told me this evening that you still loved Mark, I decided that someone had to use a little sense," she said sternly. "I figured if you still loved him, he probably still loved you—though why you've let this drag on all these years, I'll never know. You *both* belong in the Dark Ages!"

Jessica was barely aware of what Maureen was saying. Her eyes were on Mark's face. Was it possible that he really did still love her? He was looking at her as though he had just been struck by lightning.

Maureen whirled around, flipping her long mane of dark hair in an arc behind her. "Now, listen, you two. I'm going on up to my room. And I'm thinking of locking the front door so neither one of you can leave until you come to your senses," she said darkly. "You two don't have much of a track record, you know."

She stalked up the stairs, leaving a strained silence behind her.

Mark spoke first. "That's one determined granddaughter we've got. I hope you don't mind."

"Yes, she certainly is determined. And of course I don't mind." She moved toward a couch and motioned to Mark. "Why don't you sit down. She seems to be right about one thing. We do need to talk. And, Mark—thank you for what you did tonight. Not telling her about who you are, I mean. It was extremely generous. And I know it cost you."

"Thank you for telling her. That must have cost *you*. Why did you?"

She shrugged. "It was time to stop all the pretense. And, I thought, if you could be generous, so could I."

"You risked everything."

"You gave up everything."

The silence lengthened. He rose from the couch and gazed down at her, then slowly extended a hand, his eyes never leaving hers. Feeling suddenly shy, she allowed herself to be pulled to her feet.

"Do you know what I'd like to do?" he asked softly. She shook her head, afraid to speak, and he pulled her to the side of the room and switched on the radio, liberating the strains of a plaintive country song. As Patsy Cline moaned about lost love, he enfolded her in his arms.

"I'd like to dance with you," he said softly. "I've dreamed of it so often, remembered when I went to the schoolhouse social, a backwoods hillbilly, and took you away from everyone. We never did get a chance to dance together—not then, not in all these years."

He moved rhythmically around the room, and she followed as though they were welded together. His hand on her back, her cheek against his chest, felt absolutely right, as though all time had been flowing toward this moment. She was aware of the thudding of his heart through his linen shirt, was enveloped in his clean, masculine scent. For this moment she wouldn't think, wouldn't analyze— she would just experience.

The music died, and she looked up into his face. "You dance beautifully," she said.

He squeezed her tightly, then let his arm fall, and they moved together to the couch. He sat a few inches away, and both were aware of the empty space between them. Then he put his hand on her cheek and turned her face toward him, his eyes darkening until they were nearly black. "What happened to us, Jessica? How did we ever lose so much?"

"I don't know," she whispered. "So many things got in the way." She lifted her head and looked him squarely in the eyes, wondering if he could read her confusion.

His hand tightened convulsively on her cheek. His touch burned her skin, sent fire racing through her veins. He seemed to dominate the room with his dark, restless energy, and her heart twisted in her chest with a combination of longing and fear. If Maureen had been telling the truth, then he had admitted that he loved her. But was that enough to erase the long years they had been apart? Could even love surmount the doubts, the anger, the pain that had come between them?

Perhaps Mark was having the same thoughts. He dropped his hand and gave her a searching glance. "I don't know what to say, Jessica. What to do. I tried to explain to Maureen that there had never been any doubt that we loved each other. So many things got in the way—duty, guilt, pride."

"Yes," she said slowly. "And so much time has gone by. Time that has changed us both. Your life has been so different from mine, I often wonder if we're still the same people who fell in love."

"Undoubtedly we're not," he said softly. "But I will say this. No matter how much my life changed, no matter how much I changed, there was always a kernel inside me that was unalterable. It was my love for you. You think I've been pretty bad," he said, his mouth twisting in a wry grin, "a robber baron, but every time I strayed too far from my course, you were the lodestar that brought me back."

The ice that had encased Jessica's emotions for so long began to melt; she was like a frozen winter stream beneath the spring sun's tentative, searching fingers. The ice softens, cracks, breaks into crystal pieces, and the water breaks free, gurgling and gushing, irrepressible and irresistible as it rushes to its destiny, the all-embracing sea.

She reached toward him. All her feelings must have

been apparent in her face. Instantly he was on his feet, then he dropped to his knees in front of her. With a muffled cry that might have been a prayer or an oath, he buried his face in her lap, pulling her against him in a fierce, desperate motion. She tangled her fingers in his silver hair, then bent down to press her lips against his head, murmuring incoherent endearments. God, after all these years he felt just the same. He smelled just the same. The same intense energy radiated from his body. Even blindfolded, she would have recognized him.

He raised his head, looked up into her face, and gave her a blinding smile. Slowly he rose from his knees and sat beside her on the couch, very close this time, and tilted her head so that it rested on his shoulder. There was so much to say, so many questions to ask, but for the moment they were both silent, taking in the enormity of what had just happened. "You won't get away from me this time, Jessica," he said huskily.

"I don't intend to try," she said. "Oh, Mark, can it really be true? I feel as giddy as a sixteen-year-old. Shouldn't we be behaving with a little more decorum?"

"Probably." He chuckled. "But it's hard to remember that when you're so damn beautiful." He put the palm of his hand along her cheek, then guided her head so that his lips could find her mouth. The kiss was anything but decorous. Desire blazed between them, a conflagration so all-consuming that she trembled helplessly against him. Much more of this and they would be making love on the living-room couch—completely unseemly. She had known for a long time that she still loved Mark; she hadn't known that the passion would still burn as high as it had when she had lain beside him in the secluded little clearing along the creek by the schoolhouse so long ago.

She rose on shaky legs. Without a word she turned to him and grasped his hand, then led him toward the stairs.

"I hope Maureen doesn't hear us," she whispered when they reached the landing and started toward her room. "She's an understanding girl, but she's young. She knows we're in love, but I'm not sure how she'd react to you in my bed. Youngsters have a hard time believing that anyone over thirty isn't half-dead."

"Not Maureen, I'll wager," he retorted. "If we *didn't* go to your room, I wouldn't put it past her to come downstairs and chase us up here!"

She giggled, wildly, passionately happy, and opened the door to her room. It closed softly behind them, and for the first time in years she snapped the lock. It was the last time either one of them thought of or mentioned their granddaughter that night.

22

Mark turned his head to gaze at Jessica lying beside him and wondered if it could really be true. Was he dreaming? But he couldn't be; he had been awake for an hour, watching her sleeping face, and he thought he would never tire of it. She was incredibly lovely, simultaneously sensual yet peaceful in the aftermath of love. She appeared so vulnerable, so heartbreakingly fragile, with her dark lashes in stark contrast to her ivory skin, her coral lips slightly parted, her hair wild on the pillow beneath her head. His throat tightened with a surge of such exquisite tenderness that it was almost painful. She was his. To love, to cherish, to protect. He would never doubt it again.

He elevated himself on his elbow and glanced out the window, thinking that he had not felt so at peace in years. He could just see the top of a huge maple, and he noticed that the leaves were already beginning to turn. Summer was brief at this elevation. In a few days the tree would be a blaze of scarlet, and a few days later its branches would be bare. For the first time that he could remember, the awareness of such swift change didn't fill him with aching regrets. All the time one ever had was the moment one was living—and he was happy in the moment.

Jessica stirred slightly, and he tucked the sheet around her shoulders. The air coming through the open window carried the chill of early morning, and he didn't want her catching a cold. He didn't want anything at all to happen to her—ever!

He glanced at her face and saw that her eyes were open, and that they were soft with remembrance of their night of love. Bending his head, he lightly kissed her mouth. It tasted like more, and his kiss deepened. She was as fragrant as a mountain meadow, fresh and clean with a hint of roses. Eventually he drew back a few inches and smiled down into her face. "Good morning, sleepyhead."

She reached up and put a bare arm around his neck, drawing him back to her. "It can't be morning yet."

"The sun has been up for hours." He nibbled at her ear.

"It doesn't know any better," she said lazily, running one finger over his lips. "Now, *we* have no reason at all to get up—at least not right this minute."

"My dear woman, I am not nineteen years old," he said severely, running his hand over her cheek, then down to caress her breasts. Her flesh was still sweet and moist from sleep. Lowering his head, he kissed the hollow at the base of her throat, then each breast. She had been a little hesitant last night about uncovering her body, and he had immediately divined the reason: she wondered if he would find her body as desirable as he had when she was young. He hoped he'd convinced her how little it mattered. True, her skin didn't have the same elasticity, her breasts weren't quite as high and firm as they had once been, but if it was taut skin he wanted, he could have gotten it anyplace. And often had, he thought dryly. But he had never been satisfied until Jessica was once again in his arms. Had never felt whole. Her physical self was infinitely desirable to him, but it was her spirit, her soul, that had bound him to her all these years.

Her hand moved down and found him, and he gasped with pleasure. "Not nineteen?" She giggled. "You could have fooled me."

He had thought that throughout the night they had run

the gamut of moods, loving with wild desperation, sweet deliberation, unbearable tenderness, but he had been wrong. This morning they were like a couple of kids, laughing, joking, tickling, nibbling, until they were finally swept up in a vortex of passion. Whoever said that sex was the most fun you could have without laughing was mistaken, Mark thought in one of the brief respites. There was nothing wrong with laughing.

Finally they collapsed again on the bed, Jessica's head nestling trustingly on his shoulder.

"Do you realize this is only the second time we've made love in a bed?" she asked, turning to give him a kiss on the moist skin of his shoulder.

"Not the last time—I promise."

"I rather like it. The other times were nice, too, but maybe I'm getting a little too old for the ground." She spoke deliberately, as though considering the question from every angle.

"Even if we took a pillow? Anyway, 'To me, fair friend, you never can be old, for as you were when first your eye I eyed, such seems your beauty still.'"

"Still quoting Shakespeare, I see. Did you steal a book of his sonnets?"

"No." He chuckled. "I managed to buy the complete works."

For a few moments both were quiet, lost in memory. Finally she spoke slowly, reluctantly. "Mark, I suppose we do have to talk seriously."

"About the future?" His lips set firmly. "Our future is together, Jessica. If you are thinking anything else, forget it."

"No, no, not the future. I think it's the past we have to talk about. There were so many hurts, so many doubts. I think we need to get everything out in the open."

He turned toward her to push back a lock of hair, then lightly kissed her forehead. "Whatever you say. But it's not going to change anything. I'm not letting you go."

"I'm not sure you still know me, or I you. There've been

so many changes—in our lives, in us, even in the county. Look at all the housing, the stands of timber that have been cleared—so much of the 'progress' is due to you!"

"And the new schools, the new jobs, the new opportunities," he said. "Actually, though, most of the changes are due to the times. They were inevitable. I profited from them, sure, but I didn't exactly change the world," he said almost ruefully. He looked at her closely. "We'll probably never see eye to eye on certain things, sweetheart. I saw too much poverty and despair to have any heartfelt nostalgia for the old order.

"Anyway"—he grinned at her—"you've done a great job of keeping your finger in the dike. And you've certainly kept the Carter ranch safe from too much 'progress,'" he teased.

"For now."

"Maybe forever. More and more people are beginning to see things your way. We're all going to have to find ways to preserve the land and still keep the economy growing." Frowning, he gazed out the window, then back at her face. "We sound like we're addressing a town meeting. This has nothing to do with *us*, Jessica, with you and me. Not deep down, anyway."

"I think perhaps it does." Anxiety shone in her lovely eyes. "When I came to see you about Jeb, you sounded so bitter," she continued. "Bitterness corrodes the soul, makes people do things out of spite, out of some misguided sense of revenge. I'd hate to see you keep on trying to crush everything that reminded you of the past. . . ."

"I'm glad I went to see the old man," Mark said softly. "Thanks to your prodding, I think I understand a little better that he's a product of his time, just like everyone else. It's still hard to see how he justified his behavior, but in his own mind he was fair. We've made peace, of a sort. You don't have to worry on that score anymore."

"What are you going to do about him?"

"What he'll let me do—which isn't much. Maybe I can

make his last days more comfortable. Mom would have wanted that." He smiled meaningfully at her, and she smiled back, her heart brimming.

For nearly an hour they murmured together, reminiscing, explaining, drawing as close together mentally as they already were physically. The lingering bitterness, anger, and guilt of the intervening years evaporated in the heat of their newfound love.

Finally Mark sighed and sat up, swinging his long legs over the edge of the bed. "So many years wasted."

"Not wasted," she said softly. "I've come to believe no experience is ever wasted."

He gazed at her. "Well, I promise you one thing—we aren't going to waste another minute." At the look in her eyes he laughed hugely. "No, no, not now. Have mercy. I'm in the mood for some coffee."

While Mark took a quick shower and slipped back into his clothes, Jessica lolled in bed. When he was ready, he gave her an amused glance. "You aren't going downstairs like that, are you?"

"You were hogging the shower," she retorted.

"Next time we'll shower together."

"Ha! A lady needs some privacy." She clutched a robe around her, grinned over her shoulder, and disappeared into the bathroom.

Mark sank down in a chair, feeling as comfortable as a lizard on a sun-warmed rock. There was none of the strangeness, the jockeying for position and dominance, of a new relationship. In some ways he and Jessica were like an old married couple. And, conversely, the relationship was as wild and exciting, as full of potential, as though they had just met.

A few minutes later they walked sedately down the stairs.

"I smell coffee," Mark said as they approached the kitchen. "Or is that wishful thinking?"

She sniffed. "If it is, we're both doing it. I smell it, too. And biscuits?"

Maureen turned from the stove as they entered the kitchen, her eyes bright with excitement and curiosity. With her hair caught back in a scarf, her long legs and arms tanned and bare in her shorts and halter top, she looked impossibly young. Like a playful filly, full of exuberant energy that might explode into action at any moment.

Jessica felt suddenly bashful. She tightened her grip on Mark's hand. This situation was new to her. Somehow it was reversed. She should have been the one regarding Maureen with level, assessing eyes, not the other way around.

The girl flashed them a brilliant smile. "Well, it's about time you lovebirds got out of the sack. It's nearly noon. You can't live on love alone, you know."

"Maureen!" Jessica's cheeks burned. Mark's chuckle didn't help her embarrassment a bit.

"Pay no attention," he told her cheerfully. "Kids today don't know how to show respect to their elders."

"These elders need a keeper," Maureen said darkly, her sparkling eyes in contrast to her solemn words. "You're lucky I'm here to take charge of things. Come on over to the table now. I've got coffee, scrambled eggs, and muffins." She glanced confidentially at Mark and lowered her voice. "She can't cook a thing, you know."

He shook his head sadly. "Bad news. I thought she was perfect."

"You don't have to talk about me as though I'm not in the room." Jessica couldn't remember a time when she had felt so happy—not even in the beginning, when she had first fallen in love with Mark. If she were a cat, right now was the moment she'd begin to purr. The two people she loved most in the world were right here with her.

When they were seated at the table to Maureen's satisfaction, she positioned herself across from them, propped her elbows on the table, put her chin in her hands, and regarded them sternly. "All right, you two. When's the wedding?"

Jessica nearly choked on her coffee. She set the cup down carefully on the pine table. "I—I guess we didn't get around to discussing it." She glanced at Mark. He was regarding her with amused, loving eyes.

"I suggest you get married as soon as we can get everything ready," Maureen said. "We'll need to go to Boise and pick out your wedding gown. Yards and yards of white satin, I think."

"White satin!"

"Well, perhaps something more the color of your hair," Maureen said judiciously. "And we need to select my dress, too, of course. I think I'd like something in emerald chiffon. Naturally I'm to be your main attendant, but you may want a few other people, too, like Lydia. Mark, you'll need to decide on your best man. Then there's the music to consider. And flowers. The weather might hold for an outdoor wedding—maybe in our rose garden. That way we can have as many guests as we wish, and—"

"Maureen!" Jessica cut in desperately. "Slow down. We haven't even talked about marriage yet." Oh my, why was *she* the one suddenly feeling like a guilty, rebellious teenager?

"It doesn't need talking about," Mark growled. "Of course we're getting married."

"Y-yes, of course. But I thought maybe just the two of us"—she caught Maureen's outraged look and hastily amended her statement—"the three of us would go down to the courthouse, and a little afternoon suit would do just—"

Maureen threw up her hands. "No way! You two have dillydallied long enough. And after all these years I think you deserve a real wedding. And soon." She scowled across the table at the two of them. "Obviously I can't trust either of you out of my sight. Who knows what might happen this time? With your track record you can never tell. Something might come up, and you'd mess up again. I want this wedding to be held just as soon as possible."

Jessica glanced at Mark, and a tiny smile curved her lips. His eyes told her he knew just what she was thinking, and he agreed completely. It had taken over half their lives—but they wouldn't lose each other again.

"Whatever you say, Maureen," she said meekly.

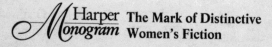

COMING NEXT MONTH

A FOREVER KIND OF LOVE by Patricia Hagan

A sweeping novel of romance, suspense, mystery, and revenge, set in the turbulent reconstruction period following the Civil War. This bestselling author tells a story of two lovers drawn together in the blaze of passion amidst a world aflame with prejudice and deceit.

THE SEASON OF LOVING by Helen Archery

A delightful Christmas romance set in Regency England. On her way to visit a family friend, Merrie Lawrence's gig runs into the Earl of Warwick's curricle. Discovering Merrie is his mother's houseguest, the earl takes an immediate dislike to her, only to discover later his overwhelming interest.

THE BASKET BRIDE by Phyllis Coe

An enthralling historical romance spun from the historic event of the "Basket Brides" who came from France in the 18th century to help settle Louisiana.

ONE MAN'S TREASURE by Catriona Flynt

Adventure, intrigue, and humor are hallmarks of this delightful historical romance. Ruth McKenna travels to Flagstaff, Arizona, to make peace with her brother, but she's too late—someone has killed him. The only person to help her is big, redheaded Gladius Blade. A nosy, hard-headed woman only adds to Blade's problems. But when he falls in love with her, he knows he is in for real trouble.

ANALISE

Analise Caldwell was the reigning belle of New Orleans. Disguised as a Confederate soldier, Union major Mark Schaeffer captured the Rebel beauty's heart as part of his mission. Stunned by his deception, Analise swore never to yield to the caresses of this Yankee spy...until he delivered an ultimatum.

ROSEWOOD

Millicent Hayes had lived all her life amid the lush woodland of Emmetsville, Texas. Bound by her duty to her crippled brother, the dark-haired innocent had never known desire...until a handsome stranger moved in next door.

BONDS OF LOVE

Katherine Devereaux was a willful, defiant beauty who had yet to meet her match in any man—until the winds of war swept the Union innocent into the arms of Confederate Captain Matthew Hampton.

LIGHT AND SHADOW

The day nobleman Jason Somerville broke into her rooms and swept her away to his ancestral estate, Carolyn Mabry began living a dangerous charade. Posing as her twin sister, Jason's wife, Carolyn thought she was helping her gentle twin. Instead she found herself drawn to the man she had so seductively deceived.

CRYSTAL HEART

A seductive beauty, Lady Lettice Kenton swore never to give her heart to any man—until she met the rugged American rebel Charles Murdock. Together on a ship bound for America, they shared a perfect passion, but danger awaited them on the shores of Boston Harbor.

If you would like to receive a HarperPaperbacks catalog, please send your name and address plus $1.00 postage/handling to:

HarperPaperbacks Catalog Request
10 East 53rd St.
New York, NY 10022

ATTENTION: ORGANIZATIONS AND CORPORATIONS

Most HarperPaperbacks are available at special quantity discounts for bulk purchases for sales promotions,premiums, or fund-raising. For information, please call or write:
Special Markets Department, HarperCollins Publishers, 10 East 53rd Street, New York, N.Y. 10022.
Telephone: (212) 207-7528. Fax: (212) 207-7222.